Pirates' Pay

a novel by
STAN BAILEY

First published by Dog Ear Publishing
4010 W. 86th Street, Ste H
Indianapolis, IN 46268
www.dogearpublishing.net

ISBN: 978-1-59858-600-8

This book is printed on acid-free paper.
This book is a work of fiction. Places, events, and situations in this book are purely
fictional and any resemblance to actual persons, living or dead, is coincidental.

Acknowledgments:

Several people gave me invaluable assistance in the creation and editing of this story. To them I am deeply indebted and grateful:

—First and foremost, my wife, Bobbie, to whom this book is dedicated. She was the first to hear each page of the story; first to read each word of the manuscript, and was the toughest editor of my career.

—My daughter, Cheryl, who proofed the final edit and found errors we had missed.

— Jim Warren, long-time sailor and now trawler cruiser, advised me on navigation issues. He called *Pirates' Pay* "a well-researched story from a writer who hopefully has a lot more to say."

—David Byrne, attorney, former federal prosecutor and friend of nearly four decades, advised me on legal issues and assured me: ``I would take this book to the beach on vacation....It's a yarn that deserves to be on the big screen."

—Kelly Sanders, a former National Guard captain who suffered and continues to recover from a traumatic brain injury (TBI), helped me to understand TBI. She earned her BS degree and specialty titles CST (cranial sacral therapist), LMT (licensed massage therapist) and RT (recreational therapist). She told me: "The emotional aspect of TBI you hit on the nail… "a wonderful story…a fine initial work."

—Don Hutton, former Coast Guard investigator and author of several books, including non-fiction books on careers in law enforcement, the military and homeland security. He gave me valuable pointers on writing and insight into the fear and courage that "Coasties" take with them into armed maneuvers against lawbreakers.

—John M. Manahan, retired master chief petty officer and special intelligence agent with the U.S. Coast Guard, whose suggestions helped me bring a measure of authenticity to the purely fictitious structure and operations of Coast Guard personnel in my story. He told me: "Stan Bailey's *Pirates' Pay* is a captivating novel. The situations and lively action depict what could happen at any moment on today's troubled seas!"

—Dana Beyerle, reporter for New York Times Regional Newspapers, gave me a U.S. Navy veteran's perspective on personnel.

—Dr. Mark Keller, professor of English, Middle Georgia State College, a friend and former college pal, whose critiques of my previous unpublished works were among the strongest encouragements to write *Pirates' Pay*, of which he notes: "Stan Bailey has proven to be a swashbuckling first novelist with *Pirates' Pay*. The book is an exceptionally good read, with just the right combination of interesting characters, suspenseful action, and themes that are both universal – such as love – and that are relevant to our own age – such as modern sea piracy."

###

Preface

Hundreds of thousands of Americans suffer traumatic brain injuries (TBI) each year, according to the Centers for Disease Control and Prevention. Many of these injuries result in death. Many others cause long-term disability.

Pirates' Pay is a totally fictitious story about pirates and prosecutors, courtroom drama and romance, adventures on the high seas and the struggle of one TBI victim who valiantly battled the effects of her injury.

The role of the U.S. Coast Guard in this story is just one example of the myriad actions of the real Guardians of the homeland: saving lives; assisting people in distress; search and rescue; interdicting illegal immigrants, and battling drug smugglers and pirates.

While this yarn is set squarely in the real world, it is totally fictitious. Comments by medical professionals in this story are not represented as medically accurate statements. The words and actions of the characters are not intended to represent the words and actions of any person, living or dead.

The situations in this story are intended to highlight in some cases what the careful reader will recognize as the recurring theme of friendship, illustrating that a friend may be an intimate associate or a close acquaintance; one who is helpful and reliable, who is on our side in a struggle, and not our enemy or foe.
–Stan Bailey

Chapter One

Elaine lay unconscious on the beach at daybreak.

She didn't hear the gulls squealing or the waves crashing. And she didn't see the first piercing rays of the sun.

She had washed ashore in the night, lying almost lifeless upon a splintered timber of some kind, perhaps a piece of wreckage from a boat or private yacht on which she went to sea.

As the tide rolled in, each wave drove her farther upon the shore, swirling and foaming, leaving pieces of shell, seaweed and an occasional minnow flipping. Strands of her long light brown hair lay buried beneath the sand.

The gentle tug against her scalp produced her first signs of consciousness. Slowly she became aware that each ebb and flow left wakes of piercing pain, prompting her eventually to open her eyes. She wiped a gritty hand across her brow and felt her eyes afire from sand and salt. Then she drew her thumb and forefinger over her eyelids and over the bridge of her nose like a squeegee. It didn't help much.

She moaned. Then she realized she was sore all over. Everything hurt, particularly her head, which burned on the outside and throbbed on the inside like strokes of a blacksmith's hammer. And something was binding her waist. She could take only short breaths without its seeming to cut into her flesh. She reached her hand down to loosen the cord or rope or whatever it was, but it wouldn't budge.

Then she turned her head over against the beam and felt excruciating pain at the base of her skull. She tried to feel the sore spot with her hand and found a huge bump with a soft and painful center. She wondered if her skull were shattered, but she slowly worked her fingers underneath the bump and held it gently in her hand, lifting her head slightly. Then she saw the sun, shining between her toes.

"Hello, Sol," she said softly. "I wonder where I am and how I got here."

She didn't remember being tied to the timber, but she realized it had kept her afloat and probably had saved her life. Now it bound her so tightly she couldn't get a full breath, and she knew she would have to break free of it to live.

"I've got to have air," she shouted at no one in particular. But the more she struggled to get free, the more frustrated she became, and that only made it more difficult to breathe. So she forced herself to hold back and try to figure out how to get loose.

"At least I'm breathing," she said softly, trying to calm her fear.

But then she felt another burst of adrenalin: She realized she couldn't remember being at sea or where she had been before she went there, and most disturbing of all, she couldn't remember her name.

She faced the sun for an instant and was blinded by its brilliance. Then she forced herself to take only fleeting glances at the glowing wafer rising out of the waves.

Eventually she saw what was binding her too tightly at the waist: a man's narrow brown leather belt. Its buckle, if it had one, was hidden behind her, buried in the sand beneath the big plank on which she lay.

She tried but was unable to reach the buckle. It wouldn't slip to the right or left, but the sand between the belt and her skin cut like a knife. She could see a bright red line beneath her navel where the sandy edge of the belt had cut her skin. She knew she had to get her weight off the buckle to remove the leather strap; so she drew her knees forward and toppled over on her left side, leaving her right arm free to search for the buckle. She quickly felt the smooth metal, with its center pin through the hole nearest the end of the belt.

"So that's why it's too tight," she whispered. "The man had a very trim waistline!"

She drew her waist in as far as she could and felt the belt loosen. Then she caught the end of it with her fingers and yanked it backward as hard as she could, but not hard enough. She tried a second and a third time, then felt the tension snap as the belt came loose.

She caught the buckle and pulled it out, freeing her from the board that had saved her life. And for the first time since she regained consciousness, she could breathe a full breath of air. She sat back up and for a while just enjoyed breathing again.

But her head still ached like her worst migraine ever – a hammering throb with each heartbeat inside the burning bump at the base of her skull.

"What I wouldn't give for a strong dose of ibuprofen," she whispered to herself.

She noticed that she was wearing a tank top and loose-fitting knit athletic pants. She couldn't check the contents of her pockets while seated, so she tried to get up and felt pain so intense that the top of her head seemed to lift off. She swooned and fell again on the sand. Suddenly she felt nauseous; so she lay quietly for several minutes, again breathing short breaths.

Then she thrust her hands to the bottoms of both front pockets. She found nothing but a little sand in her left pocket, but in her right she found a soggy five-dollar bill and three ones. She had no back pockets.

She decided to try again to stand, but this time she pulled up slowly on all-fours. She brought her knees up and leaned over, stretching her arms forward for balance. Finally she rose out of deep knee bends and stood up. Her head throbbed with sharp jabs, but she gritted her teeth, breathed a series of short breaths and moaned.

She held out her hands from her sides for balance and focused her eyes on her toes to fight off a slight blurring of her vision that had preceded her fall the first time. She took a few staggering steps away from the water toward the top edge of her now definite but lengthy shadow on the sand.

"Now what do I do?" she asked aloud but heard no answer.

"I've got to have a doctor check this bump on my head. I must get something for pain," Elaine whispered, suddenly feeling giddy again. This time she sat down more gently, but the pain in her head kicked really hard anyway.

"Ow!" she said as she came to rest in the sand. "This is definitely not cutting it. I can't stay here and suffer with my busted head, and I don't seem to be able to go anywhere else. Besides, where would I go?"

She sat leaning forward, toward the water and the rising sun, with her eyes closed, her forehead in the palms of her hands and her elbows on her knees. And she hurt all over.

"God, I've got to get help," she said aloud, almost whining. "Please, God. Where am I? Who am I? And what am I going to do?"

She felt a cool breeze from off the water's surface but heard only the gentle sloshing of the waves against the shore. Then she spotted something she couldn't identify, like maybe a mound of seaweed, lying on the flatly packed sand a long way down the shore. Whatever it was lay halfway in the water and halfway out, bobbing like a cork in the ebb and flow.

"I've got to go see what that is," Elaine said after studying the mass on the shore for a while. "Somehow," she added a good bit later.

Slowly, she leaned forward again, stretching out her arms in front of her for balance. Then she stood as before, still shakily. She looked around for something she could use for a walking cane to steady herself as she seemed again about to fall.

"This should work," she said, reaching down for a piece of slickly worn driftwood that appeared to have been, sometime in the past, a tree limb. Slowly and carefully she began her trek along the water's edge toward the mass on the beach, but sometimes the waves surprised her and washed over her bare feet.

"I wonder where my shoes are," she said then.

The sun had begun its climb and was beginning to feel uncomfortably warm when Elaine realized that she was terribly thirsty. Her mouth seemed full of cotton, which she tried in vain to spit out. She got rid of only a few grains of gritty, salty sand.

She looked back at her barefoot tracks on the beach to see how far she had come, and she spotted the timber which had been her lifeboat, floating now just off the shore.

"The tide must have changed," she said to herself. "And there goes the board that might have contained a clue to where I have come from and who I am."

She fought back the urge to expend her last reserve of energy to dash out and try to retrieve the wood, for she remembered somehow that she was or had been an excellent swimmer. But in the few seconds she considered it, the board had doubled its distance from the shore. Still she stood, with the water washing around her feet. She leaned on her driftwood walking stick for what seemed like five minutes or so, watching her plank shrink into a thin line in the distance. The gulls occasionally darted down to investigate the plank and sometimes caught it for a brief free ride.

"So much for that," she said with a sigh as she turned to resume her trek toward the mass on the beach and felt real tears welling up in her eyes for the first time in her memory. But as the tears continued, the burning eased and she wiped her eyes, one sandy, salty arm at a time.

As she drew closer to the mass on the beach, she thought she could see the back of a man's head, bobbing face down in the water, with both arms stretching out in front of him. She stopped suddenly and studied the mass more closely, but wouldn't let herself believe it was a man. If so, he almost certainly had to be dead, and she felt her heart race away like a runner on the beach as she considered that likelihood.

After a momentary stop, she hobbled forward again, then stood cold still in her tracks and screamed as she felt her driftwood stick fall out of her hand.

"No!" she shouted, partly now because she knew the mass in front of her was a dead man, and partly because she had dropped her stick. She lunged forward in the shallow water, reclaiming the stick with a bear hug.

"Gotcha!" she yelled, grasping the stick and using it to push herself back up. Then she approached the man on the sand, whose pale blue skin told her he obviously was dead. She shuddered as she tried without success to roll him over with her stick to see his face.

He was a slender man, barefoot and wearing jeans with no belt and a tank top with a tiny purple hole in the back, just above the waistline. He had thick black hair with no sign of thinning or balding, and thus far didn't look like anyone she knew.

Elaine tried again to turn the man over by placing her driftwood stick under his shoulder and lifting, but she didn't have the strength, and she was afraid she might break her stick. So she let him roll back to his original position. The water line now was several feet away, and he lay entirely on the sand.

She got down on all fours and approached him again, this time gently touching his cold dead flesh with her fingertips. Then she gritted her teeth and made a hefty shove all at once with her palms on his shoulder, and over he rolled with a whump like a waterlogged mop. He had a neat black beard with a closely cropped mustache, and there was an even bigger purple hole in the front of his shirt, in his lower abdomen, just above his belt line.

"Hmmm. He must have been shot in the back," Elaine said as she considered the hole and thought how glad she was that she still didn't recognize him.

She didn't feel good about reaching into a dead man's pockets, but she had to know if they contained any clue of his identity or whether his past somehow was intertwined with hers. She found nothing in his left pocket, and only a scrap of paper in his right which stated, "Inspected by No. 32."

"Well, they were new pants," she said. "Maybe that's a clue to where they came from and who bought them and where," she said. She reminded herself again that if she didn't get water and medical care soon, there would be another dead body in the sand: hers.

She didn't see any way to solve her own problems, but perhaps, she thought, she could cover the corpse with enough sand to keep the vultures from devouring him until the authorities could be notified – whoever and wherever the authorities were.

She decided to dig a shallow grave a short distance up on the beach so the waves wouldn't reach him and perhaps uncover him later. But digging with her hands was slow and painful. Then she found that her driftwood stick, used as a combination pick and scraper, cut easily through the sand. She soon had a trench the length of his body and she guessed about a foot and a half deep. That should be enough if she could just get him in the grave, she thought.

She crawled on her hands and knees to the body, then placed her hands under his arms and lifted him as high off the sand as she could as she attempted to stand up. Then she pulled with all her strength but moved him barely an inch. The exertion was enough to make her head hurt much worse, however. She felt giddy again, so she sat back down in the sand with the man's head in her lap.

"You're really heavy for a little guy," she whispered. "I may have dug your grave for nothing if I can't get you in it."

She knew she had to find another way. She couldn't merely leave him. If for no other reason, it would waste her painful work.

"Maybe I can sit in the sand and scoot backward by pushing with my feet and just drag you with me, you think?" she asked, now realizing that she was talking to the corpse.

"Don't answer that," she said, shuddering at the macabre nature of her task and yet finding a spark of humor in it. So long as the corpse didn't answer, she thought.

She cut tracks in the sand that looked like those of a giant dung beetle or perhaps a sea turtle, pulling some kind of cargo behind him. As she neared the front edge of the grave, she veered to one side, dragging the body along the edge. But the man's feet didn't follow the path. Instead they dropped into the grave and rolled the whole body over, carrying Elaine in with it. She screamed and suddenly found new strength to hustle non-stop out the top end of the grave.

"Well, at least for now, I'm not going with you, Sir," she spoke to the corpse again.

The sudden burst of motion cost her dearly. She now was thirstier than ever, and the sun was becoming even more uncomfortably warm.

"Maybe I spoke too soon," she said as she began to rake big double-handfuls of sand in on the body, starting with his feet and working her way up. As she got to his left shoulder she saw something she hadn't seen before.

"Wait. What's this?" she asked nobody in particular as she wiped the sand away from the side of his arm to reveal a primitive and apparently home-made tattoo: the name ELAINE in capital letters, made with uneven lines of dark blue dots.

She stopped covering the body and pondered the name and home-made tattoo of dark blue dots and wondered what they could mean.

"Elaine," she said the name softly. "I wonder who that is and whether or not I knew her. And I ... wonder..." She paused a long time. "...if I am her," she continued. "If so, this man and I must have known each other, maybe really well."

But she couldn't remember ever seeing the dead man before, and the name ELAINE struck no familiar chord in her memory. She still had no idea who she was or how she came to wash ashore on a deserted beach, strapped with a man's leather belt to a broken plank.

She closed her eyes and shook her head, but that made her headache worse, and that reminded her of the painful bump on her head and how dreadfully thirsty she had become.

"Got to get you covered up and find some water," she again spoke to the corpse as though he were still alive. She resumed scooping great handfuls of sand upon the body and soon had it covered and mounded as though it were a buried log.

"I need to leave a marker," she said, "but I can't give up my walking stick."

She looked around for something, anything, that she could use to mark the grave. Some distance from the shore she found only a piece of driftwood stump, with knots on either side.

"It's not a very fancy cross, but it will have to do," Elaine said as she bent down to pick it up. She fell forward instead on her hands and knees and noticed a hole in the chunk where a limb used to be, filled now with water. She was so thirsty that she was ready to take a chance that it was drinkable, but she managed to stop herself just before she began to lap it up. She decided instead to dip a finger in it first and taste it, but she noticed that her hands were covered with sand, and she knew they had handled the body of a dead man.

"I may as well die of one thing as another," she said to herself then, about to drink the unknown liquid. Then she thought of the pale blue skin of the corpse and decided instead to try to wipe her finger as clean as possible on her pants leg before dipping it in the water.

"OK, please, God, let this not be salty water," she said as she dipped her finger in the dark liquid and let a drop fall on her tongue. Then another. And another. And another, until she was satisfied it wasn't sea water.

"I don't know what this is, but it isn't salty," she said then, leaning down to smell of it. She caught a faint whiff of smoke and soot and maybe fresh earth, like rotted wood should smell, she told herself before drawing her lips to the water's surface.

"It may kill me, but I'll be dead soon anyway if I don't get some water," she said as she began to sip the unknown liquid. It tasted softly sweet. "And I do believe it's good old rain water," she said with a smile of satisfaction.

When she could no longer reach the surface of the water with her lips, she sat in the sand and lifted the chunk above her head and turned it gently until the liquid flowed in a wide stream into her mouth. She continued to hold the chunk aloft as the last precious drops fell on her tongue.

"Thank you, God. Now can you find me a doctor?" she asked aloud. Then in silence she pushed herself back up and stood shakily for a moment before carrying the chunk to the grave site. She stood the chunk upright on one end of the mound so the knots on either side of it made a kind of crude cross. Then she positioned the knothole at the base where it would catch water again if it rained.

"Thanks for the water, God," she said again as she realized that Elaine and God and Sol, the sun, were the only three names she knew. And she didn't remember much about any of them.

"My head! I've got to get help," she said as she touched the bump near the base of her skull and felt excruciating pain.

For the first time since she regained consciousness at daybreak, she began to search by sight the full circle of her surroundings. She hoped desperately to find anything that might help her understand and escape her dilemma. As far as she could tell, she was on a deserted island lying directly beneath the shadow of death.

She recalled that as she awoke she had heard the soft whispering of waves washing gently against the shore. As she looked toward the sea from which she had come, she saw nothing but bluish green water, pocked with whitecaps and occasional gulls. She saw no ships or boats of any kind and no land in the distance.

On either side of her stretched a wide, smooth shoreline of white sand. An area of darker soil behind it was covered with a dense thicket of low bushes which stretched behind her for as far as she could see. She saw taller trees in the distance but no sign of other life anywhere except herself and the gulls.

She considered trying to start a fire, as she had seen it done in the movies to attract attention, but there was virtually nothing on the beach that would burn, and no matches or magnifying lens to set it afire even if she could find combustible materials.

"I may as well sit here and die!" she said in exasperation.

Just as she was ready to give up, however, she heard the faint sound of some kind of engine, perhaps that of a helicopter or plane in the distance, she thought.

"I wonder if they're just flying by or are looking for me or perhaps the dead man," she said, giving voice to her hopes. She looked up and waved, just in case anyone were looking. Soon she saw a speck in the distance and could tell that it was a helicopter headed in her general direction. "They're too far away, even if they're looking for me."

But the helicopter was circling, as though flying around an island, which meant there might be someone on board searching the shoreline.

She hurried back to the mound where she had buried the dead man and had placed a crude cross as a marker. She waved her arms again wildly and yelled with all the strength she could muster. A big white helicopter with a red stripe and a circular insignia of crossed anchors with the words UNITED STATES COAST GUARD in capital letters approached from behind her. Suddenly it seemed to be directly overhead, and its rotors were whump-whump-whumping so loudly that the noise hurt her ears. A cloud of sand billowed up from the mound that topped the dead man's grave as the chopper touched down lightly in the sand. Then the rotor slowed; the engine stopped, and a man wearing dark blue coveralls and a blue bill cap waved at her, climbed out and walked toward her.

"We're here for you, Ma'am, if you need us," the man said, approaching.

"Thank God!" Elaine said and felt herself fainting, but the man rushed toward her, caught her before she hit the sand and lifted her back to her feet.

"Just lean on me, Ma'am," he said as he draped her arm over his shoulder and walked her toward the helicopter's passenger bay door.

"Do you think you can climb the steps if I help you?" he asked.

"I think so," she said as he helped her into the big chopper and she sat down. But as he closed the door and started to climb back in, she shouted, "No! Wait!"

"Is something wrong? Are you alright?" the man asked.

"Yes, something's wrong, and no, I'm not alright," she said. "I appreciate your coming to get me, and I know I need medical care for this bump on my head." She pointed a finger toward the base of her skull and continued talking: "But I need to tell you something. Do you see that chunk of driftwood over there?"

"Yes, Ma'am. I see it. In fact, it looked like a cross from the air," the man told her. "Of course, we also saw you waving at us, and you appeared to be in some kind of distress. Do you know anything about the marker – what it is and why it's there?"

"Yes. It's a grave marker. I put it there after I buried a man I found dead on the beach this morning," she said. "I didn't know him, but I could tell he had been shot, apparently in the back. I think somebody needs to investigate his death. Burying him was all I knew or was able to do."

"We'll take care of it, Ma'am," the man said. "And we'll get you something to drink while I put the dead gentleman in a body bag. Have you been on the beach here long?"

"I don't know," she said. "I was unconscious for I don't know how long, until I came to about daybreak, strapped with a man's leather belt to a piece of plank.

"I'm guessing the belt belonged to the man I buried, because he wasn't wearing one. He was kind of slim, and the belt almost wasn't long enough to go around me and the piece of plank too. But I'm pretty sure that without that plank holding me up, I would have drowned.

"So this man, whom I don't know, or somebody, saved my life. And that reminds me: I left the belt on the shore where I took it off. Do you think you can look for it and bring it with us if it's still there? It may be a clue to who the man was."

"Yes, Ma'am. I'll look for it and will get it if it's still there," he said. "Now you just sit here and relax a minute, and then we'll try to get you to a hospital."

He handed her a bottle of cold water.

"Would you rather lie down? We have a med-evac cot in the back there that's quite comfortable," he said.

"No this seat is fine, and thanks for the water," she said as she quickly opened it and drank nearly the whole bottle before stopping for air. "This is sooo good, but do you possibly have any ibuprofen or other painkiller? My head is killing me."

"You're welcome to the water, and yes Ma'am, we do have some OTC stuff. I believe it's acetaminophen, but that's about all. We don't have any medical capability on this run," he said, handing her a white plastic pill bottle. "By the way, I'm Lt. Robert McGuffy, co-pilot, but I didn't get your name."

"Thanks for the Tylenol," she said, downing two extra-strength caplets with the rest of the bottle of water. "But I didn't tell you my name."

"Well, we can get your name later for our report, but just for convenience do you mind introducing yourself? That's our pilot up there, Lt. Joe Anderson," said McGuffy.

"Hello, Ma'am. Just call me Joe," said Anderson, nodding back toward her. "We don't have many frills on this flight. We're what you might call a skeleton crew. Oh, sorry, Ma'am. I didn't mean to say that. That was an unintentional pun."

"That's all right, lieutenant, but I'm afraid I can't give you my name," she said.

"Why not?" he asked.

"Because I don't know my name," she said. "That bump on my head must have knocked out most of what I used to know. I hope it's not permanent, but that dead man out there apparently saved my life. And I hope one day to know who he is or was. As you'll notice, if you look, he has the name ELAINE tattooed on his left arm. I don't know who Elaine is, but perhaps, just maybe, that's me."

"I'm sorry, Ma'am. I didn't know," he said.

"It's OK. You couldn't have known," she said.

Moments later, she heard the back cargo bay door open, and McGuffy hefted a black plastic body bag from his shoulder over onto the floor of the helicopter. Then he climbed in, placed the bag into a separate locker, fastened the lid securely and climbed back out again.

He walked toward the beach where a line of barefoot tracks led through the sand to a man's brown leather belt, lying in the sand. He rolled the belt in a coil as he headed back to the chopper.

"Here's your belt, Ma'am," McGuffy said as he climbed back into the co-pilot's seat and handed her the belt.

"Good! You found it," she said. "Thank you, Lieutenant."

"Yes, I could see where you must have tossed it when you got unhitched from that plank, although I didn't see a plank," said McGuffy, handing.

"I must have thrown it up on the shore, because the plank I was strapped to drifted back out to sea," she said.

She held the belt in a roll for a moment against her chest, glad she had not lost it in the waves, then she gently unwound it and noticed impressions in the leather: the numerals "36" and the words Handcrafted in USA and Genuine Leather. The initials TJF were stamped into the metal buckle.

"You'll need to fasten your safety belt, Ma'am," Anderson said, starting the big chopper's engine.

"Sure," she said, first fastening the dead man's belt around her waist and then snapping the helicopter safety belt on over it.

As the big chopper lifted out and away in a cloud of swirling sand, she still was checking out her new leather belt. She rubbed her fingers over the initials TJF stamped into the metal buckle and wondered what they stood for.

She tightened the belt around her waist all the way to the last hole, and without the plank, there still was plenty of belt left over. She took a long breath and smiled. For many reasons, she was breathing much easier now.

Chapter Two

Elaine turned her face toward the window of the U.S. Coast Guard helicopter on which she was riding skyward. She was headed, she hoped, for a hospital somewhere and medical care for her excruciatingly painful head injuries. Far below she could see the apparently uninhabited island on which she had spent a stark and terrible morning and she didn't know what portion of the night.

The acetaminophen she had taken moments ago had begun to take effect. The throbbing was less intense, and the bump on the back of her head hurt only if she touched it or allowed the headrest of her seat to come in contact with it. She inadvertently leaned back one time and quickly jumped forward again, letting out a loud, "Yeow!"

"Is something wrong, Ma'am?" Anderson asked, glancing back in time to see her reach toward the back of her head.

"My head is really sore," she said. "I bumped it when I tried to lean back, and it almost sent me through the ceiling. I guess I won't do that again."

"Would you like us to adjust your headrest downward so it doesn't touch the sore place? Maybe that would help," said Anderson. "See if you can help her with that, Bob."

"Sure," said McGuffy, unhitching his own safety belt. He quickly squeezed through the narrow opening between the pilot's and co-pilot's seats, joining Elaine in the second row.

"I was hoping you could adjust the headrest from up here, Bob, by reaching back there," said Anderson, raising his eyebrows, clearly surprised at how quickly McGuffy scrambled for the second row of seats.

"I know this isn't exactly standard protocol," McGuffy told Elaine as though in self-defense, "but maybe I can help you without causing Lt. Anderson to crash the ship."

McGuffy reached quickly underneath Anderson's seat and pulled out a bright yellow life jacket with the words Coast Guard in black capital letters on the back.

"You really should be wearing a life jacket anyway," McGuffy told Elaine. "This should help you to sit forward and keep you from putting pressure on your injury."

"Thank you sir. I'm sure that will help," said Elaine.

"You're welcome," said McGuffy as he helped her strap on the life jacket and adjusted the headrest. "Is there anything else I can get for you, like some food, for instance?" McGuffy asked, boldly pushing beyond Anderson's instructions.

"Why, yes, if you have food, I guess I could use some. I have been so bothered by this headache I hadn't realized I was hungry. What do you have?" Elaine asked.

"Yeah, Bob. I want to hear this too. What do you have?" Anderson asked, looking back at McGuffy.

"Uh, we have a rations box in the back. I'll check," said McGuffy, scrambling even farther back in the helicopter. He stopped himself seconds before opening the compartment containing the corpse and opened instead a First Aid kit. Out spilled bandages, rolls of gauze and medical tape, which McGuffy hurriedly gathered and tossed back in the box and slammed it shut.

"Find anything back there for the lady to eat, Bob? And bring me something too. I'll have what she's having," Anderson shouted toward the back of the helicopter.

McGuffy slowly came back to the front of the chopper with a red face, refusing to look at either Elaine or Anderson.

"I'm sorry, Ma'am," he said finally to Elaine. "I spoke too soon. We don't have any food on this chopper I'm afraid. We usually have some emergency meals-ready-to-eat. I forgot we passed out all of those in a rescue we did yesterday, and we just plain forgot to restock. I'm sorry."

"That's all right, but you did remind me of how hungry I am, and how badly I need a doctor to take a look at my head," said Elaine. "How far are we away from your base or a hospital or something?" It was her first question about their location or destination.

"We're probably 30 to 45 minutes out from our base on the mainland," said Anderson, looking back at her. "But I'd be happy to offer you some junk food I brought with me today," he said, reaching in his shirt pocket for a package of round snack crackers with peanut butter filling.

"Oh, I couldn't take your snack. You probably were saving that for lunch," said Elaine, now suddenly ravenously hungry.

"Ma'am, rescue is part of our mission. I insist that you take these," Anderson said, passing the package back to her.

"And you'll need something to wash those down with. Here, take this," said McGuffy, handing her another bottle of water. "Now I've got to go back up front and help Lt. Anderson pilot this ship, but you call me if you need anything else."

"Sure. Thanks. And thank you, Lt. Anderson," Elaine said, opening the snack crackers.

"You're welcome. Call me Joe," said Anderson.

"And you know you can call me Bob," said McGuffy.

"And for the time being, I guess you all can call me Elaine," she said, closing her eyes, leaning back as far as she could in her seat without pressing the bump on her head, and thinking how pleased she was to have a name again – any name.

Anderson made radio contact with his home base in Miami.

"This is USCG Dolphin Unit Four-One-Niner, Lt. Joseph Anderson, to USCG Miami. Come in," Anderson said.

"USCG Miami. Go ahead Unit 419," came the dispatcher's voice.

"We are headed your way with one injured and unidentified Caucasian female, estimated late 20s or early 30s, who has sustained unknown but apparently severe head injury," said Anderson.

"Subject complains of severe headache; doesn't remember her name, but is ambulatory with some assistance. Administered acetaminophen with water and snack food. Also, we have recovered from the same site a deceased Caucasian male, approximately same age, and we are bringing him in. Cause of death unknown but subject had single gunshot wound, unknown caliber, through back and lower abdomen."

"Roger, copy, 419," said the dispatcher. "Can you confirm for the record your approximate location and the site of the rescue and recovery?"

"Copy, Miami. We have just lifted off from the rescue and recovery site, a sandbar near Cape Romano Island," said Anderson.

"Copy, 419. We'll see if we can make an appointment with a specialist to look at your injured subject when you get here. We'll get back with you. Dispatch out," said the dispatcher as the radio went silent.

"Could you understand that, Elaine?" Anderson asked. "That was our home base in Miami. They are going to try to find a specialist to look at your head injury. We are flying full throttle and will get help for you as soon as possible. How are you doing?"

"The acetaminophen is beginning to kick in, so my headache isn't as severe, but of course it's still throbbing with every heartbeat. At least it's not getting worse, and those snack crackers of yours were fantastically good, thanks!" she said. "I was beginning to get nauseous, but the crackers helped a lot. I'm feeling much better."

"Good news," said Anderson. "Just try to hold on a little longer, and I'm sure we can find you some more decent food soon."

"I'll hold on. Thanks, Lieutenant," said Elaine.

"It's Joe, remember," said Anderson, glancing back at her.

"Oh, I forgot. Thanks a lot, Joe," she said.

"You betcha," he said as the hum of the chopper's twin engines climbed to its peak pitch and stabilized.

For a fleeting instant, the blue-green waters of the gulf met a hazy sky on the distant horizon. Then as the chopper headed east toward Miami, miles of mangrove-covered islands and swamps, forests of cypress and pine, and fields of sawgrass in the vast Everglades National Park, unrolled like a dense green blanket below them.

"You said we are going to Miami?" Elaine asked. "That's a familiar name, but I don't remember anything about it or if I have ever been there. I'm not sure if I've ever been anywhere, and I can't think of any more places, either."

"Have you heard of Florida? That's a state. Miami is a city on the southeastern tip of Florida. Does that sound familiar?" Anderson asked.

"It sounds a bit familiar. I think I've heard of Florida, but I have no idea where or what it is. And I wonder if I'll ever know," Elaine said.

"I'm no doctor, Elaine, but I'll bet you will recover from your injuries and will regain your memory as well in time," said Anderson.

"I hope so," said Elaine. "But the scary part is what happens between now and then. I don't know anybody except you two guys, and I have no idea what I'll do or even be able to do until I recover. I'm just going to be at everybody's mercy, I guess."

"Well, I'm sure the specialist who will examine your injury and prescribe your treatment will have dealt with many patients in the same situation," said Anderson.

"He will be able to recommend treatments and programs and people to help you. Bob and I will take your deceased friend back there to the morgue in the FBI's Miami branch forensics lab for autopsy.

"Our experts will run a full analysis to see if we can get any clues on who he is and who may have shot him in the back. And if at all possible, we will bring his killer or killers to justice."

"Good. That's what I want. And will you keep me posted on what you find out?" asked Elaine. "I'd sure like to know what you find, not only for the sake of justice but to maybe jog my memory about who we are and what happened to us. Why were you flying over the island where you found me, by the way?"

"When we spotted you, we were running search and rescue on a list of incidents we know about, from vessels reported missing or lost at sea to known drug runners, pirates and their victims," said Anderson. "Sometimes we search for those who elude us when we interdict shipments of illegal drugs. We get all kinds of calls, hundreds of them some days, from across the Gulf and the Caribbean. Of course our unit's main territory is South Florida and the Gulf."

"We don't usually deal with people suffering from organic memory loss, though," said McGuffy. "Our drug interdiction and law enforcement units regularly investigate drug smuggling, piracy and related crimes of violence on the high seas. We work with local, state and federal law enforcement and with victims and witnesses to help find and prosecute these criminals. Our hope would be that as you recover from your injuries you will remember things that will help to bring your attackers to justice."

"So maybe we can help each other, then," said Elaine. "I would like that very much, guys. You can count on me."

"That's great, Elaine. Thanks," said Anderson.

At that point, the dispatcher from the Miami base called to say they had located a physician willing to see Elaine the moment she arrived. Dr. Jonas Sutherland, who specializes in treating patients with head injuries and memory loss, agreed to meet them at the receiving port at the landing pad of Miami General Hospital. Anderson was directed to go first to the hospital and put Elaine in the care of physicians, then to immediately bring her deceased friend to the FBI forensics lab on Causeway Island.

"Copy, Miami," said Anderson. "We should arrive at Miami General in approximately 18 minutes. Unit 419 out."

McGuffy said very little on their way in to headquarters. He had embarrassed himself when he offered Elaine food before checking first to learn that there was absolutely none on board. But as they approached Miami General, McGuffy wasted no time in making sure he didn't disappear from Elaine's life after they dropped her off at the hospital.

"Miss Elaine, I don't have a personal business card, but while we were on the way I wrote my name and address and phone number on this snapshot of my brother and me on a fishing trip," said McGuffy. "It was all I could find to write on. That's me on the left, there, and as you can see, my fish clearly weighs more than his. I just carry the photo around to prove it. You can have it. I have other copies of it at home."

"Well, thank you, Bob. I'm glad to have your phone number and your picture," said Elaine. "I hope you won't mind if I call you. You and Joe are the only two guys I know right now. You're kind of my whole world, you might say."

"Sure. Call me any time. Particularly while the doctor is trying to help you get well," said McGuffy. "I'm just glad and honored to be in your world. You can be sure I'll do all I can to help find out who did this to you and bring them to justice."

"Ditto for me, Elaine," said Anderson, not to be outdone by his co-pilot. Taking a cue from McGuffy, he slipped a snapshot of himself with his wife and two children, Rachel, 9, and Tommy, 6, from his billfold. He scratched his name and phone number on the back of the photo with a ballpoint pen and handed it to Elaine.

"I'd be happy for you to call us at any time, too, Elaine," said Anderson. "I'm sure my wife and kids would like to meet you, and I don't think I'm going too far out on a limb to invite you over to our house for a meal and maybe even a game or two of touch football when you feel up to it. But make sure you get well first. We'll check back later today, and if you're going to be stuck here in the hospital for a while, as I expect, we'll come by and see you. So you don't have to worry about Bob and me running out on you. I'm afraid you're stuck with us."

"Thanks, Joe. Thanks, Bob. My headache feels better already," said Elaine.

"You can see Miami on the horizon up ahead here," said Anderson, pointing toward the skyline through the helicopter's windshield. "You see that big white building there? That's the hospital, Miami General, and we'll be there momentarily," he said.

The skyline seemed to rush toward them as the helicopter maintained its speed. As they neared the city, Anderson turned on an ambulance beacon and siren, and the base dispatcher said the way was cleared for the landing. Seconds later they were on the pad and two hospital employees, one with a wheelchair, approached to help even as the rotor whirred slowly to a stop.

At that moment, a tall, broad-shouldered man with silver hair and a white physician's coat stepped from behind a steel-lined glass door across the hospital roof and approached the helicopter.

"I'm Jonas Sutherland, and I understand you have a patient for me," the man said, extending his hand to Anderson and McGuffy. He then smiled and waved to Elaine, who was still seated in the helicopter, smiling and waving back at them.

Anderson opened the helicopter door near Elaine, and he and McGuffy helped her out. She stood shakily for a moment on the pad before the two hospital workers helped her to sit in the wheelchair.

"I'm Dr. Sutherland," the doctor said, shaking her hand.

"Just call me Elaine, I guess, doctor. I'm afraid I don't remember my real name," she said.

"That's OK. We're going to try to do something about that, Elaine," said Sutherland. "How do you feel?"

"I've got the worst headache I've ever had and a very painful bump the size of a fist on the right side and back of my head, but other than that I feel OK, I guess," she said. "I'm just glad you could see me, Doctor, and I owe my being here to these two gentlemen." She smiled again and nodded at Anderson and McGuffy, who nodded back as they climbed aboard.

"Thanks, men. We'll do all we can to help her. Now excuse us. We've got to run," said Sutherland, who turned to the hospital workers and said, "Take her to my office suite."

Elaine was impressed at how smoothly and yet how fast the hospital workers steered her wheelchair down the halls of the hospital to the doctor's 11th-floor office. And she smiled again as she heard the helicopter on the roof crank up and speed away.

In Dr. Sutherland's office, Elaine sat in the wheelchair and waited.

Nurse Helen Martin and various assistants scurried about, readying a battery of tests to determine the precise nature of her head injury and to prepare to start her treatment. One of them stuck a thermometer in her mouth. Another strapped a blood-pressure device on her arm, and another gave her an injection. Still another asked whether and where she was hurting; shined a flashlight in her eyes, and asked whether she had nausea, dizziness, blurred vision, paralysis or tingling in arms or legs, irregular heartbeat or difficulty breathing or speaking.

"I was a bit dizzy and unsteady on my feet when I got off the helicopter, but I'm not having any of those problems now," said Elaine as aide Roberta Sanchez approached her with a clipboard and a thick stack of forms of some kind.

"That's great. Hi. I'm Roberta," said the aide. "I understand that we may call you Elaine, and I wonder if we may ask you a few housekeeping questions for our records."

"Yes, that will be alright. But I'm afraid I don't remember my real name or much of anything else for your record," said Elaine.

"That's alright, Elaine. Most of the people we see in this unit have that same problem, and I'm glad to say we help most of them to recover their memory in due time. We'll do all we can to help you, too," said Roberta.

"For record purposes, however, would I be right to assume that you are not able at this time to give us your full name, date of birth, address, phone number, or medical insurance information? Is that right?"

"That's right. I don't remember any of that," said Elaine.

"That's fine. Now as we go forward with the tests, if you find at any time that you remember any of those things, will you interrupt whatever we are doing or saying and let us know that? Will you do that for us?"

"Yes. Sure," said Elaine. "But could I ask you a question?"

"Sure. Asking questions is a good sign. What's your question?" asked Roberta.

"Can I please have something to eat? I'm starving," said Elaine.

"Eating too soon after a head injury can sometimes cause a problem, but if you're not experiencing nausea, and I understand you've already eaten some snack crackers, I don't know why not," said nurse Martin. "What can we get for you?"

"This probably sounds weird to you, but I noticed a golden arches sign across the street as we landed, and I've been wanting a double-size order of their fries and a sundae ever since. Is that out of the question?" asked Elaine.

"Oh, I'm afraid we couldn't ...," said the nurse, pausing as Sutherland walked in.

"Of course you may have fries and a sundae," said Sutherland with a smile. He reached behind his white robe for his billfold and motioned for one of the orderlies in the hallway.

"Angelo, take this $5 bill down to Mickey D's and get Elaine here a double order of fries and a sundae," he said. "What would you like on the sundae, Elaine? Peanuts? Chocolate syrup? You name it, and what would you like to drink?"

"Thanks a lot, doctor," said Elaine, surprised that he had approved her request so quickly. "Just plain vanilla on the sundae, please, and I'll have ice water to drink, but I would appreciate some ketchup for the fries if you don't mind," she said, her face lighting up like the morning sun.

"You heard that, Angelo? Bring her some ketchup and a bottle of water with her fries and ice cream," said Sutherland as he put his billfold back in his pocket, pulled up a stool in front of Elaine and sat on it.

"You know, Elaine, you've passed a lot of the tests we usually give without even taking them," said Sutherland. "You sat upright during your helicopter ride to the hospital. Normally people with a head injury like yours come in on a stretcher or gurney, because a high percentage of them have a broken neck.

"That could mean a broken or damaged spinal cord and paralysis if we move them the wrong way. In your case, we're going to do x-rays, PET scans and MRIs just to make sure, but I'm betting you don't have a neck fracture or you wouldn't have been able to come in holding up your head without excruciating pain."

"Well, doctor, I do have excruciating pain, but it's on that big, soft-centered bump on the right side and near the back of my head here," she said, pulling her blood-matted hair back gently and then grimacing as even touching her hair near the wound created flaming pain.

"We have given you an injection of mannitol to reduce the swelling, and we'll give you something for pain shortly. I understand you already had acetaminophen en route here," said Sutherland. "That's actually not a bad treatment at this stage, but we'll give you something else as we learn more about your injury."

"What about my memory, Doc?" asked Elaine. "Can you tell me whether I will ever know who I am; where I came from; how I got here; who my family is; who did this to me; and who shot and killed the man I found dead on the beach?"

"Now that's several questions. We'll answer them all in due time. For now, you have an excellent chance of regaining all or almost all of your memory, Elaine," said Sutherland.

"I understand you were unconscious for a while but you have no way of knowing for how long. We'll try to determine how long. That's important, because the shorter the period of unconsciousness, the greater the chance of recovery.

"Normally, a severe blow to the base of the skull can cause paralysis, coma, problems with heart rhythm and breathing and even death. You obviously haven't had such symptoms."

"No, doctor. Just the pain around the bump on my head and the loss of memory," said Elaine.

"Well, that's a bit of a puzzle but not an unusual situation," said Sutherland. "Let me explain it this way: Sometimes the brain is severely injured in an area other than where the skull is injured.

"Sometimes a compound skull fracture like you apparently have at the back and side of your head relieves pressure from blood and fluids that otherwise would build up there or elsewhere and cause the symptoms like paralysis and death that I've mentioned.

"The reverse also is true. Unrelieved internal bleeding from an initial and seemingly minor injury to the skull can cause serious injury elsewhere later from pressure that builds up over a period of hours or even days.

"If that occurs with you, we have methods of detecting and relieving the pressure. So obviously, this will require close monitoring for a period of days or even weeks. You will have a private room here, and until further notice consider this home."

"But doctor, I'm sure you know I have no insurance. At least, none that I know of. So I have no way to pay for what would be obviously big medical bills," said Elaine.

"Well, you seem to remember accurately the strong connection between money and medicine in this country, but in a case like yours we have policies and programs to take care of that. You don't worry yourself about any of that. Just concentrate on getting well," said Sutherland.

"Well, I don't remember much of anything about my past life. What kind of injury causes that?" asked Elaine. "I have this big bump on my head but almost none of the symptoms you mentioned. How do you explain that?"

"We know that the temporal lobes on the sides and back of the head are involved with memory," said Sutherland.

"We'll find out for certain with the x-rays and scans, but it appears that the bump to the back and side of your head was a compound fracture that allowed the brain to expand as the fluids built up. This prevented more serious injury.

"There seems to be enough direct injury to the temporal lobe to interfere with memory, but in most cases, this is an interference with recall that goes away as the brain heals. Usually this doesn't represent a destruction of the memory cells themselves. Short term memories near the time of the initial injury are the exception. Those usually are lost permanently."

"That's got to be good news for the criminals that did this, if I never remember what they look like," said Elaine, "but maybe I'll remember enough some day to bring them to justice."

"Perhaps you will, Elaine. I certainly hope so. And we're going to do all we can to help bring that about," said Sutherland.

"Does that mean that I can stay in touch with the Coast Guard investigators, particularly if I have a long hospital stay, to see if anything they find out jogs my memory on that and other things?" Elaine asked.

"You certainly may. And those Coast Guard guys wouldn't want it any other way," said Sutherland. "In fact, interactions with others and your obviously strong motivation to remember can actually aid in your recovery. We will assign people to work with you as well, and there are non-profit voluntary community programs we'll put you in touch with that can help you begin to rebuild your life as you regain your memory and search for your past."

"Thanks, Doctor," said Elaine. "For the first time since I regained consciousness this morning on the beach, I don't have a splitting headache. The pain is still there, but it's a lot better. And I've just noticed what a horrible mess I'm in. My hair must look like a worn-out mop, and I still have sand and salt all over me. Can I please have someone help me to get cleaned up a bit, although I don't have any clothes but the ones I have on."

"My assistants here will help you with that and then take you through all the scans and other tests. We'll issue you some gowns, which aren't so bad once you get used to them," said Sutherland.

Angelo was back with the sundae and fries. Elaine thanked him and Sutherland and gobbled at least a half dozen fries in her first bite.

After Elaine finished virtually all of the fries and the sundae from Micky D's, two of Dr. Sutherland's aides helped her into a shower. Moments later, clean and refreshed, she was wearing a hospital gown instead of the salty, sandy, outfit in which she had spent last night in the ocean unconscious and strapped to a plank.

"Do you feel better now, Elaine?" Sutherland asked her as she sat in front of a mirror while another aide combed her long locks of light brown hair, cropping closely and removing snippets from the area matted with dried blood around the huge bump on the side and back of her skull.

"I feel a lot better, Doctor, thanks," said Elaine. "A few hours ago, I didn't know whether I would be alive much longer, and the pain was so severe it made me nauseous. The pain in my head still is stabbing me every time my heart beats, but the nausea is gone, and I think the fries and sundae were just what the doctor ordered."

"They were indeed," said Sutherland, "and now I'm going to order you something to take away that stabbing pain you mentioned, and when it takes effect, my aides are going to run you through all those electronic scans I mentioned. I want you to eat only a light meal tonight, which they'll bring you from the kitchen. You'll be here overnight, of course, and if all goes well, you may have whatever you want for breakfast. I'll see you tomorrow morning about nine to go over your test results. We'll find out what's broke and what isn't in that noggin of yours, and we'll come up with a plan to fix it, OK?"

"OK. Fine. Thanks, Doctor," she said as two more orderlies showed up with another gurney.

"Ready for your PET scan?" one orderly asked with a smile and a cheery voice as she nodded 'yes,' and the other orderly helped her up on the gurney and placed a specially shaped foam pillow under her head and neck so as not to put pressure on the bump on her head.

Elaine studied the bright ceiling lights in the hallways as she rode the gurney from the doctor's office to what seemed like an endless series of x-rays, tests and electronic scans. Afterward, late in the afternoon, she was wheeled into what would become her private room. A woman with a notepad who identified herself as a staff psychologist was already there.

"I'm Dr. Mary Horton, a staff psychologist, and I understand we may call you Elaine," the woman said with a smile, extending her hand.

"Nice to meet you, Dr. Horton, and you may call me Elaine, although I have no idea if that's my real name," said Elaine, shaking the woman's hand.

"Well, until we know for sure, we'll just call you Elaine. It's a very pretty name, I think," Horton said.

"I like it, too," said Elaine. "I'd be happy to find out that's who I really am."

"Well, why don't you tell me how you came by the name Elaine, if you don't mind," said Mary.

"I was on a sandy island last night, unconscious and bound to a plank by a man's leather belt," said Elaine. "When I came to this morning and was finally able to get the belt off me and the plank, I noticed something a long way down the beach that I couldn't make out. I don't know why, but I felt like I needed to find out what it was.

"It took me a while, but eventually I learned that it was a dead man, who had been shot in the back. When I tried to bury him in the sand, I saw what looked like a home-made tattoo, little irregular rows of blue dots that spelled ELAINE on his left shoulder. I noticed that he had on jeans without a belt, so I'm guessing the belt binding me to the plank was his. The plank helped me float while I was unconscious, and it probably saved my life."

"I see," said Horton. "That seems like a logical conclusion. When you say the name ELAINE aloud, does it sound familiar to you or stir any memories?"

"No. It just sounds like a pretty name, and I just think it might be mine. How pleased I would be to find that it's my name. Because that would mean I had been able to untangle the mystery of my past life, and that might help me to get on with my present and future," she said.

"It's not unusual, Elaine, for lost memory to be restored gradually, a few bits at a time," said Horton. "So I'll be talking with you almost every day to see if we can help you remember the pieces of your past. Just don't give up, and be as patient as you can. I will try to make our conversations as painless as possible."

"Thanks, Doctor. I appreciate your help, and I'm sure your comments will be interesting and helpful to me," said Elaine.

"Well, I'm aware that you've had a long day, so I'll keep this our first conversation short," said Horton. "Is there anything at all you want to talk about, any feelings you want to share, any questions you have that we may be able to answer?"

"Yes, there is, Doctor. I'm glad you asked," said Elaine. "I keep feeling like my family somewhere is grieving over me, wondering where I am and what happened to me. I don't get a flashback of anyone in particular, but it seems that I have one or more children. I just know if I have children, they're missing me, and that hurts me and makes me feel like I miss them, although I don't know if I really have any children. Is there any way to find out?"

"Recovering your memory would be the best way I know, and we can't rush that process," said Horton. "Until you recover your memory, we won't know who or where or how old your children are, even if we knew you had children. So I'd suggest you try not to let that worry you."

"I'll try, but I feel so lonesome. I just hope I can get some sleep here by myself tonight," said Elaine.

"Well, just know that nurses will be on duty on this floor all night, and you may pull the call bell at any time you need anything, even if you just need to see a human face or to share thoughts or concerns," said Horton. "It's not unusual after someone has suffered a serious physical injury to feel vulnerable and threatened. So if you experience anxiety, just know it's natural and it's temporary. I'm sure you will continue to get medication for pain, and that should help you sleep as well. Dr. Sutherland will want you to be rested as he discusses the results of your tests with you tomorrow. So sleep tight and know there are a whole bunch of people who care about you and will be pulling for you, Elaine. I'm betting that's your real name, by the way. So good night and I'll see you tomorrow."

"Good night, Doctor. And thanks for caring about me."

"You're welcome, Elaine. Good night," Horton said as she walked out, leaving Elaine alone in her hospital room. But before she could feel sorry for herself, the food wagon stopped at her door and left her a standard order of chicken tenders, creamed potatoes with gravy, fruit cocktail and a cookie and a cup of decaffeinated coffee.

After her meal, Elaine flipped through the channels on the television mounted on the hospital wall but didn't like any of the choices. Then she began to check out the battery of devices she was connected to. Across the room, she could make out a monitor screen displaying what she figured were her heartbeat, breathing and other vital signs.

Through a needle taped to her left arm and a clear plastic tube she was receiving intravenously a clear liquid from a plastic pouch suspended on a stand next to her bed. Through another clear tube attached to a soft rubber cup at the base of her skull, an unsightly bloody liquid trickled slowly into a waste container hooked to the side of her bed.

"I'm hooked up pretty good," she said softly to herself. "It's a good thing I wasn't planning to go anywhere tonight."

A matronly candy striper with characteristic pink apron came by with several magazines, all of which Elaine declined. There was just enough of her headache remaining that reading was the last thing she wanted to do. Then a nurse came by and gave her an injection which she said would reduce her pain. And after a few minutes, all she wanted to do was sleep.

Nurses awoke Elaine several times through the night to make sure that she hadn't slipped into a coma. The sedative was so effective that she quickly returned to sleep between awakenings.

Chapter Three

Elaine finally awoke to the smell of food, the sound of the metal cover over her breakfast being bumped against the table on wheels on which it sat. Smiling down at her was a nurse she hadn't previously met, wearing a starched white dress uniform with a similarly starched white cap.

"Are we ready for some breakfast?" the nurse with abundant but smartly cropped silver grey hair asked with sunshine in her voice.

Elaine, still half in a daze, said nothing but almost involuntarily tried to lift and stretch both her arms, which seemed stiff and sore. But feeling the tug of the fluid tube in her left arm, she stopped half-way of a full stretch and put all of her effort into her right arm instead.

"Good morning. I'm Sarah Stone, and I understand you are Elaine. Is that right?" the nurse asked, again trying to make initial contact.

"Oh, I'm sorry, Ma'am. I must have been still half asleep. Yes, I'm Elaine," she said.

"And are we ready for breakfast?" Sarah asked again.

Elaine looked at the tray of food and said nothing, as though she were having trouble identifying the items.

"What is this?" she asked.

"Well, you have poached egg and dry toast, with margarine and fruit spread on the side if you like, and this is sliced kiwi with sour cream. This is a serving of hot oatmeal with raisins, and your drinks are papaya juice, nonfat milk and coffee," Sarah said as though she considered that a very good breakfast.

"I'm sorry, Ma'am, but I never eat poached egg. Can I please have two eggs sunny side up instead, with bacon?" asked Elaine, as though she were planning to eat her last meal before receiving the death penalty.

When there was no immediate response from the nurse, she added: "Dr. Sutherland said that if things went OK I could have whatever I want for breakfast. Does this mean I didn't do so well last night?"

Sarah laughed. She noticed that Elaine's loss of memory didn't extend to breakfast.

"You did fine last night, Elaine," said Sarah. "We just didn't know what you would want for breakfast. We thought it best to let you sleep this morning as long as possible. Dr. Sutherland wants to see you at nine, so we decided to let you sleep until eight."

Reaching for the breakfast tray and turning toward an orderly, the nurse said, "Take this and bring her two eggs sunny side up with bacon. I'm sure they have that in the kitchen."

"Oh, just swap the eggs out, please. I'd like to keep everything else," said Elaine. Sarah laughed again.

"I believe we really are hungry, aren't we?" Sarah asked.

Elaine, already devouring the oatmeal, nodded "yes" and kept eating.

An orderly Elaine recognized from yesterday afternoon as Angelo pushed a cart containing a large plasma monitor, a disc player and several other items she didn't recognize into her room, making eye contact with her as he stopped at the foot of her bed. He smiled at her but said nothing, figuring she didn't remember he was the one who went to Mickey D's for her fries and sundae the previous afternoon.

Angelo's face lit up as Elaine smiled at him and spoke.

"Hey, Angelo," she said somewhat to his surprise. "Are you bringing me a new TV to watch movies on?"

"No. No TV," Angelo replied. "Dr. Sutherland show scan pictures. You see inside head," he said, touching the side of his head with his finger, then he said, "You head."

"Oh, I see," said Elaine. "That must be to see if my head is empty inside or has any gray stuff in it," she joked.

"No. Not empty. Head have much stuff," Angelo said. "Maybe some blood. Maybe some piece broke."

"Oh, OK. You think my head is broke?" she asked, still kidding him.

Angelo looked down, avoiding eye contact with her. "Dr. Sutherland talk, not Angelo. Maybe not mucho grande broke. See scan pictures first, comprende?"

"Yes, I understand. You're not the doctor, are you? Well, thanks for what you did for me yesterday, Angelo. I appreciate it very much," said Elaine.

Angelo looked up, smiling, and made eye contact with her again.

"You like fries, ice cream, Mickey D's?" he asked.

"Very much. I don't know how to thank you, Angelo," said Elaine.

"Muchas gracias," he said. "Angelo go now," he said as he left the room.

"Muchas gracias, Angelo," she said as he left and another orderly brought in a fresh food tray with two eggs sunny side up and three slices of crisply fried bacon. Sarah and two aides checked a battery of gauges and monitors and made notations on clipboards. They shined a flashlight into her eyes again and asked her all the questions they had asked the day before. Seemingly to their surprise, she had no paralysis or tingling in arms or legs, no irregular breathing, and no irregular heartbeat. She still complained of headache but said the sedative was making the pain tolerable and less severe. They noted that some fluid had drained from the bump on the back and right side of her head during the night, which seemed to please Sarah, the nurse.

"You have near normal respiratory readings, Elaine, and drainage from the site of the trauma is sufficient to prevent pressure buildup and further injury elsewhere," said Sarah.

"I'm sure Dr. Sutherland will want to give you a more thorough report, but from what I see, you couldn't expect a more positive picture," said Sarah.

"In that case, can I please have a mirror to see how horrid my head looks from the outside?" Elaine asked.

"Yes, of course. Bring her a mirror," Sarah said to an orderly, then said to Elaine, "Dr. Sutherland will be in shortly, so you have a few minutes to freshen up if you like. But please don't get out of bed yet. The assistants are here to assist you if you need them."

Without Elaine's asking her for help, an assistant brought in a basin of warm water, a towel and a bar of soap and asked, "Would you like me to help you wash your face?"

"Is it that dirty?" Elaine asked with a smile, then before the girl could answer said, "Thank you, but I can do it. Thanks for bringing the water and the soap and towel. You all are spoiling me rotten I want you to know. I would like for you to raise the bed under my pillow a bit and help me with that drain tube on that bump on my head, however, if you don't mind."

"Sure. Let me help you," the assistant said. A few minutes later, after a face-washing and a few trips with a comb through her hair, Dr. Sutherland and Sarah and a couple of aides came into the room. Sutherland was flipping a page on the clipboard that Sarah had handed him in the hallway.

"So, you like bacon and eggs sunny side up, do you?" Sutherland asked Elaine as he stopped by her bedside. "Me too," he said, shaking her free hand. "Did you sleep well? What about the headache?"

"I slept very well, Doctor, thank you," she said. "Maybe I'm supposed to remember it, but I don't remember waking up in the night. One of the nurses told me she had awakened me every two hours. I just don't remember it. But the headache is much better."

"That's good. We'll maintain the sedation a while longer, but you aren't supposed to remember waking up, necessarily," said Sutherland. "You were heavily sedated, and your short-term memory may fade a bit for a while because of the trauma. That's totally normal for your situation. It will pass. Don't worry about it. Anything else you want to tell me or ask me before we go over your scan results?"

"No, Doctor. I guess I'm ready to hear the sad part now," said Elaine.

"Actually, Elaine, I can't always say this, but I see only good things in your scan results," Sutherland said, flipping on the plasma screen and punching up several multi-color images of what was obviously Elaine's head and its contents from several angles.

"This gets into forensic medicine a bit, Elaine, but if I were asked to testify in court, as I may be asked to do someday in the trial of whoever did this to you, I would say you were hit with a flat wooden object, such as a wide plank," said Sutherland. "Do you want to know why I say that?"

"Sure. I want to know anything and everything you can tell me, Doctor," said Elaine. "What have you found out?"

"Your skull is shattered into fragments like the spokes of a wagon wheel," said Sutherland, pointing on the screen image to fracture lines that fanned out from a central point. "This central point is the contact point with a broad, flat object like a plank. The fracture lines radiate out more than three inches in all directions, which means the plank was really wide, perhaps six or even eight inches wide. That pressed all the fragments in together, the same distance at the same time, then bounced back. That allowed the entire brain and not just the pressure point to absorb the impact. Are you following me?"

"Yes, I think so, Doctor. Go on," Elaine said.

"A rounded object, like a pipe or a pole or a baseball bat would have left an indented area, with the skull fragments pushing inward on the brain like a bullet or projectile of some sort. Such an impact could and likely would have killed you instantly," said Sutherland.

"Or if you survived, it could have left you paralyzed or in a vegetative stupor for the rest of your life. That could have been months or years," he said.

"A sharp metal object likewise would have sliced into your brain, which could and likely would have been instantly fatal. But what we have here is quite remarkable and a fact of good fortune for you, Elaine," said Sutherland

"Even though you didn't get major punctures in the membranes surrounding the brain, which we call the meninges, from skull fragments being driven inward, you did get a single, shallow puncture," said Sutherland. "The puncture, which we see right here, may have saved your life."

Sutherland pointed on the view screen to what looked like a toothpick, piercing the membrane between the brain and the skull for a short distance between two fracture lines.

"I'm guessing that's a shard of wood from a splintered plank," said Sutherland.

"A splinter may have saved my life?" asked Elaine. "Surely that couldn't be so. What do you mean?"

"You see, that puncture allowed blood and fluid to drain out that otherwise could have built up pressure and caused additional injuries elsewhere in the brain, which in turn could have made you essentially nonfunctional," said Sutherland. "There could have been a rupture or hernia in the notch between the temporal lobe and the cerebellum, which could have caused paralysis, coma, irregular heartbeat, breathing difficulty and death."

"So does that mean I dodged a bullet?" Elaine asked.

"In more ways than one, Elaine," Sutherland said. "For instance, had the plank hit you on the back of the skull, it would have smashed the brain stem, and it would have been all over for you. But that doesn't mean you're out of the woods. There are more things to be concerned about."

"Like what?" Elaine wanted to know.

"The problem with puncturing the membrane surrounding the brain is that you are at risk for a severe and debilitating infection," said Sutherland. "An infection in the meninges, which we call meningitis, usually responds to megadoses of antibiotics, but sometimes it doesn't. There's no surefire way to get the antibiotic exactly where it needs to be at the time it's needed. And over long periods of treatment, the bacteria mutate and become resistant to the antibiotic. So as I said, you're out of the ocean but not yet out of the woods."

"I see, Doctor," said Elaine. "So what are you going to do, and what can I do?"

"You need to plan to cool your heels around here for the next four to six weeks," said Sutherland. "We need to monitor you constantly, to make sure we nip any infection in the bud and to be sure there aren't hematoma and edema points or blood and fluid buildup that could cause new injuries.

"While you're healing, we just have to be alert to any changes in your symptoms that may indicate problems. Just remember those symptoms I described and let me know if you start getting any of them.

"Of course, we're going to put you through regular scans which ought to indicate any problems before they get too big to solve. And in the meantime, young lady, I want you to make as many new friends as possible. You're going to need them. Any questions?"

"Just a few, Doctor," said Elaine. "You didn't mention surgery. I guess I was wondering if you were going to go in there and get that toothpick out of my head."

"Not for a few days, Elaine, so long as the drainage from the bump on your head is sufficient to keep the pressure down," said Sutherland.

"The drainage is expelling any agents of infection that may have come from the splinter. Trying to remove it too soon could cause the infection to spread.

"You don't have any skull fragments that are out of alignment, so the fractures should heal on their own without any interference from us. So, medically and surgically, we just have to hurry up and wait. Any more questions?"

"Yes, Doctor. I couldn't help but wonder if that splinter came from the board I was strapped to or one similar to it," said Elaine. "I know the chances of finding a chip in the ocean are slim to none, but I was just wondering: if the splinter could be identified, it might be a clue to who hit me and thus may be a clue to who I am.

"The tide took that plank back out to the ocean, but it may have come back when the tide changed. I'd like to suggest that to the Coast Guard guys. What do you think?"

"That's a remarkable question to which I don't have an answer. It's a bit out of my league, but high-tech investigative techniques have brought many a criminal to justice. It just might work. I'd say give it a try for sure," said Sutherland.

"Thanks, Doctor. Just turn that splinter over to the Coast Guard if anything happens to me," said Elaine. "I haven't heard yet from the guys who rescued me. Maybe they'll contact me soon."

"A Lt. Anderson and a Lt. McGuffy already called my office this morning to find out when they could come by," said Sutherland. "I'll have my secretary call them back and tell them they can come by anytime. For the time being, however, I'd rather you stay here at home base, though. OK?"

"OK, Doctor. Will do," she said.

"Good. I'll see you about this time tomorrow. Let the nurse know if you need something for pain or have trouble sleeping," said Sutherland, who stopped a moment at the door and looked down at the floor.

"So you like eggs and bacon? I'll tell them to let you have anything you want from the kitchen," he said.

Elaine was in her hospital bed, still receiving a variety of liquids intravenously when a smartly dressed young man in a dark blue U.S. Coast Guard uniform, carrying a bouquet of pink roses, stopped at the doorway of her room.

"May I help you?" asked nurse Sarah Stone, stepping directly in front of him as though to prevent his entry unless he could justify his being there.

"I'm looking for a Miss Elaine, uh, somebody. I'm sorry, I don't know her last name, but I understand she's a patient here. I was told she could have visitors," the young soldier said.

"And who might you be?" the nurse asked him.

"I'm Lt. Robert McGuffy, Ma'am, of the U.S. Coast Guard, but you can call me Bob," he said, noticing Elaine for the first time in a bed in the far side of the room, behind the nurse, behind a mountain of medical equipment, and behind a curtain pulled only part of the way closed. "Oh, I see her. That's her there, Ma'am," McGuffy said eagerly, removing his cap and holding up the flowers for Elaine to see.

"It turns out, Bob, that you are right on both counts," Sarah said. "We do have a patient named Elaine and neither she nor we know her last name. She's right over there," the nurse said, turning to one side and stretching out her arm toward Elaine. "She can have visitors, properly identified, of course, and I suppose these are for me," Sarah said, pointing to the bouquet and wiping out her previously stern countenance with a smile and a wink at McGuffy.

"Uh, no Ma'am, not really," said McGuffy, turning bright red as he noticed Elaine cupping her free hand over her mouth to stifle a snicker. "They're for Miss Elaine."

"Well, you can show your flowers to her, and I'm sure she appreciates them, but we have a rather strict rule about leaving flowers on display in patient rooms. We have to guard against allergies as well as bacteria that may be multiplying in them," said Sarah. "But we have a botanical garden behind glass walls downstairs in our lobby. I'd be happy to have an orderly take them down there for display so visitors and our ambulatory patients can enjoy them for as long as they're fresh. Of course, Elaine isn't quite ambulatory yet, but you're welcome to visit with her here in her room if you like and if it's OK with her."

"Oh, yes Ma'am. I'm sorry. I didn't know about the rule against flowers. Now that Miss Elaine has seen them, I'd be happy for them to be put on display in the lobby," McGuffy said.

"They're beautiful, Lt. McGuffy. It was nice of you to bring them and even nicer that you remembered me," said Elaine. "Of course, I'm delighted for you to visit me, but why don't you drop that `Miss Elaine' stuff. Just call me Elaine."

"Sure, Elaine. How are you feeling? And I guess more importantly, how are you doing? What do the doctors say? And how about dropping that Lt. McGuffy stuff. Call me Bob, remember?"

"Sure, Bob. I'm still fairly heavily sedated, as you can probably tell by the way I'm slurring my words, but I'm not in a lot of pain. Dr. Sutherland seems to think I'm doing quite well for a gal who nearly got her brains knocked out," said Elaine.

"The doctor and nurse are all excited about how much gross-looking bloody crud is draining out of that huge bump on my head. They say the drainage means that stuff won't be building up pressure inside my brain that could cause even more serious damage."

"That's good news, I guess," said McGuffy. "I mean, it still sounds very serious to me."

"It sounds serious to me, too, Bob, but I feel good about Dr. Sutherland and the whole staff here," said Elaine. "They're spoiling me rotten, and I really think they've had a lot of experience working with people with serious head injuries. Bottom line, it's just going to take time."

"Like, how much time? Have they said how long it will be before you can get out of the hospital? Are they going to have to operate, I mean, like brain surgery? And do they think you will regain your memory?" asked McGuffy.

"That's several questions, but Dr. Sutherland said I should expect, in his words to 'cool my heels' here in the hospital for a month to six weeks, and he believes I should get most if not all of my memory back, with the exception of events just before and just after I was hit on the head," said Elaine.

"Oh, by the way, he thinks I was hit by some wide plank, which had splinters on it like the plank I was strapped to when I washed up on the beach. In fact, one of the splinters may have saved my life, he said."

"Naw! A splinter saved your life? How does he figure that?" asked McGuffy.

"Well, you should have seen that multi-color scan image of my head, which he had displayed on a big-screen plasma monitor," said Elaine. "He said a splinter from the plank punctured the membranes around my brain, which allowed the blood and fluid to drain out instead of to put pressure on areas that control things like arm and leg movement, heartbeat, and breathing and could even cause death."

"Wow! That does sound like you're lucky!" said McGuffy.

"Well, I'm not sure lucky is the right word. But the downside of that puncture is that I could get a deadly infection or meningitis, which still could wipe me out," said Elaine.

"But he's going to bombard me with antibiotics for a while, monitor me constantly, and remove the splinter only after he's convinced any possible infection is gone.

"Meanwhile, my skull, which was busted into a lot of little pieces, should grow back all on its own, the doctor said, without further surgery, which is totally alright with me."

"I'll bet," said McGuffy. "Well, gee, I'm glad, Elaine, that the doctor has given you a good report, and I know you'll be eager to come on through the infection and other danger zones, but I know you're a fighter from what I saw you had done on that beach, so I predict you'll whip this thing, coming through with flying colors."

"I hope so, Bob. But thank you so much, first for helping to rescue me and then for thinking about me. The flowers were beautiful, even though they wouldn't let me keep them. The thought was there, and was so sweet," she said, and suddenly she felt she was about to cry. She reached for a tissue instead and wiped her eyes.

"Is something wrong?" McGuffy asked her.

"No. Must have got an eyelash in my eye," she said.

"Well, I don't want to overstay my welcome. Maybe I ought to be going. Is there anything you want that they'll let you have? I'll be glad to get it and bring it to you," McGuffy said.

"Not really, Bob. Dr. Sutherland sent an orderly over to Mickey D's yesterday for ice cream and fries for me, and this morning he told me he would instruct the kitchen to let me have anything I liked. But I would like you to mention that splinter to the investigators and ask them for me whether there's any chance you all could find that piece of board I was strapped to when I floated ashore," said Elaine.

"I know it's just one chip on a vast ocean, with no way to find it, but I'm thinking that if it washed ashore on that island and then back out again when the tide changed, it just might wash back again when the tide reversed.

"If you could find it, it just might be possible to relate it to the splinter that's in my brain, and if so, to where it came from. And that might help find whoever used it to bash my brains out and why. And after all those `ifs,' the biggest `if' of all would be if it would help me find out who I am."

"We've got investigators assigned to your case already, Elaine," said McGuffy. "Joe and I are on the team along with several specialists. I think they may be headed back out to the island soon to try to plot the currents and see if we can back them up to the point in time and to the approximate location of where you and your deceased friend were attacked. We all want to bring whoever did this to you and him to justice."

"Thank you, Bob. That means a lot to me," said Elaine. "All the more, because I still can't do much of anything about it myself."

"You just get well, Elaine. I believe you will start to remember key facts that will help us fill in the gaps in our investigation eventually," said McGuffy. "Well, I'll be going."

McGuffy leaned over her bed for an awkward hug before nodding to the nurse and two orderlies on his way out.

"Oh, and Joe said to tell you `hi' and that he'll be by soon to see you," said McGuffy.

"Oh, OK. Thanks and tell him thanks, too," said Elaine.

"Will do. Bye now," said McGuffy.

"Bye, Bob," said Elaine as he disappeared down the hallway.

Anderson was about to enter a flower and gift shop half a block from Miami General Hospital when his cell phone rang. It was McGuffy.

"Joe, it's me, Bob. Just thought I'd save you a few bucks in case you were thinking of taking any flowers by the hospital for Elaine. I've just come from there, and they wouldn't let her keep live flowers in her room," said McGuffy.

"Oh, really? What are you, a mind-reader, clairvoyant or something?" asked Anderson. ``I was just about to go into a flower shop to buy flowers for Elaine. That's exactly what I was going to do."

"See. You owe me one," said McGuffy. "You might give her a box of chocolates instead, since she told me the doctor said she could eat any foods she likes from the hospital kitchen."

"Well, I'll bet they don't have chocolates on the patient menu. Maybe I'll give her another pack of snack crackers with peanut butter, or do you want to do that this time?" asked Anderson.

"OK. OK. I get the insinuation. Just go ahead and give her flowers. See if I care," said McGuffy as he walked into the flower shop and stood next to Anderson.

"You were spying on me!" said Anderson.

"No, I just came out of the hospital and saw you walk in here," said McGuffy. "It's no skin off my nose, no matter how you want to spend your money."

Anderson bought a book, *Scenic Florida*, and had it wrapped.

"Did you have a good visit with Elaine?" Anderson asked.

"Yes, I guess I had a good visit, except that they took my flowers away from me and put them behind the glass walls of a display case in the hospital lobby. Said they were concerned about allergies and germs or something," said McGuffy.

"Yeah? Well how's she doing? Did she remember you?" asked Anderson.

"Oh yeah, big time," said McGuffy. "Said the doctor told her she dodged a bullet and may make a nearly full recovery. Said something about a splinter's saving her life. I'm not sure I heard her right or understood what she said, but it had something to do with fluid draining out of that bump on her head instead of building up pressure inside the brain. Doctor believes she was hit by a wide plank like the one she floated to shore on. Well, hey, if you're on your way up there, let her tell you."

"Yeah, OK. Did she say she remembered anything about who did this to her and the guy that was shot in the back, I guess her husband?" asked Anderson.

"No. Said she didn't remember and may not remember things that happened right before and right after the time she was hit," said McGuffy. "But she was very much onto our trying to find the plank she floated in on. Thinks it might be a clue to what happened and who she is."

"Well, that's like finding a needle in a haystack, but I think old Morelli and company want to tackle it," said Anderson, referring to Chief Petty Officer Walter Morelli, operations officer of a special Justice Department-funded Tactical Law Enforcement Team assigned to the case.

"They took our coordinates and went back out to the island today, measuring wind and ocean currents and all, hoping to get back to the point where the attack occurred."

"Yeah, that's what I told Elaine. But frankly, it sounds like hocus-pocus to me," said McGuffy. "I mean, it's not like they left a puddle of blood on the sidewalk. What do you think? And what do they want us to do about it?"

"I think we'll do what Morelli tells us and see what shakes out," said Anderson. "I've learned not to second-guess those high-tech gurus. You never know what they might pull out of their hat."

"Well, I hope they can pull out whoever did this and send them to where the sun don't shine for a long time if not permanently," said McGuffy.

"You and me, too," said Anderson, turning to walk toward the hospital entrance. "I'll be in the office in a little while, after I drop this book off for Elaine. I guess you got Morelli's e-mail about the briefing at 1100 hours?"

"Yeah, I got it. Guess I'll see you there," said McGuffy.

"See you," said Anderson as they swapped salutes.

Chapter Four

Master Chief Petty Officer Walter Morelli was standing behind a plain wooden desk at the front of his briefing room when Anderson and McGuffy walked in about five minutes early for the scheduled briefing of his Special Tactical Law Enforcement Team.

A special Justice Department grant aimed at cleaning up drug trafficking and piracy in the Gulf of Mexico was funding the team's operations. Through a complicated patronage chain, Lieutenant Commander Jeanne Hoover, who was a licensed surgeon before she decided to make the Coast Guard her career, was named to head the team.

And she had named Morelli as her operations officer. Morelli was an experienced investigator who was handling search and rescue missions and law enforcement patrols when some members of the team were in diapers. And with Hoover's advice and approval, Morelli had assembled the rest of the team.

When Anderson and McGuffy arrived for the day's mission briefing, Hoover and the other three team members already had taken their seats. Morelli stood next to a screen on which was projected a map of the Gulf of Mexico, marked at various points by a series of red X's.

"Come in, gentlemen," Morelli greeted Anderson and McGuffy as he punched keys on a laptop computer, "and please be seated. I believe we're all here, so let's begin.

"I'll start by commending officers Anderson and McGuffy for their successful rescue on yesterday of a Caucasian female, designated for now as `Elaine,' from an uninhabited sandbar near Cape Romano Island just off the southwest Florida coast. They also retrieved from the same location the body of a deceased Caucasian male with a gunshot wound to the back. I believe we have an autopsy report on that, don't we, Commander?" Morelli asked Hoover.

"Yes we do, Chief," said Hoover, handing Morelli a printed report in a blue folder. "Ensign Hess and I completed the autopsy at 1600 hours yesterday."

"And what were your key findings?" asked Morelli.

"We believe the cause of death was drowning, precipitated by loss of consciousness from blood loss from a gunshot wound to the lower back," said Hoover. "The bullet caused moderate damage to internal organs, the left kidney and large intestine, resulting in significant blood loss from the entry point in the lower back to the exit in the lower abdomen."

"Anything else of note?" asked Morelli.

"Yes, sir, there was significant alcohol content in the blood, however below the intoxication point, and no other drugs were detected."

"Thank you, Commander, and for those who don't know it already, Cdr. Hoover is a licensed surgeon and also answers to the title of Doctor Hoover. Did you determine the approximate time of death, Doctor?" asked Morelli.

"In our judgment, the time of death was approximately 12 hours prior to the start of our examination, which would put it pre-dawn on Monday between 0300 and 0400 hours," said Hoover.

"And I believe the female subject regained consciousness shortly before 0700 hours, or about daybreak on Monday, which means she was out between three and four hours?" asked Morelli.

"That's correct," said Hoover. "And that is quite significant, because as a general rule, the shorter the period of unconsciousness the greater the likelihood of recovery, particularly memory loss, which was substantial in this case, according to her attending physician, Dr. Jonas Sutherland."

"Has Sutherland agreed to work with us in monitoring her memory recovery for possible significance in this case?" asked Morelli.

"Yes, he has," said Hoover. "In fact, he says the subject, who now calls herself Elaine, has mentioned wanting to work directly with us to try to bring to justice whoever attacked her and shot the deceased male in the back."

"Good," said Morelli. "Now what does our marine science technician, Petty Officer Patrick Meacham, have to report? Anything?"

"Yessir," said Meacham. "Petty Officer Sam Mendez, our law enforcement specialist, and I flew immediately out to the island yesterday afternoon to document tidal activity and wind and ocean current speeds and directions. We think we can project the site of the crime from the subjects' arrival on the beach backward to the time of the attack and more or less pinpoint its location."

"Are you telling me that you can determine where this crime occurred?" asked Morelli.

"From the position of the female subject and the deceased male subject on the beach and from the prevailing wind and water currents, yessir, but with some qualifications," said Meacham.

"Qualifications? You mean wiggle room?" asked Morelli.

"You might call it that, sir," said Meacham.

"Well, go on. What qualifications are we talking about?" asked Morelli.

"Well, our method presumes that the two subjects began floating on the water at almost precisely the same time and place and coincident with their substantial injuries," said Meacham. "And we assume that they were allowed to float naturally, neither hindered nor helped along by external forces other than the prevailing wind and water currents. We don't know that for certain, but we assume that."

"In other words, the female subject hit the water immediately upon her being bludgeoned by someone wielding a plank, and the deceased male drowned at almost the same time and location after being shot in the back," said Morelli.

"That's right, sir," said Meacham. "At least, those are our assumptions."

"You know what they say about assumptions, but it seems to me we have to have a starting place somewhere," said Morelli. "And if these assumptions can't be sustained in light of further investigation, we'll toss them. Is there anything else before we focus on some questions I have which I haven't heard you mention?"

Morelli looked around the room at members of the team, who for the first time had nothing to say.

"Well, I'll start with you, Sam," said Morelli. "Did you check for evidence that our Lady Elaine may have shot the deceased male, who may have considered her his significant other at some time in the past? And it's elementary I know, but did you check her for powder residue from firing the pistol or look for the spent cartridge or the projectile or the gun?"

"I arranged with Dr. Sutherland for a check for powder traces on the hands and arms of the female subject but found none," said Hoover before Mendez could answer. "It was clear that the projectile exited the deceased male subject's abdomen at the time or shortly before he drowned. It was not retained by his body and thus was never on the island."

"Lack of evidence proves nothing, but to answer your question, Pat and I did search the vicinity where they arrived on the beach and found none of the evidence you mentioned on the island," said Mendez.

"OK. Speaking of what was on the island, did anybody find the plank the female subject told Lieutenants Anderson and McGuffy she was strapped onto when she floated ashore in the early hours of yesterday morning?" asked Morelli.

Nobody answered.

"She told us she was strapped to the board by a man's leather belt, which she unhooked and tossed aside after she regained consciousness," Anderson said eventually.

"McGuffy recovered the belt, but she said the plank, with splintered ends and sides, floated back out to sea when the tide changed. From her description of it, it likely was a piece of wreckage from a yacht or a boat of fairly significant size.

"She told me when I visited her in her hospital room this morning that she considered trying to recover the plank as she saw it floating away from the shore, but she said she was afraid she'd pass out again. She said she hoped we could find it, however, because she thought it could offer significant clues to her identity as well as to the perpetrators of this crime."

"Well, Cdr. Hoover and I agree with her. So you and Lt. McGuffy will take a search team out to look for that plank today until you find it or until further notice," said Morelli. "Ensign Hess and Officers Meacham and Mendez, you will go with them. Use your measuring techniques and see if you can project where that plank should be right now, given what you already know about the wind and water currents and tidal action in the area of that island."

"Respectfully, Chief, considering we have six million square miles of ocean in the transit zone and at least a dozen vessels in some kind of distress at any given minute, there's not a high degree of likelihood that we could find a single plank, even if the entire Coast Guard were looking diligently for it," said Meacham.

"That's why we've got experts like you fellows working on it," said Morelli. "Now if there's nothing else, I have a few more questions for you to work on in your spare time:

"First, why do you suppose that a single plank of wreckage floated ashore with Lady Elaine instead of literally dozens of pieces of debris that an explosion of a boat or yacht would have produced?" asked Morelli.

"And since that wreckage wasn't found with Elaine and her friend, where do you suppose it is? Don't everybody answer at once.

"Oh, never mind. I'll work on those questions today. I've got to have something to do to keep me busy. I did take the liberty of calling for incident reports for our patrol area for the past 24 hours. And some trivia for you: we had at least three incidents of exploding or sunken vessels and at least six others are disabled and adrift at sea, one or more of them near where you found Lady Elaine and friend. In the past 24 we also have confiscated 53 pounds of marijuana and 390 pounds of cocaine on our way to rescue or otherwise help 96 people in distress, save a dozen lives, interdict and rescue another dozen would-be illegal immigrants and board nearly 200 vessels in the name of law enforcement. So it's a busy Gulf out there, and it's time we get to it, folks. It's going to be a busy day. And now I'll turn this briefing over to our commanding officer, Lt.Cdr. Jeanne Hoover."

"Thanks, Chief. Our work appears to be laid out for us," said Hoover before the team headed out for the day.

"I'll expect the diligence Chief Morelli has described from each member of this team, and for the record, I include myself, although he and I have drawn office duty today. We'll do our best here at the base to navigate a sea of government red tape having to do with the administration of our team and its mission. I'll expect you guys to present a report of your findings on Wednesday morning, that's here at 0900 tomorrow. Dismissed."

Morelli folded his laptop and the map of the Gulf of Mexico vanished from the projection screen.

"You gave them something they can cut their teeth on, Walt," said Hoover as the briefing room emptied and the two of them walked toward their office down the hall.

"I think we've all got a lot to chew on," said Morelli.

On Tuesday afternoon, Anderson, McGuffy and three other members of the Special Tactical Law Enforcement Team boarded a twin-engine Dolphin HH65 helicopter. It was the chopper Anderson and McGuffy had used in their rescue of Elaine on Monday. It was to be their mission vehicle for today.

"So where do you guys think we ought to look first?" asked Anderson. "Pardon me if I think your so-called scientific method isn't nearly sophisticated enough to find a single plank in so many square miles of water."

"No pardon necessary," said Meacham, the team's marine science guru. "I'm as skeptical as you are about that. But I will say our method is a few degrees better than throwing a dart at a map of the Gulf, which is the alternative as I see it."

"I'm afraid you're right," said Anderson. "So let's get started," he said as he took his seat in the cockpit, and the others except McGuffy, his co-pilot, climbed aboard.

"Now where is McGuffy?" Anderson asked. "I thought he walked out of the briefing room with us. Did any of you see where he went?"

"No. Maybe he went to the latrine," said Mendez.

"Well, I'd hate to do this without him, but I'm not in the mood to play baby sitter," said Anderson, starting the chopper's engine.

At that moment, over the sound of the idling helicopter engine, could be heard a man from somewhere behind them yelling something unintelligible at the top of his lungs.

In his rear-view mirrors Anderson could see a man in blue coveralls running toward their helicopter, waving one arm frantically and pulling the handle of a heavily loaded utility wagon with the other. Recognizing the man as McGuffy, Anderson killed the engine and waited.

"Do you want us to come out and play, too?" Anderson yelled out an open window as McGuffy approached the chopper's cargo bay.

"No, I want you to come outside and help me load these supplies, unless you want to spend the day flying around out there with nothing to eat," said McGuffy. "Let me correct that. Nothing to eat but peanut butter and cracker sandwiches."

"OK. OK. You learn quickly, I see," said Anderson. "Boys, let's help him unload that wagon. What do you have for us today, Bob? Steak and potatoes I hope."

"Nope. Roast 'possum in lime sauce and gator stew with swamp cabbage were all I could find in the supply bin," said McGuffy. "And I threw in a few first aid and survival kits just in case we need them."

"Well, let's hope we don't need them, and let's hope you're joking on those meals," said Anderson. Moments later, the crew had the chopper's cache of supplies loaded and were back in their seats, ready for takeoff.

"So where to, guys? Any suggestions?" Anderson asked again as he opened throttle, and with no immediate input from his crew, retraced his path of yesterday over Everglades National Park and the Ten Thousand Islands to Cape Romano.

"Actually I have done a few calculations which I'll share with you," Meacham said eventually. "We know the plank Elaine was strapped to moved quickly away from the island yesterday morning when the tide changed. For that to happen, she got unhooked from the plank shortly before the tide changed, otherwise it would have stayed on the beach as she and the dead man did. As it turned out, the tide came in just far enough and long enough to float the plank and carry it quickly back out to sea."

"Wouldn't the wind and water currents have kept the plank close to the beach, since they were sufficient to bring Elaine and the dead man ashore?" asked Anderson.

"That's a good question," said Meacham. "The plank would have hovered close to the island if the currents had remained constant, but we know from measurement listings from other points around the Gulf that what we are calling our base line currents were temporarily influenced by a squall line that crossed the transit zone shortly after you guys left the island yesterday. We think the combined currents are taking the plank roughly half the distance to Dry Tortugas each 24 hours."

"Which means?" asked Anderson.

"Which means it's going to float very close to Key West about this time tomorrow, assuming it isn't plucked out of the water by a beach bum wanting to use it as fuel for his campfire," said Meacham.

"Awesome!" said McGuffy in his first and only contribution to the conversation. "I never would have believed it."

"I still don't believe it," said Mendez, "and I helped him come up with this story. But as my compadre told you a few minutes ago, it's got to be as good a starting point as throwing a dart at a map of the Gulf."

"Well, I have to agree on that, so what do you say, we head on over to Key West, lock onto the course you guys think the plank is most likely to have taken, and rush out to meet it?" asked Anderson.

"Actually, it's very important that we do just that," said Meacham. "Since we don't know exactly what it looks like, virtually our only chance of identifying it from among maybe hundreds of others on the beach is to spot it before it gets there. A lone plank along these coordinates has a high probability of being the plank we're looking for. We have to get ahead of it and scoop it up as we meet it."

"I think that's a plan, but since we're roughly 24 hours ahead of the plank from its point of view right now, do you think we've got at least a few minutes to eat some of that swamp cabbage Bob found for us. What do you say?" asked Anderson.

"We're traveling a lot faster than the plank, so we may be only an hour or less ahead of it from our point of view," said Meacham. "But yeah, we've got time for lunch so long as we don't take too long. And if we can keep one eye on the ocean as we go."

"Bob, can you wedge yourself between the seats and make it back to the cargo bay without our landing?" Anderson asked McGuffy. "I know you can because I saw you slip like an eel back there when Elaine was in distress there yesterday. So why don't you do the honors on lunch?"

"I think I can handle that, although I want you guys to know that you don't come anywhere close to Elaine as an incentive for me to come back there," said McGuffy.

"Sounds like he's sweet on her already," said Meacham. "That's a bit swift even for you, isn't it, Bob?"

"Well, I'll just say you guys are at a distinct disadvantage compared to Joe and me in that you've not yet seen her," said McGuffy.

"Oh? You make her sound like a looker, but that doesn't mean you and Joe have an advantage over Sam and me," said Meacham.

"How do you figure that?" asked McGuffy.

"She hasn't seen us yet," Meacham said.

After lunch on packaged rations, Anderson and crew headed south from Cape Romano Island toward Dry Tortugas, where Meacham said the plank that bludgeoned Elaine was most likely bound. They didn't talk about it much, but they felt a heavy sense of futility. At least, they told themselves, their quest was theoretically possible.

They were using wind and water current data compiled earlier by Meacham and Mendez, who had traveled back to the island where Elaine washed ashore. They had calculated the point where they believed Elaine and her husband were attacked. Then they plotted the theoretical present location of the plank. Anderson said he understood they had to search a roughly outlined zone rather than a precise pinpoint.

"Well, that's a good way to put it," said Meacham. "Call it a zone instead of a point. If we had absolute precision, we could just drop a basket a few feet ahead of it and watch it float in. Then we'd be talking about the retrieval point or the target point.

"But even we don't think we're that good. So it's better to think of it as a target zone, ranging perhaps up to several hundred meters on either side of what we calculate to be its true course.

"I'm expecting that we'll fly over its true path and back several times before we spot it. We may be a little off its true course, or we may be precisely on it, but it could be hidden by a wave at the moment and at the place we look."

"That's not very encouraging, Pat," said McGuffy.

"No, but here's the good part about our method," said Meacham. "The plank is presumed to be afloat and still subject to being found until about noon tomorrow, when it floats ashore somewhere near Dry Tortugas. We don't know which shore. So we're just going to run its projected course out there and back, over and over, until we find it, or until the chief says we can throw in the towel."

"You haven't worked with Morelli before, have you?" asked Anderson.

"No, why?" asked Meacham.

"Morelli never throws in the towel," said Anderson

"Well, I guess we may as well find that plank for him, then," said Meacham.

Using the chopper's global positioning system, Anderson flew a direct line, from Cape Romano to Dry Tortugas, several times to no avail. There was no plank in sight, although they retrieved several plastic soft-drink containers and a plastic beach chair.

Anderson theorized that since the plank was described as white or cream-colored, it may have caught the light of the sun and glinted like a sun-sparkle off the water or might have appeared to be a line of white foam on the surface where a wave descended.

They had to return to their Miami base once to refuel, then returned to fly the route again and again, eventually after sunset with their headlamps gleaming.

"You don't think you're going to see a plank in the dark with those little headlights, do you?" asked McGuffy. "I hate to say it, guys, but I think this project is a lost cause."

"When Morelli says it's a lost cause, we say it, and not until then," said Anderson. "So keep your eyes peeled, guys. And Pat, keep feeding me those coordinates."

"Yessir, the coordinates will continue," Meacham said.

At that point, with the sun gone and the ocean almost pitch black, their radio crackled with static and came alive. It was Morelli.

"You can drop the search and head on in to get some shut-eye," said Morelli. "I take it you guys haven't found the plank yet."

"I'm afraid not, Chief," said Anderson. "We've made numerous passes over the calculated path, but we've essentially got nothing to report."

"Bring it on home, then," said Morelli. "We'll try again tomorrow."

"OK, Chief. Anderson out," he said as the radio went silent.

"Well, I guess we can head home, but I'd like to see us make one more pass over the coordinates I calculated," said Meacham. "I've just got a hunch this will be the time we find it."

"I'm game for another spin before we head back, although I don't have any hunches about it one way or another," said Mendez.

"Same for me," said McGuffy. "I'm just thinking we've now got one more opportunity to enjoy skunk cabbage and gator stew instead of decent food back in Miami."

"One more pass it is, and don't complain about the skunk cabbage," said Anderson, guiding the chopper out to sea again on the prescribed path, only this time manipulating the headlight beams back and forth to light a wider swath of water.

Ahead of the chopper, one swipe of the beams lit the wings of several gulls which were circling and occasionally dipping lightly in the water and flying back up again. Then one of them seemed to light on the water and stay there several seconds before flying up a short distance then back again.

"We'll I'll be a monkey's uncle," said Anderson, bringing the helicopter to a hover a respectable distance away from the gulls. "First time I've ever seen that!"

"Me, too," said McGuffy. "If you live long enough, I guess there's no telling what you might see out here."

"Yeah? What's going on? You all see something up there?" asked Meacham.

"He said he saw a monkey and his uncle, which just proves he's been out to sea too long," said Mendez. "It was bound to happen, given the stress we're under. He's finally snapped."

"I'm fine, you guys, but this is passing strange," said Anderson. "Three gulls fighting over a surf board. One rides it awhile, then the others swoop in low, and he flies off and one of them takes his place."

Meacham laughed.

"It's not what you think," said Meacham. "There's a school of small fish that have learned it's safe under the board from being gobbled by the gulls, and the gulls have learned that if they brush the board aside a bit, they get a tasty morsel for supper. It's sort of a symbiotic relationship, but not unusual in marine life."

"I think you've both made a mistake," said Mendez.

"Why do you say that?" asked McGuffy.

"Because that isn't a surf board. That's the blasted plank we've been looking for all over South Florida," said Mendez. "How about dropping your basket down and see if we can haul it aboard. If not, drop me down and I'll grab it."

"I think you're right, Sam," said Anderson, moving directly over the board, which now appeared much clearer in his view. "One basket on the way down," he said, lowering the basket slowly.

Then he moved it underneath the plank and hauled it up beneath the cargo bay door, where Meacham reached out and grabbed it. Within seconds, the plank, a wide 2x8 beam about four feet long with splintered ends and edges, was safely on board the chopper. The retrieval basket was hauled back in place and the door was shut again.

"We just got our net full, guys. Miami, here we come," said Anderson. "And I think we should give ourselves a round of applause."

For a few seconds, as Anderson opened the chopper's throttle and sped toward home base, whistles and cheers and hand-clapping filled the cab, almost drowning out the rising hum of the Dolphin's twin engines.

Chapter Five

Back in Miami, Anderson and company turned the splintered beam over to the director of the FBI lab, who placed it in a sealed evidence bag and locked it in a vault.

Early the next morning, on Wednesday, Morelli and the team's six other members climbed aboard their Dolphin chopper and headed back out across the Gulf for a fly-over of known sites of explosions or disabled or sinking vessels over the past twenty-four hours.

This wasn't a medical mission, despite the presence on board of two skilled medical service personnel: Cdr. Hoover and Ensign Hess. Morelli described the mission of the day as more of a reconnaissance trip, a search for debris from recent explosions or pirate assaults.

Morelli said he was looking specifically for ships that had either used or been on the receiving end of big-caliber weapons fire or explosives.

Since the 9-11-01 terrorist destruction of the World Trade Center towers in New York, the Coast Guard more frequently than ever before was boarding ships in the name of national security or other law enforcement interests. And frequently those exchanges involved weapons fire, physical destruction of vessels, personnel injuries and death.

The nature of these exchanges meant that ships involved in illegal activities were unlikely to report their own injuries or damages to their vessels or to call for help when attacked, because to do so could lead to their arrest and eventual imprisonment or deportation to their home country, where their treatment might very well be worse.

"So you may get to use your stethoscope yet before the day is out, Commander," Morelli told Hoover as they approached an apparently disabled Colombian freighter, leaning as though it were taking on water and making virtually no movement, although a curl of diesel smoke rose from the engine stack.

It had a gaping hole in its hull, obviously from some kind of explosion near the ship on its starboard side, and it appeared to be in danger of capsizing and sinking at any moment. There was no sign of life.

"Let's see what's down there," said Morelli, who used a portable loudspeaker to identify their chopper and crew as the Coast Guard's Special Tactical Law Enforcement Team out of Miami base headquarters.

"Can you acknowledge?" Morelli asked.

A couple of deck hands who had been left as lookouts scurried out of sight but neither they nor anyone else made a reply. Morelli repeated his call over the loudspeaker and gave notice of intent to board the vessel.

"You have apparently sustained an attack and appear disabled," Morelli said then.

"We have medical personnel on board who can render first aid and other medical services to you in case any of your passengers or crew are injured or otherwise need medical help. Is there anyone on board who can acknowledge?"

At this point, a man in khaki coveralls, with one pants leg torn in fragments and obviously blood-stained, hobbled out leaning on a single crutch. He held the crutch under his right arm and waved with his other arm as he looked up at the chopper.

The man shouted something in Spanish then nodded his head "yes" as he beckoned with both hands for them to come aboard.

Anderson kept the chopper aloft but cautiously hovered over the vessel as Hess descended by rope and spoke to the injured man in fluent Spanish. The man's face lit up as Hess spoke, and then he began to shake his head up and down rapidly and repeat an excited little chant, "Gracias! Gracias! Gracias, Senor! Gracias!"

Then the man shouted down to the lower decks and moments later a line of obviously wounded men hobbled out single file and began to gather in a circle around Hess. He said later he was explaining their mission as reconnaissance only rather than rescue, because their chopper was too small to carry more than a few passengers. But their situation and location would be reported, and Coast Guard cutters not far away could be summoned to render emergency aid, Hess told them.

Then one by one, Morelli and all of his team except Anderson followed Hess onto the deck. Anderson kept the chopper aloft a short distance away.

"They say their captain and the ship's regular leadership were killed in a heavy gun battle with a Texas-based pirate ship two days ago southwest of Tampa," said Hess.

"The assault, they said, came several hours after they had sustained heavy damage in an explosion in the edge of the shipping channel west of Dry Tortugas," said Hess.

"After the explosion, apparently of a private yacht loaded with ammonium nitrate, they turned due north out of the shipping lane and limped along instead toward Tampa. They are taking on water and are barely able to stay afloat by keeping the pumps running. They are low on food, water and medical supplies and have at least a dozen crew members too gravely injured to leave the lower decks. They want to know if we can spare them any supplies, but their most urgent request is for surgery and other medical help."

"Ensign Hess and I will see what medical assistance we can render," Hoover told Morelli. "George, tell them we are a small chopper with only minimal supplies, but we will make minimal medical services available to them for one hour, until rescue and recovery ships can get here. Ask them, if they were willing for us to board their ship, why they didn't radio for help from Clearwater, Tampa or Sarasota."

"They said they didn't radio for help because they didn't want authorities to find out what they were hauling. Then when the assault began, their captain was among the first killed, and the pirates shot up all their radios," said Hess.

"Ask them what they were hauling. I can tell by the way the ship is lying that their cargo holds now must be virtually empty," said Morelli.

"They didn't want to tell me what they were hauling, either. Maybe I can get one of them who speaks a little English to talk to you directly," said Hess.

"Pedro hablo un poco de Ingles," said one of the men who appeared not to be injured as he stepped forward.

"He says he speaks only a little English, but maybe it will be enough if he'll talk," said Hess.

"Yo hablo Espanol un poco," Morelli said to the man with considerable hesitation. "Your ship empty, no cargo. Why no cargo?"

"Texas bandito, how you say, pirates blow up ship, shoot, kill, take all cargo, throw much in water," Pedro said.

"What? What was your cargo?" asked Morelli.

"Many Mary Jane, many coca, many café," said Pedro.

"You had a load of marijuana and cocaine?" asked Morelli.

"Si, and mucho café," said Pedro.

"Café'? You mean coffee?" asked Morelli.

"Si, senor. Mucho Cowfey," said Pedro.

"I see," said Morelli. "What did the Texas pirates do with all the loot?"

"No comprende, loot," said Pedro.

"What did they do with marijuana, coke, and coffee?" Morelli asked.

"Haul away Mary Jane and coca on pirate ship," said Pedro. "Throw cowfey in water."

"Which way did the pirates go when they left? Did you see which direction they sailed?" asked Morelli.

"No sail. Diesel ship," said Pedro.

"OK. Diesel. Where did the diesel ship go? Back to Texas?" asked Morelli.

"No. Not Texas. Maybe Bahama. Maybe Miami. Pedro no say," Pedro said.

"Well, thanks a lot, Pedro. You've been a lot of help to us. Muchas gracias. Muchas gracias," said Morelli, who radioed Clearwater and Tampa units as well as a couple of nearby cutters to send medical and other humanitarian help. Hoover and Hess began a triage to treat the most severely injured first.

One of the more severely injured men on the damaged Columbian freighter sat flat on the deck and leaned against a wall of the ship, with his left shoulder wrapped in a large roll of bloody rags. He was smoking what smelled to Hoover like a marijuana cigarette, and he seemed to be in some sort of daze.

The young man, apparently in his mid-20s, had taken a rather large caliber round which almost severed his arm. He obviously had lost much blood. Hoover had Hess speak to him in Spanish, but he appeared confused and looked at him with a troubled stare.

"Tell him I'd like to unroll the bandage and have a look at his arm, but I'd first like to give him an injection for pain," said Hoover.

At this point, he spoke to them in fluent English.

"I don't understand Spanish, Ma'am. I speak English," he said with what Hoover recognized as a South Texas drawl. "I know the arm needs to be removed, and I was just about to try to do it myself, but I couldn't get any of these guys to help me. It's OK if you look at it, but don't give me anything else for pain. I've been giving myself mega doses of morphine already. Any more narcotics and I may go under and not come back."

"Bless you," said Hoover. "You may be right about your arm, but it may be possible to save it. Why don't I take a look at it before we decide?"

"That's fine. I'm guessing you're some kind of doctor?" he asked her.

"Oh, I'm sorry. I'm Dr. Jeanne Hoover, and I'm as you say, `some kind of doctor.' I'm a Coast Guard forensic medical specialist. I am a licensed physician, but I won't kid you. I've had very little experience as a surgeon," said Hoover. "So what I would propose is to see if we can stabilize your arm until we can get a Coast Guard ship here and let one of their experienced surgeons look at it. We've notified nearby bases and cutters and we should be hearing from them shortly."

"That's fine, Ma'am," said the young man, who identified himself as Jim Cummings and leaned forward as though offering his bound-up shoulder for her to see. "As I said, it's not hurtin' bad right now, of course I'm kind of knocked out on morphine and marijuana, which is a wicked combination, Ma'am, I'll tell you right now."

Hoover unwrapped the man's injured arm far enough to tell that the blood had clotted and to unwrap it further not only would inflict needless pain but perhaps could dislodge the clot and start it bleeding again.

"I'm not going to unwrap it any farther, Jim, since we have experienced surgeons on the way. I'd much rather they look at it and do whatever needs to be done in one step, which I'm really not set up here to do," said Hoover. "Do you understand me?"

"You may as well go on and say it out, Ma'am. They're going to have to cut my arm off, and you're just a little chicken-hearted about doing that yourself here in front of all these wounded sailors, aren't you, Ma'am?" Cummings asked.

"No, I'm just being honest with you, Jim," said Hoover. "I could amputate your arm, but I'm not sure I could save it. Perhaps the right doctors under the right conditions might be able to save it. And since you apparently stopped the bleeding long ago, there's nothing to be gained and only more needless pain to you for me to open it back up. If medical help were not on the way, I might very well feel differently about that. OK?"

"OK. I realize you're trying to help me, and I appreciate it," said Cummings.

"So how does a Texas cowboy wind up on a Colombian drug ship?" asked Hess.

"If you all could help me get to a more private place with your chief, I'll tell him not only how come I'm here, but also I'll put a bug in his ear about the folks that did this to us," said Cummings. "I would think with him being in law enforcement and all, he would want to hear what I could tell him."

"That he would, for sure," said Hess. "Let me put you and him together, and maybe Dr. Hoover and I can help some of the men here who are not so badly injured as you. Can I help you up?"

"Yeah, you're going to have to, it seems like. I can't put no pressure on it without it putting me in orbit sky high, and of course with all the drugs I got in me, I ain't exactly steady on my feet," said Cummings.

"That's alright. Let me help you up," said Hess, lifting him by his good arm.

"There. Hope that didn't hurt too bad," Hess said as Cummings stood wavering against a wall of the ship, shaking like a sail in a strong wind. "Come this way. Our chief is right over here, and since nobody's using your captain's cabin right now, I guess you may as well talk there. Chief, this young man, although he's injured badly and under heavy sedation, wants to talk to you privately about what happened on this ship, who did it to them and where they went."

"Well, I may as well talk to him," said Morelli. "I haven't gotten a thing out of the rest of these guys. Looks like somebody mopped them up pretty good, although I have to say it serves them right for the business they're in. Hi. I'm Coast Guard Chief Petty Officer Walter Morelli," he said, extending a hand to Cummings. "I understand you have something to tell me, and in English yet."

"Yessir," said Cummings, throwing down his marijuana cigarette and stomping it out with his shoe as he extended his good arm for a handshake. "I think I can tell you some things that would be of interest to you, being in law enforcement and all like you are."

"Good. Well why don't you for a start tell me what my associate asked you awhile ago. How does a Texas cowboy like yourself wind up on a Colombian drug ship?"

"That's just it, sir," said Cummings. "I didn't start out on no drug ship. Well, I can't really say that. I did start out on a drug ship out of Texas, Brownsville to be exact. Except I didn't know it was a drug ship at the time. I thought it was more of a vigilante, good ole' boy, pirate-type operation, where just for kicks we go out on the Gulf and scout us out some of these guys who haul drugs and illegal immigrants and stuff, you name it, and try to impress on them a more law-abiding course of action, if you get my drift. The idea I got was they was going to lighten these druggies' loads on the high seas and make the whole dadgum Gulf of Mexico into a cocaine toddy. You know, slash it open with machetes and throw it overboard. Pity them dolphins and whales and stuff if there's any there, cause they ain't going to feel a thing after they sip some of that soup."

"I get the picture. You just take the law into your own hands and inflict cowboy justice, judge, jury and executioner all in one operation. Is that about it?" asked Morelli.

Cummings broke into a wide grin and a drug-drunk giggle. He showed stained yellow teeth and filled the air with the smell of stale marijuana smoke.

"Yessir, something like that," Cummings laughed again, then grew abruptly serious. "But I didn't know them boys did what I found out they did after I got on the journey. I was not into no killing, and I for sure wasn't into no drug selling. Only drug business I was ever in was for my own use, you understand?"

"I understand. So what happened after you got on the journey as you say?"

"Well, first off, I found out they had loaded the dadgum boat with ammonium nitrate and diesel. I mean, that's a dangerous combination, I want you to know, and I wanted to be nowhere close to a boat-load of ammonium nitrate," said Cummings. "But I found out about the stuff about the third day out, and I confronted them with my complaint about being rooked into something more dangerous than fighting terrorists in Iraq. Yessir. Ammonium nitrate, or Semtex I think they call it, will kill you dead and knock you way up close to the next world. I can say that, because like everybody else, I remember what it did to that federal building in Oklahoma City, and now because I seen 'em do it to a couple's pleasure boat, a yacht you might say."

"Yeah. Tell me about that. We're real interested in that," said Morelli.

"Well, there was this cream-colored boat, pretty souped up if you ask me, with this couple on board," said Cummings. "I think they had named it *Nautilus*, but it was just a pleasure boat as far as I could see. It did have a rather big cargo hold for a pleasure boat it seemed to me. Our ship, which was several times bigger than their little yacht, we called it *The Silver Bullet* and I mean it lived up to its name. Even on diesel power it was fast, but when we opened up them twin jet auxiliary engines, we could out-drag anything on the ocean."

"Yeah, well never mind about your hot-rod; just tell me about the couple in the yacht. What happened to them?" Morelli asked.

"Well, I was going to tell you, see. They told me they came down the Mississippi through New Orleans, then hugged the coast until they reached Mobile. Then they said they headed due south, bound for Cancun," said Cummings. "But they ran into a squall that was pitching them around like a toothpick, and it pushed them away yonder off of their intended course. They wound up in the shipping lane east of Cancun and directly in the path of *The Silver Bullet*, and as it turned out, the path of the Colombian freighter, the *San Pedro,* as well.

"*The Silver Bullet* originally headed out of Brownsville toward the shipping lane just north of the western tip of Cuba. We didn't have *The Silver Bullet*'s course plotted out after that. Joe Brannigan, the captain, said sometimes he did a little business in Tampa, sometimes in Key West and even Miami or Grand Bahama Island, depending on who's buying what he had to sell and who was offering the best price, and of course depending on how busy the Coast Guard was on a given day."

"Get on with it. A squall blew the couple into your path. Then what?" asked Morelli.

"Well, we got up real close to the squall and was waitin' for them when they came through. Our captain, Brannigan, pulled up aside them and offered to help them, since they had taken on a lot of water, one of their engines went kablooey, and they had been battered up pretty good by the storm and was more or less disabled," said Cummings.

"Anyway, Brannigan offered to let them hitch onto our ship and come on board for what he told them was a big party and afterward we'd help them repair their yacht and they'd be on their way. Of course, they did come on board, and right there's when it turned ugly. I begun to have this queasy feeling in my stomach like I didn't belong on

625

this boat on this particular journey."

"What do you mean it turned ugly?" asked Morelli.

"They began to knock the man around a bit and made him drink way too much liquor, and then they began making passes at his wife or girlfriend, I don't know which, and that's when he pulled out this little pistol and began to shoot wild he was so drunk," said Cummings. "But he hit Brannigan right near the heart and almost took him out. Then the others took the gun away from him and threw him and his woman in the brig.

"And right there's when I made the stupid mistake of telling Brannigan that I didn't want no part of whatever he was up to and wanted them to put me and the couple onto their yacht and cut us free to go our own way and take our own chances," said Cummings.

"Well, sir, he did part of that. He put me in the brig with them. Unbeknownst to Brannigan's boys, though, I had a gun myself on a little scabbard under my shirt," said Cummings. "We talked, me and this yachtsman, about a plan to get us out. I was to give him my gun and then rattle the bars and tell them they had to put me somewhere else, that me and this guy couldn't get along.

"Well, Brannigan's boys said they'd let me out if I'd help them load the couple's yacht with ammonium nitrate. I told them I didn't want no part of handling no ammonium nitrate, but they just laughed at me and said I'd have to load it all in that case. Now that was a miserable job right there, but the only other option I had was to get shot on the spot, so I finally got the little cream colored boat loaded plum full of ammonium nitrate. A couple of Brannigan's boys then cut the boat loose and it was adrift in the shipping lane for a while, but we kept an eye on it from a distance until we spotted this Colombian drug boat coming around the western tip of Cuba."

"You mean the ship we're on now?" asked Morelli.

"One and the same," said Cummings. "Well Brannigan had lost a lot of blood, but he was still giving orders. He said they were going to use the yacht as bait to nab this Colombian drug boat, the *San Pedro*. Well, we just laid back and followed the yacht until the *San Pedro* took out after it, then we made as though we was trying to beat them to it. By plan, we laid back then and let the *San Pedro* pass us and cut in front of us, between us and the little yacht, which was riding way down in the water from all that ammonium nitrate.

"Well, the Colombian boat took the bait and steamed right up next to the little yacht between it and us as though to rescue it from us. And about that time, Brannigan set off the ammonium nitrate with a radio signal. It blew the yacht to smithereens and blew a big chunk out of the side of the Colombian boat, disabling it as it is now.

"Well, Brannigan followed the disabled Colombian boat, which then made a sharp turn northeast toward Tampa. It was limping along, and we followed it a couple of hours or more. Then, when Brannigan said it was time, his guys hopped aboard the drug boat like the Marines at Normandy and pretty soon had shot nearly everybody. They made havoc with the *San Pedro*, loading all their coke and marijuana onto *The Silver Bullet* and throwing nearly all of the coffee overboard. Then they put me on board the *San Pedro*, which I'm sure they expected to sink shortly, and they skedaddled south and I'm guessing they eventually went east in the shipping lane toward Miami or the Bahamas or wherever they was headed. I'm guessing they're all the way there by now."

"Is that all?" asked Morelli.

"It just about is," said Cummings, "but when Brannigan's boys was on board the *San Pedro*, I heard a couple of gunshots back on *The Silver Bullet*. I guessed it was the man and woman breaking out of the brig and trying to knock out Brannigan and Perkins. I can't tell you what happened after that, though."

"So that's the full story as far as you know? Are you sure there's nothing else?" asked Morelli.

"Yeah. Well, there is one more thing," said Cummings. "If them Coast Guard doctors ain't here soon, I'm going to have to get me a refill of that morphine and smoke another weed or two, if you care to join me."

"No, but tell me. Did you ever hear the man and woman call each other by name?" asked Morelli.

"Yeah, I did actually," said Cummings. "I know the man called the woman ELAINE a couple of times and she called him some kind of double name like Billy Joe or something," said Cummings. "No, I believe it was Tommy Joe. That's what it was. She called him Tommy Joe."

"Did you find out anything else about them, such as their last name or where they were from?" asked Morelli.

"No, I heard them say they lived somewhere up the Mississippi River, I forget the town," said Cummings. "They didn't use no last names as I can recall."

Chapter Six

A Coast Guard ship announced its approach with several blasts on its horns.

``There's the cutter," said Morelli. "Maybe you can get some help with that arm. Maybe their surgeons will be able to save it. I hope so. You've been a big help. Looks like you jumped that pirate ship just in time, Mr. Cummings. Technically you're under arrest now, but we're going to place you in the custody of that cutter's captain and his med crew, and eventually you'll be in a secure hospital room. OK?"

"Yessir, OK, well, I'd like to do whatever I can to help, after what they done did to me," said Cummings.

``What was your last address?" asked Morelli.

Cummings gave him an address and phone number of a homeless shelter in Brownsville.

"I reckon you can say I lived in Brownsville," said Cummings. ``That's where I was beach bumming when I signed up with Brannigan. I think I would have been better off bumming."

"Probably so," said Morelli, rising to greet an approaching officer from the cutter.

"We're just leaving," Morelli said as the cutter's medical team came aboard the *San Pedro*. Moments later they were transporting Cummings and other wounded sailors aboard for treatment, and Morelli and his team headed toward Miami.

"That was good fishing," Morelli said as the chopper pulled away.

"Yes, it was, Chief," said Hoover. "Cummings was really helpful to us. There may be a lot of pirates out there who'd like to see him dead because of the damning testimony he could and hopefully will give in court. So we need to keep a 24-7 watch on him until this case comes to trial. I'll call the marshals in Brownsville and see if they can keep Cummings safe for us until he can be transferred to a hospital here in Miami. I don't want the rest of those pirates to know we've even got him. They think he went down with the *San Pedro*."

As Morelli and his team rode the chopper toward Miami, Mendez said he has new insight about the crime based on Cummings' story.

"I think I can tell you now, Chief, why there was no debris on the beach where Elaine and her dead buddy washed ashore," said Mendez.

"OK. Let's hear it," said Morelli.

"Well, I figure the *Nautilus* debris must have rained out of the sky for a while. At least one plank of that debris fell on the deck of *The Silver Bullet*," said Mendez. "The rest of the debris floated eastward in the main shipping lane and by now is covering the beaches of Key West and keys farther east.

"Elaine and her then not-yet-dead husband didn't hit the water for a couple of hours or more after the *Nautilus* explosion, and after the *San Pedro* and *The Silver Bullet* had turned north toward Tampa and were off Cape Romano, probably close to where we are now.

"Remember they were armed at the time with Cummings' little pistol, which they used to break out of *The Silver Bullet*'s brig. And while Brannigan's boys were slaughtering the captain and crew of the *San Pedro*, Brannigan and Perkins were more or less alone on *The Silver Bullet*. That's when Elaine and her hubby had a final deadly showdown with them on *The Silver Bullet*'s top deck.

"My theory is that in the struggle, one of Brannigan's men, probably Perkins, picked up one of the bigger planks from the litter on the deck and whacked Elaine across the head, knocking her overboard. As the plank and her head collided, he loosened his grip, probably leaving splinters in his hands as well as in her head, and leaving tissues from them both on the plank.

"Elaine's guy was out of bullets by then, and looking down the gun barrel of Brannigan or one of his men, he knew the only way to escape summary execution after witnessing the bludgeoning of his wife was to jump overboard.

"But as he jumped, Brannigan or one of his men shot him in the back. Elaine presumably floated unconscious as her injured man labored before he died to attach her with his belt to the only piece of debris he could find: the plank that had struck her on the head.

"The crew of *The Silver Bullet* either never saw them in the water or else left them to drown before heading at top speed back toward the shipping lane to Miami."

"Excellent theory," said Morelli and the others together.

"But it seems a bit unlikely to me that the man would have lasted long enough, from the internal wounds I noted in the autopsy report, to attach his wife to the plank before he lost consciousness and they both drowned," said Hoover.

"I fully agree that the plank kept his wife at least intermittently out of the water and thus saved her life. Frankly, though, I'm skeptical about how he was able to do that.

"Given the relatively low temperature of the water and his presumably strong motivation to save her life, he may have tried to restrict his wound in some way to slow his loss of blood. So, considering those possibilities, perhaps it's a plausible theory."

"The ultimate proof of the theory will be the results of the DNA tests," said Morelli. "And I understand you'll be dealing with the lab directly on those. Is that right, Commander?" Morelli asked.

"For sure, Chief," said Hoover. "Getting that plank tested is right at the top of my agenda. And in fairness to Elaine, I think we should tell her what we have found and to invite her to our next briefing."

"Absolutely. Let's do it. I'll schedule it for tomorrow morning," said Morelli.

"I would propose that we contact Dr. Sutherland and offer to hold our briefing in a conference room in the hospital," said Hoover. "That would allow her to attend and perhaps participate in our briefing without leaving the hospital. I feel quite certain that he would prefer that. I'll contact him and suggest we meet with his patient in a conference room tomorrow morning."

"Then if there's nothing else we need to do tonight, I'll bid you guys good night," said Morelli as his team scattered to their own pursuits for the evening.

Hoover called Sutherland and arranged for the team to meet the following morning in a hospital conference room. Sutherland said he would be glad for Elaine to attend the briefing if she felt up to it and if she wanted to. He said he would leave her participation in the briefing totally up to her.

The next morning, which was Thursday, the team stood and applauded as Elaine walked into the briefing room.

"Right this way, Ma'am. May I call you Elaine?" asked Morelli, motioning for her to be seated in the first chair on his right.

"Sure. Elaine's fine," she said, smiling broadly and nodding at Anderson and McGuffy, whom she recognized as her rescuers from the shore of an uninhabited island on Monday morning.

"Elaine, we're really glad you could join us this morning," said Morelli, "and I'd be pleased if you'd sit here by me. If the rest of you will take your seats, we'll begin."

Lt. Thomas Nichols of the headquarters office came in just as the meeting was about to start. Dr. Mary Horton, the hospital's staff psychologist, sat in the back of the room.

"Lt. Nichols of the headquarters office has joined us at my request on short notice this morning," said Morelli, "so Lt. Nichols, if it won't put you on the spot, I'd like to call on you first to give us a report on some of the items on which our team has asked for your help, and of course mention any other matters you care to address. I understand you have several other appointments and will have to leave shortly, is that right?"

"Yessir, that's right, Chief," said Nichols.

"Then go ahead. Tell us what you have," said Morelli.

"All right. First, you asked us to alert hospitals in Florida and elsewhere in the region that a suspected pirate and drug kingpin by the name of Joe Brannigan, a Caucasian male from Brownsville, TX, had been shot near the heart with a small caliber pistol and would likely be seeking medical care," said Nichols.

"Emergency rooms in virtually all of the places you mentioned reported persons shot in the upper portions of their bodies over the past weekend but none fit the description you gave us. We took the liberty of also contacting surgeons of all types licensed by the State of Florida and who are on hospital staffs or are in private practice, and again we found numerous reports of gunshot wounds but as best we could determine, none of them was a Caucasian male from Texas. We will continue to monitor these in case our suspect may seek medical help later in the week, perhaps using an alias."

"That's fine, Lieutenant," said Morelli. "Stay on it if you will and let us know. Also, we'd appreciate it if you could monitor Florida ports for Brannigan's ship, named *The Silver Bullet*, which we know is fully armed and dangerous. This outfit is bad news even if Brannigan has left it for medical care or is incapacitated and no longer is serving as captain.

"Our team would appreciate some backup support to be held at the ready in case we locate the ship and see fit to board it and take its crew into custody on murder, kidnapping, piracy and drug smuggling charges."

"We anticipated the need for substantial support, and we have a cutter under the command of Capt. Bart Ellis, armed and standing by in Miami to lead the assault. Two other cutters are on standby for support. We also are running surveillance to locate the ship and to determine if it is hauling contraband of any type or is operating under an alias documentation number."

"Thank you, Lieutenant, for that report and for the support of the headquarters office in this endeavor," said Morelli. "We appreciate and likely will sorely need your help."

"That's what we're here for, Chief, Commander," said Nichols, acknowledging Hoover's presence. "Now if I may be excused, I'm running late for another appointment."

"Certainly, Lieutenant," said Hoover. "It's likely we'll be in touch with you on other aspects of this case, but that's all for now." Nichols saluted and hurriedly left the room.

Morelli noticed Horton in the back of the room and spoke to her.

"Ma'am, this is a law enforcement briefing and may involve sensitive matters at issue in an on-going criminal investigation. May we ask you to identify yourself?" Morelli asked.

"Certainly, Chief," said the woman, rising. "My apologies for barging in on your meeting unannounced and uninvited. I'm Dr. Mary Horton, the staff psychologist assigned to work with Elaine, whom you obviously know is undergoing treatment here at Miami General for head and brain injury, and is undergoing psychological and general therapy for memory loss.

"Dr. Jonas Sutherland, the supervising surgeon, asked me to attend your meeting and to be of any possible help to you and to Elaine. Our protocols require me to consider anything said at your meeting to be privileged and absolutely confidential except to other members of the hospital staff directly involved in her treatment or therapy."

"In that case, Dr. Horton, why don't you come on up to the table and join us," said Morelli. "We certainly want to work as closely as possible with you and the other hospital staff in helping Elaine to get well and to regain her memory. We're eager for her and for you to help us bring to justice those who have injured her and killed the man we believe was her husband and destroyed their yacht."

"Thanks, Chief Morelli. In that event, I'll join you at the table," said Horton, taking a seat next to Anderson. "For your information, it is our opinion that Elaine is making splendid physical and emotional progress, and we believe that dealing with these issues involving crimes against her and her husband will help her regain access to memories of her past."

"Good," said Morelli, quickly introducing members of his team. He identified Anderson and McGuffy as having rescued Elaine from the island and having recovered her supposed husband's body.

Morelli then called on McGuffy to present the plank they had found floating in the ocean and was believed to have been used to shatter her skull.

At this point, Morelli handed the plank, sealed in a clear plastic evidence bag, to McGuffy, who passed it on to Elaine.

She was all smiles at first, then tears welled up in her eyes as she held the plank, at arms length at first, then tightly close to her chest.

Morelli didn't anticipate her emotional response and for a few moments stood awkwardly silent.

"Let's give her another round of applause, folks," said Anderson, standing up and handing Elaine his handkerchief as the applause continued.

"Thank you," said Elaine, regaining her composure. "I want you to know I am aware that this plank didn't just jump in the helicopter, but was found after many hours of diligent searching, for which I am deeply grateful. I really believe that this plank will be the key to helping me regain my past and face my future, and I thank you for it."

Elaine pointed to one end of the plank, which still had traces of her blood and hair caught among the splinters, and there was a worn spot on each side of it where she was attached to it for several hours by a leather belt.

"I expect that a lab analysis of this plank will show traces of tissue from the belt, which Lt. Anderson recovered for me from the island where he and Lt. McGuffy rescued me on Monday morning," said Elaine. "Now if we could find other pieces of wood like this, perhaps they would show what happened to me and to the man I found on the beach, whom I still don't remember. I can only guess at this point that he was my husband. I have been told by Dr. Sutherland that there is a splinter of wood still in the edge of my brain. At some point, he expects to remove the splinter, which lab tests may show has come from a plank like this. And I can only hope that you people will find some way to tie these facts to whoever did this to me and bring them to justice."

"That's our hope as well, Elaine," said Morelli. "We will share more of our discoveries as we go forward, but in summary fashion I will tell you that we have found a man who witnessed much of what happened to you on the high seas. And based on what he told us, let me ask you if you know anyone named Tommy Joe."

Elaine's eyes squinted and she wrinkled her brow in concentration for a moment then shook her head, "no."

"I'm sorry," she said. "I don't remember anyone by that name."

"What about the name *Nautilus*?" Morelli asked.

"It seems like a name in a story I read a long time ago," said Elaine. "For some reason, it seems that it was the name of a huge underwater boat or submarine, and its captain had a funny name, like Milo or Minnow or something. I remember reading that story in about the eighth grade, I believe.

"I know that the story was so interesting that I immediately wanted to go for a ride in a submarine, and after that I became very interested in boats. I had pictures of ships and boats of all kinds on the walls of my room, which I guess was a bit unusual for a girl. I believe I had one picture of a submarine named *Nautilus*, although it was not the ship Captain Zeno piloted. It was a real ship, powered by atomic energy, and I don't remember the captain's name."

"Excellent, Elaine," said Mary Horton. "Now try again to remember the name of the captain in the story you read about the *Nautilus*. You almost got it just now, but not quite. You said the captain was Milo or Minnow and later you said it was Zeno. Do you want to try again? You're real close."

"I know the names I used were incorrect, but I just can't seem to hit it exactly," said Elaine. "I know it was something like Memo or maybe Leno, but I know that wasn't it, either. I just can't seem to get it right."

"That's OK, Elaine," said Horton. "Just relax and maybe it will come to you correctly after a while. Chief Morelli, I'm sorry I intruded on your presentation. I'll be quiet."

"No, Dr. Horton," said Morelli. "You're doing exactly what I was hoping you could do. Our case will be much easier to prove in court if Elaine regains her memory and can testify as a witness for the prosecution. So please continue to speak up at any time you think it's appropriate."

"Thank you, Chief," said Horton.

"OK, Elaine, I'm going to give you one more name, and I'd like you to tell us what, if anything, it means to you," said Morelli. "The name is Joe Brannigan."

"Joe Brannigan," said Elaine, again furrowing her brow as though trying to remember but once again coming up empty. "No, I don't recognize that name. Sorry."

"That's fine. Don't let it bother you," said Morelli. "Now let me ask you a final question. Did you ever ride on a boat named *Nautilus*, as far as you know?"

"Well, now that's a very interesting question. When I try to think about the name *Nautilus*, I see it on the side of the ship in a picture in the book I told you about, and then I see it on the side of the ship, the nuclear-powered submarine, in the picture I had on the wall of my room," said Elaine. "And I seem to see it on another boat, a cream-colored yacht, at a dock somewhere. I guess that may have been my boat. I know I had a framed photo of the boat, with me and several others, I don't know who, on board, waving at the camera. And that photo, I'm not sure if it was made at the dock or on the sea or if I completely imagined it. But I believe that was a real boat. I'm pretty sure I must have been on it at least once or perhaps many times, but I just can't remember."

"That's good, Elaine. You're doing fine. Just don't let it bother you, OK?" asked Horton. "Just relax, and let it come back at its own speed. It'll come back eventually."

"Sure, Elaine, we don't want to rush you," said Morelli. "Now, since we want you to find your own pace, I won't give you the details just yet of what a man we talked to told us about what he saw happening to you and to your friend or perhaps your husband, he wasn't really sure about that. Thanks for being with us today, and now I want to discuss a few matters with members of our team before adjourning this meeting."

"Chief, I wonder if this might be a good time for Elaine and me to leave the room, since it is clear that you will be discussing matters about which Elaine hasn't yet recovered her memory," said Horton. "But if you will keep us informed of your future meetings, I'm sure we can make the conference room here available to you, and both Elaine and I will be happy to help."

"Thanks, Dr. Horton," said Morelli. "I believe your suggestion is well-taken. Thanks for your help today, and thank you, Elaine, for being here and inspiring our team to work diligently to bring your attackers to justice. We'll send you a memo on our next briefing."

"Thank you, Chief Morelli," said Elaine. "I appreciate the work of you and your team on my behalf. Please let me know whenever I may be of help. And I think I've just remembered the captain's name."

"Which captain?" asked Morelli.

"The *Nautilus* captain," said Elaine. "It's Nemo! You said you would send me a memo, and I immediately remembered. It's Captain Nemo! Captain of the *Nautilus*!"

"Well, is that amazing or not? You're right! It was Nemo," said Morelli. "Team, I think this calls for another round of applause. What do you say?"

Horton and the team stood and cheered and applauded as she and Elaine left the room.

Chapter Seven

Morelli and his team spent the rest of the day flying a saturation search pattern over the Miami harbor and vicinity, checking ships entering or leaving the harbor as well as those loading or unloading. They came up "dry" with nothing that matched the description of *The Silver Bullet*.

"Perhaps we ought to move farther out, and then if we find nothing, head over to Nassau and on up to Grand Bahama Island," Morelli said eventually. "What do you say, Sam? Any suggestions?"

"You're on target, Chief. We've covered the area pretty good, so I'd say we need to move a little farther out," said Mendez.

"Let's do it," said Morelli, nodding to Anderson, who flew farther south of the Miami harbor. They spotted at least two ships headed out to sea and one inbound toward Miami, but one that caught Morelli's eye was anchored about five miles out.

"Let's check that one a bit closer, guys," said Morelli. "If it's the ship we're looking for, I'd rather we didn't fly in close enough to tip our hand that we've spotted them. So see what you can see using binoculars on a rapid fly-by."

"Well, you don't see that every day," said Hess, using his binoculars. "They've got some kind of tarpaulin or blanket hanging over the bow as though it's covering up something."

"What do you suspect they're trying to hide?" asked Morelli.

"Well, if that's the pirate ship, and if they've got the name *Silver Bullet* painted in crude letters on the side like some pirate ships I've seen, then that's what they're covering up," said Hess.

"Well, let's do a fly-by, still a good ways out but a bit closer, to see if we see any signs of recent gunshots," said Morelli.

"Bingo," said Hess. "There do appear to be gunshot holes in the main window of the captain's cabin and on the wall beneath it as well as on the top deck, which seems to be fairly well-littered with pieces of white or cream-colored debris of some kind."

"Notice that there's a yacht docked to their ship," said Hoover. "A man wearing dark slacks, a tan coat and a dark green shirt with no tie is getting out of the yacht and boarding the ship. He's carrying a small black bag of some sort."

"Yeah, and I'm pretty sure I saw that yacht heading out of the harbor a little while ago," said Morelli. "Let's see if we can figure out what he's up to."

In a few minutes, the man with the small black bag returned to the yacht and it pulled away, heading back toward Miami.

"Let's follow that dude a good distance away from him but see where he goes," said Morelli. Moments later the yacht approached a private pier near Key Biscayne.

"If I were a betting man, which I sometimes am, I'd say we've found our quarry," Morelli said. "They're anchored a few miles out, and they're bringing in a doctor, probably a little while each day, to check on the pirate captain Brannigan's near-heart experience. That dude with the black bag may be a doctor who has lost his license because of drug violations or who knows what else and is very well known to the kingpins. That may be the reason we could find no licensed surgeon who treated Brannigan."

"You've mentioned several strong indicators that sound like pay-dirt to me, Chief," said Mendez. "Why don't we shut them down?"

"That's a lot easier said than done, as you know," said Morelli. "But it may be just about time to do it. If we can do a little reconnaissance first and establish for certain that this is *The Silver Bullet*, then I'm ready to alert headquarters and get the green light to take them over by force."

"Well, I've got a plan for establishing their identity," said Mendez.

"Let's hear it," said Morelli.

"Suppose we put a grappling hook on a long rope and fly over the ship and snag their tarp," said Mendez. "I'll bet we'll have all the ID we need."

"Sounds like a plan, Sam. Let's do it," said Morelli.

Moments later, as the team flew over the ship with the grappling hook dangling, the tarp was ripped away, revealing the words SILVER BULLET in hand-painted letters on the side of the ship.

"One down," said Mendez as he drew in the rope and hook, and the chopper headed away from the pirate ship at a rapid clip. "Now what, Chief?"

"Now we alert headquarters that we're ready to move on them according to a plan Cdr. Hoover and I filed Tuesday afternoon while you guys were plank hunting," said Morelli, radioing headquarters. Lt. Nichols took the call.

"Lieutenant, this is Walt Morelli on behalf of Lt. Cdr. Hoover and the Special Tactical Law Enforcement Team. We suggest you pass this on up, but we're ready to put in motion our Operation Knight Raiders," said Morelli. "As our operations plan filed Tuesday shows, we're counting on headquarters to alert the commanders of three cutters in the area to provide a base and support for the operation."

"Understood, Chief, Commander," said Nichols. "I have been briefed on your operation. The cutter captains have their positions relative to *The Silver Bullet*, and alerts will go out momentarily. Capt. Roy Rodriguez, our base operations chief, will monitor your operation and will remain on standby. You may proceed."

"Well, by way of preliminary report, the suspected pirate ship, *The Silver Bullet*, is anchored about five miles south of Miami harbor," said Morelli. "We've observed a yacht bringing what we believe to be a doctor to the ship, staying with the pirates for a few minutes, then returning to the Key Biscayne area, perhaps a private residence. We'll try to get the name and ID number of the yacht and the address of the residence if we can before we hand off any follow-up arrests to you guys at headquarters."

"I'll send a chopper to your location, and we'll follow the doctor," said Nichols.

"Our chopper is leaving headquarters as we speak. Give them five minutes. Nichols out."

Morelli had barely hung up his receiver when he saw a chopper with the characteristic red stripe heading across Biscayne Bay. Moments later, the chopper pilot radioed Morelli about what charges should be lodged against the so-called doctor.

"You don't have to charge him immediately, but coordinate with Lt. Nichols, who will remain in touch with us," said Morelli. "We expect to have evidence within the next 12 to 24 hours to support charges of conspiracy after the fact on murder, assault, piracy within U.S. coastal waters, destruction of private property and drug trafficking. That ought to be enough to hold him for a few days."

Ensign Hess, using binoculars, read out an ID number on the yacht and a street and residence number from the rather substantial house adjoining the pier.

"It's a house befitting a drug kingpin," said Morelli, "or a crooked doctor, maybe both."

"Yessir, we'll take it from here," said the chopper pilot as Morelli gave the word to return to headquarters for a briefing.

"I thought we were readying for an attack on *The Silver Bullet*," said Hess.

"We are. That's why we need to head home for a few hours," said Morelli. "I'll explain everything to you momentarily, so I won't have to compete with the chopper's noise to make myself heard."

Morelli and the team were soon at his briefing room in the federal administrative building. He opened his laptop computer and the map of the Gulf was back on the screen.

"*The Silver Bullet* is anchored here, at a spot we'll mark `SB' in red letters," said Morelli. "The cutter *Red Eagle*, whose skipper is Commander Bart Ellis, will be positioned here off the pirates' port side as the base for our assault teams. Two other cutters will be positioned to the pirates' starboard. One cutter, we'll designate as `C,' will draw alongside them. The third cutter we'll call `D,' will cut in front of them to block their exit if they try to get away. We'll use substantial firepower from all three cutters if necessary to restrain the pirate ship. This will be a multi-directional operation which should prove quite persuasive. Are there any questions thus far?"

"If that pirate ship is as fast as Cummings said it was with its jet backup engines, that may turn out to be a tough plan to execute, Chief," said Hess.

"Yes. What's your question?" asked Morelli.

"How do we overcome the potential disadvantage of going against a ship that is likely to easily outrun us if he chooses?" asked Hess.

"Well, that's the beautiful part of our Operation Knight Raiders," said Morelli. "We do it at night, spelled without the K. The cutters will run darkened ship, and we will be close enough to reach out and touch them before they know we're anywhere near. Our assault force will be three six-member Search and Seizure (SAS) teams. We expect them to be on board before the pirates know they're even on the way. Any more questions?"

"I've got one, Chief," said Mendez. "We can't drop planks and walk over, and we can't swing over on ropes. So how do our SAS teams get on board the pirate ship without being mowed down by automatic weapons fire?"

"Actually we can swing over on ropes, but not directly from the cutters," said Morelli. "The SAS teams will slide off the sides of the *Red Eagle* in inflatable go-fast boats, which will sneak up on the stern of the pirate ship.

"Just before the SAS teams board over the rail with grappling hooks, we will shine a battery of searchlights into the pirates' bridge, which will effectively blind them. And you didn't ask this, but I'll tell you anyway: the young men and women in our SAS teams are as brave as any knights in armor ever were, but every single one of them will feel at risk, and each will feel a healthy dose of fear. They will not only feel at risk, they will be at risk – from the churning propellers of the ship, from the slippery ropes and from the black sea below if they fall. And yes, each one is at risk of being shot."

Silence descended like a veil over the briefing room. And after a while, Morelli asked for a final time: "Any more questions?"

"Where will we be – I mean our Special Tactical Law Enforcement Team — during the battle?" asked Meacham, who had turned pale and appeared visibly shaken by Morelli's stark remarks.

"We'll be in our chopper, which will remain well out of range of any expected weapons fire, although we don't know exactly what the pirates have and whether they remain battle-ready after their assault on the *San Pedro*," said Morelli. "It's possible that they'll be on the lower decks, nursing their wounds, and won't put up much of a fight. But we can't bet on that. If they choose to resist arrest, after the bullets stop flying, our team will go in and process the ship for evidence. So relax, Patrick. You won't be on the front line this time."

"Thanks, Chief," said Meacham, breathing an audible sigh of relief.

"You bet," said Morelli. "Anybody else?"

"I've got a question, Chief," said Anderson. "You said the cutters will be running darkened ship. Will our chopper be dark as well? And what about the phase of the moon? I hadn't thought to check it to see how much light we'll have."

"Our chopper will be far enough away that it should attract no attention, but I would expect us to keep unnecessary lights off," said Morelli. "We're real close to a new moon, which should give us nearly total darkness. We lucked up on that. Now, if there's nothing else, take time for chow and be back here at 2100 hours. Operation Knight Raiders will commence at 2130. That is all."

The moonless night was pitch black when Morelli gave the signal for the three cutters in Operation Knight Raiders to move quietly into positions near the anchored pirate ship. Moments later, skippers of all three cutters signaled they were in place.

"We're a few minutes early by my time, so stand by," Morelli told them. "Cdr. Hoover insists we initiate according to the plan."

"Roger. Standing by," said Cdr. Bart Ellis, who took the time to swap some banter with Morelli.

"Chief, aren't you too old for this kind of work? I thought you'd be sitting in your rocker on your front porch by this time," said Ellis, who had worked numerous operations with Morelli in past years.

"Old is a matter of mind over matter," said Morelli. "If you've still got your mind, it don't matter."

"You got that right," said Ellis. "So are you of a mind to tell me how to do my job in this operation?"

"Anything I don't know, I'll ask my boss, Cdr. Hoover, who's sitting right here. And she suggests that you impress on those SAS teams that we'd really rather place those pirates under arrest than to send them down to Davy Jones' locker," said Morelli. "You know she's a licensed M.D., and killing doesn't exactly fit her doctor's oath."

"I hear you, and I can assure you both that we'd much rather let a judge and jury put these guys away than to have us risk our necks to do it," said Ellis.

"I'm sure those SAS teams have been given strong warnings about the risk of dying from friendly fire if they start firing those automatic weapons in a steel-hulled ship," said Morelli.

"They know that, and they're going to be careful. Was there anything else from advice central?" asked Ellis, as the other two cutter captains chimed in that they were awaiting Morelli's signal to commence the take-over.

"Yeah, one more thing," said Morelli. "Remind your SAS teams that *The Silver Bullet* may be loaded with good evidence we can use against those pirates in court. Capturing that evidence is at least as important as capturing the pirates, because without that evidence, we may not be able to prove they're pirates."

"I hear you," said Ellis. "So what evidence should we be on the lookout for?"

"We can tell the top deck is still littered with debris from the explosion of our girl Elaine's yacht," said Morelli. "We think if we can haul back a load of those splintered beams, we can absolutely match them with the beam we recovered that they used to whack her in the head."

"Gotcha covered," said Ellis. "When we put them all down, one way or another, we'll have a major deck-cleaning and will bring back a cargo bin full of that stuff. What else?"

"Well, we know that Brannigan himself, the pirate captain, may be on board, suffering from a small caliber pistol wound close to the heart," said Morelli. "We'd like to recover that gun. And try to keep them from throwing good evidence into the ocean. We need the evidence. We want to permanently nail these dudes, not just give them a ride to Miami."

"I hear you loud and clear, Walt," said Ellis. "I'm glad we can help. So when do we move?"

"The time has come. Move at will," said Morelli.

"Good, Walt. We're going in," said Ellis. "Ellis out."

Morelli and his team watched from their chopper as three six-member SAS teams teams slipped silently into the water off the starboard side of the *Red Eagle*.

Even the thin sliver of the new moon that could have been seen on a clear night was obscured by a dense layer of fog that almost hid *The Silver Bullet* from view.

Virtually invisible in the darkness, the SAS teams rode inflatable go-fast boats to the stern of the anchored pirate ship and gently tossed grappling hooks over the rail. They knew that if their presence became known and the vessel's propellers were engaged, they could be ground into sausage.

To lessen the chance that the SAS teams would be seen, as the first six went over the rail, a blaze of light from several batteries of searchlights lit the bridge of the pirate ship brighter than the blast of a welder's torch at high noon. Fast on the heels of the first six SAS team members came six more and then a final wave of six more, without a round's being fired and without any of them being seen.

"You are being boarded by U.S. Coast Guard SAS teams and are ordered to stand down and submit to arrest," said Lt. William Morris, commander of the SAS teams, over a portable loudspeaker.

There was no reply and no sign of opposition as the SAS teams occupied the top deck of the pirate ship in a matter of seconds, without incident.

"You are cautioned to lay down your weapons and put your hands behind your heads or be considered hostile," Morris said then. "We intend to place each of you under arrest to face trial on charges of murder, kidnapping, piracy in U.S. coastal waters, and drug trafficking. You are advised to surrender and submit peaceably or you will be taken into custody by force. We are preparing to enter the lower decks. What is your response?"

There was no reply and no sounds indicated anyone was aboard.

Morris stood to one side of a door leading to the lower decks and gently opened it. Then he kicked it open with his foot and again stepped to one side. Again there was no response.

"If any of you has been wounded or is otherwise incapacitated, we will see that you are provided immediate medical help," said Morris. "We have an experienced medical staff on board the Coast Guard cutter *Red Eagle*, which waits a short distance away. We urge you not to sacrifice your health and your lives needlessly."

Again there was no response, but as Morris stepped into the doorway and attempted to walk down a few steps to the second deck, a barrage of machinegun fire hit him in the chest, knocking him flat on his back. Into the doorway sped a half-dozen more SAS team members, who sprinkled selected bales of marijuana with high-powered rifle fire.

Several of the suspected pirates, who had been hiding behind bales of marijuana and bags of cocaine began to roll out onto the deck, dead or obviously seriously injured. At least three SAS team members took shots in an arm or leg during the exchange.

Morris, who was injured but not fatally, because his body armor wasn't pierced, climbed to his feet and returned to the doorway, this time successfully entering onto the second deck.

"Where is your captain? Who is in charge here?" Morris bellowed over the loud-speaker. But there was no reply.

By this time all three SAS teams had reached the second deck, which was quiet and apparently had been neutralized. So Morris gave the order to descend to the third and lowest deck. Before opening the massive wooden door leading down to the third deck, however, Morris fired a barrage of rounds into it, effectively destroying it as it fell off the hinges like a wad of splinters. Morris then ran through the doorway armed with a .45 caliber revolver, rolling over on the deck as he fired in a sequence of single shots at a row of marijuana bales that had been arranged as a kind of walled fort.

Morris, with his weapon drawn, then crawled behind a barricade of bales where a pirate who had run out of ammunition whacked him over the head with an empty pistol.

Morris's helmet held and the pistol blow bounced off his head. Morris then returned the favor, swinging his pistol like a blacksmith's hammer against the pirate's head. The pistol struck the pirate above his right jaw, shattering his skull. Blood spurted in all directions like juice from an over-ripe watermelon.

"Enough!" one pirate yelled at this point. "Hold your fire. We're coming out!" he said, throwing out a pistol and standing with his hands over his head.

"Get behind me," said Morris. "How about the rest of you? Are we done here, or would you like a second helping. We have more troops on the way. Just say the word."

"We're through," said a man who weighed at least 250 pounds, with a blood-stained long-sleeved shirt wrapped around his upper body. He spoke in a raspy voice barely above a whisper.

"I'm Joe Brannigan. I need a doctor," he said to Morris, then turning toward a row of barricades on either side and behind him, he said, "Give it up, boys. Come on out and lay down your guns." At least a dozen men who hadn't yet received any injuries filed out, laid their guns down, and put their hands over their heads.

Suddenly, SAS team members swarmed around Brannigan's men, searched them for weapons and anything else in their pockets, placed leg and wrist cuffs on them and declared them under arrest.

The bloodiest part of their mission accomplished, the SAS teams helped transfer the injured, including three of their own number and Brannigan, the pirate chief, to the *Red Eagle*, where emergency medical teams were standing by and where Cdr. Hoover and Ensign Hess also put their medical skills to good use.

Pirates who were not injured were taken in cuffs aboard the cutter designated "C" and were locked in the brig for their transfer to a federal penal facility in Miami. Six pirates killed in the skirmish were loaded aboard the cutter dubbed "D" for transfer to a morgue in Miami.

Morelli and his team then landed their chopper on the neutralized pirate ship's landing pad and began to process the ship for evidence.

As the cutters prepared to head back toward Miami, Morelli's radio came alive. It was Ellis.

"I think we're done here, Chief," said Ellis. "Can we help you with anything else?"

"No, thanks, Bart. We're done except to look for evidence, and my guys are here to handle that. We've got it covered I think," said Morelli. "That was a heckuva spectacular take-down of that den of pirates, by the way."

"You think so? Well, our SAS teams are good, as you can now judge for yourself," said Ellis. "Too bad three of them took slugs, but I think they'll recover OK. I was wondering, since you're going to need the evidence in federal court, if you'd like me to put the pirate ship in tow and anchor it for you at the Coast Guard pier at the headquarters office in Miami."

"It would be really helpful to us if you could do that," said Morelli. "I'm sure it would be a lot more convenient."

"Then count it done," said Ellis. "Do you think we can weigh anchor and drive it in on its own power?" asked Ellis.

"Well, they had to get it there some way. I'm assuming it was on their own power," said Morelli. "Do you want us to try to start the engines and let you know if they're operational?"

"Naw, that's alright. Just go ahead and process it for evidence before our guys start piddling in it," said Ellis.

"Will do, Bart. Can you give us 30 minutes?" asked Morelli.

"Thirty minutes it is, Walt. Will you need us to haul the evidence back, or do you have that covered, too?"

"We've got that covered I believe, Bart. Thanks again for a splendid operation, and again, I'm sorry three SAS team members got hurt," said Morelli.

"That goes with the territory, Walt. We just suck it up and do our duty. Always prepared, you know," said Ellis.

"Right. I know the Coast Guard motto, too. So I'll call you momentarily," said Morelli.

Morelli and his team except for Cdr. Hoover and Ensign Hess went throughout the pirate ship searching for evidence. Mendez checked the brig and found a man's wallet with no money or cards left in it but with the initials TJF embossed on an inside flap. Anderson checked the pilot's cabin and found a log book of *The Silver Bullet* with a page in the back that listed the names and addresses of its crew.

Meacham checked the cargo hold and noted that it was full of marijuana, cocaine and a few sacks of coffee beans. Mendez found a physician's note on Brannigan's gunshot wound .

Morelli checked the ship's engine room and found its two auxiliary jet engines, just as Cummings had described them, apparently in operating condition but not engaged. Morelli also found a hand-drawn wiring diagram which someone apparently dropped in haste on the floor in an adjacent fuse room. Morelli glanced at it and couldn't understand what he was looking at, so he folded it and put it in his pocket.

"It looks like they've souped up this baby with all kinds of unconventional connections. I'd sure like to take those two jet engines for a spin, but maybe in another life," Morelli muttered to himself.

McGuffy gathered a huge pile of splintered cream-colored planks from the top deck and packed them in a cargo bin on the chopper.

"Well, guys, make one more quick pass to see if we've missed anything, then let's hand this crate over to Capt. Ellis," said Morelli. "I'm going to take another look at that engine room. I can't figure out how those bubbas make those jets work the way they're depicted on their wiring diagram, but I guess it's like a teen-ager with a hot rod. When they say `Watch this!' you never know if it's going to work or be the last thing they ever say. But knowing all that, I'd still like to take her for a spin. I'm just a teenager at heart, I guess."

Moments later, Morelli and his team had completed the evidence search of the pirate ship and were aboard their chopper, headed toward Miami. Morelli put in a call to Ellis.

"You can have it now, Bart. Let me know when you get it to the dock so we can put a security seal on it. It appears to be operable, but your plan to tow it sounds OK, too. That's up to you," said Morelli.

"We've got it covered, Walt. We'll need it on its own power in the harbor, so we may as well go ahead and power her up. We'll take it from here. It was a pleasure working with you guys," said Ellis.

"Same here, Bart. Morelli out."

Chapter Eight

When Morelli and his team had lifted off the pirate ship and headed for Miami, Ellis called the SAS teams and his crew together for a round of verbal and literal pats on the back.

"You guys did a bang-up good job, no pun intended," said Ellis. "We're sorry three of you got hurt, but that goes with the territory, and it could have been much worse. Anyhow, the doctors tell me you'll all recover. We have an excellent medical team on the *Red Eagle*, but I want the three of you who were injured to go home and spend a few weeks on R&R when they run you out of the hospital.

"Now we've got a lighter part of this mission still hanging, and that's to crank up that pirate ship and see what it'll do on the open seas. Morelli said a turncoat member of the pirate crew claimed *The Silver Bullet* has twin jet auxiliary engines, and when they're revved to top speed, it'll in his words `out-drag anything on the ocean.'

"Now I know all of you guys are either teenagers in fact or teenagers at heart. So if there's any of you with plans to one day pilot a Coast Guard ship, you may just want to do all your drag-racing behind the wheel of something other than a Government Issue boat. This may be your chance. Do I have any volunteers to take the old *Silver Bullet* for a spin before showing us your skill at steering it to safe haven at the headquarters pier?"

About six hands went up, but Ellis chose two lieutenants for the mission.

Meanwhile, as Morelli and his team neared Miami, he handed the folded hand-drawn wiring diagram from *The Silver Bullet* to Mendez.

"See what you can make of this, Sam," said Morelli. "I must be getting old, but for the life of me, I can't see how those jet engines could work hooked up like that. Do you see what I mean?"

"I certainly do, Chief," said Mendez after no more than a glance at the hand-drawn diagram. "I don't know if it was just their ignorance or if they intended to hook them up that way, but those engines definitely won't work like that."

"Hmmm. Well, those guys aren't overburdened with gray matter between their ears, or they never would have tangled with the Coast Guard, but that's too dumb even for those guys, don't you think?" Morelli asked.

"Definitely right, Chief," said Mendez. "I'd say that's a deliberate short-circuit. They must have just wanted to make it hard for us to get it to port."

Morelli put in a call to Ellis.

"Come in, Bart. This is Morelli," he said. "Have your guys gone over to start *The Silver Bullet* yet?"

"Yeah, they should be climbing aboard over there about now. Why do you ask?" asked Ellis.

"There's something really strange about a wiring diagram I picked up on the floor of a fuse room next to those two jet engines. My folks and I think those engines won't start hooked up like that. It's more like a deliberate short-circuit, I guess just to make it as hard as possible for us to anchor it at the pier in Miami. So you may want to try to rewire it or just skip trying to crank those engines. We can always hire a tug to push it up to the dock."

"Your suggestion is noted," said Ellis. "But my guys want to take it for a little spin to see what those jets will do. I hope you don't mind. If they get a short-circuit, I guess they'll…" Ellis stopped in mid-sentence and let out with a stream of profanity that blistered even Morelli's ears.

"I've got to stop them, Walt! Stand by!" Ellis yelled, then grabbing another radio unit, he shouted to his two men now boarding *The Silver Bullet*: "Don't start those engines, guys, whatever you do. They've been…"

At that moment, a horrific explosion blew *The Silver Bullet* into a cloud of tiny fragments at least 150 feet in the air. Powerful shock waves rocked the *Red Eagle*, which sat uncomfortably close by but not in direct danger.

"Booby-trapped!" Ellis finally completed his sentence.

"What was that?" Morrelli asked over the radio as the blast lit up the sky for miles. "Bart, are you guys OK?"

"I just lost two good men," said Ellis. "That was one megablast of an explosion, and I hope you guys got all the evidence you needed before she blew. I'm afraid my two guys and what used to be that pirate boat have shipped straight into Davy Jones's locker."

"Say it ain't so, Bart," said Morelli. "Those pirates not only booby-trapped it, they must have saved a sizeable bin of that ammonium nitrate for just this eventuality. It was a dangerous and dastardly thing to do. Too bad those pirates weren't on board when she blew."

Ellis cursed again.

"I sure hate it about your men, Bart. That just makes me want to put those SOBs behind bars even more, you know what I mean?" asked Morelli.

"I know what you mean, Walt. I feel the same way, but I think bars are too good for them," said Ellis. "It's times like these that I'm glad they reinstituted the federal death penalty."

"Yeah, I hear you," said Morelli. "I'm just glad we got a cargo bin or two of evidence before it detonated. We may want to sift through the fragments that rain down in the area for a while. If you want to do any sifting yourself, have at it. And call us if you need us."

"Will do, Walt. Ellis out."

The explosion and the resulting deaths of two Coast Guard sailors attracted substantial local and national media attention. The deaths by Coast Guard gunfire of six suspected pirates and the arrests of more than a dozen others, some severely injured, increased widespread interest in the incident.

The Coast Guard's provision of medical care and humanitarian aid to survivors of the suspected pirates' violent assault on the *San Pedro* also grabbed headlines.

News reports mentioned that the suspected pirates killed the captain and most of the crew of the Colombian ship and left most of the rest severely injured. They also reported that the suspected pirates confiscated a private yacht from an unidentified couple on the high seas, loaded it with ammonium nitrate and blew it up near the *San Pedro*, knocking a huge hole in the Colombian ship's hull.

The reports said the suspected pirates then made away with the *San Pedro's* substantial stash of marijuana and cocaine and a few bags of coffee.

There was scant mention of the couple on the yacht except that authorities still were trying to identify the man, who was shot and killed, and the woman, who was being treated at an undisclosed location for serious but unspecified injuries.

"You hear that, Boss?" asked Vincent Perkins, top sidekick to suspected pirate captain Joe Brannigan, who was in a medical lockup on board the *Red Eagle*. Perkins, his first mate, now in an adjoining medical cell, took several slugs from the Coast Guard SAS teams when they took over the suspected pirate ship. A row of steel security bars separated the two rooms, which had one TV set that could be seen from both rooms.

"Did I hear, what?" asked Brannigan, in a raspy voice barely above a whisper.

"TV said that woman we knocked off after we blew up that yacht is being treated somewhere, they said 'an undisclosed location, for serious but unspecified injuries.' I thought I knocked that wench overboard with a plank," said Perkins. "I know I still have my hands full of splinters from the effort, but if that story's right, she apparently got to shore somehow and might get well and could show up in court to testify against us."

"Get real, Vince," said Brannigan. "They got enough evidence against us already to throw us under the jail. What you worried about her for?"

"'Cause I ain't necessarily guilty of everything that happened on that *Silver Bullet* ride," said Perkins. "Anyways, they got to prove it on us. But if she shows up in court and points me out, it's all over for me. I won't be under the jail. I'll be on the blasted death gurney."

"I 'spect that's where we're all going to be, Vince, unless we can figure out a way to break out of here," said Brannigan. "Except I ain't wanting to break out until I can get well from this bullet hole next to my heart. I mean that two-bit mob doctor that came out here and looked at me on the boat this afternoon don't know beans about no heart surgery. He was right on one thing, though."

"What's that, Boss?" asked Perkins.

"He said I had a powerful infection, and if the pain is any indication, there's no question about that," said Brannigan. "He gave me a megashot of antibiotics and said that's all he could do until he could get someplace where he could do some surgery. He said there may be an abscess in there that will have to be cut out. Of course, we got kind of interrupted from that. Maybe these Coast Guard doctors will be able to operate on me. Anyways, that woman you hit over the head is the least of my worries. There's not a thing happened to her or her old man that she can blame on me."

"You got to be kidding me. I mean, if she shows up in court, she can blame the whole kit and caboodle on you, and me too," said Perkins. "That's what I was getting to. Don't you think we ought to get word to some of the boys back in Brownsville to do some snooping and find her and finish the job I started?"

"I got too much hurtin' around my heart right now, Vince, to worry about her. Maybe if I get well, I could put her somewhere on my list. But, like I said, I've got bigger fish to fry right now. You want to worry about her, you worry about her. Don't bother me with it. You got that, Vince? Don't bloody bother me!"

"Don't get sore," said Perkins. "I was just trying to look out for us, you know?"

Brannigan aimed a blast of profanity at Perkins and told him, "I done been sore for nearly a week now, and I don't think either one of us can stand much more of your looking out for us. So let it be. You hear me?"

"OK, Boss. Sorry I bothered you with it," said Perkins. "I guess if a feller wants anything done he has to do it hisself."

U.S. Attorney Joseph Barton put down his copy of Friday morning's *Miami Herald* after reading an in-depth report of the Thursday night explosion of a suspected pirate ship a few miles south of the Miami Harbor.

The story mentioned that Coast Guard doctors treated those injured in a gun battle between the suspected pirates and Coast Guard SAS teams who took over their ship. The news report also mentioned that the suspected pirates earlier had massacred the crew of a Colombian freighter loaded with marijuana and cocaine off the coast southwest of Tampa.

There was scant mention in the news story of the suspected pirates' assault several days earlier on an unidentified couple and the destruction of their private yacht.

"Margaret, get Master Chief Walter Morelli, on the line for me please," Barton told his secretary on the intercom.

"Right away, sir," the secretary said. "Is anything wrong?"

"That's precisely what I want to find out," said Barton, the newly appointed U.S. attorney in Miami on his first day on the job. "Have you read the morning paper?"

"Oh, you mean the piece about the pirate ship exploding near the harbor?" she asked. "Yessir, I saw it, and it was all over the network and local TV news as well. It didn't mention our office at all on any of the reports I saw, though."

"That's just it," said Barton. "I suspect the Justice Department may call on us at any moment to show that we're keeping a tight rein on this investigation of, by and for the Coast Guard. The explosion that killed those two sailors may well have been part of a botched operation which in any event has cost numerous lives. Washington is anxious enough about us down here in the land of hanging chads without adding a runaway Coast Guard unit to the mix. Let me know when you get Morelli on the line."

"Morelli here,"said Morelli as the phone rang in his office.

"Chief, this is U.S. Attorney Joseph Barton. I've been reading about your anti-pirate, anti-drug operations just south of the harbor, which apparently have resulted in the loss of a ship and the deaths of numerous people, including two young sailors. I was wondering if I could trouble you for a first-person account of your adventures to me and my staff," said Barton.

"Certainly, Mr. Barton," said Morelli. "Perhaps I am remiss in not already having called you to offer you and your staff a preliminary report. I'm well aware that the task of prosecuting the lawbreakers in this bloody business will fall to your office. Our Special Tactical Law Enforcement Team is quite eager to cooperate with your office in every way possible to get successful prosecutions and to bring these guys to justice.

"To that end, Sir, we are taking great pains to gather a rather large body of physical evidence, which is being processed in the FBI's branch forensics laboratory here in Miami. It will be processed and turned over to your office in a condition ready for use in court. I would be glad to come to your office right now or later, as you prefer. Or perhaps you would rather come to my office or to the lab and take a preliminary look at the evidence yourself, first-hand."

"Yes, I would rather come to the lab, wherever the evidence is being held after processing," said Barton. "I will tell you up front, however, Chief, that if the remainder of the evidence is no more secure than was the so-called pirate ship and its reported large cache of contraband marijuana and cocaine, not to mention the two young sailors who lost their lives, then I have some rather substantial concerns about your conduct of this whole operation. Why don't you prepare to show me within the hour the evidence you still have left in your custody?"

"That will be fine, Mr. Barton," said Morelli. "Your office and mine are both rather close to our lab. I will be at the lab in five minutes, and if you'll join me there, I'll show you our evidence as soon as you can get there. Is there anything else?"

"Not at this time, Chief," said Barton. "I'll be right over. It'll take me a bit longer than five minutes, but I'll meet you there shortly."

"We'll be happy to wait for you sir. See you there," said Morelli, who hung up first.

"Was that some heavy-handed bureaucrat wanting to look over our shoulder?" asked Lt. Cdr. Hoover.

"You might say that," said Morelli. "It was the new U.S. attorney, Joseph Barton. His name and picture were in the paper today. This is his first day on the job, and if I read him right, he wants a report from us on our mission in general and on the piracy case specifically. And he wants us to meet him in the lab in a few minutes and show him the evidence we've gathered."

"Well, we'd better hustle, then," said Hoover. "We don't want to keep our new top federal lawyer waiting."

"My thought exactly, especially when it's going to be his office's job to take the evidence we gather and prosecute these pirates," said Morelli as he picked up a file from his desk and tucked it under his arm.

"Actually, we're meeting Barton at a good time," said Hoover. "He can sort out some of the red tape that doctors on the *Red Eagle* are getting tangled up in."

"What kind of red tape?" asked Morelli.

"Some of them insist that their medical treatment of injured piracy suspects takes precedence over their gathering evidence against them for their prosecution. It's a legal question, not a medical question as I see it. Barton should be the one to sort it out."

"Well, Commander, it seems to me we need to ask Mr. Barton to make it clear to Capt. Ellis, since they're on his ship, that our team has jurisdiction over medical personnel treating anyone charged with the crimes we're investigating in this case," said Morelli.

"I agree with you," said Hoover as they arrived at the FBI lab ahead of Barton, giving Morelli time for a little housekeeping. He put in a call to Bart Ellis.

"Bart, this is Morelli. How's the weather?"

"Hey, Walt," said Ellis. "Weather is fine, but we both know you didn't cut your nap short to talk about the weather. What's up?"

"You know me too well," said Morelli. "I'll cut to the chase. I'm expecting the U.S. attorney on my doorstep any minute. I've got to give him an accounting of everything we've done in this investigation, if we can call it that, and what we have to show for it.

"As you very well know, you've done the lion's share of the real work in this case, serving as our SAS teams' base last night and providing medical care afterward. I need to report our operation to the federal lawyers in terms you can live with. You get my drift?"

"Doesn't sound much like drift, Walt. Sounds like the guy's chewing your tail and you're heading away full throttle. Am I right?" asked Ellis.

"Yeah, yeah. Now hear me out," said Morelli. "We need a written account from you as soon as possible on our take-over of the pirate ship, complete with a body count and ID's on the dead, including your two guys that lost their lives; a hospital count, condition reports and ID's on the injured, including the three injured SAS team members, and a head count and ID's on those in custody without injuries. You got all of that?"

"I've got all of that all typed out neatly in my ship's log. What's your fax number and I'll shoot it to you," said Ellis. "Anything else?"

"Yeah, one more thing," said Morelli. "Our team chief, Commander Hoover, tells me that the doctors on your ship are moving ahead with surgery on those injured pirates without waiting for her to process them for evidence. We would request, since they're on your ship, to make it clear to the doctors that they're under Cdr. Hoover's command as regards their treatment of any patient or client connected to this investigation. Do you think you can handle that for us?"

"I can speak to them, Walt, but I can't promise you that it will do any good," said Ellis. "As you should well know by now, doctors are a lot like lawyers. They're independent cusses who pretty much do what they want to, no matter who tells them what."

"I know that, Bart. Hey, this is Jeanne," said Hoover into the receiver. "I want to make sure that we don't lose evidence because of some doctor's lofty, exaggerated sense of ethics. A case in point is the suspected pirate captain's first mate, Vincent somebody I believe, who seemed in the cursory exam I was able to give him yesterday to have multiple splinters in his hands, as well as gunshot wounds in his hip, calf and shoulder.

"I think there's an excellent chance that he's the culprit who hit Elaine, the female victim, with that splintered plank, trying with all his might to kill her. I think he will survive the gunshot wounds easily enough, but we need to match those splinters in his hands if we can to the splintered board on which Elaine floated ashore.

"And we need to match the DNA from this dude to any DNA that might still be on the plank. In short, Bart, we need the evidence, and we can and should be able to obtain it without compromising his medical care in any way."

"Your point is well taken," said Ellis. "I'll speak to them and see what I can do."

"Well, you might remind them that they will comply with the protocols of our mission or they'll be skating close to a court-martial," said Hoover.

"I wouldn't threaten them, if I were you," said Ellis. "Suppose I remind them that they are under my authority on this ship and that you will be on board and will speak for me on all matters pertaining to their treatment of the suspected pirates?"

"Couldn't have said it better myself," said Hoover. "Thanks a bunch, Bart. We owe you one."

"Morelli owes me a heckuva lot more than one, but you've got it. Now what else can I do for you fine folks today?" asked Ellis.

"That's about it, I guess. Is there anything we can do for you?" asked Hoover.

"Yes, now that you mention it, there is something you can do for me," said Ellis.

"What's that?" asked Hoover.

"I have taken the liberty of contacting the headquarters office about transferring custody of your pirates to the federal brig, with the injured going to whatever secure medical facilities they can find available," said Ellis. "As I'm sure you know, the *Red Eagle* isn't exactly a hospital or long-term prison ship, and I would like to return to our first mission of patrol and enforcement as soon as possible. So I would appreciate it if you could sign off on these piracy custody transfers, since you and your team have a stake in being able to process them for evidence as well as to have them nearby as potential witnesses in federal court."

"Well, I would have appreciated a contact before you called them, but I have no problem with your washing us out of your hair," said Hoover. "When do you expect to make the transfers?"

"Headquarters said they could probably make arrangements today, begin the transfers Saturday and complete them by Sunday afternoon," said Ellis. "Would that interfere in any way with you or your team's schedules?"

"Not that I know of," said Hoover. "We're happy to clear out and let you have your ship back as soon as possible. You've been a huge help to us in this mission, and we can't thank you enough for that."

"Good. We're on the same page, then," said Ellis. "As usual, we're prepared to serve. Glad we could be of help. Try to keep Morelli awake. I've gotta run. Ellis out."

Morelli had just hung up the radio receiver when in through the front door of the lab walked Barton and his top assistant, Milton Richards. A fax machine on a nearby desk began to hum, and Morelli checked it, noting that a copy of Ellis' log entry on the take-over of *The Silver Bullet* was coming in.

Morelli glanced at the first page and noticed that, high in the report, Ellis had listed the casualties of the operation. The transmission ended and the fax machine stopped just as Hoover and Morelli greeted the federal lawyers and shook hands with them.

Morelli then reached toward the now silent fax machine and picked up the three pages of Ellis' log entry, which was signed, dated and notarized at the bottom of the third page.

"I believe you will find this report helpful, Mr. Barton," Hoover said as Morelli handed the report to him. "I am prepared to supplement Capt. Ellis' report with whatever additional information you may need, Sir."

Morelli showed Barton and Richards the catalog of evidence in the case, which was contained in clear, sealed bags and described in detail on log sheets identifying each item as to place and time of recovery as well as to its complete chain of custody.

The evidence included the splintered plank, containing the DNA of Elaine and one person yet to be identified. There were several pieces of debris, which seemed clearly to match the other plank in shape and paint color, and the fragment of a page from the log book of a yacht named *Nautilus*.

"It all seems to be in order," Barton said at the conclusion of the lab tour. "I trust that the remaining evidence will be processed and catalogued in like manner and that you will notify my office whenever processing is complete."

"We will keep you posted, Sir," said Hoover and Morelli together as Barton and his assistant departed.

Morelli breathed a sigh of relief as the federal lawyers left the lab. Then he alerted Anderson and McGuffy to fly Hoover and Hess over to the *Red Eagle*. They were to supervise the medical treatment of injured piracy suspects and the gathering of medical evidence for use against them in federal court.

Several doctors had gone ahead with surgery and other treatment procedures, which they contended should take ethical precedence over the gathering of evidence.

Hoover stepped off the chopper and was quickly escorted to Capt. Ellis' cabin, and almost immediately an alert whistle sounded on all decks.

"Now hear this. This is Capt. Bart Ellis," came the captain's voice over the loud-speakers. "All physicians and other medical services personnel are to report to my cabin immediately. That is all."

Moments later, a half-dozen or more doctors and several nurses and assistants gathered outside Ellis' cabin and were invited in.

"This shouldn't take long, folks, but it is both important and urgent," said Ellis. "Please be advised that your medical practice on board this ship is under my authority and direction. As I'm sure you're aware, we are in the midst of an on-going criminal investigation into alleged piracy, drug trafficking, murder, and a half-dozen other charges against some reluctant passengers on this ship, some of whom are among the injured.

"It is imperative that we do not compromise forensic evidence against these suspects during surgery or other treatment procedures. So that we don't work at cross-purposes, Cdr. Jeanne Hoover will speak for me as to the procedures you are to follow. For those of you who may not have met her, she is a licensed surgeon and forensic medical specialist as well as chief of the Special Tactical Law Enforcement Team investigating this piracy and drug-trafficking case. Give her your attention and your cooperation. You will hear her now."

"Thank you Captain," said Hoover, stepping forward to address the doctors. "The requirements are clear. You are to conscientiously care for the injured without destroying or compromising potential evidence. It is important that you accomplish both missions. If you have questions, I will answer them now. If you have questions later, bring them to me. If you find that you are unable to adhere to these requirements, I will expect you to surrender your authorization to practice medicine on this ship. Am I clear? Are there any questions?"

All was quiet except for a low murmur.

"Good. That is all," said Hoover.

"You are dismissed," said Ellis, as the doctors and other medical personnel, including Hoover, left the captain's cabin and headed to the ship's infirmary and surgery center.

Hoover addressed the medical crew there:

"In the brief time you have had to examine the injured, I trust you triaged and met the needs of those most seriously injured first," said Hoover. "I understand that some of you remained on board during the night and are aware of their current conditions. Are there any who are in critical condition?"

"I have one who's critical," said a doctor in the back of the room.

"OK. Give me your name and the name of your patient, with a brief description and pertinent details of the injury and condition," said Hoover.

"I'm Dr. Arlene Davis. My patient is Joseph Brannigan, Caucasian male, age 44, with gunshot wound to the chest," she said. "The projectile, from a small-caliber pistol, is lodged near the heart with substantial abscess, and in my opinion, substantial risk of septic shock. Patient is receiving IV antibiotics, morphine and anti-inflammatory medication."

"Thank you, Doctor. Is surgery indicated?" asked Hoover.

"As I said, Commander, I believe there is substantial risk of septic shock with this patient," said Davis. "I assumed you realized we're talking a substantial risk of death here, whether or not we do surgery."

"You know what you do when you assume, Doctor," said Hoover. "You make an ass out of you and me. For the record, I know that septic shock isn't dropping a hairdryer into your bath water. I'll repeat my question. Try your best to answer it. Is surgery indicated?"

"Not at this time," said Davis. "My recommendation is to keep him on the strongest antibiotics we've got for another eight hours or so, and if the infection shows signs of waning at that point, continue antibiotics for an additional eight hours and operate in mid-morning on Saturday."

"And if the infection remains high after eight more hours of antibiotics?" asked Hoover.

"In that event, reluctantly, I'd say we should do a blood transfusion and proceed with surgery at 8 p.m. tonight," said Davis.

"If you proceed with surgery, do you have the assistance you need or should we arrange for a heart specialist to come aboard to help you?" asked Hoover.

"If the infection remains strong after eight hours, I would appreciate the assistance of a heart specialist," said Davis. "If the infection comes under control, I would do the surgery myself with such assistance as we have on board."

"Good. Do you agree with me, Doctor, that in the intervening eight hours, our investigators could question Mr. Brannigan, with his attorneys present, of course, for thirty minutes to an hour without in any way interfering with the medical treatment you have outlined?" asked Hoover.

"I would rather you not weaken my patient further by subjecting him to interrogation prior to what can only be described as high-risk surgery," said Davis.

"I will note your objection in the written record, Doctor, and will invite you to be present throughout our questioning of him to further monitor his condition and to make such objections as you think necessary," said Hoover. "I will be present also, and in the event you and I disagree as to whether questioning should proceed, my opinion will prevail."

Looking over the group of doctors, Hoover asked again, "Are there any others in critical condition?"

"I have one, Commander," said another doctor. "I'm Thomas Carter. My patient is Vincent Perkins, Caucasian male, age 30, has projectile wounds from large-caliber automatic weapons fire in his left hip, right calf and left shoulder. All the projectiles appear to have exited his body, but muscles in all three wound areas will require substantial repair as soon as possible."

"Thank you, Dr. Carter. I made my own examination of Mr. Perkins Thursday afternoon and I agree fully with your assessment," said Hoover. "I also noted that Mr. Perkins has retained several prominent splinters in his hands. Our investigators believe there is a high probability that Mr. Perkins retains these splinters from tightly grasping the plank he used to whack a woman on the head, attempting to kill her. We have obtained what we believe is the plank he used. The splinters in Mr. Perkins' hands, we believe, constitute strong evidence that he wielded the plank that not only fractured her skull but pierced the outer membrane covering her brain. In short, Doctor, we believe those splinters are vital evidence that we simply must have. It is my opinion that we can extract the splinters in Mr. Perkins' hands prior to surgery without any interference at all with repairs to his bullet wounds. Do you agree?"

"Yes, Commander, I agree," said Carter. "The splinters can be removed without hindering the repairs. In fact, I would be happy for you to remove or to supervise the removal of the splinters immediately, before they extract themselves more or less automatically. I see no problem in delaying surgery until you have removed the splinters."

"Good, Doctor. I will proceed to remove the splinters as soon as we're done here, and I'll inform you when I'm done," said Hoover. "Is there anyone else?"

When no one else spoke up, Hoover said, "You may proceed. Post me on your progress and call on me if you need me. That is all."

Vincent Perkins was asleep when Cdr. Jeanne Hoover, M.D., knocked softly on his medical cell door on Friday morning and called his name. A security guard outside in the hallway stepped aside so she could enter the cell if she chose to.

"Mr. Perkins, I am Dr. Jeanne Hoover and I'd like to visit with you a few moments if that's alright with you. How do you feel this morning?" asked Hoover.

"I'm so sore I can hardly breathe," said Perkins. "I guess you could say I'm not feeling too well this morning. Besides the hurt places — and I've got several of them in my shoulder and my leg and my butt — I've also got a mean headache."

"Oh, well I hope they're giving you something for pain. If not I'll get you something," said Hoover. "Do you know what they're giving you and when they last gave it to you?"

"Yessm, it was morphine, about 30 minutes to an hour or so ago, and I guess it's got me kind of knocked out, but it ain't knocked out the pain much. So's if you can get me something extra, I guess I could stand your visit, so long as I don't have to talk much. Even talking makes it worse."

"Oh, well, I'm sorry about that, Mr. Perkins. We'll try to keep talking to a minimum," said Hoover. "I can see by your chart that Dr. Carter has authorized some additional pain medication for you if you need it, so we'll go ahead with that. And how about if I come in and take a quick look at your wounds, Mr. Perkins?"

"Aw-right," said Perkins, staring now at the ceiling as Hoover motioned for the security guard to open the cell and a nurse temporarily boosted the morphine flow.

"Good, Mr. Perkins," said Hoover, who walked quickly to his bedside. "Now I have spoken to Dr. Carter and he will be by after a while and do some repairs on your injured shoulder, hip and calf. I'm sure he'll put you to sleep for that, so you won't be in pain during surgery. But I'd like to see your hands if you don't mind, to see how those splinters I saw last night are doing. Are they showing signs of infection, can you tell?"

"Them splinters are the least of my worries, Ma'am," said Perkins. "You can go ahead and take them out if you want to, but you know where I'm really hurtin' is my butt. I'm sorry to be so plain about it to you, Ma'am, but you done asked me how I was doing. I reckon I was supposed to tell you."

"That's right, Mr. Perkins," said Hoover. "I asked you and you told me, now let's look at those hands."

Hoover examined Perkins' hands, and several prominent splinters were beginning to abscess.

"I'll go ahead and take those out of your hands, Mr. Perkins. They look like they're getting infected. And we don't want them to interfere in any way with your other injuries, OK?" asked Hoover.

"OK," said Perkins as Hoover left the cell and quickly came back with a wash basin of warm water, a couple of folded towels, some alcohol, hydrogen peroxide, iodine and various stainless steel scissors, pliers and large needles.

"OK, now give me your right hand first, palm up and open your fingers, Mr. Perkins, all right?" asked Hoover.

Perkins grunted and opened his right hand on the towel as Hoover bathed it with a liberal dash of alcohol. She then nicked the open end of the splinter injuries with a large pin and poured in peroxide, which bubbled profusely and loosened the splinters so that they slid out quickly with a little prodding from the pliers. In a couple of minutes, Hoover had removed several splinters from Perkins' right hand and a few from his left. Then she painted the wounds with iodide and put the splinters in a plastic zipper-lock bag.

"Now, that wasn't so bad was it, Mr. Perkins?" Hoover asked, and Perkins, who had already dozed off to sleep again, made no reply. "Thanks. I'll see you later," she said as she made a brief entry on Perkins' chart and the guard let her out of his cell.

U.S. Attorney Joe Barton sent Milton Richards to interview Brannigan in his hospital cell that afternoon. Brannigan had used his one allowed phone call to call Jeb Smoot, a lawyer he knew in Brownsville, TX. Smoot and Richards worked out the interview time as 1500 hours Friday to give Smoot time on short notice to catch a plane to Miami and report to Richards' office.

Smoot wore jeans and a brown blazer over a bright red shirt with oversize collar and no tie, a black western hat and black boots. He arrived at Richards' office about 1445.

"I'm Jeb Smoot," he told Richards' secretary in the outer office. "Can you tell him for me, Ma'am, that I'm here to do business?"

Richards heard Smoot's remark and came out to greet him.

"Mr. Smoot, I'm Milton Richards," he said, extending his hand. "Glad you could be here on such short notice. I've arranged for a couple of our investigative team members to take us by helicopter out to the ship where Mr. Brannigan, your client, is being held in a secure medical cell. Do you need to freshen up after your travel before we board the chopper?"

"I'm fine, Mr. Richards," said Smoot. "And as I told your secretary to tell you, I'm here to do business."

"Yes, I heard your comment through the office door," said Richards. "Is that just a general comment, or do you have a proposal in mind?"

"That depends on you, Mr. Richards," said Smoot. "If you value my client's testimony in court in support of your prosecution of the surviving members of the crew of *The Silver Bullet* on whatever charges may be pending against them, you should be prepared to offer him immunity from prosecution on those charges."

"Oh, so you're willing to throw the survivors of Brannigan's crew to the sharks to save his hide?" asked Richards. "I figured you might have considered them all in the same boat, in fact the same pirate boat, Mr. Brannigan's pirate boat, *The Silver Bullet*, to be exact, and thus to plead a common defense for them all. Instead, it seems that you want to barter away their rights to assert his."

"Their rights are not my concern, Mr. Richards," said Smoot. "Joe Brannigan's my client, and he's the only one I represent."

"Well, let's talk about your client, Mr. Smoot," said Richards.

"That's what I came here from Texas to do, Mr. Richards," said Smoot as Richards' secretary knocked softly and opened the door slightly.

"Pardon me, gentlemen, but I believe the Coast Guard chopper is waiting to take you to the *Red Eagle*," she said.

"Thanks, Frances," said Richards, picking up his brief case and buttoning his coat. "This way, Mr. Smoot. The pad is just a few steps outside the back door."

Anderson and McGuffy already had the chopper's engines running when Smoot and Richards boarded. As they lifted up and over the harbor, Smoot said to Richards, "You wanted to discuss my client, I believe."

"That's right, Mr. Smoot," said Richards. "Your client, in addition to having a small-caliber bullet lodged close to his heart and is facing surgery, is charged with piracy, murder, kidnapping, drug trafficking and theft and destruction of property, among other crimes. What do you say about that? Or would you rather wait until a stenographer is present to answer?"

"I'll say it now. I'll say it when you get a stenographer, doesn't matter. My client is not guilty, period, of those or any other charges," said Smoot.

"I don't know how prosecutors work in Texas, Mr. Smoot," said Richards, "but in federal jurisdictions in Florida, we usually offer some recommendations of leniency to lesser figures in a common criminal enterprise in exchange for their testimony against those at the top instead of vice-versa as you are apparently urging us to do."

"Perhaps that is the procedure the government uses when it has insufficient evidence to convict without the testimony of co-conspirators," said Smoot. "In this case, there is simply no evidence that my client committed any of the crimes you mentioned, because my client has committed no crime at all."

"Gentlemen, we're approaching the *Red Eagle* and will touch down shortly," said Anderson, bringing the chopper to a stop on the cutter's pad as Richards and Smoot stepped down and turned toward the cabin of Capt. Bart Ellis.

"We'll continue this later, Mr. Smoot," said Richards as Ellis greeted them and directed them toward the ship's infirmary and its secure medical cells.

"Your client is being transferred to Miami General Hospital for surgery at mid-morning tomorrow if he makes good progress today against an infection," Ellis told Smoot. "If the infection is no better by tonight, however, he is to be operated on board my ship tonight."

"That's my understanding as well, Captain," said Smoot as they arrived at the infirmary and were met by Hoover and Brannigan's physician, Dr. Arlene Davis.

"Mr. Smoot, I'm Cdr. Jeanne Hoover, the forensic medical specialist and commanding officer of the team investigating the activities of your client, Joe Brannigan," Hoover said. "Under the authority of Capt. Ellis, since he commands this ship, I will be present during the interview to monitor its effects, if any, on your client's medical condition."

"Mr. Smoot, I'm Dr. Arlene Davis, the physician rendering medical assistance and treatment to your client. I also will be present during the interview of Mr. Brannigan, and for the record, I have objected to it as ill-timed and likely to cause needless and harmful stress to him, coming as it does just prior to his surgery."

"I disagree with Dr. Davis, Mr. Smoot," said Hoover. "Brannigan is responding positively to antibiotics, and the medication he is receiving for pain is lowering his physical and emotional stress to manageable and harmless levels. And under Capt. Ellis' authority, my opinion will prevail."

"Well, in that case, I will absolutely forbid my client to talk to you at all, Mr. Richards," said Smoot. "We'll see you in court."

"Indeed we shall, Mr. Smoot," said Richards. "But you might be interested to know that as we waited for you to arrive from Texas today, agents of our office and the Coast Guard investigative team interviewed and took sworn statements from several surviving crew members of the pirate ship *The Silver Bullet*. Virtually all of them have identified your client as its captain and as the architect and leader of the massive campaign of bloody violence, kidnapping, murder and destruction he waged across the Gulf of Mexico.

"Badly injured survivors of the Colombian ship *San Pedro* have given us similar statements. Perhaps you should reconsider your earlier statement that you are here to do business."

"You're bluffing, Richards," said Smoot. "I happen to know that the *San Pedro* sank in the Gulf two days ago. You couldn't possibly have interviewed its crew today."

"Our investigators were aboard the *San Pedro* several days ago, Mr. Smoot," said Richards. "We recovered numerous items of physical evidence as well as the bodies of several members of its crew, who were gunned down in *The Silver Bullet*'s brazen piracy. *San Pedro* crewmen who were severely wounded but survived have described *The Silver Bullet*'s merciless and bloody assault in great detail, including Brannigan's role in directing the charge."

"All of that is of no consequence or concern to me and my client," said Smoot. "What the crew of *The Silver Bullet* did after my client was shot in an act of rebellion and mutiny cannot be laid to his charge."

"You don't listen well, do you Mr. Smoot ?" asked Hoover. "We have evidence that Brannigan personally ordered the kidnapping of a man and a woman on a private yacht before there was any opposition from any member of his crew. And the only hostile act against Brannigan came not from members of a mutinous crew but from the man whose wife was being assaulted. There is simply no evidence of a mutiny. The only member of *The Silver Bullet*'s crew who verbally took up for the man and his wife was thrown in the brig with them. He was pleading for mercy for himself and the couple, not physically or verbally leading a rebellion."

"You must be talking about the mutiny kingpin, Jim Cummings, who my client says was shot and left for dead and eventually went down with the *San Pedro*," said Smoot. "After leading the rebellion, in which he got his arm almost shot off, he boarded the Colombian ship but was hurt too severely to leave it. He was left to bleed to death or go down with the ship, whichever came first. It made no difference."

"Your client is feeding you bad information, Mr. Smoot," said Hoover. "There was no mutiny, which means Brannigan is personally responsible for every crime that occurred on his ship, and there is a long list of them. In fact, Brannigan remained in command of *The Silver Bullet* despite his gunshot wound up to the moment the Coast Guard SAS teams occupied it Thursday night and took him into custody," said Hoover. "Brannigan also was in command, although he had been forced to surrender, when *The Silver Bullet*'s auxiliary engines were booby-trapped to explode. That means he's responsible for the deaths of two Coast Guard sailors. So Mr. Smoot, your claim of mutiny as a defense of your client is without any basis in fact, and we have ample evidence to show it."

"We'll see whether a jury will believe the testimony of Colombian drug lords and mutinous crewmen over my client," said Smoot. "But if you think your evidence is so cotton-picking strong, why do you need to talk to my client at all? Are you looking for a confession?" asked Smoot.

"If you really are ready to do business, Mr. Smoot, a confession and guilty pleas from your client would save the taxpayers a lot of money, and I would on their behalf recommend leniency on the sentence," said Richards.

"Then perhaps we need to see what he says about that," said Smoot as the three of them walked up to the steel bars of the hospital cell where Brannigan lay asleep with an IV device in his arm.

Chapter Nine

Dr. Arlene Davis spoke softly to her patient, Joe Brannigan, who lay sleeping in a hospital bed behind the steel bars of the Coast Guard cutter *Red Eagle*'s secure medical cells.

"Mr. Brannigan, I'm your surgeon, Dr. Arlene Davis," she said. "As you know, I have scheduled surgery for you tomorrow morning at a hospital in Miami if the infection you have been battling continues to diminish today. With me here now is your attorney, Mr. Smoot from Texas, and some government folks, all of whom are here to see you and talk to you. Do you feel like talking with them now?"

"Who?" asked Brannigan in a gruff, almost angry voice.

"Your lawyer, Mr. Smoot, and some government folks, a Mr. Richards of the U.S. attorney's office, and Cdr. Hoover, a Coast Guard investigator," said Davis. "They want to talk to you if you feel like talking to them. How do you feel?"

"Well, you woke me up out of a sound sleep! How am I supposed to feel?" Brannigan asked. "Who are you?"

"I'm Dr. Davis, your physician, as I just told you," she said. "Perhaps you don't remember me. You have been under rather strong sedation for pain. Are you in pain right now, Mr. Brannigan?"

"Pain? Yes, I'm in pain. I'm in terrible pain. With every breath, I'm in pain. I've been shot, woman, right next to my heart! What kind of doctor are you, anyway? Of course I'm in pain! Ohhhh, Lordy!" said Brannigan, whose angry tirade ended with a loud moan. Then Smoot spoke to him.

"Joe, this is Jeb Smoot of Brownsville. You know, you called me this morning and wanted me to be your lawyer. Do you still want me to be your lawyer, or are you in too much pain or under too much morphine to talk about legal matters right now?" asked Smoot.

At this point, Brannigan raised his head off the pillow and looked directly into the face of Smoot, who had stepped closer to his bedside.

"Jeb!" Brannigan said, obviously recognizing his lawyer and feebly extending his right hand, which was visibly trembling. "Why didn't you say it was you? What brings you to these parts?"

"I just told you!" said Smoot. "You said on the phone you wanted me to represent you in some kind of government investigation or something. Don't you remember? You called me early this morning."

"Oh, yeah. I'm sorry, Jeb. My head's a little messed up with drugs right now," said Brannigan. "I remember now. The blasted government's trying to hang a piracy and murder charge on me which I had nothing to do with, and I want you to get them out of my hair. You understand? What took you so long?"

"I got here as quick as I could, Joe. Now if you still want me to represent you, I recommend that you plead the Fifth Amendment on anything they ask you. And if they want to go forward with any questions right now, I'm going to file a request with the federal judge for a restraining order against them. You're obviously too sedated right now to think clearly or to talk coherently," said Smoot. "So why don't we clear out and let you get some more sleep. You'll need to be rested for your surgery. Maybe you and I can talk after you come out of the recovery room and hopefully are feeling better. So I'm going to go now, Joe. OK? I'll check with you later."

"OK, Jeb. Thanks for coming. Maybe I'll feel like talking later, I don't know," said Brannigan, who leaned back on his pillow and closed his eyes again.

"Well, I think you can see, Mr. Brannigan is in no condition to be interrogated right now," said Davis. "Do you agree, Cdr. Hoover?"

"I will accept your diagnosis for now, Dr. Davis, but unless he has been given far more morphine than his chart indicates, I would question whether he has been coached to give incoherent responses," said Hoover. "I repeat, however, we will accept your diagnosis for now."

"I don't appreciate your insinuation, Cdr. Hoover, that Mr. Brannigan was coached by me or by Dr. Davis to give false or misleading answers, and I'm sure Dr. Davis doesn't appreciate it, either," said Smoot. "It appears that this is just one more indication that the government intends to hold my client guilty in a kangaroo court until he proves himself innocent."

"We respect your right to maintain your client's innocence unless and until he is proven guilty, Mr. Smoot," said Richards. "But you have to know that the government has a mountain of evidence implicating your client on a variety of charges, some of which, I might add, carry the death penalty upon conviction. For the second time, Mr. Smoot, I suggest that you consider again your earlier statement that you have come to do business.

"Unless you and your client are prepared to be more cooperative than you have been up to now, about the only business left to transact is for your client to plead guilty as charged and beg the court for mercy not to impose the death penalty."

"We'll see you in court, Mr. Richards," said Smoot with a sneer. "I am ready to return to the mainland if you don't mind."

Hoover nodded to an ensign who had accompanied them to the infirmary, and he escorted them quickly back to Ellis' cabin.

"Back so soon?" Ellis asked.

"We didn't transact very much business, Captain," said Hoover. "But thanks for your hospitality. If you will alert our chopper pilot, we're ready to return to the mainland."

"Sure thing, Commander," said Ellis as Hoover, Richards and Smoot turned to board the chopper for the flight back to Miami.

When they arrived at Richards' office, Smoot placed one of his business cards on Richards' desk.

"When the government is ready to do business, give me a call," Smoot told Richards. "I maintain on my client's behalf that the government has no credible evidence connecting him to any of the list of crimes you have drawn up out of thin air, and I will ask the court shortly to release him on his own recognizance pending any proceedings you intend to bring against him."

"Mr. Smoot, I know you have a reputation to live up to as some kind of cock of the walk, but your empty crowing is wasting one of the last opportunities your client is likely to get to avoid the death penalty," said Richards. "I am prepared to recommend a sentence of life in prison upon his guilty plea, but that option won't remain open to him indefinitely. I intend to present our case to the federal grand jury starting Monday."

"You know my client has a right to see and examine the evidence you claim to have against him," said Smoot. "Where is the evidence that he ordered or was in any way responsible for the take-over and destruction of the Colombian ship and the deaths and assaults you contend occurred aboard it?"

"Our evidence, Mr. Smoot, as we have indicated before, is the testimony of several people who witnessed those events," said Richards. "Many of these witnesses are the people Brannigan signed up as members of his crew. Several of them are ready to testify that Brannigan alone was in command of *The Silver Bullet.*"

"I don't care to debate you any longer, Mr. Richards. Good day!" said Smoot as he left Richards' office, slamming the door behind him. Smoot then went to the federal court clerk's office and filed a petition for Brannigan's release. Before Smoot could get out of the federal building, however, a security officer at the door stopped him.

"Judge Francis Steele wants to see you in his chambers, Mr. Smoot," the officer said. "And it might be a good idea to remove your hat when you go in. You can take the elevator over there. He's on the third floor."

Smoot took the security officer's advice and removed his hat as he got off the elevator and rang the buzzer near the door to the judge's chamber. The lock mechanism hummed and clicked, and a muffled female voice came over a small speaker near the buzzer:

"Come in, please."

"Have a seat, Mr. Smoot," said a woman behind a large mahogany desk as he walked in holding his hat. "Judge will see you shortly," she said.

Five minutes and then ten minutes passed, and Smoot grew fidgety. He looked repeatedly at the large office clock on the wall above the head of the woman at the desk, apparently the judge's secretary. The clock read ten minutes to five.

Smoot heard the buzzer ring again outside the door he had just entered, and this time he saw the secretary as she pressed a button on her desk and said, "Come in, please."

In walked Richards, the assistant U.S. attorney, who looked as surprised to see Smoot as Smoot was to see him.

"Have a seat, Mr. Richards," the woman said. "Judge will see you shortly. Have you two gentlemen met?"

"Yes, we've met," said Richards, nodding to Smoot, who stared straight at the clock and said nothing. At that moment, a door behind and to one side of the secretary's desk opened, and a tall, broad-shouldered man, whose black hair had the merest tinge of gray, stepped into the outer office.

"I'm Francis Steele," he said, shaking hands with Richards first, then Smoot. "Come in, gentlemen," he said, turning back toward the door from which he had just come.

"I've just received your petition, Mr. Smoot, for your client Joseph Brannigan's release on his own signature pending trial, and I'm prepared to act on it promptly if you're serious about it," said Steele.

"I am wondering, however, after viewing the government's preliminary report on the evidence against your client, what makes you think you can get away with toying frivolously with this court, Mr. Smoot?" asked Steele, looking Smoot directly in the eye.

"It was not my intention to toy frivolously with the court, Your Honor," said Smoot, still holding his hat. "My client has a right under the federal Constitution to be free of excessive bail, even following the filing of federal charges against him. My client, being completely innocent of the government's charges, has a right to be presumed innocent by this court unless and until he's proven guilty, Your Honor. Surely you do not intend to usurp the role of the jury and find him guilty without benefit of trial."

"We're not talking about guilt or innocence at this juncture, Mr. Smoot," said Steele. "You have petitioned this court for your client's release on his own signature. Surely you know that it is this court's duty to assess a fair and reasonable bail, one that is not unduly burdensome but sufficient to ensure your client's presence in court for trial. Have you seen a copy of the government's complaint?"

"I have seen it, Your Honor, but it is made up out of whole cloth. There's not a shred of evidence to back it up. I think it's time for Mr. Richards to put up or shut up," said Smoot.

"Your Honor, for the record, the United States has a mountain of evidence that bail for Brannigan should be denied altogether because no amount of bail would assure his presence in court," said Richards.

"The rules this court must follow extend protections in both directions, to the government as well as to your client, Mr. Smoot," said Steele. "But giving you the benefit of my severe doubts as to your seriousness, I'll schedule a Rule 5 initial appearance and a detention hearing for your client at seven tonight. Have him here, Mr. Smoot, and we'll proceed."

"But, Your Honor, my client is suffering from a bullet wound near his heart and is quite unable to attend a hearing tonight. Perhaps in a couple of weeks, following surgery to remove the bullet, he could make an appearance at that time," said Smoot.

"You can't have it both ways, Mr. Smoot," said Steele. "If you want him released pending trial, we'll have to hear why you think release without bond is reasonable. I won't release him on any amount of bail without a hearing, and certainly not on his own signature.

"My probation officer has completed his report, copies of which I'll furnish to counsel momentarily, and I'll hear your evidence at 7 p.m., gentlemen."

Steele stood up, signaling to Smoot and Richards that their conference with the judge was over. As they left the federal building, Smoot asked Richards if Brannigan could be flown by helicopter from the *Red Eagle* to the courthouse for the hearing before Steele.

"Your client has made a miraculous recovery from his gunshot wound, I see," said Richards.

"My client is deathly ill, Mr. Richards, but so long as his IV remains intact, he should be able to sit in a wheelchair for the hearing without significantly worsening his condition," said Smoot. "My question is, can he be flown to the courthouse?"

"We'll fly him here if that's what you want, Mr. Smoot, but your request confirms Dr. Hoover's suspicion that Brannigan's condition is somewhat flexible to fit the whim of his lawyer," said Richards. "I'll ask a deputy marshal to go with you, and I'll get Anderson and McGuffy to fly you out to the *Red Eagle*. You can observe every minute of Brannigan's flight to the courthouse."

Later, when Smoot arrived on the *Red Eagle*, Brannigan seemed surprised that Smoot wanted him to fly in his condition, but he offered no objection.

"I reckon I can do it, if you think it's necessary, Jeb," Brannigan said as he was hurriedly dressed and placed in a wheelchair with his IV suspended from a hook. The apparatus was locked in place for the chopper ride to the mainland, then Brannigan was wheeled swiftly to the federal courthouse and Steele's courtroom.

Promptly at 7 p.m., Steele entered the courtroom.

"Gentlemen, I'll hear you now," said the judge as Richards stood up to address him.

"Your Honor, this man, Joe Brannigan, is directly responsible for the deaths of more than a dozen people, including two Coast Guard sailors who died in his booby-trapped ship," said Richards.

"I'm sure Your Honor has read our preliminary report of the substantial evidence of Brannigan's acts of piracy, murder, kidnapping and destruction of property, as well as trafficking in cocaine, marijuana and other contraband.   It is the government's position that no amount of bail is likely to ensure his presence in court. Therefore, we respectfully request that bail be denied."

"I'll hear you now, Mr. Smoot," said Steele.

"Your Honor, as you can plainly see, my client is quite ill and physically fragile, and is no threat to anyone," said Smoot, standing behind Brannigan's wheelchair. "His physician as well as the Coast Guard's own medical expert, Dr. Hoover, have stated in affidavits that I'll present to the court that my client needs three to six weeks of recovery and rehabilitation. This means he is absolutely no escape risk. He should be released on his own signature."

"Have you read the probation report, Mr. Smoot?" asked Steele. "Your client has no prior convictions and no ties that we can find to any community. Tell me why he's not a potential flight risk."

"Other than what I've already told you, Your Honor, I have no additional evidence," said Smoot.

"Thank you, gentlemen," said Steele, quickly scanning the documents offered by both lawyers before addressing them again.

"The court takes judicial notice that drug trafficking is an enterprise that involves billions of dollars in the Gulf region each year," said Steele, "and despite the fragile condition of your client, Mr. Smoot, his presence here on short notice is evidence that he could move to any location of his choice.

"Under those circumstances, Mr. Brannigan, I believe it only fair that bond either be denied altogether for you, or that cash bond in the amount of $1 billion be deposited with the clerk of this court before you can be released prior to trial. Giving your flamboyant counsel Mr. Smoot the benefit of the doubt that your petition is serious, I will set your bail at $1 billion, that's with a B, Mr. Brannigan. Are there any other pre-trial matters I need to take up at this time, gentlemen?" Steele asked.

When neither Richards nor Smoot responded, Steele added, "I hope it isn't necessary, Mr. Smoot, for me to impress upon you again that you are not to file frivolous motions with this court. You are to take this case seriously or be held in contempt. Am I clear?"

"Yes, Your Honor," said Smoot. "It wasn't my intention to be disrespectful of the court but rather to represent the best interests of my client, which I intend to continue to do as conscientiously and as well as I am able.'"

"See that you do that, Mr. Smoot. That is all," said Steele who stood up and left the courtroom.

Chapter Ten

Joe Brannigan's surgery went well on Saturday morning at a second-floor surgical suite at Miami General Hospital. Dr. Arlene Davis, who had given him preliminary care aboard the Coast Guard cutter *Red Eagle*, was in charge of the surgery to remove a small-caliber bullet lodged near his heart.

Jeb Smoot, wearing his black felt hat, waited in the lobby near the recovery room for Brannigan to come out from under anesthesia. A hospital security officer stood outside the door.

Upstairs on the third floor, also in a secure medical cell, was Vincent Perkins, *The Silver Bullet*'s second in command. He had undergone surgery on Friday on board the *Red Eagle* to repair bullet wounds in his left hip, left shoulder and right calf. Dr. Thomas Carter, the surgeon, then had him transferred to Miami General for several days of recuperation.

U.S. Attorney Joseph Barton and his assistants visited more than two dozen members of the crew of the suspected pirate ship *The Silver Bullet*, some in special federal cells in local jails. Others were recuperating from injuries in secure medical cells in Miami General and other local hospitals. Barton and his assistants told the suspected pirates that they had a right to remain silent; that they had a right to the assistance of counsel, and that an attorney would be appointed and paid by the federal court to represent them if they lacked money to hire a lawyer. Barton filed a list of those in each category with the federal court.

On Saturday afternoon, Dr. Jonas Sutherland, a brain injury specialist at Miami General Hospital, stopped by the private room of the patient he knew only as Elaine to check on her recovery

"So how are we feeling today, Elaine?" asked Sutherland.

"Just fine, Doctor," said Elaine, who was sitting up in bed, leaning back against two big pillows, reading a book on "Scenic Florida Vacations."

"Good. What are you reading?" asked Sutherland.

"It's called Scenic Florida Vacations, but I'll confess I'm more looking at the pictures than reading," said Elaine.

"There's nothing wrong with looking at pictures. I do that a lot myself," said Sutherland. "In fact, I think I have a copy of that book on my coffee table at home. So what have you learned about Florida?"

"I guess the biggest thing I've learned is that Florida is a place, not an item like a flower or a piece of bread," said Elaine. "And I'm learning a little about all the little places that fit inside Florida like the pieces of cereal in my breakfast bowl."

"Well, have you seen anything in the book that looks familiar, which you may have visited before?" asked Sutherland.

"Not really, but when I saw the rocket and space center, I thought immediately of the name CAPE KENNEDY," said Elaine. "I couldn't explain it, but the words CAPE KENNEDY kept running through my head, and when I saw a picture of a rocket on the launch pad, I remembered hearing a man's voice counting backward and then the words, "We have lift-off.""

"I had looked at all the pictures several times before I noticed the words CAPE KENNEDY next to the pictures. I don't know what it means, but it was exciting and frustrating to me all at the same time. I figured I was getting a fragment of my memory back, but I couldn't go beyond it and get anything else. And that was very frustrating."

"So what did you do when you got frustrated?" asked Sutherland.

"I just got very angry for a while and threw the book on the floor and finally just closed my eyes and let the words and pictures flow by, until finally they stopped, and I picked up the book and didn't look at it any more all day," said Elaine. "And then when I tried to go to sleep that night, it was Wednesday night I believe, I couldn't go to sleep until I looked at the Cape Kennedy pictures again. And then something really strange happened. I remembered that after the man stopped counting backward and said `Liftoff,' the rocket spewed out a lot of smoke and went out of sight into the sky. I just remembered vividly seeing that rocket take off some time in the past. I don't know if I was actually there and I saw it in person, or if I saw it on TV. Anyway, I didn't get angry this time. I just put the book on the table and soon dozed off to sleep."

"Well, I'd say you made and continue to make really great progress, Elaine," said Sutherland. "How are your headaches and other pains?"

"I have not had any headaches since I remembered the rocket launch," said Elaine, "although it's still very sore around that splinter, and it causes me a really sharp pain if I bump it even lightly."

"Well, I've got good news," said Sutherland. "As of this morning, your tests came back totally negative for bacterial infection in the vicinity of the splinter. So I'd like for you to be ready early Monday morning for surgery to remove that splinter. I think it's about time."

"That's great, Doctor," said Elaine. "But do you remember something I told you when my first brain scan showed that the splinter had punctured the membrane around my brain?"

"Well, now I guess it's my turn to lose memory," said Sutherland. "I can't say that I do remember what you told me. Perhaps you need to tell me again."

"I told you, Doctor, that if the splinter were removed and anything happened to me, to give the splinter to the Coast Guard investigators, because I believe they can trace the splinter in my brain to the plank used by a pirate to whack me on the head. And that might be just the evidence needed to convict him and send him to prison."

"Oh, yes, I do remember now," said Sutherland. "Well, I don't plan on anything happening to you, but you've got my promise. When the splinter comes out, I'm going to have the investigating team's medical specialist, Cdr. Hoover, on hand to receive it as evidence. You see, I'd like to see whoever did this to you go to prison, too. You can count on it."

"Good, Doctor. I'll be ready on Monday morning," said Elaine.

"I'll see you then, but there's no reason to waste the weekend," said Sutherland. "I'm going to suggest to our psychologist, Mary Horton, that she help you plan some social and spiritual activities for tonight and tomorrow. I want you to begin to build relationships with folks other than just us here at the hospital. We all treasure our relationship with you, but we want you to have a rich and full life in the future, and that means finding a new set of friends."

"Friends," said Elaine. "I guess I'm not really sure what friends are."

"That's what we all want you to find out," said Sutherland. "I'll send Mary up in a little while, and I'll see you bright and early on Monday. OK?"

"OK, Dr. Sutherland. I'll see you Monday."

Sutherland told Horton to help Elaine plan some social and spiritual activities for the weekend and for later in the week following her surgery.

"She's free to leave the hospital for a while each day or night if she wants to, so long as you're with her and it's reasonably close by, so that she could return to the hospital quickly in case she needed to," Sutherland told Horton.

"Certainly, Doctor. I'll go by her room right away," said Horton, closing a folder which contained information sheets on several private organizations that offered a variety of services to people recovering from mild to severe brain injuries.

Moments later, Horton stopped by Elaine's room to follow up on Sutherland's instructions.

"Hello, Elaine. How are you today?" asked Horton. "You mind if I visit with you for a few minutes?"

"Oh, not at all, Dr. Horton. Come in and have a seat," said Elaine. "I guess Dr. Sutherland told you that I have recovered a few more fragments of my lost memory, and I'm trying to hold my excitement down to the level of eager instead of impatient, if you know what I mean."

"I know exactly what you mean, Elaine," said Horton. "Dr. Sutherland mentioned that you had made some progress, particularly by learning to be patient while you recover your memory. That will be a valuable lesson that really will speed up rather than delay the process. So I would encourage you to use that lesson as you go forward from here. Dr. Sutherland mentioned that you will undergo surgery on Monday morning to remove the splinter, and that he would like for me to help you plan some social and spiritual activities for tonight and tomorrow, and for later in the week after your surgery.

"I'm going to be glad to get rid of that splinter," said Elaine. "I have been unable to touch the area where it entered without experiencing horrible pain. So maybe I'll be able to do more, not less, after I get it removed."

"I hope so, Elaine," said Horton. "So what activities do you think you would enjoy? Let's just think first in terms of this afternoon, then we'll plan something for later if you feel up to it. So what do you say? What would you like to do?" asked Horton.

"Oh, goodness, it's been so long since I went out anyplace, and I can't remember the last time I went anywhere to meet people," said Elaine. "I think we'd better take this voyage a bit slow until I can get my sea legs."

Horton laughed.

"Oh, I see you used a nautical metaphor. That's interesting," said Horton. "It may be that you were once involved in sailing or otherwise were on the sea."

"Yeah, maybe I was," said Elaine. "I know I remembered the story about Captain Nemo and his submarine, the *Nautilus*. And of course I washed ashore from being somewhere out in the Gulf, so I must have had a strong interest in the sea."

"I would say there's an excellent chance of it," said Horton. "So perhaps we could go walking on the beach or on a boardwalk near the beach and maybe stop around sunset for a meal at a seafood place. Do you think you would enjoy that?"

"Definitely!" said Elaine. "Under one condition."

"What's that?" asked Horton.

"If I could call Lt. McGuffy, who helped to rescue me from that sandbar island, and see if he would like to go walking with us," said Elaine.

"Why, I think that would be wonderful. And it's on such short notice, if he were not able to see you tonight, perhaps he could join us tomorrow sometime or an afternoon or night next week," said Horton. "Why don't you call him?"

"I think I will," said Elaine, retrieving McGuffy's photo and phone number from the drawer of the night table near her bed. She dialed his number and waited. It rang several times and then played a recorded message: "This is Bob. I'm sorry I missed your call. Please leave your name and number at the tone, and I'll call you back."

"Bob, this is Elaine," she said at the tone. "I was hoping I could see you again, at your convenience of course. I'm going to be away from the hospital for a little while, so please call again if I'm not here when you call. I miss you. Bye!"

"He's not in," said Elaine as she hung up the phone. "But maybe Lt. Anderson is in. I know he's married and has two kids, but he said his family would like to meet me sometime, so this is as good a time as any. I think I'll call him. Do you think that would be alright?"

"Surely, it would be alright, if he told you to," said Horton. "Again, however, it's kind of short notice, so I suggest you make it another time at his and his family's convenience if they've made other plans for tonight."

"Wonderful. I'll do it," said Elaine, again picking up the phone and this time retrieving Anderson's photo and phone number from her night table.

She dialed Anderson's number and a boy answered.

"Anderson residence. This is Tommy. Who's calling?" he asked.

"Tommy, I'm Elaine. You don't know me, but I'd like to speak to your Mom or Dad if either of them is in," she said.

"Dad isn't in right now. He's at work," said Tommy.

"Who is it, Tommy?" came a woman's voice faintly, as though coming from another room.

"It's some woman named Elaine. She wants to speak to you or Dad," said Tommy, 6, handing the phone to his mother as she walked into the living room from the kitchen.

"You know I've told you not to tell anyone on the phone that your father isn't in, Tommy! You know that!" she said sternly in a coarse whisper, taking the phone. "Uh, hello. This is Ruth Anderson. Who's calling, please?"

"Ruth. Ms. Anderson. My name is Elaine. I don't know if your husband has mentioned me, but he and Lt. Bob McGuffy rescued me from a sandbar island in the Gulf on Monday. I'm calling from Miami General Hospital, where I am recovering from a brain injury. Did I hear Tommy say Lt. Anderson isn't in?" asked Elaine.

"Why, yes, Elaine. Joe did mention you, as a matter of fact, and he said he invited you to visit us sometime," said Ruth. "I will gladly join in his invitation, Elaine. We'd all like to meet you as soon as you are able. Oh, and you heard Tommy right. Joe isn't here right now. I think he was flying a helicopter today in connection with your case in some way, but I wasn't supposed to tell you that. I guess Tommy gets it from me. How can we help you, Elaine?"

"Well, my doctors say I'm ready for some social and spiritual activities, so long as my psychologist, Dr. Mary Horton, goes with me and we don't get too far away from Miami General, in case I have to rush back for some reason," said Elaine. "I'm sorry to impose on you like this, but I'm about to get cabin fever here in this hospital, particularly since Lt. Anderson and Lt. McGuffy are about the only people I know in the world except for the hospital staff. I don't know if you are aware that my brain injury, temporarily I hope, wiped out all my memories of my past life."

"Well, Joe did say something like that about you," said Ruth. "But just let me say, Elaine, that my kids and I would love to see you and have you visit us at any time whatsoever, including right now or as soon as you can get here. Is your psychologist close by, so I can give her directions to our place?"

"She's right here. I'll put her on," said Elaine, handing the phone to Horton.

"This is Mary Horton, Elaine's psychological counselor," she said. "I've heard your conversation with Elaine, and I'd underscore her comment that we don't want to impose on you on short notice. But I could drive Elaine over for a brief visit this afternoon or evening, at your convenience."

"Well, Dr. Horton, I'll repeat what I told Elaine. You all just come on over whenever you like. I'm sure we can find something around here to feed you, so long as Elaine doesn't have to have too much of a special diet or anything," said Ruth. "My husband should be home in about an hour or so. It won't hurt a thing to surprise him; so you and Elaine come over when you can. We'll be right here, and that includes Tommy and Rachel."

"Thank you, Ms. Anderson. We'll be over within the hour, but I'd rather we not impose on you for dinner on such short notice. Perhaps later, OK?" asked Horton after Ruth gave her directions to the Anderson home.

"That's up to you and Elaine entirely, Doctor. We'll be looking for you shortly," said Ruth as she hung up the phone.

"I'm so excited about seeing Lt. Anderson again, although he insists that I call him Joe," said Elaine after making arrangements to visit Anderson and his family. "And I'll get to meet his wife and kids, and that should be exciting as well."

"Yes, I think this will be a good experience for you, Elaine," said Horton. "It's likely to be an emotional experience, since an injury such as yours has placed powerful stresses upon you, and it's likely that you have suffered emotional as well as physical injuries. So don't be surprised if during your visit you feel exaggerated emotional highs and lows. It's OK and natural to laugh or shed a few tears, as you feel like it. You are among friends, so relax as much as possible and just let it happen, without apology."

"There's that word 'friends' again. Dr. Sutherland used it, and I told him I'm not sure exactly what it means," said Elaine. "He told me that's what he wants me to learn."

"Yes, we do want you to know what friends are, and we want you to find and cultivate many new friendships as you recover," said Horton. "While you are visiting with the Anderson family, don't be surprised if they place you at the center of attention. The kids, especially, will want to know about your injury and probably will ask you questions that the adults would hesitate to ask. Don't feel that you have the burden of carrying the entire conversation. You should strive to listen to their comments at least as much as you share about yourself. You may want to ask a few questions of them about things like school work or hobbies or other activities, such as entertainment and leisure."

"I don't know why I didn't think of it before, but we need to call Ms. Anderson and tell her that it will be at least an hour before we come by," said Elaine. "And then, Dr. Horton, I need you to help me to look as close to presentable as possible. And by that, I mean some clothes other than hospital clothes and this bandage on my head that makes it look like some kind of beehive. Do you think an hour is enough time for a make-over?"

"We can do a lot in an hour, but the family knows you've had a severe injury, so you shouldn't feel that you have to disguise that fact, Elaine," said Horton. "Let's do what we can and not fret about the rest. We can work on the bandage and your hair first. I'll get a couple of our aides up here to fit you with a new, smaller and flesh-toned bandage over the injury. And they should be able to do a bit of snipping and combing and maybe a bit of curling to put more pizzazz in your hairdo.

"And I don't mean to invade your privacy, Elaine, but you and I are the same height and look to be about the same weight and shape; so we'll run by my apartment and you can have your pick of my wardrobe. The hospital will reimburse me if I file for it, but I think I'd much rather consider it a gift to a friend. What do you say?"

"There's that word again, Doctor," said Elaine. "I still don't know what the word 'friend' means, but it just has to be something or someone who is really, really nice. If you would do that for me as a friend, you must be a really good friend. That's all I can say," she said as she reached for a tissue and broke into a deep and unexpected sob.

"I like your plan very much, Doctor. Thank you," she said eventually. "You are really, really nice to me. Nobody ever did anything like that for me, except maybe Joe and Bob, who rescued me from the island. And…" she broke into laughter, "I'm going to get to see Joe and his family tonight!"

"Yes, you are, but we have work to do," said Horton, who started calling aides and explaining the urgency of their new assignments. Moments later, Elaine had swapped her hospital gown for green coveralls, and the best word to describe her makeover was miraculous.

"Now, go with me to the lobby and wait for me," said Horton. "I'll get my car out of the parking deck and be by for you shortly, and then we'll go clothes-hunting."

"OK, Doctor. I'll wait for you," said Elaine.

Horton returned with her car and moments later they were at Horton's apartment. She opened two sliding wooden panels in opposite directions in her bedroom closet to reveal a substantial wardrobe.

"There you are, Elaine," said Horton. "See if you can find something that you like, and it's yours."

"Oh, my goodness!" said Elaine, obviously impressed with the selection. "It would take me all day to make up my mind with that many choices, and I know we only have a few minutes. You obviously know what you have, and I don't. Plus, I'm not at all sure what's appropriate. So why don't you select one that you really don't like very much, and I won't feel so bad about accepting it."

"Now that's not what my offer was all about," said Horton. "Nobody's holding a gun on me to make me give you an outfit. But I'm sure Dr. Sutherland expected me to take the practical steps necessary to help you feel better about yourself on your first social outing since your injury. That's certainly part of my mission, and I'm happy to do it, Elaine. Anyway, we don't have much time, so let me suggest a couple of options and you choose between them. How's that?"

"That's fine, Doctor," said Elaine. "I'm sure whatever you select would suit me fine."

"Well, most of your choices have been made by the weather. It's very late summer, but it's still too hot in Miami to wear anything with sleeves to a casual outing, so everything from here back is automatically eliminated," said Horton. "And call me Mary. We can dispense with `Doctor' for a while. Now here are things I would wear to the supermarket or to a ballgame, but I think those are a bit too plain. So somewhere in between the two extremes should be something to suit you. But choose what you like, and I'm sure it will be OK."

"Thank you, Doctor. I mean Mary. I think I see the outfit I like," said Elaine, who chose a pair of long white pants and a matching white short-sleeved blouse with wide sky-blue collar. She took the outfit off the rack and asked Horton, "Can I try it on?"

"Surely!" said Horton. "But you're going to need the white sandals there to go with it, so put them on too and we'll see how you look. I already know you're going to look splendid. I am so rarely able to wear that, I've just got to see it on you before I comment. So try it on. I've got to freshen up a bit and make my own selection so we can hurry out of here."

Elaine removed the white pants suit from the hanger and quickly had it and the white sandals on.

"OK. Tell me what you think," she said as Horton came out smiling, obviously favorably impressed.

"It's just like I thought," said Horton. "It looks splendid on you, or rather you look splendid in it. And I must say, it looks much better on you than it does on me. I do like it, but I almost never wear it, because I almost never go anywhere that I feel it's appropriate. And I guess, deep down, I never feel quite as bold and adventuresome as I think it makes me appear.

"I would say you couldn't have made a better choice for a visit to the home of a Coast Guard pilot and his family. So now I've got to choose something for myself, and then we'll be on our way. You may wait for me in the living room, where you might enjoy looking at some of the books there on the coffee table."

Horton knew she couldn't match Elaine's choice of outfits, and she told herself that she had to preserve her image as a doctor, a psychologist at that. But Elaine's choice inspired her to rule out any of the dozen or more summer dresses on her rack which she otherwise might have worn, and instead she chose a plain tan pants suit with a broad white collar and tan loafers with gold rope ties.

"Well, now's your chance to get even," Horton said as she walked into the living room. "What do you think?"

Elaine closed her book and stood, not knowing what to say but wanting desperately not to offend her counselor. Finally she remembered to smile, then shook her head up and down as the most positive gesture she could come up with, then she said, "Splendid!"

It was a few minutes after five on Saturday afternoon when Elaine and her counselor, Mary Horton, arrived at Anderson's residence and rang the doorbell.

Anderson's daughter, nine-year-old Rachel, answered the door and told them to come in.

"Mom had to run to the supermarket, but she'll be right back," said Rachel. "Are you…?"

"I'm Dr. Mary Horton and this is Elaine," Horton said.

"Dr. Horton, Elaine, come in. Mom said you would be by. Come in, please. I'm Rachel," she said as she held the door open for them. "Please have a seat. Mom should be back in a few minutes. Can I get you something to drink?"

"No, thanks," said Horton and Elaine in unison. "Maybe later," said Horton.

"Well, let me know if you change your minds," said Rachel. "We have ice water and our family favorite, which you could probably guess is Florida orange juice."

"Yes, I was just looking at some beautiful pictures of Florida orange groves this morning," said Elaine. "That made me remember how much I used to like orange juice, but I haven't had any lately. I may want to try some later, though."

"You just say the word and I'll get it for you," Rachel said as she heard the sounds of a car turning in the driveway. "Oh, I think I hear Mom coming in now," Rachel said as a car door slammed and Anderson's wife, Ruth, came in through the back door to the kitchen.

"We have company I see," said Ruth. "And I guess you're . . ."

"Mom, this is Dr. Horton and this is Elaine, you know, the lady that . . ."

"Yes. Yes. Dr. Horton and Elaine. We're so glad you could be with us," said Ruth, extending her hand as the other two women stood and they exchanged greetings.

"Please make yourselves comfortable and we'll have dinner shortly. Joe phoned home a little while ago and he's also on his way. I hope you won't consider me really weird and mean, but I wanted to surprise him. And I really went out on a limb on this, but since he and Bob McGuffy fly together all the time as they did today, I took the liberty of suggesting that he invite Bob to come by here and have dinner with us before he goes home, so he'll be in for a surprise, too."

"That's fine with us, Ruth. May I call you Ruth? And please call me Mary," said Horton. "We just hope we didn't inconvenience you too much, coming in on you with such short notice."

"No, it wasn't an inconvenience at all, and please call me Ruth," she said, taking two hot extra large supreme pizzas from their boxes and placing them on different shelves in her oven, which she set at 180 degrees.

At that point, Lt. Anderson and Lt. McGuffy arrived, and seeing the extra vehicle in the driveway, Anderson parked instead on the curb. Then he and McGuffy got out and walked to Anderson's front door, which opened immediately. Tommy had heard the car doors slam and hurried outside to welcome his father and best friend Bob.

"Daddy's home! And Bob, too!" Tommy shouted as his father scooped him up and gave him a bear hug.

"And Tommy's home, too, I see," said Anderson, mussing up his son's hair as he placed him back down on the sidewalk.

"Dad, we have visitors. It's supposed to be a surprise," Tommy said. "It's a pretty woman who hurt her head and another woman who's a doctor."

Anderson and McGuffy took off their caps as they came in, still in their Coast Guard coveralls, as Elaine and Horton stood again to be welcomed.

"Boys, meet Dr. Horton, excuse me, Mary, and her friend, Elaine, whom I believe you've already met," said Ruth. "It was supposed to be a surprise, but I think Tommy took care of that."

"Hello, Mary, and Elaine," said Anderson, shaking hands with both women. "You're looking well, Elaine, and I hope you are healing and feeling better, too."

"Yes, thanks, I am," said Elaine. "Hey, guys!"

"Hey, Elaine, you're a total knock-out in that outfit, I want you to know," said McGuffy. "How in the world are you doing?" he asked, smiling broadly and extending both arms wide to embrace her. Elaine returned the embrace, and both she and McGuffy blushed. Eventually, McGuffy asked, "And how are you, Dr. Horton?" and shook her hand.

"I'm fine, thanks, Lt. McGuffy," said Horton.

"Something smells really good in the kitchen. Maybe we should check it out," McGuffy said then and Horton smiled.

"Bob, you've been here enough to know we're having our traditional Saturday night meal," said Ruth. "For the rest of you, we're having pizza, both thin and thick crust. So if you need to freshen up before dinner, the rest rooms are down the hall and Rachel has set our plates for us in the dining room. So go ahead and be seated, wherever you like, no assigned seats, and we'll have the pizzas out in a jiffy. There's also a salad bowl and choice of dressing on the counter. We'll be around with your drinks in a moment and Joe will lead us in a blessing when everyone's seated."

The Anderson family and guests were quickly seated except Ruth and Rachel, who offered them a choice of soft drinks, juice, coffee, tea or ice water.

"Hey, Mom!" said Tommy as everyone was seated and Anderson was about to say the blessing. "I thought we were going to have a dessert. Where's the dessert?"

"Bow your head, Tommy," said Anderson. "We'll have Mom check on the dessert later. And if you have any more questions, you should raise your hand first. OK?"

"OK, Dad," said Tommy, bowing his head.

"Thank you God for our food and our guests, and especially for helping Elaine get better. Amen," Anderson prayed.

"OK, folks, let's not let this pizza get cold. Dig in," said Anderson as he cut the pizza into pieces with a rotary slicer. Then he handed the spatula first to Elaine and told her to use it and pass it.

Tommy, chewing vigorously, looked at his Dad and raised his hand.

"What is it, Tommy?" Anderson asked.

"Can I ask Miss Elaine how she hurt her head, and does it still hurt, and did she forget a lot of stuff, and is she ever going to remember her family and stuff, and...?"

"Tommy!" said Anderson. "That's enough! Now you just..."

"Joe, let me answer that," said Elaine. "Tommy, I will answer your questions after dinner, OK? So let's just eat our pizza, and then you and I can talk. You remind me of my little boy, who was also named Tommy. I, I, I......I don't....I mean...I've just remembered!" she said, suddenly sobbing.

``Did I say something wrong, Miss Elaine?" asked Tommy.

"No, Tommy. I'm sorry. I'm not crying because of what you said," said Elaine. ``I'm crying because I just now for the first time remembered someone in my family, my little boy. I don't know where he is, and I know he doesn't know where I am. But you have helped me remember him, Tommy, so maybe we can talk more after dinner, OK?"

But before Tommy could answer, Elaine began to weep again.

"I'm sorry to interrupt everyone's meal. Excuse me please," said Elaine, placing her napkin over her mouth as she rose to leave the room. McGuffy got up, too, but

Horton stood in front of him, holding up her open palm as a school safety officer might have done to halt traffic.

``I'll check on her, Bob," Horton said softly, barely above a whisper. ``I'm sure she'll be fine. You all go ahead with your meal."

Everyone quietly exchanged awkward glances, then Ruth eventually got up and went to the refrigerator as those who remained at the table were finishing their second slice of pizza. She returned with a key lime pie sliced in 16 small slices.

"Tommy, since you wanted to know about dessert, would you like to help me serve everyone a slice of key lime pie?" Ruth asked her son.

"Yippee! Can I get two slices if I help?" asked Tommy as Anderson made a mock frown at him.

"Let's see if you drop a slice, first, Tommy," said his mother. "Then we'll offer our guests the first choice of an extra slice. Anyway, I just happen to have some macadamia nut cookies in the jar over there which you might like if you're still hungry after the pie."

"Can I get one of the extra slices if I help?" asked McGuffy.

"No, sorry, you're not a guest, Bob. We've adopted you as part of the family," said Ruth.

"Aw shucks!" said McGuffy. "Doesn't friendship count for anything around here?"

At that point, Elaine and Horton returned to their seats at the table.

``Friendship counts for a lot, and right now I'm glad to be among friends," said Elaine with a timid smile and a sniffle. "Dr. Sutherland says he wants me to find and cultivate new friends besides just the hospital staff, and I told him I'm not sure I remembered the meaning of the word. I think you folks are the very ones who can help to teach me."

"We'll certainly try, Elaine," said Ruth. "And you just know that each of us is proud to be your friend."

"Me, too, Miss Elaine," said Tommy. "Would you like the first slice of key lime pie?"

"Well, that's awfully kind of you, Tommy!" said Elaine. "I'm really proud to have you as my friend."

"Thanks, Miss Elaine," said Tommy. "And Bob, you can be next, because I guess we should put friends ahead of the family. And after you finish your pie, you can be part of the family again, Bob."

Everyone laughed.

"This is turning into a real lesson on courtesy and friendship for us all," said Mary, in her first comment of the meal. "May I be your friend, too, Tommy?"

"Sure, Doctor Mary," said Tommy. "You can be next. Here's your pie."

Mary laughed. "Thank you, Tommy. It's OK if you just call me Mary or Miss Mary if you like. Or you can call me Miss Horton or Dr. Horton. And why don't you serve your Mom, next, because she brought us the pie in the first place."

"OK, Mom. And you can have one of the extra pieces, even if you are part of the family," said Tommy.

"Hey, well don't Rachel and I count as part of the family around here? What do we get?" asked Anderson.

"You can wash the dishes, Dad, and Rachel can help," said Tommy. "But you can eat your pie first. Here's yours, Dad, and Rachel, you're last."

"What's new? Isn't that what sisters are for?" asked Rachel. "Wait until you want to play my CD's."

"Well, you can still have a cookie," said Tommy.

"Well, if everyone's about finished, why don't we move into the living room?" Anderson suggested. "And Elaine, we'll try not to pile too many questions on you, but I think we'd all like to hear as much of your adventure as you care to tell us. And please tell us if we ask anything that's particularly difficult for you to share, and we'd encourage you to pass on that. And turn about is fair play, so you feel free to ask us anything you'd like to know about us. We're kind of boring, compared to you. But we'll bore you with as many details about the Anderson family as you can stand."

"The same goes for the McGuffy family, Elaine, although the rest of them aren't here to defend themselves. So this might be the best time to talk about them," said McGuffy.

"Why don't we just hear from the one McGuffy that's here?" asked Elaine.

"I'd say one McGuffy is enough," said Anderson, slapping McGuffy on the back as he walked past him. "Why don't we continue this in the living room after a five-minute break, which will give Rachel and me just enough time to load the dishwasher. That's where those of us in the caboose get to spend some real quality time."

"Tommy, since you wanted to know how I hurt my head and whether it still hurts; and whether I forgot a lot of stuff as you call it, and whether I'm ever going to remember my family again, why don't you sit here by me, and I'll try to answer your questions," said Elaine as she sat about midway of the living room sofa.

"OK, Miss Elaine," said Tommy, quickly taking a seat on her left.

"And since you actually helped me to remember my little boy, who also is named Tommy, let's take your last question first," said Elaine. "Until I said your name a while ago, Tommy, I didn't remember my Tommy or anyone else in my family at all. I still don't know how old or how big he is or how he looks today or where he lives, and I don't know anyone else in my family, or even if there are any other members of my family. But my doctors, including Dr. Horton over there, tell me I'll probably remember them someday, and that I'll just have to be patient until then."

"Do you think you might have a daughter, too, somewhere that you don't remember?" asked Rachel.

"I just don't know, Rachel," said Elaine. "I would be delighted to know I had a daughter as pretty and polite as you, but right now I don't know if I have a daughter at all. I just don't remember anyone else in my family right now."

"Do you mind if I sit on the other side of you there, Elaine, just in case you decide you want to know anything about the McGuffy family?" McGuffy asked as Elaine smiled at him and patted the sofa on her right.

"Sure, Bob, sit right here," she said as McGuffy sat down.

"Now what did you want to know?" asked McGuffy.

"Let's save your question, Bob, or rather your answers, until I finish answering Tommy's questions," said Elaine. "Is that alright?"

"Yep, I'll wait," said McGuffy. "Besides, I want to know the answers to Tommy's questions, too."

"OK, let's see, Tommy, you wanted to know if I forgot a lot of stuff," said Elaine. "The answer is `yes,' I forgot almost everything and everyone I once knew. I have tried every way I know to remember, but so far I haven't, except for my Tommy. But I'm going to keep trying, and maybe it will come back to me soon."

"Does your head still hurt?" asked Tommy.

"Yes, it still hurts, but not nearly as much as it was hurting when your Dad and Bob rescued me from a sandbar island on Monday and took me to the hospital," said Elaine. "My doctors and nurses at Miami General Hospital have been taking very good care of me and have been giving me shots or pills to make my pain go away. That has been helping a lot."

"So how did your head get hurt?" asked Tommy.

"That's a hard question, Tommy," said Elaine. "Since I don't remember what happened to me, we have to try to find someone who saw what happened, or we have to try to figure out what happened by the kind of injury I have. So far, no one has told us they saw what happened, but we've got some really good and smart people, like your Dad and Bob, who are working on figuring out just how I got hurt."

"You mean Dad and Bob are helping to find out how you got hurt?" asked Tommy.

"That's exactly right, Tommy," said Elaine. "They've been helping to find out how I got hurt ever since they rescued me from the sandbar island on Monday morning. The waves washed me up on the shore, and they in their rescue helicopter found me and flew me to the hospital."

"Wow, Dad and Bob must be super-heroes, then!" said Tommy.

"Yes, I think they are kind of like super-heroes, because they saved my life," said Elaine.

"Well, we're not really super-heroes, Tommy," said Anderson. "Bob and I were just doing our jobs. But that's why we have the U.S. Coast Guard, to find and to rescue people who have been hurt on ships out in the ocean, like Elaine was. We think someone may have hit her on the head with a big piece of wood, and knocked her off a boat into the water. She floated ashore on a piece of wood and survived. But Bob and I go after the bad guys and lock them up in jail. We get the guys who do bad things like what they did to Miss Elaine."

"Dad, did you and Bob find the bad people that hurt Miss Elaine?" asked Tommy.

"Yes, Tommy, we found some people who we're pretty sure are pirates and drug peddlers who have hurt her and others and have done many other very bad things, like blowing up a boat that killed two sailors. We've already locked them up, but they still have to have a trial," said Anderson. "They're in jail right now, and they're going to stay there until we can have a trial for them in court before a jury and a judge."

"Like the lady judge on TV?" asked Tommy.

"Someone like that, although it will be Judge Steele, Judge Francis Steele," said Anderson.

"Judge Francis, the man of steel, like Superman?" asked Tommy.

"Well, he can't fly over tall buildings with a single bound, but he does wear a black robe," said Anderson, "You might say he's a man of steel, because he doesn't bend even a little bit from what he knows is right."

"Oh, OK," said Tommy. "But if he wears a black robe, he might be Batman."

"Not really, Tommy," said Anderson. "He's a federal court judge, Judge Steele."

"You should have quit when you were ahead, Joe," said McGuffy. "Let me try it. Tommy, remember when you said your Dad and I are super-heroes?"

"Yeah," said Tommy.

"Well, you were kind of right," said McGuffy. "Your Dad and I really DO fly over tall buildings and many miles of the ocean in our helicopter, and we really do bring bad guys back to jail. But we also bring really good people, like Miss Elaine here, to the hospital so they can get well and can visit their friends, like she's doing with us here tonight."

"Wow! That's really good," said Tommy.

"I think so, too, Tommy," said Elaine. "I agree with you. I think they're real super-heroes."

"Elaine, I think your remembering your little boy, also named Tommy, is a really significant achievement," said Horton. "Why don't you just put your mind in neutral and see what happens."

"What do you mean, put my mind in neutral?" asked Elaine.

"Just relax. Don't try to push yourself to remember anything else right now. See if a picture of your little boy, Tommy, will come to mind. If it doesn't, don't let that bother you. It will come in due time. But if you begin to recall an image, just observe it closely and see what else comes to mind."

"Well, I'm sorry. I'm just drawing a blank, although I do see dimly a little boy, about six or seven years old, wearing a striped knit shirt," said Elaine. "There seems to be some trees, maybe oak trees but not big ones, behind him and off to the side of them. And there's a blue pickup truck parked in the shade of one of the trees. It looks like a really old model, like an antique."

"Are you familiar enough with vehicles to recognize a particular year?" asked Anderson.

"No, but I can describe it for you," said Elaine. "The headlights are rimmed with chrome and are kind of rounded outward instead of straight and flat. The grill on the front of the truck is made up of chrome horizontal strips that also are rounded outward, and the space between the chrome strips is about the same as the width of the strips themselves."

"Take a look at this vehicle right here, Elaine," said Anderson, picking up a book on antique cars from the coffee table and opening it to the 1956 Chevrolets.

"That's it exactly!" said Elaine. "So if Tommy was six in 1956, that must mean he was born in 1950, which means he's now 56 years old! How can that be? I'm only 34. How can I have a son that's 22 years older than I am? I was born in 1972.

"Wow, Elaine! Do you realize what you just said?" asked McGuffy. "You had not remembered your age or birthday before now, had you?"

"No, not before now," said Elaine. "But that's obviously impossible. So I think my mind is playing tricks on me, and I don't want to do this any more. Let's talk about something else. This is making me really nervous. I'd like to apologize to you all. Even though I suggested that we talk about the questions Tommy had, I was not aware that I was going to remember my own son and then find out that he was 22 years older than me. That unnerved me for a moment, but I've just thought of a possible explanation that I ought to mention, just to get it out in the open, if you'll permit me to."

"Please go on if you like, Elaine," said Ruth. "Mary said it awhile ago. You're among friends here. So just let it happen like it happens and don't worry about it."

"Well, Joe, you're the antique car buff, but it just occurred to me that just because the pickup was a 1956 model doesn't mean that the boy I could see was as old as the truck. It's just as likely that the truck was ancient when he was born. It just means somebody in our family liked antique cars. It may be simply a collector's item, or it may be the family vehicle. It's a relief to realize that its age has nothing to do with my son's age. So please forgive me for reacting the way I did."

"It's quite natural, Elaine, as I told you. Don't let it bother you, but I think it may very well be time we were leaving," said Horton. "It's been a pleasant visit, Ruth, and one I'm sure Elaine will treasure as time goes on. So thanks so much for having us. You have precious children. We'd like to feel that we didn't wear out our welcome and could visit with you again as Elaine's recovery continues."

"We will insist on it," said Anderson as Elaine and Mary got up to go.

"Be sure to come back to see us, Miss Elaine," said Rachel.

"Me, too," said Tommy.

"Me three," said McGuffy. "But I may not be able to wait that long. In fact, I promise I'll come by the hospital to tell you more about the McGuffy family as soon as you feel like it."

"You all are welcome to come by my room in Miami General at any time, including Monday afternoon after my surgery," said Elaine. "I'll probably be groggy for a while, but I should be talking sober eventually."

"I'll see you then, if not sooner," said McGuffy. "Which reminds me. Don't we have Sunday this week? Why do we have to waste Sunday? Why don't I come by for you tomorrow for church, Elaine, then we can have a meal at a restaurant somewhere?"

"That sounds delightful, Bob, if it's alright with Mary, I mean Dr. Horton," said Elaine.

"It's fine," said Horton. "What time will you be by?"

"Well, I sometimes sleep late on Sunday, but the morning service is at 11," said McGuffy. "So I'll be by about 10:30, if that's alright."

"That's fine. I'll be at Elaine's room in the hospital then by 10, and we can all go in my car, Bob, if you can trust my driving," said Horton, "and can give me directions."

"Be happy to, Mary, I mean Doctor," said McGuffy. "In fact, if I can hitch a ride with you tonight, I'll start trusting you right now. I'm without wheels, since I came home with Joe for supper. He usually lets me off at my place, which is about 10 blocks from here. So I'd appreciate it if you can drop me off."

"Surely, just tell me where to turn," said Horton. And after another round of good-byes, the visit to the Anderson family was officially over. After dropping McGuffy off at his place, Elaine went by Horton's apartment where at Horton's insistence, Elaine borrowed another outfit from her wardrobe to wear to McGuffy's church on Sunday.

When they arrived at the hospital, Elaine volunteered to get out and go up to her 11th-floor room unaccompanied, but Horton insisted on parking in the deck and walking with her all the way. Guards on duty at the hospital entrance waved them on through the checkpoints.

"I'd never forgive myself, and the hospital likely wouldn't either, if something happened to you on my watch," said Horton, as they got off the elevator on the 11th floor and walked to Elaine's room.

"Well, good night Mary, or Doctor, I guess, since you're my doctor again now," said Elaine as they swapped hugs. "Thanks for walking me to my room, and thanks for going with me tonight. I really enjoyed the evening."

"Thank you, Elaine. I enjoyed it, too, and I'm glad to be your friend," said Horton. "So good night. See you in the morning."

The next day, Mary Horton arrived at Elaine's room on the 11th floor of Miami General Hospital at 10 a.m., just as planned. They met McGuffy in the lobby and rode in Mary's Lexus to McGuffy's church.

"It's quite a ways out but worth the drive," said Bob, sitting in the back seat with Elaine. "Go left, then take your first right about a block from here on SW 27th Avenue and go straight ahead about 20 blocks or so. That will put you in the big metropolis of Davie. You'll see the sign of the Davie Independent Baptist Church. Just follow the arrow."

"That is quite a ways out as you say, Bob," said Mary.

"You'll be pleased, I promise," said Bob. "They're good, friendly folks, and Pastor Hanson preaches straight from the Bible. Now being a psychologist and all, you may prefer a church where they preach psychological theory and stuff. No offense, Mary, but psychological theories may have their place, like in hospitals maybe, where people like Elaine here need help with what's going on in their head. But those theories are as empty of real spiritual truth and what's going on in a person's heart as a cup full of tea leaves or a sign of the Zodiac, which in my humble opinion are pure superstition and hogwash."

"I think I agree with you on tea leaves and horoscopes, Bob," said Mary. "But sometimes we have to remember that plain spiritual truth without love is, as the Apostle Paul said, no more significant than the noise of a gong or the clash of a cymbal. In other words, it has to be applied to the needs of people to be real. We need to temper spiritual truth with compassion for people, all people, not just those that are friendly to us."

"Now that's real insight, Mary. You would like Pastor Hanson. No, I predict you *will* like Pastor Hanson, and that he'll like you, too. You talk just like him. What church do you go to?"

"I go to a United Methodist Church in the downtown area, and I believe our congregation and pastor model true Christianity to a respectable degree," said Mary. "Not as much as we should, I'm sure, but we try."

"Yeah, us too," said Bob, now realizing that Elaine had said nothing at all. He considered asking her about her church preference but decided she would join the conversation if and when she wished without any prodding from him. Mary also considered inviting Elaine to comment on her church or religious preferences, but, like Bob, decided not to press her for a comment in case it might be an area of missing memories and thus cause her discomfort to be asked about it.

"So aren't you guys going to ask me about my religion?" Elaine asked as they approached a plain wooden sign that read "Davie Independent Baptist Church." Beneath those words was an arrow pointing to a small white frame building in the edge of what appeared to be a horse pasture.

"Oh, I'm sure we didn't want to be too nosey, Elaine," said Mary. "We felt you'd bring it up if you wished, without any prodding by us."

"Well, you may be surprised to know that even lying on the beach of that deserted island, with my head booming with pain like a base drum, I had a keen sense of God's presence with me," said Elaine.

"There was no one there to talk to but God and the dead man, the morning sunshine and the gulls. I had forgotten everybody and everything else. But as the sun warmed my face I spoke to the sun, and I prayed to God for water and for help. He sent me water in the base of an old stump, and help in the form of Bob and Joe. So I don't know how that fits your idea of religion, but it's mine, at least for now. I'm sure I must have been a believer before I got hit on the head because I heard him so clearly in my heart."

"That's a beautiful testimony, Elaine," said Mary. "Maybe as you worship God this morning with Bob and his church, God will reveal more of himself to you and more of your past life as well. I'll certainly be praying for that to happen in his time."

"Me too, Elaine. That was beautiful," said Bob.

A man in khaki pants with a short-sleeved shirt printed with green palm trees said "Welcome! Over there, please." He handed them three bulletins and motioned them toward the next parking space on the grass near the small white building. Mary parked the car as directed, and a man in a dark suit, whose face and hairline looked faintly like Richard Nixon, approached them and spoke.

"Howdy folks! It's so good to see you this morning. Hey, Bob! I almost didn't recognize you without your Jeep. Who are these good folks here?"

"Pastor, I'd like you to meet my friend Elaine and her friend Mary, who owns the fancy car and kindly gave us a ride to church this morning," said Bob as the preacher shook hands with them.

"Well, you just take them on inside there where the air conditioning will make them a little more comfortable. This sun is sure wicked today, but it's so good to have you with us, Elaine and Mary, and you too, Bob," the preacher said.

Inside the sanctuary, virtually every one of the roughly 35 people present was shaking hands and greeting everyone else. Finally, a young barefoot boy in short blue pants and a white T-shirt climbed a ladder to the belfry and rang the church bell 11 times, then Hanson walked to the pulpit and raised his hands.

"Let's pray," he said as the congregation grew quiet. After a prayer lasting several minutes, he said, "Be seated, please," and everyone, including him, sat down. After a series of announcements and hymns, Hanson stood again at the pulpit and delivered a rousing, 35-minute sermon, followed by an invitation hymn and a closing prayer. Then the boy who had rung the bell climbed back to the belfry and rang the bell 12 times.

"Let's go eat, folks. See you back here tonight at 6:30," Hanson said as he stepped back to shake hands with those leaving the sanctuary.

"Come back to see us, Elaine, Mary, and you too, Bob," Hansen told them as they left. Then with prodding from their stomachs, their attention switched from spiritual matters to food, so they talked about several options for lunch and settled on a popular Italian restaurant in the downtown area for their noon meal.

Chapter Eleven

While Elaine and friends dined, accused pirate Vincent Perkins was enjoying a visit from two of his brothers, Mose and Marty, and two friends, Jack Bostwick and Cyrus Snead, all from Brownsville, TX, his home town.

The security guard at the hospital entrance made them all walk through a metal detector, which they cleared, and made them list their names, addresses and phone numbers on the visitor's roster, which they signed.

"Only two of you at a time can visit him, doctor's orders," the guard told them. "Rest of you can wait here and use their passes when they get back. He's in Secure Unit 310. Visits are limited to 15 minutes."

"Wow! Old Vince must be shot up pretty bad," said Marty, Vincent's younger brother, who picked up one of the passes. "I figured they'd have him fixed up by now."

"Well, a .45 makes a wicked hole, but I 'spect it ain't entirely medical, his restricted visits and all," said Mose, eldest of the Perkins brothers, who got the second pass, boarded the elevator with Marty and pressed the third-floor button.

"We've got to break him out of here, Mose," said Marty as the elevator hummed and began the ascent. "I figure this hospital security is the weak link in the chain. If we don't get him out while he's in here, we're looking at busting him out of a federal pen, which won't be no piece of cake, that's for sure."

"You may be right, Little Brother, on the weak link part, and you're definitely right on the federal pen part, but if we bust him out before he's well enough to travel hard, we might wind up losing him and us, too, in one of these Florida swamps," said Mose. "I say we got to case the joint carefully, know exactly what's got to come down for us to get him out safe and get him out alive. And he's got to be well enough that he don't slow us down none. I mean, we've got to do this right or we're all sunk. So you do what I tell you, and we'll all be better off. You listening to me?"

"OK, Mose. I'm listening," said Marty. "Let's just don't waste any good chances, that's all I'm saying. You dig?"

"Shut up. We're here," Mose said as the elevator stopped on the third floor and the door opened. An arrow on the wall pointed to the left underneath the words, SECURE UNITS 300-310.

"This way," said Mose as he and Marty followed the arrow. An armed guard stood outside the door marked 310. They showed him their passes and were allowed inside.

Vincent was lying on his right side in his hospital bed, with his injured left hip and left shoulder facing up, which was the least painful position he could find.

"Well if it ain't my no-good brothers!" Vincent said in a low, moaning voice as Mose and Marty walked in. "It's about time you got here. What kept you?"

"Hey, Vince, Ol' Buddy. Got yer rear end about shot off, did you?" Mose said, extending his hand for a brotherly handshake.

"Hey, don't you go touching nothing! I ain't got nothing that ain't sore, and that's with them keeping me pumped full of morphine. Did you bring me any good weed?" Vincent asked.

"Get real, Vince. We couldn't bring no weed in no hospital. You know that," said Marty. "We come to get you out. You ready to go?"

"Wish I could say otherwise, Marty, but as you can well see, I ain't in no shape to travel," said Vincent. "What I'd rather have you do is to do some snooping and see if you can find that woman I knocked off the boat with a plank upside her head after we blew up her yacht. I thought for sure I splattered her head pretty good, but after what I heard 'em say on TV, I ain't so sure. They ain't mentioned it lately, but right after the Coast Guard took us over, the TV said an unidentified woman on the yacht was being treated for 'unspecified injuries at an unspecified location.' Like I told you on the phone, I want you boys to find her and finish the job I started. 'Cause if she shows up in court and points me out, it's all over for me. I'll be on death row for sure. Brannigan's going down on most of the stuff the feds have got on us, but she's the only witness besides possibly Brannigan that saw me knock her in the head."

"So you want us to find a woman you don't know the name of, being treated for an injury you don't know the kind of, at a place you don't know the whereabouts of. Is that all, Vince?" asked Mose. "That's kind of a tall order, don't you think?"

"It's a tall order, yer right. That's why I called you boys," said Vincent. "I ain't never seen you be looking for a stray heifer that you didn't find her or what was left of her by sundown. That's all I'm asking. So don't come belly-aching about it being no tall order."

"Well, do you have any foggy notion of where this wench is at? Or are you, as usual, clueless about the whole thing?" asked Marty.

"Do I have to draw you a picture?" asked Vincent. "The Coast Guard unit that got us is based in Miami. I know that, because it only took them a few minutes to get me here from the Gulf. If they brought me here, there's a fair chance they brought the others here, at least until they ran out of space, and Miami General's a big hospital.

"And guess what, the U.S. attorney that's going to be prosecuting this case is also based here, along with the federal court that's going to try us. I know that, because I done talked to Brannigan's lawyer, Jeb Smoot.

"I thought Smoot might agree to represent all of us on Brannigan's crew, because he's a real smart lawyer. But he said, 'No,' he ain't representing nobody but Brannigan. He said a Miami doctor who treated Brannigan on board *The Silver Bullet* and got hisself arrested had even been trying to get him to represent him and he refused even to represent him.

"Anyway, if that court case is going to go on here in Miami, which it is, where you reckon the feds are going to want their witnesses kept so they can get to them quick if they need them? Why, right here in Miami, of course. And if they're getting medical treatment, like this old gal I whacked in the head, then where reckon she's going to be? Why, right here in Miami General somewhere, I'd bet.

"Like I asked you while ago: Do I got to paint you a picture? I guess if you want anything done, you got to do it yourself. If you can't do a simple thing like I asked you to, then you may as well get on back to Brownsville!"

"Cool down, Vince. Cool down!" said Mose. "We ain't said we can't do it, have we?"

"You just as same as said it, bellyaching about it being a tall order," said Vincent. "I mean, either fish or cut bait. I'm laying up here hurting, and I got to have some relief."

"OK, Vince. We're in. We're your brothers, OK? I could say you ought to have thought about getting shot before you signed on with Brannigan, but what's done is done. Now cool down and describe this woman for us. What did she look like?" asked Mose.

"She was awesomely good-looking before I hit her, if I do say so," said Vincent. "Kind of tall for a woman but not too tall. Long, brownish blonde hair. And a dead give-away: if she's still alive she's bound to have one gollywhopper of a bandage on her head. You get the picture?"

"Oh, yeah. Sure, there would be a bandage. Should have thought about that. Piece of cake," said Marty. "You just rest easy, there, Vince. We're on it big time. Let's go, Mose. Got to get started."

"OK, Vince, we're going," said Mose. "Jack and Cyrus are downstairs waiting for us to get back with the visitation passes. I'll send them up to see you, and they're here to help if and when you're ready for us to bust you out. But this wench you want whacked again, me and Marty can handle that. I figure the fewer cooks in the kitchen, the better the stew, unless and until we need them. OK? So don't give them no hard time when they come up here to see you. I don't want them doing no volunteer vigilante stuff unless and until I give the signal. OK?"

"OK, Mose. Thanks for coming. You too, Marty. And you be careful, Little Brother," said Vincent. "One of us getting shot in the rear is enough."

"OK, Vince. I'm cool. You rest easy, now you hear?" asked Marty.

"Yeah, you boys be good. Bye, now," said Vincent as his two brothers left his room, nodding to the guard on their way out.

After lunch, Elaine convinced Bob and Mary that she wanted to spend the afternoon by herself in her hospital room, to prepare emotionally for tomorrow's surgery to remove the wooden splinter lodged in her brain.

"What time is your surgery, Elaine?" asked Bob. "I for sure want to be there whenever I can be."

"Dr. Sutherland didn't give me an exact time, but he said it would be early Monday morning," said Elaine.

"I took the liberty of checking the chart, and the 11th-floor surgery suite was reserved for 7 a.m.," said Mary. "I'm sure you'll be prepped for surgery around 6:30 a.m., so if you want to see her before they put her under anesthesia, Bob, you might want to get here by then."

"Dr. Sutherland promised me he would present the splinter once it's removed to Cdr. Hoover, who will take custody of it as evidence," said Elaine. "I'm counting on her being here to do that."

"Oh, if she said she'll be here, she'll be here. You can count on that. And maybe I can convince her that she needs my assistance, so I'll have a ready excuse for being here in the recovery room instead of punching in over at the office," said Bob as they arrived at the hospital.

Mary drove under the canopy of the admitting entrance to Miami General Hospital and let Bob and Elaine out.

"I'll be with you as you go under anesthesia tomorrow morning, Elaine, and when you come out, probably about 10 or so," said Mary. "That's after they stop serving breakfast; so I'll try to get the kitchen to hold a plate for you. Of course, you may not feel like eating that soon after surgery."

"Thanks for looking out for me, Mary," said Elaine. "I'm usually ready for food, no matter what."

After swapping hugs and goodbyes, Mary drove away in her Lexus; Bob left in his Jeep; and Elaine boarded the elevator, which was visible through the glass walls of the cafeteria across the hall to hospital workers, visitors and others having a late lunch or killing time with conversation and coffee. Elaine turned quite a few heads as she walked by.

Two nurse's aides finishing a late lunch watched Elaine as she walked past the cafeteria windows, stopped at the elevator, pushed the 'up' button, and waited for the elevator doors to open.

"Who is that woman with the head bandage?" one of them asked. "I've seen her a lot lately, either on the elevator or in the lobby."

"Oh, she's that woman that was attacked by pirates out in the Gulf," said the other aide. "You know, the news said they blew up her yacht, shot and killed her husband and then knocked her overboard with a plank. Somehow she survived, but they say she's lost most of her memory as a result. Isn't that horrible?"

"Yeah, it's horrible, but it's better than being dead. Sounds like she's lucky to be alive," said the first aide. "I wonder what they're doing to help her regain her memory."

"I understand she's being treated at Dr. Sutherland's brain injury clinic up on the 11th floor," the other aide said. "If anybody can help her, he can. He's supposed to be really good."

"Yeah, that's what I hear."

Four men seated at a nearby table, dressed alike in jeans, boots and western-style shirts, listened intently to the aides' conversation and exchanged glances but said nothing. They watched Elaine board the elevator, saw the doors close and the indicator light switch from pointing downward to pointing upward.

"There goes our gal," said Mose Perkins, nodding to his younger brother, Marty. "You're the point man on this, Marty," he said. "Give her time to get to her room, maybe five minutes, then you ride up to the 11th floor and see what you can find out. Now don't do nothing rash on this first trip.

"Remember what I told you about casing the joint first. We've got to know who's on that floor and where, and whether you can get inside her room and whack her without alerting the others.

"And I want you to scout this out without being seen or detected. Then you've got to come down the stairs in case security gets onto you and they lock down the elevators. And if the elevator locks down with you in it, you know how to remove a panel in the ceiling and get on top of it, right?"

"Right," said Marty. "What else?"

"Same thing I told you to start with. The key to a successful operation is careful surveillance, then careful planning. So case the joint, then come back and tell me what you've got, and we'll work out a plan. Don't, repeat, don't, go off half-cocked on your own. You got that, Marty? Clear it with me first. Now get with it. She's getting off on the eleventh floor right now. See the light on top of the elevator is pointing down now, indicating it has unloaded her and is starting back. Wait another minute or two, give her time to get in her room, then get up there on the sly and scout her without being seen. Now go."

Marty waited in front of the elevator by the cafeteria for another couple of minutes, then boarded it and pressed the button for the eleventh floor.

Elaine had left the elevator and had gone straight to her room, but a soft-drink machine she had walked past in the hallway near the elevator reminded her that she had become quite thirsty. She first thought about telling an aide at the nurse's station that she wanted a soft drink sent to her room. But she was enjoying her new sense of independence and didn't want to put anyone to any trouble on a Sunday afternoon. So she got one of her three one-dollar bills out of the top drawer of her night stand and fed it to the machine, swapping the dollar for a diet Dr. Pepper and two quarters in change.

She popped the top and took a sip, then she heard the elevator door open and close behind her. She turned around to see who had gotten on or off and saw no one. Then she noticed that the indicator light above the door continued to point upward instead of downward, as it was supposed to do when the elevator began to descend. She wondered if that meant someone was on the elevator, waiting just behind the closed doors, manually keeping them closed, and keeping the elevator on the 11th floor.

"Who would do that, and why?" Elaine mumbled to herself as she felt an emotional wave sweeping over her, first of uncertainty, then of fear. She realized instantly that the only hospital staff members on the 11th floor on Sunday afternoon were a nurse and two aides, and their station was a long way down the hall near her room. So instinctively she began to run back toward her room.

"Someone's playing with the elevator door," Elaine told the nurse and aides as she ran past the nurses' station. "I think you ought to notify security."

Once inside her room, Elaine closed the door and propped a straight chair underneath the knob. She was breathing heavily now, and her heart was racing. Suddenly her headache returned and she felt nauseous. She sat on a low sofa in her room and sipped her soft drink, then she began to relax a bit and slowly she felt better. Outside her room, at the nurses' station, she could hear the sound of a man's voice and those of the nurse and aides but couldn't make out what they were saying.

The voices grew louder as they approached her room, then there was a soft knock on her door.

"Elaine, this is the nurse. The man from security is here. He wants to talk to you," she said. Then Elaine moved the chair away and opened the door.

"Hello, Ma'am. I'm Keith Evans, hospital security. I'd like to ask you a couple of questions if I may," he said.

"Sure," said Elaine, breathing normally now. "What do you want to know?"

"The nurse said you ran to your room and suggested she call security because someone was playing, your words, playing with the elevator doors. Is that right?" he asked.

"Yes, Sir," said Elaine. "I had just gotten off the elevator about five minutes earlier. I came to my room to get some money and was back at the drink machine when I heard the elevator doors open and close, but nobody got on or off, and the indicator light stayed pointing up. I thought that meant someone may have followed me up and was on the elevator manually overriding the automatic door, keeping it from opening and keeping the indicator light pointing up instead of pointing down like it does when the elevator is about to start back down. I couldn't imagine who would be doing that or why, but it scared me and I ran to my room. You see, I'm in the hospital for injuries I received in an attack, and I'm a bit skittish."

"Yes, Ma'am," said Evans. "But we halted the elevator and walked up the stairs to check it up here, and as you can see, the indicator is pointing downward now and nobody is on the elevator. I just wonder if you were mistaken about anything you told me just now."

"No, Sir. I'm completely certain that the indicator light continued to point up and the doors kept starting to open again and again but remained closed after they opened and closed initially," said Elaine. "Maybe it was a mechanical malfunction, but I know what I saw and heard."

"Yes, Ma'am," said Evans. "Well, I'm going to re-start the elevator and ride it back down. And you be sure to call us," he told the nurse, "if it does anything unusual again. Thanks for letting us know."

"Thank you, officer," said the nurse as Evans boarded the elevator and went back to the first floor lobby, where Mose Perkins, Jack Bostwick and Cyrus Snead sat watching him get off the elevator.

"There's that security guy getting off now," said Mose. "But where's Marty? You think we ought to ride up to that 11th floor and see if Marty needs any help getting back down?"

"I'm sure he climbed out the top of that elevator when security locked it down and he's taking a while to get back. Maybe we ought to go check on him," said Jack.

"Maybe so, Jack. Why don't you and Cyrus go check on him," said Mose. "I'll get me another cup of coffee and wait on you here."

"OK, Mose, we're on it," said Jack.

"Right. Be right back," said Cyrus, as he and Jack left the cafeteria and boarded the elevator for the 11th floor.

On the way, Jack Bostwick pushed upward on a removable panel in the ceiling of the elevator and slid it to one side.

"Give me a boost, and I'll stick my head through and see if I can see anything," Jack said to Cyrus Snead. Snead locked his hands in front of him to make a kind of step. Jack caught the ceiling panel on either side of the opening, and, using Cyrus' hands as a step, pushed himself up and soon was peering into the blackness of the elevator shaft above.

"I can't see a blasted thing up here," said Jack. "We should have thought to bring a flashlight."

"You don't need a flashlight," said a voice somewhere above the elevator ceiling. "And you're lucky you're Jack Bostwick and not a security guard, or your head would be considerably rearranged by now."

"Marty!" said Jack, thankful that he wasn't a security guard. "What are you doing up here, hibernating?"

"No, and if you'll get down I'll get down too before the doors open on the 11th floor and a guard gets both of us," said Marty.

"What do we do when the doors open on the 11th floor?" asked Jack.

"Just push the third floor button, which is where Vince is, and we'll all get off there," said Marty. "If security stops us, we can say we were checking on Vince and forgot to get passes. If it's the same guy who was on duty when we were there earlier, he should recognize us."

When the elevator stopped on the 11th floor, Marty, Cyrus and Jack were all back inside it again. They stood motionless against the front walls and waited for the doors to open and close. Then Marty pushed the button for the third floor and the elevator was on its way back down. Jack got the ceiling panel back in place just as the doors opened on the third floor.

"Well, so far, so good," said Marty. "But let's not push our luck. Let's get off here and walk back downstairs to the cafeteria."

"Well, so much for covert actions," said Jack, heading for the stairway. "I thought the whole idea was to scout out the 11th floor without attracting attention. You sure blew that plan to kingdom come, though, didn't you, Marty?" asked Jack.

"That was the plan, you're right," said Marty. "But you know what happens to the best laid plans. Anyway, I don't think any harm was done. The guard didn't find me on the 11th floor, and the gals up there never saw me, either. I never dreamed our target would be getting a drink from the soft drink machine instead of going to her room when the elevator doors opened on the 11th floor. But she was, and I just had to find a way to deal with it, which I did. And all I've got to do now is give her a chance to get settled in her room, and I'll try it again."

"Yeah, but now you've got them all jittery, hospital security included," said Jack. "It may get sticky if they put a watch on that elevator, which they very well may do."

"You sound like Mose," said Marty. "He'll rake me over the coals, which should be bad enough without my having to listen to you, too. So zip it, Jack."

"I'm just telling you like it is, little man," said Jack. "Take it or leave it."

Marty, Jack and Cyrus walked down the stairs from the third floor, entered the cafeteria and headed for a table next to the window where Mose sat sipping a cup of stale coffee.

"At least none of us is dead yet," said Mose, shaking his head. "Any more shenanigans like this, and I'll be dead of a heart attack. Now sit down and keep your traps shut. I've got to think."

Chapter Twelve

Elaine finished her drink and changed out of the dress she had borrowed from Mary into a pair of hospital green coveralls. She hung up the dress in the closet and admired it for a while, then wondered how long it would be before she could buy a dress of her own.

She knew she would be without a job for an indefinite time, and she would have to apply for food stamps and a government assistance check to make it until she could find a job. And finding a job would be a big problem, because she couldn't remember anything she used to do for a living or whether she had ever worked for a living. She didn't even know if she knew how to do anything that would land her a job.

"What if I was rich on inherited money and never had to work?" she wondered. "That would be an ironic bummer. A curse of riches, you might say," she mumbled to herself. "And a bigger curse would be having money galore somewhere and not being able to get it, and the bank having to turn it over to the state as unclaimed property!"

Elaine closed the closet door and sat on the small sofa in her hospital room and told herself for the zillionth time, "You can't get depressed. The only way out is forward!"

She positioned her special pillow behind her head so it wouldn't put pressure on the bump on her head or on the sharp splinter at the center of it. Then she closed her eyes for a moment but opened them again immediately and checked the door to make sure it was secure. It was closed with a chair propped underneath the knob. But she still wondered who had been playing with the elevator door a few minutes ago and why. It could only be someone interested in harming her again, perhaps killing her this time, she feared.

Or was it just a mechanical malfunction, an elevator that opened and closed its doors by itself? That didn't seem plausible.

"I'm going to keep that door propped shut, just to make sure," she whispered softly, closing her eyes again. This time her thoughts turned to the image she had seen last night of a little boy, her little boy, named Tommy.

"I wish I knew if that's the way he looks today or, if not, how long ago he looked like that," said Elaine, again talking to herself. "And I'd really like to know where that was, because that might give me a clue about where I lived and about anyone else I've forgotten."

Elaine had leaned forward, with her forehead on her open hands and her elbows on her knees, when the phone on her dresser rang.

"This is Elaine," she said, picking up the receiver.

"Elaine, this is Commander Hoover. How are you doing?" came the voice on the phone.

"Oh, Commander, I'm fine. I'm going to get the splinter out of my head tomorrow morning, I guess you've heard," said Elaine.

"Yes. Yes, I've heard. That's what I'm calling about," said Hoover. "Dr. Sutherland told me he had scheduled your surgery for 7 a.m. and that you'd be in preparation around 6:30. Is that your understanding?"

"Yes, and I'm really glad you called. I wanted to ask you to please be present during the surgery so you can take custody of the splinter when Dr. Sutherland removes it," said Elaine. "I'm convinced that could be really important evidence against whoever did this to me, and I would want you to make sure it was processed and protected so it could be used for that purpose. Is that a problem?"

"No problem at all," said Hoover. "In fact, Dr. Sutherland called me about it and suggested that I call you to make sure it was alright for me to be present during your surgery. He said he wants me to be on hand to preserve that splinter as evidence, just as you said. We're thinking along the same lines."

"Great! I certainly have no objection to your being present during my surgery, and I really hope you can be there," said Elaine. "Dr. Sutherland already has told me he would make sure that it is retrieved and preserved. So your call is good news to me. Thanks."

"That's our job, Elaine, but it's more than that," said Hoover. "I'm going to confess that you've won a soft spot in our hearts, not just mine but the hearts of Chief Morelli and the whole team. We're really pulling for you, Elaine, and it has become almost a blood oath for us to nail the cowardly scoundrel or scoundrels that did this to you and shot in the back the man who was possibly your husband. Cleaning out such crud from the Gulf is a big part of what we took an oath to do when we signed on with the Coast Guard and particularly our Special Tactical Law Enforcement Team. I hope I'm not sounding too gung ho for you."

"Well, I'm sitting here with a hole in my head and a stick in my brain. How gung ho do you think I am?" asked Elaine. "As you know, I have no memory of being hit, much less who hit me, and as far as I know, whoever hit me may be the only witness except for that puny little splinter. So, yeah, I want you to take good care of that splinter, Commander."

"You can count on it, Elaine, and you can count on us," said Hoover. "I'll see you at 6:30 tomorrow morning."

"Good. See you then," said Elaine, hanging up the phone.

Downstairs in the hospital cafeteria, Mose Perkins sat at a table for a long time on this particular Sunday afternoon, watching the elevator doors open and close. Occasionally doctors wearing surgical coats, nurses in uniform, and visitors dressed in a variety of ways got on or off.

"We'll sit at the table over yonder so as not to disturb your calculatin,' Mose," said Marty after a while. "I can tell we are making you nervous."

"I am getting a bit nervous, you're right," said Mose, "but I don't think you boys have anything to do with it."

"Well, what's wrong then?" asked Cyrus. "It ain't like you to get all jittery. Is something going on that we don't know about?"

"Something's going on, alright," said Mose. "And I don't know if you boys noticed them or not, but every once in a while I have seen a security guard getting on the elevator. In fact, I've seen at least six in the last 30 minutes."

"Well, hey, it's a big hospital, Mose, and a lot of folks like Vince are being held on federal charges," said Jack. "You would expect to see guards getting on and off the elevator from time to time."

"Yeah, you would," said Mose. "That's what's bothering me. They're all getting on. I ain't seen a one getting off. That means at least six more guards went up than come down. That can only mean that they're wise to us and are slowly beefing up security. For all we know, they've got this place bugged to high heaven. They may have a tape recording of every blasted thing we've said, in Vince's room as well as here in the cafeteria. Did you ever think of that?"

"No, Mose, we ain't," said Marty. "That's what we've got you here for. Are you telling us you're chickening out?"

Mose frowned angrily and slammed the table with his fist.

"No, dad-blast-it, Marty, I ain't chickening out!" said Mose in a voice loud enough that folks at several nearby tables stopped what they were doing and looked their way. "I'm doing what I came to do: think! And I just might be keeping us all from being shot full of lead like old Vince up there. Except I wouldn't bet on our getting out of here as lucky as Vince. They've got us outnumbered at least two to one, maybe more. And I ain't sure I like them odds. You get me?"

"Yeah, Mose, we get you," said Marty.

"Yeah, Mose," said Jack and Cyrus together.

About that time, three more armed guards got on the elevator and the doors closed.

"You see that?" asked Mose. "More guards! I tell you, I don't like it. Something ain't right!"

"Well, hey, if you think it ain't the right time, we can ease off and try it again later," said Marty. "Sometime when they're least expecting it. You know what I mean?"

"Yeah, Mose. If you think it ain't right, that's good enough for us. I ain't hankering to visit no graveyard any time soon," said Jack.

"Me, neither," said Cyrus.

"OK. We're on the same page, then," said Mose, sipping the last swig of cold coffee and making an even uglier face than usual. "Well, let's clear out of here and go on back to the hotel until it cools off some."

"That's a good idea, Mose," said Marty as the four of them left the hospital together.

A nurse knocked on the door of Elaine's hospital room precisely at 6 a.m. on Monday and told her it was time to prepare for surgery. Dr. Jonas Sutherland had scheduled surgery at 7 a.m. to remove the wooden splinter that had punctured the lining of her brain and remained stuck there while she was given antibiotics for several days to guard against infection.

"Well, the time has finally come to get rid of that thing," said Elaine, suddenly noticing that she was hungry and remembering that she couldn't eat until after her surgery at least an hour from now.

"I should have sent out for a pizza at about 11:30 last night," she told the nurse, who took her pulse and blood pressure and marked it on her chart.

"There'll be plenty of time for pizza after your surgery," said the nurse. "But Dr. Sutherland has ordered several new MRI and PET scans, so we can go ahead with those. That should help you pass the time."

"Oh, I was kidding about the pizza," said Elaine. "Dr. Horton said she'd have the kitchen save me a breakfast plate which I can have after my surgery; so I'm sure that's sufficient. At least that's something I can look forward to."

Two hospital workers brought a gurney into Elaine's room and helped her get on it. Then they helped her position her special pillow behind her head for the ride to the imaging room. She had been through the giant revolving tube machines before, but each time she slid into them she felt claustrophobic and helpless, and this time was no exception. However, the scans went quickly and she was soon back in her room, waiting.

Lt. McGuffy arrived around 6:30 a.m., followed in rapid succession by Dr. Horton, Cdr. Hoover, and last of all, Dr. Sutherland.

"How's Wonder Woman this morning?" asked McGuffy, smiling widely as he stuck his head into Elaine's room. He was carrying a gold foil smiley face balloon floating atop a gold string with a big yellow ribbon bow at the bottom.

"I don't feel like doing any superhuman feats, but I'm glad to finally be about to get this wooden beam out of my head," said Elaine, smiling back. "Thanks for coming, and bringing the balloon, Bob. You're really sweet!"

"Well, I'm a fast learner," said McGuffy, handing her the balloon. "You remember I brought you flowers when you first got here, and they wouldn't let you have them because they were afraid of allergies? Well, so far they haven't found anyone allergic to gold foil and yellow ribbons."

"I remember the flowers, and you're sweet for remembering me again, Bob," said Elaine, turning to greet Horton and Hoover and then Sutherland as he walked in.

"Morning, Elaine. Morning, all," said Sutherland, extending his hand to her and the others. "Are we about ready for the big event?"

"I believe so, Doctor," said Elaine as Horton, the nurse, an anesthesiologist and a couple of assistants with one voice replied, "We're ready."

"Then let's roll on down to the launch pad, and we'll let Elaine do the Cape Canaveral countdown as we get under way," said Sutherland. "And we'll see if she can get all the way down to 'liftoff'."

"I'll try," said Elaine, laughing as she rolled down the hallway with her balloon trailing along. She breathed a big sigh of relief and was considerably less anxious now that Sutherland was on hand and had added a bit of amusement to her morning.

Moments later, Sutherland and his team were ready to proceed. They all had on their surgical masks and gloves, and as the anesthesiologists gave the signal, Sutherland said, "The time is now T minus ten seconds and counting, ten, nine, eight, you're on, Elaine. Pick up the count, six, five, four…"

"Three, two, one…" said Elaine, feebly, as her hand fell limp and her balloon floated up to the ceiling.

"And we have liftoff," said Sutherland, who then positioned a series of clamps to hold her head stationary during surgery.

An image of Elaine's head was projected on a giant screen, showing the internal divisions of her brain and its stem. A sharp object with jagged edges only a few centimeters wide and barely two inches in length cut diagonally upward across the base of her skull.

"There's our splinter," said Horton as Sutherland opened an area directly above it, grasped the wooden intruder with a forceps and gently tugged on it. But it didn't budge.

"Well, I hope I don't have to destroy the splinter as I remove it, but it has begun to seat itself in place, which is the brain's way of sealing it off permanently," said Sutherland. "I would rather not reopen the wound, because it will start the flow of fluids again as well as renew the risk of infection, but we may not have an option."

Sutherland then opened the area above the splinter a bit wider and bright red blood began to flow around it. He then locked another forceps around the splinter and this time pulled steadily with considerable force. Suddenly it moved a centimeter or so as Sutherland temporarily released his grasp. But when he tugged on it again, it came out quickly all the way.

"Do you have your evidence bag handy, Cdr. Hoover?" asked Sutherland, holding up the locked forceps with the splinter in its jaws.

"Right here, Doctor," she said, holding open a zippered plastic bag as Sutherland dropped the splinter in and Hoover sealed it and placed it in the large front pocket of her surgical coat. "That should help send one cowardly murderer to the penitentiary."

"Or to death row," said Sutherland.

Roughly two hours later, Elaine could hear voices she recognized but couldn't tell what they were saying. They seemed faint and soft as though they were trying not to awaken her. And when they grew momentarily quiet, she would drift off to sleep again, only to re-awaken at the next word someone spoke. Eventually she understood bits and pieces of what was being said.

"Well she's been asleep close to two hours. She should be waking up pretty soon," said Cdr. Hoover, who sat in a chair at the foot of Elaine's bed. "I saw her stir a bit just now, so she's probably on her way out."

"I wonder how she'll feel when she first wakes up," said McGuffy, who had retrieved the gold foil smiley face balloon from the surgery center and had tied it to the railing of Elaine's hospital bed.

"It's hard to predict," said Hoover. "Sometimes they react to the anesthesia, particularly if they sneak food after midnight, which they usually lose first thing after they wake up. And sometimes they snap out of it with no significant adverse effects. It varies with the individual and of course with the anesthetic."

Elaine, with her eyes still closed, listened but made no effort to talk or to let anyone know she was awake. That was because she still felt as though she was on the edge of a dream world, and she was trying to gauge whether she was nauseous and if so, how severely.

She thought of the plate Dr. Horton had promised to ask the kitchen to hold for her if it were past breakfast hour when she came to. But the thought of breakfast inspired more nausea than hunger. There was a violent and involuntary heaving in her abdomen, and she seemed right on the edge of throwing up.

Suddenly she was fully awake. Her head was throbbing severely, and the thought of food made her really nauseous. But then she remembered the hour a full week ago this morning when she was hauled up in a helicopter, rescued from a deserted sandbar island, and fed peanut butter and cracker sandwiches. And suddenly she wanted peanut butter and cracker sandwiches.

"Elaine, how do you feel? Can I get you something?" asked Hoover, who got up and approached her bedside.

"Hey, Commander. It looks like I lived through it. I assume Dr. Sutherland got that stick out of my head alright. Did he?" Elaine asked, skipping any mention of food.

"It's right here," said Hoover, holding up the sealed plastic bag containing the splinter for Elaine to see. "I'm going to guard it with my life. What can I get for you?"

"I'd like some ice water, please, if you don't mind," said Elaine, and Hoover said, "Certainly. Pour her about half a glass from that pitcher on the table there by you, Lt. McGuffy."

"Hey, Elaine. Welcome back to the land of the living," said McGuffy, passing the cup of water to Hoover, who passed it on to Elaine. "What would you like for me to get for you?"

"Hey, Bob. I'm glad to be back, thanks. And you'll never believe what I'd like for you to get for me, if you don't mind, and if it's not too much trouble," said Elaine.

"Speak the word, and for you, it's done," said McGuffy. "So long as it's legal in Florida, of course."

"I think it passes that test, but the Health Department may frown on it," said Elaine. "How about some of those peanut butter and cracker sandwiches Lt. Anderson gave me on the island last week. Do you think you could find some for me?"

"I'll check the snack machine in the hall down there by the elevator, which should have some," said McGuffy, checking his pockets for change. "I'll be right back," he said as he left the room in a hurry and ran smack into Anderson and his wife, Ruth, and kids Tommy and Rachel, who were standing just outside the door to Elaine's room. They had heard the conversation about the peanut butter and cracker sandwiches but had remained in the hallway because Elaine's room seemed to have all the visitors it could hold for the moment.

"Is this what you're looking for?" Anderson said eventually, reaching in his shirt pocket and pulling out a small package of peanut butter and cracker sandwiches just like those he had given Elaine the day of her rescue from the island. "I always carry a pack in my pocket in case I have to scrounge for lunch. I'm happy to oblige, Elaine," said Anderson, passing the sandwiches on to her.

About that time, McGuffy came in from the hall with an identical package of peanut butter and cracker sandwiches.

"Well, I'll be!" said McGuffy, noticing that Elaine was already munching a sandwich just like the ones he had. Then he knew Anderson had beaten him to the punch again. "Talk about bad timing. I must be the king of bad timing!" said McGuffy.

"It does look like I beat you to the punch again, Old Buddy," said Anderson, laughing as Elaine was already devouring the third sandwich from the pack.

"Don't let him make you feel bad, Bob. Just hold on to those crackers, because I'm going to want a second helping in a minute, I'm sure," said Elaine, washing down each bite with a big sip of ice water.

About that time Dr. Sutherland walked in.

"Well, Elaine, you have proved the adage that each person reacts differently to anesthesia," said Sutherland. "I think you're the first patient I've had to ask for peanut butter and cracker sandwiches after surgery. Which went well, by the way."

"Great, Doctor. Thanks. Now what do we do?" asked Elaine.

"You will need to wear a softer but fuller bandage for a few days, because you will have drainage. But that's a good thing, because if liquid builds up inside the brain, it tends to exert unwanted and potentially damaging pressure. In fact, if the drainage stops, let me know and we'll check to see if there's a blockage or if it has stopped simply because the breach has healed. I can tell that your healing is well underway, but we aren't there yet," said Sutherland.

"What precautions should I take to keep the healing going?" asked Elaine.

"You know, of course, not to bump that bump of yours, because the skull is still open there, and until the skull bone knits back, the brain is quite vulnerable. I can see signs that the skull bone is mending, but it will be a few weeks before it will have healed entirely. So stay out of the boxing ring," said Sutherland.

"I think I can manage that. Now what can I do about activities outside the hospital, such as social events?" asked Elaine.

"It's very important and part of your emotional as well as your continued physical healing to continue to build friendships for the life that's ahead of you," said Sutherland. "You're doing quite well, I must say. Dr. Horton tells me that you're relating well to people and are learning a lot about friendship. Keep it up," said Sutherland.

"I've had some very good teachers," said Elaine.

"Yes, you have," said Sutherland. "Doctor Horton, you're giving her excellent counsel and assistance. Keep that up. Any more questions, Elaine?"

"Just one. When can I get my own apartment?" asked Elaine. "I don't want to seem ungrateful for the hospitality here, but I'm growing a bit weary of spending so much time in my room. I was just wondering if I could check out an apartment somewhere close by."

"That's a reasonable question, and I see no reason why we can't move in that direction," said Sutherland. "But there are several other steps you'll need to take on the way. I'll ask Dr. Horton to help you sign up for Human Resources assistance and to introduce you to some of the private community outreach programs for TBI folks. They will help you to adjust socially and to handle chores like finding a suitable job. You will need a job, of course, before you can pay rent on an apartment.

"So go ahead with the preliminary steps I've outlined, and in a week or so, we'll see how you're adapting. You should remember that you are still in need of close medical monitoring; so I want you to remain close by so that we can act immediately if there's any interruption in your progress. I believe you're on the road to recovery, but problems sometimes are late arriving. So stick close with us a while longer."

"OK, Doctor," said Elaine. "But is there any way I can begin to shop for some new clothes to wear, other than hospital gowns and coveralls. Dr. Horton has gone away out of her way, I'm sure, to help me up to now. But I just hate to put her to any more trouble."

"Of course," said Sutherland. "You will find that some of the private community programs have volunteers and even paid staff in some cases to help persons recovering from brain injuries with such things as those you have mentioned, including selecting and purchasing a new wardrobe. In some cases they are able to provide food and housing and other essentials. We also have some limited funds available here at the hospital for that purpose. Dr. Horton, see me about a budget for some clothes for Elaine so she can trade in those green coveralls."

"Yes, certainly, Dr. Sutherland. But I want you to know that Elaine has been absolutely no trouble," said Horton. "Thanks for the offer of funds to buy her some new clothes, though. I'm sure she's ready to get started on that task, and I'll be happy to continue to help her with it."

"Fine. Carry on,"said Sutherland, turning to leave.

"OK, Doctor. Thanks so much," said Elaine. "And thanks to all of you, particularly to you Tommy, and to you Rachel." Anderson's kids insisted on giving her hugs before they left.

"Thanks so much for coming to see me, all of you," Elaine told them. "Thanks again for coming by."

"I'll call you this afternoon sometime," said McGuffy, extending his hand as he started to leave, but Elaine reached up both arms to hug him instead.

"Please do call me, Bob," she said, smiling as she looked him in the eye. "I'll look forward to your call. Thanks for coming by and for bringing me that smiley face balloon. That was the start of what I'm sure is going to be a really fine day for me. And without that start, it might have been otherwise."

"Glad to do it, Elaine," said McGuffy, "I'm glad you're through that surgery and are feeling better. I'll check you this afternoon." He handed her the still unopened pack of peanut butter and cracker sandwiches he had gotten from the snack machine.

"I'm going to get this splinter over to the lab," said Hoover, as she started to leave. "I can't wait to find out what the lab folks say about matching tissues and splinters. And I'll let you know the results as soon as I know. Hang in there, Elaine. See you later."

"Bye, Commander," said Elaine as her room once again was free of visitors, except for McGuffy's balloon, which continued to smile down at her from the ceiling.

Chapter Thirteen

Cdr. Jeanne Hoover filled out an evidence tag and attached it to the zipped and sealed plastic bag in which she had placed the jagged wooden splinter that had been surgically removed from Elaine's fractured skull.

Hoover presented the sealed bag to Michael Means, director of the Miami branch FBI lab. She told Means that she wanted tests run to compare the splinter with similar but smaller splinters removed from the hands of Vincent Perkins, the second in command of the suspected pirate ship, *The Silver Bullet*.

"I want to know if both sets of these splinters in fact came from the same beam or whether they are merely similar," said Hoover. "Also, I'd like to know whether the beam contains any hair or other human tissue deposited on it when it struck Elaine's skull. If so, I want it compared to Elaine's actual hair and tissue, which you have on file. In short, I want DNA tests run to determine if the tissue and hair on the beam are in fact Elaine's. Are you with me thus far?"

"Yes, I think so," said Means, scribbling notes on a pad. "You want to know if the beam we have was the beam that struck her and caused her injuries."

"Exactly. You've got it. Now the really vital part," said Hoover. "I want DNA from the splinters from Perkins' hands to be compared with DNA from tissue from the opposite end of the beam, where he would have held it as he swung it at Elaine's head. Have you got that?"

"Yes, you want to know if Perkins swung the beam that struck Elaine's head, causing her injuries," said Means.

"You've got it. How long before you can give me the results?" asked Hoover.

"Certainly before the day is out, and perhaps as soon as shortly after lunch," said Means.

"Good. Get on it. Let me know when you have it," said Hoover.

"We're on it and we'll give you a shout," said Means, as Hoover left the lab and returned to her office in the Coast Guard headquarters building.

She spoke to Morelli on her way into the office and gave him a quick report on Elaine's surgery.

"I was present throughout the surgery, which went really successfully, by the way, and I walked away with the big prize: the splinter, which I've turned over to Mike Means at the FBI lab," said Hoover.

"Good show," said Morelli. "You let him know we need the results immediately, I hope."

"He says he can have the results by this afternoon. That's immediate enough," said Hoover. "I'll probably start checking with him first thing after lunch."

"That sounds about right. Let me know as soon as you find out," said Morelli.

"Will do, chief. Speaking of lunch, care to join me for a sandwich?" asked Hoover. "I'm buying."

"You know I never turn down food, Commander," said Morelli. "Particularly when the boss is buying, I'm not about to argue with the boss."

After lunch, Morelli and Hoover returned to their office, and a couple of hours later Hoover headed for the lab.

"I don't mean to rush you," she told Means as she walked in, "but I just had to see how you are coming on analyzing those splinters I left you this morning."

"I was just about to call you," said Means, handing her a stack of letter-sized sheets stapled together at a top corner. "We finished our analysis an hour or so ago and I've just finished proofing our report. I think you'll be pleased."

"Good! Do you want to give me a verbal summary or would you rather I just read the printed version myself?" asked Hoover.

"When the news is this good, I'd relish an opportunity to tell you in person," said Means. "Of course, I would expect you to go over the written version and let me know if you have questions about any of our findings or if you wish additional findings besides those we made. But in a nutshell, Commander, I'd say we're batting 1,000."

"Excellent. Let me hear it!" said Hoover.

"Well, first we checked the origins of the splinters in the victim Elaine's head and in the hands of her suspected attacker, Vincent Perkins, and found them to be identical," said Means. "I use the term `identical' advisedly. These are not just splinters of a similar type from a similar source, but splinters that once were attached to the same board at specific locations.

"To say it another way, we found the exact places on the plank where each of the splinters once was attached. They not only match when viewed with the naked eye. They match microscopically as well.

"We have made color slides of each splinter, magnified substantially at the point where each was once attached to the plank. We can say to a degree of certainty beyond any reasonable question that the plank wielded by Perkins struck Elaine and drove a splinter into her brain."

"I was hoping you could be that certain, Mr. Means," said Hoover. "The jury will have to render its verdict based on facts that are true beyond a reasonable doubt."

"We believe the facts are now known virtually beyond all doubt," said Means. "But there's more, which serves only to underscore what I've already stated.

"The hair and other tissues found on the board are an exact match to the hair and tissues we have on file from the victim Elaine and her suspected attacker, Perkins."

"Let's pretend we're in court, and you're asked whether you are certain the plank we will offer as evidence was the source both of the splinters in Perkins' hands and in Elaine's brain. What would be your answer?" asked Hoover.

"Absolutely!" said Means. "I would say the chances that this many matches could occur without their identities being as I have described them would range into the trillions to one."

"That's great, Mr. Means," said Hoover. "I can't wait to tell Chief Morelli and our Special Tactical Law Enforcement Team, and of course, the U. S. attorney, Joseph Barton. I can assure you, we're all looking forward to presenting this evidence to the judge and jury. Congratulations on great work."

"Thanks. We like it when our findings are this clear, which isn't always the case," said Means. "We couldn't have done it without the tremendous work you folks have done in gathering the evidence for us to examine."

"Well, that may be. But I like to think of our work as a team effort, where each part is vital to the outcome," said Horton. "How soon could you be ready to testify and present your findings to the grand jury? I understand Barton was going to the grand jury sometime this afternoon to begin an initial presentation of our case."

"I'm ready right now, Commander," said Means. "Tell Mr. Barton to just give me a call when he's ready."

"Will do," said Hoover. "I'm sure it will be soon."

Barton and his chief deputy, Milton Richards, began on Monday afternoon parading a stream of witnesses, in what they had nicknamed the Gulf Pirates case, before the federal grand jury. The first witness was forensics lab director Michael Means, who testified that strong forensic evidence connected Vincent Perkins to the attempted murder of the victim Elaine. Means and Hoover led grand jurors on a step-by-step tour of the evidence against Perkins.

Other witnesses testified in detail about the alleged piracy and other alleged crimes, including kidnapping, murder, theft, destruction of property, destruction of federal evidence, and drug trafficking by Joe Brannigan, captain of the alleged pirate ship, *The Silver Bullet*, and Perkins, his second-in-command.

There also was testimony that Brannigan ordered *The Silver Bullet* booby-trapped to blow up if anyone attempted to power up the ship after it had been taken over by Coast Guard SAS teams. Witnesses to the blast testified that the ship exploded, taking the lives of two Coast Guard sailors and destroying the ship's cargo of thousands of pounds of cocaine, marijuana and other contraband. Grand jurors were allowed to see and examine a couple of large bags of the drug-rich debris from the explosion, which was dipped from the ocean by the crew of the cutter *Red Eagle*.

Detailed testimony about the suspected piracy episode in the Gulf came primarily from former members of Brannigan's crew, many of them badly injured, who testified on the recommendation of their court-appointed attorneys after Barton and Richards offered to recommend lighter sentences for them in exchange for their testimony against Brannigan and Perkins.

Barton the previous afternoon had ordered beefed-up security at Miami General Hospital, where Brannigan, Perkins and others involved in the alleged piracy and related crimes were hospitalized in secure medical cells for treatment of gunshot wounds.

The FBI, at Barton's request, had monitored the conversations between Brannigan, Perkins and others in the hospital with their friends, family members, and alleged co-

conspirators but not their conversations with their attorneys, either private or court-appointed.

Perkins and two of his brothers and two of his friends, all from Brownsville, TX, were overheard and taped by the FBI talking about plans to break Perkins out of custody. They also were taped discussing a second attempt to kill Elaine, the woman Perkins allegedly bludgeoned with a splintered beam on board *The Silver Bullet*, knocked overboard and left for dead. After hearing their recorded comments, Barton called for extra security at the hospital, which was provided by the U.S. Marshals Service.

"I want Elaine under 24-hour security protection and Brannigan and Perkins under 24-hour armed guard," Barton told the Marshals Service in the federal building, which responded by sending in the requested additional security personnel one or two at a time on Sunday afternoon.

Perkins' older brother Mose, however, had noticed the additional security officers arriving at the hospital and promptly called off any attack or escape plans until what they considered a more opportune time. Security at the hospital continued to tighten.

Barton said in a strongly worded memo that he wanted no one except for authorized personnel to be allowed access to the 11th floor of the hospital where Elaine was undergoing treatment, nor to the second and third floors, where Brannigan and Perkins were being held in secure medical cells and treated for gunshot wounds.

Hoover and her team members as well as medical and security personnel were among those with access to the restricted floors. They were issued special identification cards containing an electronic chip which produced a three-dimensional digital image of the authorized holder when scanned by any other authorized guard's hand-held scanning device.

McGuffy went by the FBI office and got his new ID card, but after hearing of the potential threat on Elaine's life and the talk of Brannigan's and Perkins' possible attempt to escape, he called Elaine Monday afternoon after her surgery and suggested she not leave the safety of her room.

"I'll come by and spend time with you if you like, Elaine," said McGuffy. "But I don't think this is the time for you to venture outside. Perkins is the scum of the earth as far as I am concerned, and we both know he would gladly kill you or have you killed, with his brothers and his buddies doing his dirty work."

"I agree with you, Bob," said Elaine. "I shudder to think that those guys were watching me come in yesterday and one of them actually came to the 11th floor. I'm not sure what I would have done if he had come after me up here instead of playing games with the elevator door. I know I would have tried to defend myself, but I'm not likely to have been much of a match against that hoodlum."

"Well, you won't have to deal with that question again, Elaine," said McGuffy. "I understand that several armed agents were sent to the 11th floor, and I'm sure you've seen them by now."

"Yes, there are two agents outside the elevator doors on this floor and one at the nurse's station just outside my door. So I feel a lot safer," said Elaine. "But if you wanted to come up for a little while this afternoon, I'm sure they would not object, and I would enjoy your company."

"Well, is there anything I can bring with me?" asked McGuffy. "I'll probably come up around three, if that's alright, and spend an hour or so with you. What do you think?"

"I would be delighted, but you don't need to bring anything but yourself," said Elaine. "Your balloon is still smiling down on me from a corner of the ceiling."

"Well, I'm going to try to jump through the security hoops and come see you," said McGuffy. "If I don't hit a snag, I should be up there in about five minutes."

"OK, Bob. Thanks. I'll look for you," said Elaine.

The tightened security was having its effects on the Perkins brothers.

"Well, Mose, what are we going to do?" Marty Perkins asked his older brother as they sat in a Miami Beach hotel on Monday afternoon with friends Jack Bostwick and Cyrus Snead.

"You sure were right about yesterday not being the right time to spring Vince or to finish killing the woman he hit on the head with a plank. The hospital over there is swarming with FBI agents and armed security guards. They're still out in force, so now what do we do?"

"We'll just have to find another way," said Mose. "Vince is counting on us to keep him from being executed, which is very likely to happen if that woman he hit testifies against him in court. We're his only hope."

"That, I realize," said Marty. "My question is, what are we going to do? Or maybe a better question is, is there anything we can do?"

"I don't know the answer to that question, but I know how we can find out," said Mose. "Suppose you and me go over there and visit old Vince again. I don't expect they'll let us through, but maybe we can see what their ID system is all about. Then maybe we can outsmart it."

"What about us?" asked Jack. "Have me and Cyrus come all this way from Texas to help spring Vince, and you're telling us you don't need us. If that's how you feel, we may as well go on back to Brownsville right now."

"Well, now that may not be a bad idea," said Mose. "I don't see any chance we can spring him. And he's still so sore from them three 45-caliber bullet holes that he couldn't travel even if we could get him out of the hospital alive. What I'm saying is, whacking that old gal is about all we've got left, and me and Marty can do that. Plus, if you and Cyrus go on back, that will cut our expenses half in two. You boys don't realize how much it's costing me to put you all up in this fancy hotel."

"If you feel that way about us, Mose, we're gone. I mean, we're outa here," said Cyrus. "Is that what you're telling us? You want us to go?"

"That's what I'm telling you," said Mose. "Thanks for coming, but we just had a change in plans."

"You're really serious about us cutting out, ain't you Mose?" asked Cyrus.

"Serious as a saddle sore, Cy. But it ain't personal," said Mose.

"You sure you ain't making a mistake, like maybe one that's going to get you and Marty and maybe Vince, too, killed?" asked Jack.

"We just have to take our chances, Jack," said Mose. "At least I won't have you and Cyrus getting killed on my conscience."

"If that's the way you want it, Mose, we'll see you in Brownsville. Look us up when you get back, you hear?" asked Jack.

"Yeah, sure. Will do. Brownsville for sure," said Mose as Jack and Cyrus left the hotel. "Now you go with me, Little Brother," he said to Marty.

Mose and Marty went into the hospital lobby and were stopped at the checkpoint by a security guard, who made them walk through a metal detector, which they cleared.

"Where you boys headed?" the guard asked, and Mose said, "We want to visit our brother, Vince Perkins, on the third floor."

"Third floor's closed. Sorry," the guard said. "You'll have to come back later. Can't guarantee you can get in, but I can guarantee you not today."

"Sure, I understand. But what about the sixth floor? Marty and I also have a friend on the sixth floor," Mose lied. "Can we visit him?"

"That depends," said the guard.

"On what?" asked Mose.

"On whether the hospital security officer on that floor will give you clearance," said the guard.

"What do I do to get clearance?" asked Mose.

"You ring the floor officer on that phone at that desk over there. When he answers, give him your name and the name and room number of the person you want to visit. He will check with the nurse on duty to see if the person in that room is who you said it was and whether he or she is allowed to have visitors and wishes to have a visit from you. If so, you're cleared to visit as soon as the security officer on that floor can accompany you. He'll then come down here and escort you up there. So what's your friend's name on the sixth floor?" the guard asked.

"Oh, forget it. We'll see him some other time," said Mose.

"Yeah, he probably wouldn't want to see us, anyway," said Marty as he and Mose walked back through the lobby and out of the hospital.

"Now that's what I call tight security," said Mose.

"So what are we going to do, Mose?" Marty asked as they left the hospital.

"First thing we're going to do is get away from here and check our clothes and shoes real good and make sure we ain't bugged," said Mose. "Let's walk down by the beach. We can talk there, and if they've got them high-powered directional mikes monitoring us, the waves will wipe out what we're saying. Take off your boots now, why don't you, and I'll take a look at them. And let's check each other over good for bugs."

When Mose and Marty found no bugging devices anywhere on their boots or clothes, they walked together toward the beach and then along the water's edge, where low waves washed the shore. And for a long time, they said nothing.

"I'm afraid we've done ruined every chance Vince had of avoiding Death Row," Mose said eventually. "I should have realized at the time, but I didn't, that the government was bugging us, not only to pick up on our plans to bust Vince out of custody but also Vince's flat statements that he hit the woman up side the head with a plank. He even mentioned that we, meaning Vince himself and Brannigan and the rest of the crew, blowed up the woman's yacht."

"Yeah, I do remember that," said Marty. "And even scarier, he said he thought he splattered her head pretty good and said he wanted me and you to find her and finish the job. That right there is trying to get us to kill her, and I'll just bet you that's soliciting murder or something, certainly a separate federal felony. We'll be lucky if we don't get arrested next time we go in that hospital. I think we done screwed up big time, Mose. What do you think?"

"I'm afraid you're right, Marty, but we can't abandon Vince," said Mose. "He's in a heap of hurt right now, and you remember he said he doesn't have one of them court-appointed lawyers yet to look after his legal rights. So if we cut out, he'll be out by himself and pretty much on a greased rail to the death chamber."

"You're absolutely right I know, Mose, but I don't see how me and you getting shot is going to help old Vince one little bit, do you?" asked Marty. "It looks to me like he's all but fried right now, and I ain't really hankering to go with him. I mean, it's kind of like what you told him when he said he was sore from getting shot up. You said he ought to have thought of that when he signed on with Brannigan."

"Yeah, I know I told him that, and I know it's true," said Mose. "But that still don't mean we can just roll over and play dead. It don't mean we can desert our flesh-and-blood brother, Marty! You understand me?"

"Yeah, Mose, I understand. Which gets me back to my original question. What are we going to do?" asked Marty.

"Well, I been thinking," said Mose. "We can't even get in to see him anymore, but we might be able to get in touch with old Jeb Smoot, Brannigan's lawyer. I know he ain't representing Vince and ain't about to, but Vince said he talked to him. Maybe we can get him to give us some information or ideas on how we can help him."

"Yeah, but how are we going to contact Smoot?" asked Marty. "He's not going to be in his Brownsville office, you know. He's bound to be here in Miami somewhere."

"I know that, but I'm pretty sure I saw him getting on an elevator in the lobby of our hotel yesterday," said Mose. "I didn't get a good look at him, but if it was him, he was wearing his trademark black hat, and I'll bet it was him."

"Well, why don't we go on back to the hotel and ask the desk clerk if he's registered here?" asked Marty.

"Just what I was about to do, Little Brother," said Mose as they entered the hotel and approached the clerk. "Sir, can you tell me if there's a Jeb Smoot registered here?"

"I'll check," said the clerk, punching some keys on a computer keyboard and looking at the screen.

"Yessir, he's registered here. Shall I ring him for you?" asked the clerk.

"Yeah, if you don't mind. Tell him Mose and Marty Perkins are in the lobby and would like to talk to him. And ask him if he wants us to come up there or would he be willing to come down here."

"I won't be able to give him a message, Sir," said the clerk. "I can only ring his room if you like. Then you can talk to him on the house phone there on the counter if he's in and wishes to talk to you. Or if he's out, you may leave a recorded message."

"O.K., ring him then," said Mose as the clerk punched a number and motioned for him to pick up the receiver of the house phone.

"He's on the line, Sir," said the clerk.

"Jeb Smoot," came the answer.

"Jeb, this is Mose Perkins. I'm down here in the lobby with my little brother, Marty, and we'd sure like to talk to you if you could spare us a few minutes," said Mose.

"I don't know any Mose or Marty Perkins," said Smoot. "Who are you and what do you want?"

"We're brothers to Vince Perkins, who was Joe Brannigan's second in command on *The Silver Bullet*. I understand you're representing Brannigan," said Mose.

"That's right. What can I do for you?" asked Smoot.

"Well, they done got security so tight over at the hospital, where Vince and Brannigan are being treated for gunshot wounds, that Marty and me can't even get in to see Vince no more, and of course, we're his family. Ain't there some legal rights we got to talk to him?"

"It's not my place to school you or him on your legal rights. I'm representing Brannigan, and I'm not available to represent any of the other parties in this case, your brother Vince included," said Smoot.

"Oh, we're not trying to hire you to represent him, Mr. Smoot," said Mose. "We understand Vince is supposed to get one of them court-appointed lawyers, since he don't have nobody to represent him and ain't in no position right now to hire anybody. But if he's got an appointed lawyer coming, he ain't got here yet."

"Then what do you want from me?" asked Smoot.

"We were hoping you could at least give us some information that would help us defend our brother," said Mose. "You're just about our last hope, Mr. Smoot. I'm sure Brannigan has told you some things that involved my brother, Vince, since they left out of Brownsville together. Any information at all might help us. I know Vince said you mentioned that some doctor treating Brannigan on board his ship got arrested and had asked you to represent him."

"I turned him down. But what business is that of yours?" asked Smoot.

"Well, maybe you could ask Brannigan what the doctor's name was. He might have found a lawyer by now, and maybe that lawyer could help us," said Mose.

"I'll tell you the doctor's name. It's Clay Houston. Lived over on Key Biscayne. I don't think he's much of a doctor, particularly since he lost his license in a drug case. But he's got a mansion I'm sure he built with drug money, and if you want to talk to him, be my guest," said Smoot, reading out the doctor's cell phone number. "I ain't going to be calling him. I understand, though, that he's maybe going to testify for the government in this case and say whatever they want him to say to save his own hide. Well, here's a little free advice: Stay away from him. He's into so much crooked stuff it's amazing the government is letting him walk around. I figure they wouldn't unless he's giving them what they want. Consider yourself warned. Now I've got work to do. Forget I spoke to you."

"OK, Mr. Smoot. Thanks," said Mose as he hung up the phone.

Chapter Fourteen

Mose Perkins called Dr. Clay Houston's residence in Key Biscayne and got a recorded message in a man's voice: "This is Dr. Houston. Leave your name and number and a brief message and I'll call you back."

"This is Mose Perkins, brother of Vincent Perkins of *The Silver Bullet*. Vince is in federal custody in Miami General Hospital. He doesn't have a lawyer yet, so I was hoping you might have some information that would help his defense. Please call me as soon as possible," Mose said, left his cell phone number and hung up.

No sooner had Mose hung up than his phone rang. It was Houston, calling on his cell phone.

"This is Clay Houston. How can I help you, Mr. Perkins?" he asked.

"I'm not sure, Dr. Houston, but I'm sure the government has both my phone and yours tapped. Would it be possible for us to meet somewhere, such as on the beach here in Miami Beach, and talk?" asked Mose.

"Oh, I'm certain our cell phones are secure, Mr. Perkins. But I'm not sure I could be of any help to you or your brother," said Houston. "You may not know this, but I lost my license to practice medicine about four years ago. Perhaps I should say I willingly chose not to practice.

"I was accused of drug trafficking, which the government never proved. But through a compromise my lawyer worked out with the government, I paid a $100,000 fine and surrendered my license in lieu of an extended trial that would have destroyed my practice anyway. There were certain other elements of the agreement that I am not at liberty to go into detail about."

"I see," said Mose. "Then why were you trying to hire Jeb Smoot to represent you?"

"Oh, so Jeb gave you my number. I wondered how you got it, since it hasn't been listed in years," said Houston. "I was arrested last week and jailed like a common criminal, without bond for several days I might add, which was substantially at odds with the agreement I had with the government. The government last week said I was being arrested on charges ranging from piracy and murder to drug trafficking and kidnapping. I was also accused in effect of practicing medicine without a license by coming aboard Brannigan's ship and treating his gunshot wound."

"Well, you did, didn't you?" asked Mose. "Treat Brannigan, I mean. My brother, Vince, said you did."

"I came aboard the ship, Mr. Perkins, true. But the government has no evidence at all of what I did aboard that ship. My license to practice medicine is a state license. I surrendered it four years ago without any mark against it rather than go through a proceeding that might have gone adversely to me. I can resume my practice at any time on proper notice to the Florida Board of Medical Examiners. Any complaint of unlawful practice would have to be brought before that board. The only complainant last week was the federal government, which had absolutely no evidence to support such a complaint at the time I was arrested. So it was mutually agreed that the government's complaint be dismissed."

"So if the government agreed to drop the complaint, why were you kept in jail several days?" asked Mose.

"That was my question," said Houston. "That's when I contacted Mr. Smoot on the advice of a friend. My previous attorney was disbarred last year, so I was temporarily without representation. When Mr. Smoot was unable to represent me, I found another attorney, who was able to secure my release."

"So you're free, now, right?" asked Mose.

"No, not exactly. I'm actually free on $100,000 bond," said Houston. "You see, the government says the piracy, murder, kidnapping and drug trafficking charges are based on new evidence, totally apart from my practicing or not practicing medicine. The new charges are based on my visiting the ship you mentioned, *The Silver Bullet*, shortly before it was taken over by Coast Guard SAS teams and exploded with an ammonium nitrate and diesel booby trap that killed two sailors when it blew up."

"So are you being accused of piracy and all that parade of crimes they're charging Brannigan and my brother, Vince, with?" asked Mose.

"That's about the size of it, Mr. Perkins," said Houston. "The government says I'm an accessory after the fact because I allegedly went on board *The Silver Bullet* in aid of the alleged pirates, Brannigan and Perkins, and of course the rest of the crew as well."

"Well, it strikes me that you and my brother can be of mutual benefit to each other, Dr. Houston," said Mose.

"How do you figure that?" asked Houston.

"It seems that you badly need an eye-witness who will testify that you provided no treatment whatever to Brannigan and my brother, Vince Perkins," said Mose.

"My brother, being second-in-command to Brannigan, was with him all the time and could testify in great detail about what you said and did. However, he needs an eye-witness who will testify that Brannigan was in total charge of the ship and that Vince was merely following Brannigan's orders on any alleged criminal activity.

"Such testimony would tend to sink Brannigan's defense that he was some kind of victim of mutiny led by my brother, Vince. As I said, you and Vince may be in a position to help one another."

"Are you saying that your brother, Vincent, will testify that I came on board but didn't offer any medical treatment to Brannigan, to your brother, nor to anyone else?" asked Houston.

"That depends, Dr. Houston," said Mose.

"On what?" asked Houston.

"On whether Vince can count on your testimony that Brannigan was in complete control of the ship and was not the victim of any mutiny led by my brother at any of the times when you were on board *The Silver Bullet*," said Mose.

"Didn't you tell me a moment ago that your brother, Vince, told you that I had treated Brannigan?" asked Houston.

"I may have said something like that, and Vince at one point may have said something like that, but we obviously didn't know what we were talking about, did we, Dr. Houston? You were *not* practicing medicine on Brannigan, were you, Dr. Houston? Ain't that right, Dr. Houston?" asked Mose.

"I don't have to prove that I wasn't practicing medicine, Mr. Perkins," said Houston. "The government has to prove I was practicing medicine if it wants to hang those charges on me."

"And one way for the government to prove you were practicing medicine is with the eye-witness testimony of my brother, Vince," said Mose. "But, of course, if my brother doesn't remember seeing you practicing medicine on Brannigan or anyone else, that might be of considerable benefit to you, don't you think, Dr. Houston?"

"Well, how do I know that your brother's bad memory won't improve, or perhaps that his good memory won't deteriorate, under the pressure of a federal prosecutor's examination?" asked Houston.

"Like I said, Dr. Houston. It seems that we need to work as a team, or rather that you and Vince need to work as a team, to each other's mutual benefit," said Mose. "On my brother, Vince's behalf, I think I can arrange an understanding that will be to the benefit of both of you. But, of course, I would first need an understanding of what your testimony will be. And beyond that, we'd probably just have to trust each other, wouldn't we?"

"I guess so," said Houston. "So if it will help your brother's memory, I am quite sure and am prepared to testify that Brannigan was in complete control of *The Silver Bullet* and that your brother, Vince, was completely obedient to his orders each and every time I was on board. And just for the record, that is the complete truth as I know it."

"That's good, but it seems to me that if my brother tells the complete truth, you will be charged for sure with far more than just practicing medicine without a license; you will be charged with aiding and abetting a string of crimes, including kidnapping, murder, piracy, destruction of private property and drug trafficking," said Mose. "It seems to me, therefore, that you, Dr. Houston, may be at great risk of going to the death chamber, and in view of that risk, that you may need to do a wee bit more to even up the balance scales."

"Like what, Mr. Perkins?" asked Houston.

"We'll let you know, Dr. Houston. We'll let you know," said Mose as he hung up the phone.

Lt. Bob McGuffy presented his special electronic ID card to the security guard in the lobby of Miami General Hospital.

"Where to, son?" asked the guard.

"11th floor, please," said McGuffy.

"Goin' to see that pretty woman with the bump on her head, are we?" the guard asked.

"Yessir. That I am," said McGuffy. "And you're sure right about her being pretty. She had successful surgery this morning to remove a big wooden splinter from her brain, so she shouldn't have that bump much longer."

"Well, let's hope not," said the guard. "You're free to go, son. How long you planning to be up there?"

"I told her about an hour. It's a minute or so before three now, so I'll be back around four or so. Is that all right?" asked McGuffy.

"Oh, for sure it's all right. Doc didn't put no limits on her visitors, so long as they clear security. And you passed with flying colors," said the guard. "So hug her one time for me."

"Right. Be happy to," said McGuffy, heading for the elevator. "See you!"

When McGuffy stepped off the elevator on the 11th floor, two guards stopped him and asked to see his special ID card, which he produced.

"You'll need to show this to the guard outside the nurses' station if you plan to visit the patient in her room," one guard said. "You should wear it on your front shirt pocket while you are on this floor."

"OK, thanks," said McGuffy, clamping the card to his shirt pocket as he walked toward Elaine's room. He stopped briefly at the nurse's station, showed the card to the guard, then knocked softly on her door.

"Come in," said Elaine as McGuffy pushed the door open and walked toward the small sofa where she was seated, looking over the book on Florida scenes which Lt. Anderson had given her. She stood to greet McGuffy. "Bob! Thanks for coming by. It's so good to see you."

"So good to see you!" said McGuffy, opening his arms wide as they exchanged a big hug. "That was for me, but the guard downstairs asked me to give you this," McGuffy said, giving her another big hug as they both laughed.

"We must always obey security officers, mustn't we?" asked Elaine.

"My motto exactly," said McGuffy. "So tell me how you feel after getting that piece of deck floor out of your brain."

"I can tell it's out, that's for sure," said Elaine. "There's actually a bit more throbbing, for which I'm taking some pain medication, but there's none of the usual sharp pain that comes with the least bit of pressure on that big bump on my head. I can actually touch it without much sensitivity at all."

"That's great, Elaine. I'm glad," said McGuffy. "I saw you looking at that book of Florida scenes. Were you getting any more memories back, or were you thinking of Lt. Anderson, who gave you the book?"

"Do I detect a bit of jealousy?" asked Elaine. "Sure, I was thinking of Lt. Anderson, but not the way I think of you. He's a very thoughtful friend, and I value his friendship highly, both his and his wife's and that of their delightful kids."

"So how do you think of me?" asked McGuffy. "As second-place peanut butter and crackers sandwich runner?"

"No, silly. You're the smiley face that brightens my day," said Elaine. "The one who gives me hugs, when everyone else merely offers me a handshake. The one who's concerned about my security, when everyone else lets the guards worry about it. The one who comes to my room to keep me company, when everyone else is somewhere else. Do you get the picture, Lt. McGuffy?"

"Name is Bob," said McGuffy, turning bright red in the face. "That's the picture I was hoping to see. Now your smiley face has brightened my day. I guess we're even. So what about my question about whether you're getting any more memories back?"

"Actually, I think I am," said Elaine. "I keep hearing myself calling my son Tommy. He appears to be about six or seven years of age as I picture him, but I don't know if that's real or just a creation of my mind, searching for a real Tommy that's separated from me or for an imaginary Tommy that fills a void in my memory."

"What about the man you found on the beach, who had been shot in the back? Do you have any memory of him? After all, it was his home-made tattoo that gave us your name as ELAINE. And I'm sensing that you feel very much at home with the name ELAINE now. Is that right?"

"Yes, I do feel very much at home with the name ELAINE. It's like that's who I am, and it isn't a matter of my accepting it. It's more than a name. It's me. Without it, I'm not real. So, yes, the name ELAINE and I are one reality."

"But what about the man with ELAINE tattooed on his arm?" asked McGuffy. "Without him, we wouldn't have the name. Then who would you be? Do you ever think of that?"

"Yes, I do think that if I hadn't found his body on the beach, in an important sense I wouldn't be here. Someone else would be here, perhaps, but not me," said Elaine.

"Well, if he hadn't strapped you to that plank with his belt, you almost certainly wouldn't be here. But do you have any memories at all of a past life with a man with the name ELAINE tattooed on his arm?" asked McGuffy. "Isn't it possible that you've just clung to the name on his arm like you clung to the driftwood plank. Isn't it possible that he's really not part of your past life, although he was at the heart of your new identity?"

"It's theoretically possible, Bob, but that's what I mean when I say the name ELAINE. It's like a whole reality just below the surface, waiting to break through. It's a reality that seems so right that it just has to be true."

"Well, I read one time that when a person loses their memory and there's no organic reason for it, there may be a psychological reason," said McGuffy. "If the reality of your past is so unpleasant that you have closed it off, that rather than your brain injury may be the reason you can't remember it."

"Yes, Dr. Horton and Dr. Sutherland have told me something like that. They have said there may be something in my past so unpleasant that I've blocked it off, but otherwise I should recover virtually all of my other memories," said Elaine. "There are two exceptions, however. They said I am unlikely ever to recover memories of things that occurred just before and just after my injury. That means that I am unlikely ever to remember Vincent Perkins swinging that plank and hitting me in the head. That makes me really angry, because I can never testify against him in court."

As Elaine grew angry, McGuffy saw an expression on her face he hadn't seen before. Her eyes seemed to be fixed on a point in space rather than on anything in her hospital room. She seemed to be grinding her teeth together and breathing rapidly, and her brow was wrinkled in a frowning scowl.

"At the suggestion of Petty Officer Sam Mendez, I have brought a few pictures with me, Elaine, including one of this man right here," said McGuffy, showing Elaine a close-up photo of Vincent Perkins. "Does this look like anyone you've ever seen before?"

"Vince!" said Elaine as her frown faded and a look of satisfaction came over her face. "That's the guy all the others called 'Vince,' and he's the one that told my husband, Tommy Joe, and me to come on board the ship from our yacht. Told us there was a party going on, and Captain Brannigan wanted us to attend. Then he made my husband drink too much, kept pouring liquor down him until he couldn't stand up. Then he began picking at me and making crude remarks. It's all coming back to me now. Tommy Joe is my husband!"

"Elaine! Is this really happening?" asked McGuffy as he and Elaine sat on a small sofa in her hospital room, marveling that giant pieces of her past memories seemed to be falling into focus.

"Yes, Bob, it appears to be happening," said Elaine. "My past is becoming clearer. The fog is finally lifting around the fringes at least, and that gives me hope that the doors to the rest of my past may be just ahead."

"Well, while it's coming back to you, shouldn't you just keep telling me about it to keep it flowing?" asked McGuffy. "I mean, there seems to be something about the combination of fear and anger that you feel over some figures of your past, along with the security and trust you obviously feel here in this hospital room with me by your side, and with the nurse and the guard just outside the door, that has released these memories, don't you think?"

"I don't know for sure, Bob, but I know that all of what you said plus the picture of Vince you showed me seems to have jogged my memory. But I'm guessing it was the picture of Vince that really broke through," said Elaine. "So what do you think I should do now, Bob? Do you think it would really help me to remember more if I kept on talking like I am now, telling you everything I can remember, since it seems to be coming back to me? And would you mind or would you be bored silly if I did that?"

"I'm definitely not going to be bored," said McGuffy. "I'm certainly no memory expert, and I may be selfish to say this, but I would love to hear as much of your life story as you care to tell me," said McGuffy. "I guess I'd say stop if it causes you great pain for any reason at any point, because that otherwise might cause you to seal off those memories and then close the door to all the rest."

"Is that a yes?" asked Elaine.

"Yes, it's a yes," said McGuffy, looking straight into her eyes, smiling broadly and nodding his head vigorously up and down. "I want to hear everything about you, so go ahead."

"Do you have any more pictures?" she asked.

"Yes, I happen to have a couple more," said McGuffy. He handed her another photograph. "Do you know this guy?"

"Why, that's old Brannigan himself!" she said. "He ran the ship, barking out orders even after my husband shot him and narrowly missed his heart, they said. But Vince was his enforcer. When Brannigan gave an order, Vince saw that it was carried out."

"So Vince made your husband drink too much liquor, but Brannigan gave the order to pour it down him? Is that what you're telling me?" asked McGuffy.

"Right!" said Elaine. "Brannigan kept saying, `I think he's still thirsty. Give him another drink, boys. I can't have no guest of mine going thirsty!' and then a couple of them would hold him and Vince would push the bottle in his mouth and turn it upside down. I thought several times they were going to drown him. Then my husband grabbed a gun and started firing it at everyone in sight. He was so drunk, his aim was so bad, that not a single shot hit anyone except the one that hit Brannigan, who was standing right in front of him. He couldn't miss that big tub of blubber."

"So Brannigan was not giving the orders from a distance? He was right up at the scene of the mischief?" asked McGuffy.

"That's exactly right," said Elaine. "Then after Brannigan got shot, he whacked my husband with the barrel of his pistol, told them to lock me and Tommy Joe up in their brig, and then they led Brannigan away bleeding really bad."

"I have one more photograph, Elaine," said McGuffy, who showed her a third photo and asked, "Does this look like anyone you know or have seen before?"

"Cummings!" she said. "He was the closest thing to decency on that pirate ship. He was the only one that took up for my husband and me when they were mistreating us.

"They were pushing Tommy Joe around and hitting him with their fists, and one of them was holding my arms behind me so I couldn't get away.

"He turned me loose fast when I kicked him in the groin, though, and then another one got me and threw me down on the deck, and then they all began to pick on me and make crude comments about me. Cummings tried to get Brannigan to let him and Tommy Joe and me get back on our yacht, the *Nautilus*, and go our own way. But Brannigan wouldn't hear of it, and he told Vince to throw Cummings in the brig with us."

"What happened after that?" asked McGuffy.

"Well, we stayed in the brig a long time, but Cummings had a small gun hid under his shirt, which he let Tommy Joe have as part of a plan to break out," said Elaine.

"Then when Cummings said he wanted no part of any killing, they made him load our yacht with ammonium nitrate.

"I don't know where Cummings went after that. I never saw him again. But Vince said Brannigan wanted our yacht to be used as bait to attract a Colombian freighter which they figured was hauling drugs of some kind.

"Sure enough, the freighter took the bait. When it was right up by the *Nautilus*, they exploded the ammonium nitrate, which knocked a huge hole in the hull of the freighter. Of course, the explosion also filled the sky full of debris from our yacht, which was dropping down all over the top deck and into the ocean like hailstones or a meteor shower or something."

"So then what happened? Did you and Tommy Joe decide to break out of the brig?" asked McGuffy.

"We did," said Elaine. "A couple of hours after the explosion, Brannigan gave the orders for his crew to board the freighter. They left in a wave and there was nonstop gunfire for what seemed like 10 minutes, although it probably wasn't that long.

"Then all you could hear was silence on board *The Silver Bullet*, which was what Brannigan called his ship, and there were loud moans from those who were merely shot up and not killed on board the freighter.

"When it got real quiet on *The Silver Bullet*, Tommy Joe said that would be the best time to try to break out of the brig if we ever hoped to get away. He was convinced they were going to keep us as toys or playthings for a while and then execute us. So while they were attacking the freighter, they left only one teen-age boy guarding us.

"Tommy Joe was able to get the boy to come up real close to the cell door, then he grabbed his keys, unlocked the cell, pushed the boy inside and locked it back, then threw the keys overboard.

"Tommy Joe said he figured Brannigan and Vince were both cowards and would have been about the only ones still on board *The Silver Bullet* while the bloody fighting was going on over on the Colombian ship. So he figured Brannigan and Vince were holed up in the captain's cabin, which they were, we found out after we escaped from the brig.

"Tommy Joe said he only had two bullets left, and he thought he could take care of Brannigan and Vince both with those two bullets. Then he planned to rev up *The Silver Bullet*'s engines and pull away while Brannigan's crew was still on the freighter.

"But of course, Tommy Joe, bless his heart, was not a very good shot, except for that one shot that hit Brannigan close to his heart early on. Brannigan and Vince knew Tommy Joe was out of bullets, so I really think they were planning to play with us like a cat plays with a mouse after it has caught him."

"So what did they do, Elaine?" asked McGuffy.

"They taunted Tommy Joe," said Elaine. "They made fun of him, called him 'a great big brave man going to protect his little woman from the bad guys, and Brannigan said, 'except he ain't got no bullets. Ain't that a shame? He ain't got no bullets! Too bad!'"

"Then what, Elaine?" asked McGuffy, realizing that her account was nearing the point where Vince would have whacked her on the head and Brannigan would have shot her husband in the back, and thus her memory was likely to fade and go blank at any moment. But she kept talking:

"Well, Tommy Joe fired his two shots, and of course they missed. He really didn't have any more bullets. His gun was empty. So he tossed it there on the top deck and held up his hands. 'Don't shoot!' he yelled, but Brannigan fired a shot over his head and then fired another shot into the deck next to Tommy Joe's feet. 'I'm going to let you find out what a bullet next to the heart feels like, but first I want to see you dance! Are you ready to dance for us, little man?' Brannigan asked him. But Tommy Joe just looked him in the eye and called him a 'two-bit coward.'"

"What was Vince doing during this time?" asked McGuffy.

"He had used up all his bullets, too, and was standing near me with a big plank drawn back like a baseball bat over my head," said Elaine. "He had backed me into a corner and I couldn't see any way out. I figured if I tried to make a run for it, it would startle Brannigan and he would kill Tommy Joe cold blood. Then Brannigan said, `Why don't we let the little man see what's going to happen to his woman before we shoot him, Vince? What do you say?' And Vince said, `Yeah, good idea, boss.' And then a wave rocked the boat and the gun Tommy Joe had thrown down slid across the deck to within a few feet of where I was standing. I thought I could dive for it and pick it up and maybe throw it at Vince."

"Then what happened, Elaine?" asked McGuffy.

"That's all I remember, Bob. I don't remember diving for the gun. I don't know if I ever did. The next thing I remember was coming to on the beach, strapped to a plank with a belt that had the initials 'TJF' on it. And for the first time since then, I now know what the 'F' stood for."

"What's that, Elaine?" asked McGuffy.

"Foster. I'm the widow of Thomas Joseph Foster of Hannibal, Missouri," she said as a wave of deep sadness came over her and tears filled her eyes. "Now I know that the man in the morgue with a bullet hole through him is my husband."

"I'm so sorry about his death, Elaine. Or should I now call you Mrs. Foster?" asked McGuffy.

"No, Bob. Remember what I told you. I'm Elaine. Always have been. Always will be. Just call me Elaine, OK?"

"OK, Elaine," said McGuffy, extending his hand for a handshake. "Nice to meet you."

"Nice to meet you, too," said Elaine, refusing the handshake and wrapping both of her arms around him tightly. "Why don't you stick around awhile longer if you've nothing better to do?"

"I believe I will," said McGuffy, returning the hug.

Elaine Foster leaned back on the small sofa in her hospital room and clasped her hands behind her head. Normally she would have used a special pillow behind her head to protect the bump where her skull was shattered.

The injury was still sensitive and sore after the surgery that morning to remove a splinter that had punctured the membranes surrounding her brain. But it was a dull, throbbing pain, not the sharp-as-a-knife piercing pain that she had lived with for the past week.

McGuffy sat beside her on the sofa, with his hands in copycat fashion also cupped behind his head.

"Are you making fun of me?" Elaine asked McGuffy after a few moments of silence.

"Not at all," said McGuffy. "I do this all the time. It actually helps me concentrate when I'm fighting distractions and want to give serious thought to something. I assumed you were doing the same thing, and that I was the distraction. I had just thought that this is another indication of how much we are alike."

"So if we're alike, what would you guess I'm thinking about right now?" asked Elaine.

"Oh, I'm not a mind-reader. I have no idea what you're thinking about. Maybe that I'm totally boring and that you'd like me to leave?" asked McGuffy.

"No, silly. Be serious. What am I thinking right now? Best guess," said Elaine.

"Um, let's see. You pretty well gave us the history of your encounter with pirates," said McGuffy. "So maybe you were going to go backward from there and tell how you and your husband came to be out in the Gulf of Mexico all alone to get yourself picked off by pirates. Maybe you were going to tell where you were headed when you were kidnapped, and where you came from. And ultimately, I'll bet you were going to tell about the family you left behind, particularly your son, Tommy. Am I right?"

"You're right. All those things are running through my head, but not all of them are of equal weight and power. One thing is burning a hole in my head, trying to push its way through, and yet it's still hiding in the fog. I can't see through it."

"You can't see through it yet, you mean," said McGuffy.

"Huh?" asked Elaine.

"You can't see through it yet. You said, 'I can't see through it.' But I happen to believe you will see through it. You just haven't done it yet," said McGuffy.

"Well, yes, that's right I guess. We have to keep it positive, don't we?" asked Elaine. "So I'll just say I'm trying to see my little son, Tommy. I keep calling him and calling him, but he doesn't answer. I don't know why he doesn't answer, but he doesn't."

"Don't let it get you up tight, Elaine," said McGuffy. "Just relax, like your Doctor Horton told you that night we were over at Joe's house and his Tommy made you think of your Tommy. And you know, eventually you were able to picture him as a six- or seven-year-old. So don't rush it, and maybe it will happen again."

"Yeah, I hope so," said Elaine. "After all I've remembered about the pirates, Brannigan and Vince and all the rest, I don't understand why I can't remember Tommy more clearly. And it scares me that I keep calling him, but he doesn't answer. You know what I mean, Bob?"

"Yeah, Elaine. I guess it would scare me, too, if I was calling my kid and he wouldn't answer. But you just have to take the doctor's advice and relax. Your memories are going to come back if you'll just not lock them up with fear. And when you talk about being scared, you're talking about fear. You know that, don't you? It's fear, Elaine. Pure fear."

"You know I'm no psychologist, but I practice what I've learned about fear in my job all the time," said McGuffy. "I get scared a lot in the Coast Guard, but I don't let it paralyze me. I just stay on course, no matter what. And just like flying a chopper through a thunderstorm or a squall, you eventually come out on the other side of it. And guess what. When you break through, the sun is always shining. Always, Elaine. Do you hear?"

"Yeah, Bob. I hear. And thanks. You're right. I got scared, I guess, and sort of dropped anchor when I should have opened the throttle and gone full speed ahead. In the *Nautilus*, sometimes Tommy Joe and I went through really bad weather and got tossed around like a chip. But we stuck to our course as best we could, confident that our craft was seaworthy, and eventually we got through it.

"I know it's the same in life, but I tend to forget. Sometimes I seem stuck in the bad times, and it seems that I'm not moving at all. But I know that these times too will pass. Fair weather always returns, eventually, doesn't it? I'm really sure, deep down, that it will this time, too, Bob. So thanks for sticking with me while the going's rough. You're my navigation star, so I know where I'm going, thanks to you. But it looks like I'll have to carry my albatross a while longer."

"Yeah, I'm not sure what you just said, but I think I agree with it," said McGuffy.

"You're sweet," said Elaine.

"Why don't I get us something to drink out of the machine out there?" asked McGuffy. "I'm a little thirsty, and maybe a little rest break would help our concentration."

"Yeah, it might," said Elaine.

"What would you like?" asked McGuffy. "I think I'm going to have a diet Dr. Pepper."

"Really? Maybe we are a lot alike. Diet Dr. Pepper's my favorite," said Elaine.

"Mine, too. Diet Dr. Pepper it is. Be right back."

McGuffy handed Elaine her drink then sat beside her on the sofa. They sipped their drinks, but neither of them spoke for a long while.

"A penny for your thoughts," McGuffy said eventually.

"Well, I did like you suggested and just relaxed," said Elaine. "I tried not to think of my son, just in case I was pushing too hard to understand why I could picture myself calling him but I couldn't picture him answering."

"What happened?" asked McGuffy.

"Nothing, really, but I got a picture of our place in Hannibal, Missouri, and I'm pretty sure that's where I saw Tommy when he was six or seven years years of age," said Elaine. "The picture that came to me that night at Joe's is coming back to me. Tommy was barefoot on a dirt surface of some kind, like maybe in a park or playground, and there were some small oak trees with a blue 1956 Chevrolet pickup parked nearby. I can see he wore a little short-sleeved knit shirt with dark green and yellow stripes going horizontally. And I can hear me calling him, over and over again, but he doesn't answer. I seem to be stuck at that point, and I don't know why."

"Go back to the doctor's advice, Elaine. Try it again. Just relax and see if your mind opens that picture of Tommy or goes someplace else," said McGuffy.

"OK, I'm relaxing, thinking of nothing," said Elaine, "and Tommy's standing there barefoot, with frayed, faded, cutoff jeans. So I guess I'll just say, 'Hey, Tommy!' out loud and see what happens. 'Hey, Tommy!' ... It's not working. I guess I'll just try to forget about Tommy and see what else pops up."

"Where's your husband? Where's Tommy Joe?" McGuffy asked.

"Oh, he's at work over at the boat plant," said Elaine. "What time is it? Nearly four o'clock. He won't get off for at least another hour. Sometimes he has to work late."

"The boat plant?" asked McGuffy.

"Yeah, you know, Fisher King, where our yacht, the *Nautilus*, was built. It's not really our yacht. It belongs to the company, but as a special reward for loyalty and good work, the boss allows employees on extremely rare occasions to take it on vacation trips and such," said Elaine. "For us, Tommy had just completed fifteen years with the company and he had saved up a month's vacation time. For us, it was to have been our second honeymoon. We had planned to go to Cancun."

"That sounds like a really nice thing for a boss to do. Why would he do that for Tommy Joe?" asked McGuffy, who decided to play along in the conversation without calling attention to the fact that Elaine apparently had dropped into a trance-like state, deep into her memory of a previous time in her life. He listened and let her talk:

"It was mine and Tommy Joe's dream to own a yacht like that, but of course there was no way we could ever afford it," said Elaine. "We got the trip because I think his boss was afraid if he didn't do something really nice for him, Tommy Joe would start looking around and checking other boat-building companies in Hannibal. And he could have had his pick of supervisory jobs at two other places in town that I know of. I mean, he was that good."

"How did the boss get a yacht like that. It sounds pretty expensive?" said McGuffy.

"It was very expensive. It was a million-dollar ship if it cost a dime. But it was built there at Fisher King by company employees, who got credits toward a trip for working on it on their own time," said Elaine. "There was talk that one day Fisher King might add yachts to its product line, and the *Nautilus* was a kind of prototype. But of course that never happened. You see, the boat companies in Hannibal build small fishing boats and pleasure boats mostly, like the ones you see farmers and fishermen pulling on a trailer behind their pickup truck or SUV.

"As Tommy Joe got nearer to his 15-year anniversary with the company, though, he talked all the time about his upcoming trip on the *Nautilus* – a name I suggested, by the way. And Tommy Joe would say he was going to take his sweetheart to Cancun when it came his turn to use the yacht.

"And the other employees would say, 'Yeah, and what would your wife be doing while you were gone?' and he would say, 'I would take her with me,' and they would ask, 'How could you keep two women on one yacht without getting shot by both of them?' and he would say, 'There wouldn't be two women. You see, I'm married to my sweetheart. Elaine is both my sweetheart and my wife.' It was great to hear him say that, and the *Nautilus* really was a magnificent boat."

"I wish I could have seen it," said McGuffy.

"Yeah, I wish you could have too," Elaine said as the phone rang.

"This is Elaine," she said as she picked up the receiver.

"This is security downstairs. Is that McGuffy guy from the Coast Guard still up there?" came the voice on the phone.

"Yes, he is. He's right here. Do you want to talk to him?" asked Elaine.

"No, not necessarily, if everything's alright. He told me he planned to be up there an hour, which would have been around four o'clock. It's almost five and we haven't seen hide nor hair of him. I just wondered if something was wrong," the security guard said.

"No. Nothing is wrong," said Elaine. "I have just . . . just . . .I'm sorry, sir," she said as she began to sob deeply.

"Are you sure nothing's wrong, Ma'am?" asked the guard. "I mean, I can hear you crying. Has he done anything to hurt you?"

"No. It's just me getting emotional over some memories of my past coming back," said Elaine, sniffing. "I can see a guard in the hallway outside my room and there are two others down the hall at the elevator. If anything were wrong, I would be scream-ing and all three of them would come to my aid, I'm pretty sure. Thanks for checking on me though, Sir. It makes me feel really safe and secure."

"That's the way we want to keep it, Ma'am," said the guard. "Just checking. Sorry to interrupt you."

"I was just about to leave, officer," McGuffy said into the phone. "Give us just a few more minutes, OK?"

"Well, did you give her that hug I asked you to?" asked the guard.

"Sure did, but I can repeat it if you like, just for good measure," said McGuffy.

"No, one's enough. You might get carried away," said the guard. "See you soon."

"Yessir. See you," said McGuffy as he handed the phone back to Elaine and she hung it up.

"Wow! Can you believe what I've just done?" Elaine asked McGuffy. "I must have talked your ears full! And I absolutely can't explain it. Somehow, it seemed that I was in our home in Hannibal, like in the kitchen or the edge of the dining room. Those two rooms kind of ran together in our house. And you were sitting in a dining chair, having a cup of coffee or something and waiting on Tommy Joe. I don't know if you were an insurance salesman or somebody he worked with or what. But it sure did seem real."

"How long ago do you expect that was in real time, Elaine?" asked McGuffy.

"Maybe a year or 18 months or so at the most," said Elaine. "I thought I was supposed to remember the distant events first and the recent events last. Seems like I've got it just reversed, except for my remembering Captain Nemo of the original *Nautilus*, which would have been a long, long time ago, pretty early in my childhood, actually. And really, my memory of our son, Tommy, was quite a number of years ago. But I can't, I mean I haven't yet been able to remember him completely. And suddenly, Bob, I'm just really, really tired. You know? I don't want to hurt your feelings, but I think I need to be by myself a while."

"No hurt feelings," said McGuffy. "I was about to suggest that I need to leave and let you take a rest for a while. You've made a lot of progress this afternoon. Don't rush it. I'll be back whenever I can get some time off, like maybe tomorrow after work, as long as it's OK with you."

"It's always OK with me, Bob. Just come by when you can. I know you have work to do, so I don't expect you to spend all your free time with me, but I'll take as much of it as you can spare," said Elaine.

"You've got it," said McGuffy as he got up to leave. Elaine got up as well and they exchanged hugs. Then for just a moment, they held each other close and looked each other in the eyes but said nothing. In words, that is. But McGuffy defied his fears and did what he had wanted to do for several days: He gave her a passionate kiss on the lips. Then as he drew away, she leaned forward against him and gave him an equally passionate kiss in return.

"You'd better go," she told him as he turned to leave. "But be back soon."

"My name isn't Arnold, but I'll be back," McGuffy said as he walked out of Elaine's room and punched the 'down' button on the elevator.

"It's about time you came down from up there, son," said the guard at the lobby entrance as McGuffy approached the checkpoint. "Another minute or two and I was about to send a couple of officers up there to check on you."

"Another minute or two and perhaps you should've," said McGuffy, grinning even more widely than usual as he walked out of the hospital lobby to the parking deck.

Chapter Fifteen

Elaine Foster was all alone in her hospital room with her thoughts after McGuffy left.

Weary from her unsuccessful efforts to remember her son and saddened by the memory that her husband, Tommy Joe, had been shot in the back and killed by pirates, she drifted off to sleep shortly after her evening meal. Sometime in the night, however, she was awakened by the image of her small son, as she had visualized him around the age of six or seven, greatly distressed and yelling to her, "Momma!" She was unable to answer him except with a loud moan into her pillow.

A nurse ran into her room from the hallway.

"Elaine! What's wrong?" asked the nurse, who saw her face down in the pillow and feared she couldn't turn her head around and was suffocating. Suddenly Elaine whirled around and sat up in bed, bumping forehead to forehead with the nurse and letting out a loud howl of pain.

"What's wrong, Elaine?" asked the nurse, who tried to wipe Elaine's forehead with a damp cloth.

"My son was calling for me for a change and I couldn't answer him," said Elaine. "He was so real, as though he was on the floor here by my bed. I could see him down there, but he was like in a pit of some kind and couldn't get out and I couldn't reach far enough down to catch him by the hand. He had this pained look on his face and kept shouting, 'Momma! Momma!' And I couldn't say anything at all to him."

"There's no child in the floor, Elaine. You were having a dream, maybe a nightmare if you want to call it that. And I'm afraid you also may have a severe headache. I know I do," said the nurse, rubbing the bump on her forehead where she and Elaine collided.

"I'm sorry I bumped you, Ma'am," said Elaine. "I felt like I was suffocating and I had to struggle to get up so I could keep breathing."

"Well, your face was rather deep down in your pillow," said the nurse. "I thought you were suffocating, too. But it's all over now. Would you like a sedative to relax you a little, wipe away part of that headache, and maybe get some sleep?"

"That would be good," said Elaine. The nurse left the room and returned in a few minutes with a hypodermic needle. She gave Elaine an injection and she soon drifted off to sleep again. This time she slept until morning and her phone rang before the hospital had served breakfast. It was McGuffy.

"Hey, Sleeping Beauty! Time to get up and at `em!" said McGuffy's cheerful voice on the phone. "Did you get a good nap?"

"I was having a pretty good nap until some inconsiderate person called me on the phone before breakfast," said Elaine.

"Sorry about that. I just couldn't stand the thought of going off to work, as I'm about to do, and spending the day without hearing your voice," said McGuffy. "I hope I didn't disturb you too much."

"No, I was kidding about waking me. I actually had just woke up, I guess, when the nurse came in to get me ready for breakfast," said Elaine. "And you're sweet to call. Now my day will be brighter because of the sunshine in your voice."

"So how did you sleep? OK? Did you get any more of your memory back?" asked McGuffy.

"I woke up once in a nightmare, but I slept OK after that," said Elaine. "I thought Tommy was calling me for a change, from down inside some kind of pit, and I couldn't make a sound and couldn't reach far enough down to touch him. So I woke up moaning and bumped the nurse on her forehead. She said it was a bad dream, and I guess that's all it was. At least, I hope so. I'd hate to think I lost my son without ever meeting him."

"Yeah, that sounds like a nightmare instead of reality," said McGuffy. "Just cool it today, and I'll be by to see you this afternoon. I'm going to skip lunch, so I can see you about four-thirty if that's all right."

"Oh, don't skip your lunch, Bob. I want to see you as early as possible all right, but I'd rather you not be famished when you come by. Please tell me you'll get something to eat," said Elaine.

"OK. I promise to bum a couple of packs of peanut butter and cracker sandwiches from Joe. How's that?" asked McGuffy.

"You're impossible, that's how's that," said Elaine.

"You're right. Have a good day. See you at four-thirty," said McGuffy, hanging up the phone.

"Impossible!" said Elaine, smiling broadly and looking out the window as the first rays of the morning sun broke through.

When McGuffy got to work, Hoover and Morelli were already there. Other members of the Special Tactical Law Enforcement Team were taking a turn at patrolling the area south of the Miami harbor where the pirate ship *The Silver Bullet* and its substantial stash of cocaine and marijuana had exploded last week.

Quite a few small boats and their eager crews had clustered around the debris site like piranha around raw meat, dipping in a variety of small nets and hauling in their catch. Where the scavengers could be caught, their contraband was confiscated, but much of it found its way quickly to the streets of Miami.

"It's about time you got here, Lieutenant, don't you agree?" Hoover asked McGuffy as he walked in, hung his bill cap on a coat tree, and headed for the coffee pot on a counter near his desk.

"I was at work on special team business outside the office, Commander," said McGuffy, pouring himself a mug of coffee. "I'd be happy to furnish you with the details if you're interested."

"Yes, I'm quite interested in seeing just how creative you're going to be this time," said Hoover, who already had poured herself a cup of coffee and was using a red plastic stir stick to disperse two containers of creamer and a packet of sweetener in it. "I think we ought to hear the full story."

"I'll give 10-to-1 odds that his special team business had to do with a certain brownish-blonde female who has been consuming great gobs of the lieutenant's time, not to mention his thoughts, dreams and did I say daydreams?" asked Morelli.

"I'll have you know that I have been up many hours during the night making phone calls and doing Internet research on the Foster family of Hannibal, Missouri. And with only a fraction of my usual quantity of sleep, I checked moments ago on the post-surgical condition of one, Elaine Foster, whose deceased husband, she has disclosed to me, was an experienced boat-builder at Fisher King, a boat manufacturing firm in Hannibal."

"Really!?" Hoover asked in apparent disbelief. "Are you kidding me?"

"Wo! Is that right?" asked Morelli. "That's amazing! When did you find out? And what else did you learn?"

"I found out for sure yesterday that her husband's name was Tommy Joe Foster; that he worked for a boat-building company in Hannibal, Missouri, the town where they lived and where their yacht was made," said McGuffy. "Adding what I found on the Internet to that, and I pretty much have unraveled the story of Elaine's past life. I took the liberty of typing out a written account of what she told me during my visit to her hospital room yesterday afternoon, which you'll find in the folder there. And then what I learned from the Internet is in a separate report. It's all here in this folder, complete with class snapshots of her and her husband, Tommy Joe, in their high school yearbook, Class of 1990, which I downloaded from the Internet. But I would strongly urge that Elaine not be given, at least for now, any of the information I have learned from the Internet or by phone from people I've contacted in Hannibal. I think she should be given time to recover her memory about these matters on her own. I think it wouldn't be good for her to learn too much about her past too soon."

"I would agree with you, Lt. McGuffy, although I'm no expert on recovering memory," said Morelli. "I'd like to hear what our good doctor says about that. What about it, Commander?"

"You're right as far as I know," said Hoover. "But I am no more an expert on recovering memory than you all are. I'd say, now that she's remembering, we need to let her move at her own pace. We can perhaps facilitate her recovery with things like familiar photos, newspaper clippings or yearbook snapshots, but if we tell her facts that she can't yet access, it could confuse her and even slow down her recovery, I would think."

"My thoughts, exactly," said Morelli. "Good work, Lieutenant. It does my heart good to see such enthusiasm about one's work and duties, although in this case I think it could be said that you had a rather attractive incentive. Would you agree?"

"Definitely," said McGuffy. "One of the most attractive incentives I've ever met in this line of work."

"I'll read your written report later, but why don't you get a refill on your coffee and tell us the highlights?" asked Hoover.

"I'd be happy to," said McGuffy. "Pull up a chair."

Hoover and Morelli turned their chairs facing McGuffy's and told him to go ahead.

"I think I'll just walk you through my research chronologically. First thing I looked for was the phone and street address of Tommy Joe Foster, which I found immediately. Then I called the number from my cell phone, and it answered in a woman's voice, I believe it was Elaine, which said, `We can't take your call right now; please leave your name and number.'"

"Did you leave your name and number?" asked Morelli.

"I did," said McGuffy. "I identified myself as Lt. Robert McGuffy of the U.S. Coast Guard's Miami district. I didn't give any hint of my purpose in calling, but I left my cell phone number with the request to `please call.' I figured that if I said I was trying to reach family members, it would be obvious that I was trying to locate the next of kin. I didn't think that was appropriate at this stage. I wanted to find out through other sources the names and contact information of any relatives that would need to be notified."

"I take it no one has called you back," said Morelli.

"Not at this time," said McGuffy.

"What else did you find?" asked Morelli.

"I checked the Hannibal *Courier-Post* newspaper archives and found a list of the Class of 1990 with their photos," said McGuffy. "The class roll included both Thomas Joseph Foster and Anna Elaine Preston. There were no other Elaines, so I figured Elaine Preston was our Elaine. Then I checked the society pages for June of 1990 and found our couple's engagement announcement. A few weeks later there was a report of their wedding at the local Presbyterian church, which listed the parents of both the bride and groom as well as two maids named Preston and a best man named Foster."

"Good, then what did you do?" asked Morelli.

"I searched the city directory and found the addresses and phone numbers of both sets of parents. I didn't call either of them, but their phone numbers are listed in my report, and I would guess we would need to notify them soon of Tommy Joe's death as well as give them a condition report on Elaine. But I thought it more appropriate that you do that, Chief, or you, Commander," said McGuffy.

"We can notify the relatives, Lieutenant, but let's get down to brass tacks," said Hoover. "Did you find out whether our adventurous yachting couple notified anyone anywhere of their plans to go to Cancun and back? We already know they didn't notify us, as they should have, of their launch and destination as well as their course settings and emergency contact information."

"I talked to Tommy Joe's boss, a man named Jeffrey Sides, CEO of the Fisher King boat manufacturing company in Hannibal where he worked," said McGuffy. "He said Tommy Joe's family and work associates gave him and Elaine a big going-away launch party, which they referred to as `the start of their second honeymoon,' and no one was to get any report from them for at least 30 days. He said family members at the launch included Elaine's mother and Tommy Joe's father. Apparently her father and his mother are deceased."

"Did you tell him that Tommy Joe is dead and that Elaine is in the hospital recovering from a brain injury?" asked Morelli.

"No. Again, I thought it best for you or the Commander to handle that," said McGuffy.

"Right. Did Tommy Joe's boss ask why the Coast Guard was looking for him?" asked Morelli.

"No. When I identified myself as Lt. McGuffy of the U.S. Coast Guard and asked if he had an employee named Tommy Joe Foster, the man immediately said, `What's happened to him? Is he in some kind of drug trade trouble?' and I told him, `No, Sir. We're verifying some information,' and he said, `Surely he didn't falsify his ID to the Coast Guard,' and I told him he didn't."

"What about children? Was there any mention of children?" asked Hoover.

"Yes and no," said McGuffy. "Tommy Joe's boss didn't mention it, so I asked him. He said their only son, Tommy Joe Jr., was killed in 1998 at age seven in an auto accident involving a drunk driver. They had a daughter, born with a heart defect, the year after their son died. She lived only about three weeks, the man said. I thanked him for the information and told him that someone would perhaps contact him later."

"Thank you, Lieutenant," said Hoover. "Now I guess Chief and I've got some work to do, and you do, too."

"What do you mean? Is there something you want me to do?" asked McGuffy.

"Yes, I want you to get over to that hospital and see that you spend as much of the day with Elaine as she will tolerate," said Hoover. "Chief and I will notify the next of kin."

"Thanks, and if you don't mind, I'm going to contact Elaine's doctors and bring them up to speed. They need to know what we now know, and maybe they can help us find the best time and way to break the news to Elaine," said McGuffy.

"Or maybe they can be there for her when she figures it out on her own," said Morelli.

"Yes, I guess that is possible, too," said McGuffy. He made several copies of his written report and furnished copies to Hoover, Morelli and other members of their team, as well as to Elaine's doctors, Sutherland and Horton. Sutherland asked him to come by his office and discuss his findings.

"I'll have Dr. Horton here when you come by so you don't have to discuss it twice," said Sutherland. "Can you come on over now?"

"Yes, in fact, Cdr. Hoover asked me to spend as much time with Elaine today as needed, so I'll be right over," said McGuffy. Moments later he arrived at Sutherland's outer office.

"Come on in, Lt. McGuffy," said Sutherland, hanging up his phone after calling Horton. "Dr. Horton is on her way. My Goodness, you're quick! You must have run all the way over here."

"I guess I was walking pretty fast, Sir," said McGuffy. "I appreciate your letting me tell you and Dr. Horton what I learned from and about Elaine yesterday afternoon after her surgery. I came right over because I didn't want to keep you both waiting, and of course, I wanted to go ahead and surprise Elaine by showing up this morning instead of this afternoon as she was expecting. The way she was recovering so much of her memory yesterday afternoon, I was hoping and even expecting that she might get virtually all of it back today. And I guess I was kind of hoping to be there when she did."

"Understood, Lt. McGuffy, and appreciated, too," said Sutherland. "I'm sure you have been a significant support for her."

At that moment, Horton walked in and shook hands with Sutherland and McGuffy.

"Good morning, Lieutenant, Doctor. What's this good news I hear we have on Elaine?" Horton asked.

"I have it right here, Ma'am, and I think it's pretty good news, although some parts of it are rather sad," said McGuffy, handing them folders containing Elaine's recollections and in a separate section, the results of his telephone and Internet research.

"I kept the two parts separate because I was concerned about how difficult it might be for her to accept and deal with some of these matters if we told her all at once or even if she suddenly remembered them all," said McGuffy.

"That's probably a wise decision, Lieutenant. Why don't you give us a whirlwind tour of what Elaine has remembered up to now and then what you have learned by your research," said Sutherland.

"Well, I think her biggest breakthrough came after I showed her photos of the captain and co-captain of the pirate ship, *The Silver Bullet*. She immediately called them by name, and then she began to tell us what they had done to her and her husband and she remembered that they had blown up their yacht," said McGuffy. "She didn't remember being hit over the head or seeing her husband shot. But she understood enough about her memory loss to realize that she likely would not be able to testify against them in court as to those crimes because she simply didn't remember seeing them happen. And that fact seemed to make her really angry, which in turn, seemed to bring her memory back right away."

"So she had a virtually full recovery of memory up to an abrupt point just prior to her injury, is that right?" asked Horton.

"Yes, Ma'am," said McGuffy. "And at that time she remembered her husband's full name as Tommy Joe Foster. Shortly after that, she remembered that they had lived in Hannibal, Missouri, and that he worked for a boat manufacturing company there where the company yacht they were using, the *Nautilus*, had been built."

"Was she emotional at all concerning her husband's death?" asked Horton.

"Yes, she seemed very sad, and her eyes filled with tears. She had pretty much decided, I think, and had accepted long before that, that Tommy Joe was her husband and that he had been shot in the back and killed. She didn't recognize him, and she didn't remember before then that his last name was Foster," said McGuffy.

"During all this, she recalled having a son, Tommy Joe Jr., who was six or seven years old," said McGuffy. "She said she had a strong impression of calling for him over and over again, but that he never answered. Then last night, she had a nightmare where she saw and heard her son calling for her, but this time she couldn't answer. I learned through a phone call to Tommy Joe's employer that Elaine and her husband had a son who was killed at the age of seven by a drunk driver in a car wreck in 1998, and that they had a daughter born with a heart defect about a year later who lived only about three weeks."

"That's why the boy didn't answer and in her nightmare she couldn't answer," said Sutherland. "That memory and the memory of the death of their infant daughter were just too painful, so she painted them out of her past. She may have some real difficulty accepting those bitter facts, and that could slow down or stop her recovery of other memories. So we have to go really slow and easy in this area and give her all the emotional support we can if she begins to recall those memories."

"Yes, we do," said Horton. "And Lt. McGuffy, you have been such a strong support to her up to now, I would nominate you to be her main support for the immediate future if not longer, if you're willing and available for the task."

"For sure," said McGuffy. "As long as Cdr. Hoover will let me stay over here with Elaine, I will be glad to be here and to be whatever support to her that I can. But I'm not sure I know how to help her deal with such things as the death of her children."

"Your presence and your touch, Lt. McGuffy, are worth more to her in those times, I believe, than all the other information Dr. Sutherland and I might be able to offer. Dr. Sutherland and I will, of course, be available to you and to her throughout her remaining recovery, to give specific advice when you want and need it. But it's obvious that she feels very secure with you. She relates well to you, and that's why her major memory recoveries have been when you have been present and were interacting with her."

"She's not expecting you until this afternoon, but why don't you go on over to her room and surprise her," said Sutherland. "And we're close by if you need us. Let her talk about her past when she wants to."

"And mostly, then, I should just listen?" asked McGuffy.

"Just listen, and offer her a shoulder if she needs one," said Horton.

"Right. I can do that. I've got two shoulders. Should be able to spare one of them," said McGuffy, grinning. "Thanks to both of you for letting me do this. Elaine in the past week has come to mean a lot to me. And if I can help her recover, that's what I want to do."

"I think we get the picture, Lt. McGuffy," said Sutherland. "She's come to mean a lot to all of us around here, and we're just glad you're here when we all need you."

"That's the Coast Guard motto, Sir. Always prepared," said McGuffy.

"She couldn't have happened to a nicer guy," said Horton.

"Now you're embarrassing me. I'll leave on that note," said McGuffy, rising to leave as Sutherland and Horton laughed.

"Keep us posted," said Sutherland.

McGuffy knocked on Elaine's door a few minutes before nine on the Tuesday morning after her surgery, just as she was finishing her breakfast and was reading a copy of *The Miami Herald*.

"Come in," she said, not looking up from her paper. Then as she reached for her cup of coffee to take a sip, she saw McGuffy out of the corner of her eye.

"Bob!" she virtually shouted. "What are you doing here? I didn't expect to see you until you got off work this afternoon. Is the Coast Guard taking a holiday or something?"

"No. I'm taking a holiday," said McGuffy, rolling his bill cap flat and placing it on a table. "Well, not really. Cdr. Hoover said she was so pleased with your progress yesterday, during the time I spent with you, that she wants me to spend all day with you today. Or, as she put it, to stay with you as long as you were willing to put up with me. Can you actually believe that?"

"I'm not sure I can believe that, Bob," said Elaine. "I mean, that's fabulous! And I'm afraid you're stuck with me all day."

"Well, I guess I'm stuck good and proper, then, Commander's orders," said McGuffy. "All I can say is, it's tough work, but somebody's got to do it. And to think, the government pays me to do this. Pinch me. I must be dreaming."

"I'll pinch you if you don't stand over there out of the way while I change her bandage," said nurse Helen Martin, pulling a curtain between Elaine and McGuffy.

"Oh, sorry," said McGuffy, quickly taking a couple of steps back. "How's this?"

"That's fine. Just stay put for a few minutes, then you can have the rest of the day with her, Lieutenant," said the nurse.

Just then an orderly came by for Elaine's tray, and the nurse began changing her bandage.

"Are we experiencing any pain this morning, Elaine?" asked the nurse.

"Just a bit of throbbing, but much better than yesterday," said Elaine. "I'm thinking some extra-strength acetaminophen just might do the trick. And that breakfast was so good, I had pretty much ignored the pain until you mentioned it."

"Here you are," the nurse said, handing her two caplets in a small paper cup and a fresh cup of ice water. "Looks like you're healing nicely, so I'm using a much smaller bandage today. Maybe real soon you won't need a bandage at all. Doc said you might want to go for a walk outside the hospital today if you feel up to it, and, of course, if you can persuade Lt. McGuffy to go with you, and if you don't go too far away."

"Sounds like a lot of 'ifs' to me. So how far is too far?" asked Elaine. "I sure would like to go walking down by the water."

"Oh, the water is just a skip and a hop beyond the hospital," said the nurse. "And just down the way from that is the Vizcaya Museum and Gardens. That's a beautiful old mansion, if you've never seen it, with lots of statues and other art, and the orchids are breathtaking. So if you can twist Lt. McGuffy's arm and get him to go with you, you should have a really nice outing."

"It sounds really great to me. Bob, what about it?" asked Elaine.

"If you like it, I like it. Do you still have that white pants outfit Dr. Horton found for you the other day, so you don't have to wear those hospital green coveralls. I just remembered you haven't been shopping yet for real clothes," said McGuffy.

"Yes, I think those white pants I wore to Lt. Anderson's would do in a tight, and this is as close to a tight as I want to be," said Elaine. "We won't be in the water, or I'd need a two-piece swimsuit. But those white pants will be fine for a stroll along the water's edge. You reminded me, though. I'll need to put clothes shopping on my to-do list for tomorrow for sure. That is, if I can work out another small matter, which I have to put on my list before shopping."

"What small matter?" asked McGuffy.

"Money," said Elaine.

"Oh, yeah, money," said McGuffy. "Money tends to get on the list before everything, doesn't it. Well, that's one thing I'm real short on right now. I've got a pocket full of credit cards, but no money."

At that moment, Dr. Horton walked in.

"Did someone say 'money'?" she asked. "I'll take a large helping of that."

"We're not dishing it out. We're trying to figure out how and where to dish it in," said McGuffy.

"Yeah, the nurse was telling us about that Vizcaya mansion and garden. I wonder if it has any money trees," said Elaine, who suddenly put her hand to her forehead and sat down abruptly on the sofa.

"Is something wrong?" asked Horton, walking to Elaine's side and putting her hand on her shoulder. But Elaine leaned forward, covered her face with both hands and said nothing.

"Yeah, Elaine. What's wrong?" asked McGuffy. "Is your head hurting?"

"No. I'm fine," said Elaine after a while. "I just remembered. Tommy Joe and I had a joint bank account in Hannibal. We withdrew a good bit of cash before we launched the *Nautilus*, and we spent a fair amount of it on our way down the Mississippi River to the Gulf. But I know we didn't close out the account. I know we had money left, which I could spend if I could figure out how to access it. But I don't have a check book with me. It would have been destroyed when the *Nautilus* was blown up. And I certainly don't remember our account number. So I'm kind of shut out of my own money."

Horton and McGuffy exchanged glances but said nothing. Then after what seemed like a long wait, McGuffy nodded to Horton, and she took the cue:

"Elaine, is there anyone you know in Hannibal who maybe could go to the bank for you?" Horton asked.

"My two sisters, Angela and Marcia, still live there. I guess I could call one of them. And, of course, Mom is there," said Elaine. "I think I still remember Mom's number. Let's see, it was…What was our area code?…It was…If I could just…"

At that moment, the phone in Elaine's hospital room rang and she answered, "Hello."

"Elaine Foster, please," came a woman's voice on the phone.

"This is Elaine," she said.

"Elaine, this is your Mom," she said. Then her voice broke into deep sobs for a while, and eventually she asked Elaine, "How are you? I mean, a woman from the Coast Guard, a Dr. Hoover, I believe, called me just now and told me you were in a hospital in Miami. She said you're safe and in good condition in the hospital there. She said you were seriously injured and temporarily lost some of your memory but are rapidly regaining it. Is that right? And how's Tommy Joe and the yacht. She didn't mention him or the boat."

"We were attacked by pirates, Mom," said Elaine. "The boat was blown up, and I don't know if they've notified Tommy Joe's dad yet or not, but…"

Elaine at that point burst into tears and wept loudly, as though all her grief over the death of her husband picked this minute to break forth like a geyser.

"He's dead, Mom. The pirates shot him in the back," she said, and cried again loudly. Then she handed the phone to Horton as McGuffy sat down beside her, put her head on his shoulder, and hugged her close to him.

"Just let it all out, Elaine," said McGuffy. "You can call your Mom back later."

For several minutes, Elaine wept from deep within as McGuffy held her. Then the nurse wiped her face and forehead with a damp cloth and handed her several tissues.

"Is Mom still on the phone?" she asked then.

"Ma'am, are you still there?" asked Horton, who hadn't hung up the phone.

"Yes, I'm still here. Who's there with Elaine? I heard a man's voice," said Elaine's mother, Emma Preston. "I'm glad somebody could be there to comfort her about Tommy Joe. They had so looked forward to this trip. It was to be their second honeymoon."

"Yes, Ma'am, we know,' said Horton. "And that was Lt. Bob McGuffy you heard on the phone. He's a young Coast Guard pilot who helped to rescue Elaine from a sandbar Monday was a week ago. He's here with her, as of course are members of our medical staff, and he has been a real friend to Elaine. It was after Elaine's surgery yesterday, when Lt. McGuffy was with her, that she remembered Tommy Joe's last name and that they lived and worked in Hannibal. That made it possible for us to call you and others in Hannibal."

"Was someone going to notify Mr. Foster, Tommy Joe's dad?" asked Elaine's mother.

"I'm sure the Coast Guard officer that is handling the investigation into the piracy case has or will shortly notify Tommy Joe's father," said Horton. "I'm going to give the phone back to Elaine now, Ma'am. Here she is." Elaine stood as Horton handed her the phone.

"Hey, Mom. I wish we could have been together and hugged each other through that crying spell, but we both had to get it out of our system," said Elaine. "Now I've got some really important things I need for you to do for me. You still have the key that I gave you to our house, don't you?"

"Yes, I keep it right here in the top desk drawer," said Ms. Preston.

"Well, I want you to get it and get somebody to drive you to our house. Get a taxi if you can't find anyone else to do it. But I need you to do this as soon as you can. OK, Mom?" asked Elaine.

"OK, Elaine. What do you need?" asked her mother.

"I want you to go into my little office there in the kitchen and open the top right drawer and get my checkbook and then call me back and read me the balance, OK?" asked Elaine. "Then I want you to read off the row of numbers at the bottom of the check. And in that same drawer are two credit cards. I'll want you to read me the numbers and expiration dates off of them, too. Now can you do that?"

"Yes. I see Tommy Joe's dad driving in the driveway now. That must mean somebody has told him. Wait, I think he's coming to the door," said Emma. "I'm going to put the phone down and let him in. Just a minute."

Elaine could hear her father-in-law talking to her mother:

"Come here, girl, and give me a hug," said the man's voice, in a kind of moaning wail, on the phone. "We've got to go through this together, Emma," he said.

"Yes, I know we do, Spencer," she said. "I've got Elaine on the phone. I guess they told you she's fine but has had a brain injury and is in the hospital. She needs her checkbook and credit cards. Can you drive me to her place so I can get them for her?"

"You bet I can," Spencer Foster said; then into the phone to Elaine, he said, "Hey, girl. You hang in there. Me and your mom are going to get you some money, and then we're going to get the next flight out of here to come see you. OK?"

"OK, Papa Spence. Thanks. I'll be looking for you. You all be careful."

"OK. Bye now," Foster said and hung up the phone.

"Well, I believe the fog is finally clearing," said Elaine to McGuffy as she hung up the phone and sat again on the small sofa in her hospital room. "It's kind of amazing. I had no trouble just now remembering Mom and my sisters and the bank account, but that was the first time I had thought of any of them or the bank since I got hurt. It was just as though they didn't exist."

"You remembered when you became aware of the need to remember," said Horton. "That doesn't mean the fog is going to clear away instantly, but it's a good sign that you're headed toward a virtually full recovery of your long-term memory."

"So what else do you need to remember that hasn't come up yet?" asked McGuffy. "Did you happen to have a wardrobe or did you take most of your clothes with you on the *Nautilus*?"

"I don't remember what I left at home, except I know we didn't pack any winter coats or anything," said Elaine. "But I know we bought a lot of new items just for the trip. I'll bet that's why Tommy Joe had that `Inspected by No. 32' ticket in his pocket when he washed ashore. That was probably the first time he had worn those jeans on the trip. It was the first time he had ever worn them, and his last."

"Probably so. It makes sense," said McGuffy. "So what else are you remembering about Hannibal and the folks there?"

"Oh, let's see. Well, I remember Tommy Joe when we were really little, I guess it was even before we started kindergarten," said Elaine. "We lived next door to each other, and we used to play outside together, under the shade of a big oak tree. The tree really belonged to Tommy Joe's folks, but it reached way over and shaded half of our backyard during portions of the day. So early in the morning we'd play in his yard, and in the afternoon we'd play in mine. Our toys were strewed in both places."

"Did you ever make mud pies?" asked Horton.

"Oh, yes. And Tommy Joe's dad had a hunting dog on a leash, and the dog would scratch up nearly all of the grass around his house so he'd have fresh cool dirt to lie in when it got hot. And Tommy Joe would take the little shovel I got to dig sand on the beach and dig dirt with it from around his dad's dog house. That's how we got the dirt for mud pies."

"Interesting. What else?" asked McGuffy.

"Well, I remember how Tommy Joe got brand new jeans and a new shirt and a fresh haircut when we started first grade. And I got new shoes and a new dress, and Mama fixed my hair up real nice with a little bow in it," said Elaine.

"Anything else?" asked McGuffy.

"Oh, let's see. We used to go to the movies downtown on Saturday mornings, at first with our parents while they shopped, then eventually by ourselves by the time we were in junior high," said Elaine.

"So you were childhood friends, and it sounds like childhood sweethearts, too, is that right?" asked Horton.

"That's right. I was literally the girl next door and he was the boy next door," said Elaine. "Our folks wouldn't let us go steady, so after we started dating, we'd go with others just so our parents wouldn't think we were getting too serious. But we were. Serious, I mean. Especially when we got up in the eighth or ninth grade. Tommy Joe was in the eighth grade, I believe, when he took a ballpoint pen and a big old hairpin and made a home-made tattoo out of blue dots on his arm. It spelled out my name, Elaine, but one or two of the dots got infected, and for a long time it looked like `Blaine,' and they would kid him about being in love with Blaine Evans, another guy in our class. That would usually end up with him in a fist fight with somebody, so for a while he kept the whole tattoo covered up with a bandage. I thought it was funny, but of course I didn't want him to get hurt. He could usually take care of himself in a fight. Several of the girls wanted to date him, and some of them did. I didn't let him know it bothered me unless he went out with the same girl several times, then I'd put my foot down."

"Interesting. Jealous, then, were you?" asked McGuffy.

"I guess you could say I was pretty jealous about Tommy Joe, and I was feeling a little guilty about that. I know jealousy isn't love, but I was wondering if I was getting to care too much about him. So I dated the same football player three times, and then Tommy Joe put his foot down. So I knew if it was jealousy, Tommy Joe had a case of it for me, too, and I guess that made me feel better."

"Did Tommy Joe play football?" asked McGuffy.

"Yeah, he played right bench and left out. He tried hard, but he was just too small and he wasn't that fast on his feet, so the coach didn't use him much," said Elaine. "He wasn't much better at basketball, But of course, I played basketball my last three years at Hannibal High. So we had that in common.

"They called the guys' team the Pirates and the girls' team the Lady Pirates. And if either team had a bad year, they'd call the guys the *Titanic*s and the girls Totally Sinkable. You know, after the Unsinkable Molly Brown? Hannibal is the birthplace, you know, of Margaret Brown, a survivor of the *Titanic*."

"No, I didn't know," said McGuffy as Elaine continued without a stop.

"Which is kind of amazing, now that I think about it, looking back," she said, "because I was into collecting posters and models of ships, including the original *Nautilus* and the first nuclear sub *Nautilus*, and even the *Titanic*. And I guess you can say I am kind of unsinkable, too, since I survived our own little *Nautilus*. It wasn't the *Titanic*, but maybe Molly and I do have a few things in common."

"Sounds that way," said Horton. "So you're remembering your high school years. What came next?"

"Well, Tommy Joe went on the co-op program, working for Mr. Sides at Fisher King while he went to college and got his degree in industrial arts and design," said Elaine. "I think I influenced him to get into that, because I thought it would help him build ships, which was my passion. Except for the *Nautilus*, though, he never built a ship. Just boats."

"What did you do?" asked Horton.

"I actually enrolled in the same classes with him and was planning to get the same degree, but I guess I was hearing wedding bells more than ship bells that summer," said Elaine. "Anyway, right after our high school graduation, Tommy Joe and I got engaged and right after that we got married. And straight away I got pregnant with Tommy Jr. and decided to drop out of college and raise babies. Tommy Jr. was born the following March and I never went back to school. But I also never got pregnant again…well, not until we lost Tommy Jr. in 1998, and then….Oh, my goodness!"

Elaine jumped to her feet, put both her hands over her face and threw her head back as though she were looking at the ceiling. But she shut both eyes, clenched her teeth tightly and said over and over again, "Oh, my goodness! My goodness!" and then, "Tommy, my sweet baby, where are you?"

Horton nodded to McGuffy, who immediately recognized his cue, stood up in front of Elaine and drew her close to him.

"It's all right, Elaine. We're here for you," said McGuffy, now holding her tightly as she cried, but deep waves of anguish drowned out everything McGuffy and Horton said to her.

"We're right here, Elaine," McGuffy said as the loudness of her wails diminished somewhat. "We're not going anywhere, OK? We're right here. Just let it all out."

Elaine continued to cry out, "My sweet Tommy! Where are you, baby?" and then in a suddenly angry tone to Horton, "What have you done with him?" She pulled away from McGuffy and asked him even more angrily and loudly, "What have you done with him?"

"You need to calm down, Elaine, and then we can tell you," said Horton, wetting a towel in the lavatory and wiping Elaine's forehead and the sides of her face. Elaine grew suddenly quiet, reached for the wet towel and threw it across the room. Then she faced Horton and asked again angrily, "What have you done with Tommy?"

"We have not harmed Tommy, Elaine. Come on now, and calm down," said Horton.

Elaine then stormed out of the room and yelled into the hallway toward the nursing station, "Has Tommy been out here?" Then she noticed the armed security officer outside the door to her hospital room and asked him, "Have you seen Tommy?"

"No Ma'am," the guard said. "I haven't seen him, Ma'am. But if you will sit down there a moment, I'll see if I can help you find him."

"Good! Good! Finally somebody is willing to help me!" said Elaine, breathing heavily.

"Just sit down right here, Ma'am," the guard said, pointing toward a straight chair in the hall.

Elaine sat down as the guard asked her to, and then she asked him, "Can I have a Diet Dr. Pepper while I wait?"

"I'll get you a Diet Dr. Pepper, Elaine," said McGuffy, coming out of her room to see if he could find a way to get through to her. "And would you like some peanut butter and cracker sandwiches, too?"

"Yes," said Elaine, in an uncharacteristically curt tone.

Moments later, McGuffy was back with the drink and sandwiches and opened the wrapper for her. Elaine began to nibble on one of the sandwiches and took a sip of her drink.

"Bob, why are we out here in the hall? Why don't we go back in my room?" she asked in a totally different tone of voice.

Elaine then dried her own tears on her sleeves and went back into her room, visibly calmer now, and sat back down on the sofa. McGuffy sat back down beside her and waited before saying anything. Finally he asked, "Do you feel better now, Elaine?"

"Yes, a little, and I'm real sorry Bob, and you, too, Mary. I don't know what came over me. I just kind of lost it, I guess," Elaine said.

"It's alright, Elaine, we understand," said Horton.

"I don't know why I said and did that," said Elaine. "I know Tommy is dead. I remember his funeral now. It was and still is the saddest day of my life."

"Is there anything else that you remember about your past, Elaine?" Horton asked when Elaine had calmed down and had stopped weeping.

"Oh, I don't know. I'm so tired, I just want to be quiet for a while, I guess," said Elaine. "I'm glad I remembered Tommy and what really happened to him, though, because over and over again, I was forever seeing him reach up to me and hearing him call when I couldn't answer him or reach him. It was a torment I couldn't seem to escape. I think now that I've told it, it may not be so overpowering. I hope not."

"We hope not, too, Elaine," said Horton. "So what do you see now?"

"I see Tommy playing with a ball in our front yard there in Hannibal," said Elaine.

"Did it roll into the street, and he was hit by a car when he went after it?" asked McGuffy.

"No, he was never in the street," said Elaine. "Tommy Joe had fixed Tommy Jr. a little basketball goal on the front wall of the garage, because we had a paved drive leading in from the street and he could bounce his ball on it.

"Our street wasn't really a street like a city street, because it used to be a highway that led from Hannibal out into the country before that area out there settled. At first there were just scattered houses along that highway, but eventually new houses were built in between the older houses.

"Our house was one of the last built, so it was built I guess in not the best location. It was near a sharp curve in the highway. We didn't think anything about its being a dangerous location when we moved there, but a lot of drivers missed the curve and came into our yard.

"So Tommy Joe put up some wooden posts with red reflectors in the edge of our lawn, in a straight line that looked in the distance like it was perpendicular to the street or that it was completely blocking the street. The reflectors would show up in a driver's headlights at night. So any driver paying attention would know they were about to hit the posts, and so they would turn with the curve and stay safely on the road.

"But one afternoon, just before dark, Tommy was out playing with his ball, and it rolled out pretty close to where the posts were. He ran to get his ball, and this drunk driver, without his lights on, came speeding down that highway and missed the turn.

"He hit the posts and tore them out of the ground, then he ran over Tommy and just kept on going through a neighbor's yard, finally coming to a stop against a big oak tree. He wasn't wearing his seat belt, so he was impaled on the steering wheel and killed. Police said the alcohol content in his blood was more than three times the legal limit.

"Tommy had severe injuries and died in my arms within a very few minutes," said Elaine, breaking into deep crying again and couldn't continue. "I'm sorry," she said after a while, then she wiped her tears and tried again in agony to tell her story.

"I've got to tell this and get past it or it will torment me forever," she said. "Little Tommy was in terrific pain, screaming 'Momma! Momma!' at the top of his lungs. Then suddenly his eyes rolled back and he stopped breathing. And I yelled 'Tommy! Tommy!' several times, but I don't know if he ever heard me. Anyway, that's what I have kept seeing and hearing in my nightmare."

"It should be much better now, Elaine, since you've brought it up into your conscious mind and dealt with it," said Horton. "Your grief was so great you had sealed off your memory of it to protect yourself from the pain."

"Is there anything else you remember that you want to tell us?" asked McGuffy as he slid closer to Elaine and put his arm around her shoulder. "If so, you may as well go on and get it out. We're here for you, Elaine. You can tell us anything you want to, anything that's bothering you, anything at all. Was there anything else?"

"Oh, let's see. I know we had the funeral for little Tommy, and for a long time afterward I was almost delirious, and then I would sink into deep depression. I couldn't sleep. I couldn't eat. I lost a lot of weight and began to look like a skeleton.

"But Tommy Joe started getting me to go to the boat shop with him. He knew how much I liked boats, and I actually started helping him and doing whatever needed to be done in the boat shop, at no pay. I was just there because I enjoyed being around boats, and because it helped me work through my grief.

"And then pretty soon I was pregnant again, and I didn't feel like going to the boat shop. But I found things to do at home, reading, painting and crafts, and eventually I felt alive again. But when beautiful little Anna Carol was born the next year, I had grief to deal with all over again. She was born with a severe heart defect, which the doctors said they couldn't repair, and she only lived about three weeks.

"We had the funeral, and somehow I was able to accept her death much easier than Tommy's. I remember thinking she was in a better place and she went there before suffering a lot of hurt. That made me feel better, just thinking that.

"And I was able to return to the boat shop and worked hard, really hard. I just poured all I had into that work, and it was satisfying to me, and that also helped me to heal. It worked. Now I remember those days as boat shop days more than Anna Carol days, but of course there's still a big hole in my heart where little Anna Carol used to be. I just know that Tommy Joe and I together helped each other live through it."

"What else do you remember, Elaine," asked Horton.

"Well, not a lot before we started a couple of years ago building the company yacht, which was named *Nautilus* on my suggestion," said Elaine. "Because of my love of ships, particularly Captain Nemo and his *Nautilus*, I worked nearly full time without pay for a pretty good while. Mr. Sides said he wanted the *Nautilus* to belong to the employees, and if we would work on it on our own time, he would pay us in shares of the yacht. So we eventually owned several shares. Mr. Sides told me if I ever wanted a job building boats, I was hired. He said except for Tommy Joe, I was his best employee, and since he didn't have to pay me, I probably topped out Tommy Joe. That made me feel good."

"Well, you know, part of the recovery process for a brain-injured person, Elaine, is finding or re-learning job skills," said Horton. "Perhaps you could talk to Mr. Sides about going to work at his boat shop when you return to Hannibal. I'm guessing you will want to return to Hannibal."

"Oh, I hadn't thought that far ahead," said Elaine. "But that's where Mom and Papa Spence live, and my two sisters, Angela and Marcia, and Tommy Joe's brother, J.T. You might say, my whole family lives there, so it would be the most logical place for me to live, but I'm not going to cross that bridge just yet. I know I've got more recovery to do, and you, Mary, and Dr. Sutherland, my two doctors, are here. So, for the time being at least, you all are stuck with me."

"Does that include me, too, Elaine?" asked McGuffy, who had said almost nothing during her recollection session.

"Especially that includes you," said Elaine, giving McGuffy a warm smile.

"I was just checking," said McGuffy, who also smiled and breathed an audible sigh.

Chapter Sixteen

"Do you still want to go walking down by the water and maybe visit the Viscaya Museum and Gardens?" McGuffy asked Elaine.

"Oh, I think so, definitely, but it's almost lunch time now. So maybe we can go first thing after lunch," said Elaine, "and I'd like to spend most of the afternoon out of the hospital if that's OK with you, Mary."

"I see nothing to prevent you from taking the afternoon, Elaine, so long as you're feeling OK and there is no problem with excessive drainage from your wound," said Horton. "I'd say don't overdo it, but an afternoon out should be fine, assuming Lt. McGuffy goes with you and is prepared to bring you back quickly if you have any unexpected difficulty."

Elaine and McGuffy decided to have lunch in the hospital cafeteria by special arrangement with the kitchen, but before they left her room, the phone rang.

"This is Elaine," she answered.

"Elaine, this is your Mom. I've got those numbers for you. Do you have something to write them down with?" asked the voice on the phone.

"Oh, hey, Mom. Thanks for getting them for me," said Elaine, reaching for a pad and a pen from the top drawer of her night stand. "Yes. Go ahead when you're ready. I have a pad and pen."

Elaine's mother read out her bank balance as $3,562 and change. Then she read out her account number on the bottom of the check, then the numbers and expiration dates of both credit cards.

"Was there anything else you needed, Elaine?" her mother asked.

"No, Mom. That should do it, but let me give you the cell phone number of my friend Lt. McGuffy in case you need to contact me this afternoon while I'm out of my room. And if you and Papa Spence are able to fly to Miami to see me, I would appreciate it if you'd bring my checkbook and both of the credit cards with you, even though I already have the numbers now. Can you do that?" asked Elaine. "But just be very careful, and don't leave them where someone can swipe them, OK?"

"OK. Well, Spence has already called and reserved tickets for me and him on the 8 p.m. flight out," said Ms. Preston. "We'll change planes in Atlanta, but we've got a two-hour lay-over there, and of course the time zone changes, so we'll get to Miami around midnight or a little after I guess. I know you won't still be up at that time, but Spence has got us rooms at a motel near the airport. So we'll not disturb you until after breakfast time tomorrow."

"But you won't disturb me," said Elaine. ``I'll probably still be awake anyway, wondering how you're doing. So go ahead and call me when you get to the motel. OK?"

"Well, if you insist. But I'll just say, `Elaine, it's me. We're here. Good night.' So you can go on back to sleep," said Ms. Preston.

"So I guess I'll see you all at my room on the 11th floor of Miami General Hospital about nine tomorrow morning, then, right?" asked Elaine.

"That's the plan," said Ms. Preston.

"OK, Mom. Thanks for getting me the numbers. And you're going to remember to bring the checkbook and the cards anyway, right?" asked Elaine.

"I told you, didn't I? They're all right here in my purse with your friend's cell phone number, where they're going to stay until I see you tomorrow. Well, I got to go. I think Spence and I are going to go shopping. We both have to pick up a few things for the trip," said Ms. Preston. "I've gotta go. He's already got the motor running and he just blew the horn. Oh, by the way, we're going to have lunch' in town together. There's the horn again. Bye!"

"Bye, Mom," said Elaine, smiling broadly as she hung up the phone and left with McGuffy for the hospital cafeteria. Two security guards rode down with them and stayed on duty near their table while they ate.

"Well, you've come a long way since yesterday, Elaine," McGuffy told her. "Now that you've got these key memories back, do you think that's it, or are you expecting other things from your past to crop up from time to time?" asked McGuffy.

"Oh, I expect there will be things I remember from time to time that I hadn't remembered in a long time, like we all do, I mean just like I did before my injury," said Elaine. "But, Bob, I feel like I'm free of an incredibly heavy burden. My mind had locked me out of my past, and yet it would send just enough through to torment me. I certainly hope that is over."

"Yeah, I hope so too," said McGuffy. "And it's all coming together at a good time, too, because you're more likely to be able to be a good witness in court now that you've got your memory back."

"You mean we're about ready to go to court in the piracy case? I figured that might be weeks or months away," said Elaine. "I haven't heard anything about there being even an indictment out on these guys."

"Oh, there is no indictment. You're right," said McGuffy. "But I spoke with Milton Richards of the U.S. attorney's office this morning. He said the evidence is really strong, which means they're breezing through the presentation to the grand jury, and he thinks they'll have an indictment by the weekend."

"You mean by Friday night? They don't work on Saturdays and Sundays, do they?" asked Elaine.

"In this case, it could be Saturday or Sunday if it takes them that long," said McGuffy. "Barton's pushing straight through the weekend with it, no matter what, because he knows this is a really big fish. He knows the eyes of the nation are on him, especially the eyes of the big brass in Washington he wants to impress."

"Do you mean the President?" Elaine asked.

"The President and the attorney general on down," said McGuffy."

"Well, even when he gets an indictment, assuming he gets one, won't it still take several weeks for them to get ready for trial, and then weeks after that to try the case?" asked Elaine.

"That sometimes happens, and the defense lawyers are going to yell and scream if they have to go full speed ahead with the trial, but from what Richards said, Judge Steele is not all that impressed with their dallying. Oh, he'll give them a fair trial, but the evidence is so strong that the result is virtually inevitable," said McGuffy.

"Under those conditions, the judge isn't likely to give them much time to play stalling games, particularly with the prosecution pushing to go ahead with the trial. Richards told me there'll probably be a preliminary hearing or an arraignment next week, then the judge will read the charges and ask the lawyers on both sides how long they need to get ready for trial. Richards said Barton will stand up and say, 'The United States is ready, Your Honor'."

"And then the defense lawyers will wail and howl that they need at least six months and want to move the trial to Lower Slobovia because there has been such saturation press coverage that their low-life clients can't get a fair trial in Miami."

"And then what?" asked Elaine. "Will Judge Steele grant the delay?"

"Richards said he's likely to say, 'Having reviewed the government's evidence in this case, and the evidence presented by the defense relating to fair trial issues, the court will grant the parties two weeks to prepare for trial and one week to exchange lists of witnesses. The motion for change of venue is denied'," said McGuffy.

"Richards said that's the judge's way of saying the axe of judgment is close to their necks and is shortly going to fall. He said he can hear Barton now, telling the jury, 'You ladies and gentlemen can send the murdering, drug-trafficking pirates of the Gulf of Mexico and the Caribbean a message: 'You're not welcome here. We hang pirates!'"

"Well, I hope Mr. Richards isn't over-estimating the strength of our case," said Elaine. "I mean, I want to see those murdering scoundrels come to justice, too, but I'm still painfully aware that I have not an iota's recollection of being hit with that beam that busted my head. I can't testify in court that Vince Perkins hit me and knocked me overboard to drown in the Gulf, because I simply don't remember it. And that scares me a lot, Bob. I just hope the scientific evidence is strong enough to get them."

"It is, Elaine. Richards said Barton told him the case is open and shut. So you don't worry about testifying," said McGuffy. "Besides, you saw enough before you were hit to put them away for the rest of their natural lives, even if you can't remember Vince hitting you.

"Well, I see you have about finished your lunch. Are you ready for a walk down by the water and over to the Vizcaya Museum and Gardens?"

"Yes, but I'm itching to know if I can go to the bank and access any of my money," said Elaine. "I don't know why, but I just feel like I would feel a lot better if I wasn't flat broke. Uh, make that almost broke. I think I still have a couple of dollars or so of that money that was in my pants pocket when I washed ashore. I plan to keep the rest of that and frame it as a memento of our *Nautilus'* first and final voyage."

"Well, the way I understand it, you're released to my custody, and I say, if you want to go to a bank, you can go to a bank. I think there are at least three big ones within sight of the hospital entrance. So take your pick," said McGuffy.

The two security guards that followed Elaine and McGuffy into the cafeteria suddenly were standing by their table and informed them that they had checked out the Vizcaya Museum and Gardens and would remain on duty near them if they chose to spend part of their afternoon there.

At McGuffy's request, the guards also went with them to a bank less than a block from the hospital so Elaine could request a wire transfer of money from her bank account in Hannibal. The bank turned her down because she couldn't prove her identity.

Moments later, McGuffy's cell phone rang. It was Helen Petree, a former classmate of Elaine's who worked at the Bank of Hannibal.

"Hello, Elaine?" said a woman's voice.

``Just a moment, Ma'am. It's for you," said McGuffy, handing Elaine the phone.

``Are you alright? Your mom's here, said you needed to talk to me. I told her I'd be delighted," said Helen. "I want you to know, you are a celebrity around here today. People are calling you 'The Unsinkable Elaine Foster'. You made the front page of the *Courier-Post*, and of course we're all heart-broken about Tommy Joe. We're so sorry about that. But tell me how I'm lucky enough to be on the phone with a celebrity, who's also an old friend?"

"Watch that 'old' part, but you've heard that old saying about 'a friend in need is a friend indeed'?" asked Elaine.

"Yes, I've heard that. But how in the world are you doing?"

"Helen, I'm making good progress, but I'm a long way from well," said Elaine. "And right now, I'm the proverbial friend in need. I mean, when the pirates attacked Tommy Joe and me, kidnapped us and blew up our yacht, I lost all my ID cards, credit cards, driver's license, wholesale club card, the works, you name it. And telling it like it is, I'm flat broke."

"Well, what can I do?" asked Helen. "Do you want me to wire you some money, or maybe send it to you by way of a bank near you, or to your hospital, I guess? The paper said you were hospitalized with a traumatic brain injury."

"Yes, I have what they call TBI. And yes, I need you to find a way to get me some money here. But forget the bank near me stuff. I've just been turned down by one of those big-shot big-city banks. They didn't even want to talk to me and my friend here, Bob McGuffy, about getting somebody from the Bank of Hannibal on the line," said Elaine. "I mean, it didn't leave a good flavor in my opinion for the banking industry."

"Well, let's see if we can change that," said Helen. "Now, for my record, I need to verify two recent transactions to your account, either a check or a deposit. Can you give me that? I mean I have to fill out a written report."

"I can tell you that my balance in checking is $3,562, and my Mom has my checkbook, so she can give you as many check numbers and amounts as you need for further verification," said Elaine.

"OK, Elaine. I'll accept that, since I'm absolutely positive I'm talking to you and because your Mom is standing right here. Now Ms. Preston, do you have Elaine's checkbook?"

"I have it," said Emma, retrieving the checkbook from her purse and handing it to Helen.

"OK. I have verified your account and you have access to it," said Helen. "Now how much money do you need, and where do I need to send it? Perhaps we could send it to your friend's account in his bank, with his permission of course."

"I need $1,000, and let me find out his bank. What's your bank, Bob? She says she can send my money to your account, if it's OK with you," said Elaine.

"My bank is People's Credit Union of Dade County," said McGuffy. "They financed my Jeep when I bought it, and they take out my payments automatically. And it's definitely OK to send me the money. That old account won't know what to do with $1,000 worth of fresh, green money.'"

"OK, Helen, send it to the People's Credit Union of Dade County," said Elaine. "What's your account number, Bob?" McGuffy gave her the number. "Now how soon can we write checks on it?"

"Ordinarily, we say wait 24 hours," said Helen. "We're not a corresponding bank with your bank or we could speed it up. But I believe some of the banks in our network may correspond with People's Credit, so I'll make a call or two and see if I can get you an emergency expedite on it. If you'll stand by I'll let you know in about five minutes."

In less than three minutes, McGuffy's cell phone rang again. Elaine answered. It was Helen.

"Elaine, it's clear. You can write checks or get cash from an ATM immediately," said Helen. "Our president, Mr. Hall, is standing here right beside me, and he has been pulling a few strings of his own. So he's the reason it cleared so fast. Would you like to speak to him?"

"Definitely! To tell him thanks, for sure!" said Elaine.

"I'll let you do that. Here he is," said Helen, handing the phone to her boss.

"Is this the Unsinkable Elaine Foster?" asked Hall. "This is Roger Hall, one of the little people."

"Oh, Mr. Hall, thank you, thank you, thank you! You don't know how much this means to me," said Elaine.

"I happen to know a little bit about what it feels like to be broke myself," said Hall. "It happened to me in Vegas one night, but we won't go there. You know what they say about Vegas. Now, have I squared up the banking profession with you?"

"Definitely. Definitely," said Elaine.

"Well, I've been reading about our celebrity. And, no, I don't mean Molly Brown or even Mark Twain. I'm talking about you," said Hall. "So get well and come by to see me when you get back in town. I've got an idea for a yacht, if we could come up with a name for it, that is. Maybe you could suggest a name."

"Like how about, *Nautilus* 2?" asked Elaine.

"Yeah, something like that," said Hall.

"Thanks again, Mr. Hall. And can I say goodbye to Helen?" asked Elaine.

"Sure. Here she is," said Hall.

"Hey, Elaine. Glad we could fix you up. I heard Mr. Hall mention the yacht. I know that got your attention," said Helen."

"You're right! Thanks again, Helen. And bye for now. I hope to see you soon," said Elaine as the conversation ended.

McGuffy and Elaine then strolled over to the Vizcaya Museum and Gardens and for a long time silently soaked up its spectacular beauty, then Elaine suggested they find a bench in the shade and rest their feet.

"You know, Bob, this horrible nightmare may be about over for me," said Elaine. "And I'm not talking about the mountain of sadness I've still got to climb. You know, Tommy Joe's funeral, which we've got to make arrangements for, and then at some point, maybe sooner than you think, there'll be separation from the good friends I've made here in Miami in the past couple of weeks when I go back to Hannibal and try to rebuild my life."

"Well, if you're not talking about that mountain of sadness as you call it, what are you talking about?" McGuffy asked.

"I'm talking about the nightmare of walking around with a crushed skull with a splinter sticking in my brain. I'm talking about not knowing from one minute to the next whether I'll bleed to death during the night, or turn into a vegetable, where I see everything going on around me but I can't say anything back to let folks know I'm still alive in there," said Elaine.

"I'm talking about not knowing who I am or where I came from or where I'm going. I'm talking about being totally dependent, like a baby needing a diaper change, with no car, no driver's license, no checkbook or credit card, no job, no phone, no clothes except what some kind-hearted soul gives me. I'm talking about that nightmare, Bob. And that's what I'm thankful to the Good Lord may be about over."

"Wow! That must have hurt coming out! That was a mighty long list," said McGuffy.

"Yes, and a very powerful and intimidating list, Bob, when you see it from my side of the experience," said Elaine. "And I know that there are still several items on that list I've got to work through, but at least I have hope now, and realistic opportunities, I believe, to reclaim my life."

"And you have some very devoted friends who pledge to be right there by your side, pulling for you, and even pushing you if you need us to," said McGuffy.

"I remember your saying once that Dr. Sutherland wanted you to discover the meaning of the word 'friend' and that he wanted you to have a large group of new friends as you recover your memory. And I know you kept mentioning, whenever the word 'friend' came up in conversation, that you were still trying to learn what being a friend or having a friend is all about. Do you think you have a handle on what a friend is now?"

"Well, I'm not sure. I think I know a lot more about friendship, because I've seen what I consider friendship exhibited to me in so many ways since I've been in the hospital here," said Elaine. "There are the kindnesses shown me by Dr. Sutherland and Dr. Horton and the nurses and staff, and really before that, when you and Lt. Anderson rescued me from that sandbar island. Why do you ask?"

"Well, it's just that you mean more to me than I would ever have imagined just a few days ago when I saw you on that island," said McGuffy. "That wasn't friendship that day. That was duty. I was just doing my job. But really soon after that, I knew I wasn't just living out the Coast Guard motto. I found myself really wanting to be your friend, and trying hard to be your friend. And what made it so nice is that it seemed you wanted to be my friend, too."

"Well, that's how I feel, Bob. So what's the problem?" asked Elaine.

"Well, with your talking about going back to Hannibal and all, I get all queasy inside, because I'm just afraid that will mean you'll move away and go back to your old friends in Hannibal, or maybe find a new set of friends in Hannibal, and I won't see you again. I mean, that would just tear me up big time, Elaine, if I thought I would never see you again."

"Well, hey! There are things like planes and helicopters and buses and cars that go from here to there on a regular basis. And I think it can even be done on a yacht, even though right now I don't have a yacht. But I wouldn't mind trying it sometime, if I ever am so blessed to be aboard another yacht," said Elaine. "But I want you to know, that no matter how many old friends I go back to in Hannibal or how many new ones I find, there aren't any of them who have the place in my heart that you have, Lt. McGuffy."

"Don't call me that," said McGuffy. "I'm Bob, remember?"

"Sure, I remember," said Elaine. "I said that to make a point."

"What was your point?" asked McGuffy.

"My point was that it would be absolutely preposterous for me, even with all the trouble I've had remembering my past, to forget your name is Bob after calling you Bob literally dozens of times over the past week," said Elaine. "Do you really think I would forget and call you Lt. McGuffy?" asked Elaine.

"No," said McGuffy.

"No, exactly," said Elaine. "It would be preposterous. And my point is, it's even more preposterous to think I'd forget my very best friend in the whole world just because I made a trip to the town where I was born and grew up."

"I would very much like to think that's true," said McGuffy. "But my point is, I don't know that for sure."

"Well, I'm telling you that's true for sure. What do I need to do to convince you?" asked Elaine.

"Well, you used that word `friend' again," said McGuffy. "You said or strongly implied that I'm, in your words, your 'very best friend in the whole world.' What do you mean when you say I'm your very best friend in the whole world?"

"OK, as the poet once said, 'Let me count the ways' that you are my friend," said Elaine. "In just the past few days, you have kept me company when I was lonely; listened to me when I was burdened and scared and needed someone to talk to; held me and reassured me when my heart was breaking and I was crying my eyes out; you have cheered me up when I was depressed; brought me a smiley-face balloon and flowers and Diet Dr. Peppers and peanut butter sandwiches, just when I needed each of those things; you have invited me to worship with you when I was in a spiritual desert; you helped me deal with the banks when I needed money, and you have given your day to me today, when you could have been out rescuing other lost souls from the sea. Bob, nobody else can match your record as a friend to me. You don't have to worry that I'll ever forget you, whether I go back to Hannibal or go to Timbuktu or stay in Miami, which I've got to do for at least the next several weeks, Dr. Sutherland's orders, you know. Does that make it any clearer to you?"

"It helps a bit," said McGuffy. "But you have to know that I'm ready for my friendship — I should say our friendship — to go even beyond that."

"What are you saying, Bob?" asked Elaine.

"I'm not sure I really know myself what I'm saying," said McGuffy. "I do know, Elaine, that when I'm with you, emotionally I just melt with a joy I can't explain. Being with you is like being in the sunshine when everywhere else around you it's pouring down rain."

"It's that way being with you, too, Bob," said Elaine. "But what do you mean, a friendship that goes beyond that?"

"I already answered that question," said McGuffy. "The answer is, 'I don't know what I mean.' But I'll try to explain what I mean. It's like this, Elaine. When I'm with you, I feel that I'm receiving from you even more than I'm giving, just because you're there. Whether I give you my company, my shoulder or my smiley face, your smile repays me ten times over. I just keep running a deficit with you.

"In other words, Elaine, I'm not giving you anything that's really costing me anything that you don't repay ten times over just by being there. What I think I'm talking about, when I say I'm ready for our friendship to be more than that, is that I'm ready to do what's best for you, even if it's not what's best for me.

"In other words, if my friendship is really true and real, I'll be ready and willing to do even what hurts me, if it helps and benefits you. I'm not a psychologist, but I know you will be grieving for a while over the death of your husband, particularly since you were childhood sweethearts.

"For me to come into your life so soon and make a power play for your heart after you've regained that painful memory makes me feel almost like I'm a looter, pilfering what was left in a home hit by a hurricane. Do you understand that?"

"I think so, Bob, and you don't need to feel that way," said Elaine. "I wasn't exactly born yesterday. I know I'm going to be in grief for a long time over the loss of the man who was my sweetheart in kindergarten and every day since then. That's why I described the funeral coming up as a mountain of sadness.

"But please don't withdraw your friendship at a time when I really may need it most. I mean, a hurricane has hit, and my life is a shambles. Thanks to you and the other real friends I've met here in Miami, I have an opportunity to rebuild my life and a realistic hope that I can do it. You have given me the emotional steam to say, `I think I can. No, I know I can.' Am I getting through to you, Bob?"

"Yes, I hear you," said McGuffy. "And I shudder to think this, much less to say it, Elaine, but I'm willing to bow out of your life altogether if it would be truly better for you to return to Hannibal and your old friends, or even to make new ones as you rebuild your life instead of locking onto somebody who just happened to fly over in a chopper one day and helped to airlift you off a sandbar. Am I getting through to you?"

"Of course," said Elaine. "But you know what you said a while back about getting that queasy feeling in your stomach if you thought you'd never see me again? Well, that's how I'm feeling about you right now, especially since you're talking about doing something so devastating to me as to pull away just because you think you aren't good for me right now.

"If you want to pull away because you think that's best for you, my idea of friendship says you should be free to do that. I mean, you don't owe me anything. But if you are considering pulling away from me because you think that would be best for me, then I think I should get a vote…no, make that a veto, on that proposal. And I'm willing to give you that same privilege with me, I promise."

"That covers a lot of ground, Elaine. It seems fair enough in theory. I don't know how it's going to work out in practice, though," said McGuffy.

"What do you mean? Give me an example," said Elaine.

"OK. I'll give you an example: feeling the way I feel about you, my heart tells me to stick with you like glue every minute from now on, for as long as you're willing to put up with me," said McGuffy.

"But because I want you to have the life you're entitled to build through your own choices, I feel that maybe I should step aside while you go back to Hannibal, if that's where you choose to build your future life, until your broken heart has healed and you know what it is saying to you. Then, if you decide later, on your own, to leave Hannibal and come 2,000 miles looking for a lonesome Coast Guard lieutenant, that would be your free choice instead of an accident of the wind and tide."

"I don't believe in accident and chance, Bob," said Elaine. "The God I spoke to on the day I drifted ashore on that sandbar has a plan for me which I expect to learn and to live in the days ahead.

"He answered my prayer for water when I was dying of thirst, and he sent two guys in a helicopter to get me medical help when I asked him for a doctor.

"The chance that I would survive a crushed skull without losing my brains and my life and float across the Gulf of Mexico on the plank that hit me is infinitesimally small. It wouldn't have happened in a million years if chance was all I had going for me, Bob.

"And I don't think you came to that sandbar island a week ago Monday by chance, either. I think we both had a divine appointment. Neither of us made this journey by accident."

"I'd like very much to believe that, Elaine," said McGuffy. "And one day I may believe it. I'm not ruling it out. I do believe in divine appointments. And our becoming friends may be one of them. But I'd like for you to do what you think you should do about going back to Hannibal without my vote."

"That's fair enough," said Elaine. "Now let me tell you what I plan to do, and you tell me if you want to veto anything or make a counter-suggestion."

"OK. What do you plan to do?" asked McGuffy.

"I plan to make arrangements for Tommy Joe's funeral when Mom and Papa Spence get here tomorrow," said Elaine. "I think we're all going to want to bury him in Hannibal, although he might very well have voted to make it simple by cremating his body with a brief ceremony here and then to have a memorial service in Hannibal later.

"But I'm expecting to travel to Hannibal for a full funeral ceremony. Then I'll come back to Miami, and when Dr. Sutherland dismisses me from the hospital in maybe another week or two, I'll find some kind of rehab or community support facility where I can live until the piracy trial is over.

"Since I'll be a witness for the federal government, there may be some witness protection funds available to help me, I don't know. I'll see if I can pass a driving test and get my license, maybe using a rental car at first. Then I'll see if I can buy a reliable used car to get me around to places while I'm here.

"When the piracy trial is over, you and I can assess where our relationship is at that time. That may be a couple of months or so from now, and that will be soon enough to be making decisions that are going to determine our future, don't you think?"

"That sounds like a very good plan to me, and in line with it, I have a proposal that is totally for my benefit, but you're free to veto it if you like," said McGuffy.

"No, if it's for your benefit, I don't get a veto, remember?" asked Elaine. "If it's what you think is best for me, that's when I get a veto. If it's what you think is best for you, you should just go ahead and do it, without consulting me."

"That's exactly what I was hoping you would say. This is totally for my benefit," said McGuffy, reaching his arms around Elaine, drawing her close and giving her a passionate kiss. Then as McGuffy began to pull away, Elaine leaned forward and gave McGuffy an even more passionate kiss.

"I take it that wasn't a veto," said McGuffy.

"I'd call it a tie vote," said Elaine as their two security guards exchanged glances and smiled.

Chapter Seventeen

Elaine wanted to view the physical evidence that the Team had gathered in the piracy case, so they came by Morelli's office before going back to the hospital. Morelli unlocked the vaults and took her on a tour of the virtual mountain of evidence gathered in the case.

Elaine was impressed. The evidence seemed strong enough to convict her attackers, even without her eye-witness testimony in court. She was less concerned now that she still had no memory of being hit by a plank or of seeing her husband get shot in the back.

Elaine told Morelli that her mother and father-in-law were flying in to help plan her husband's funeral, and Morelli offered to help with transportation. He said Barton had authorized him to use witness protection funds to fly Elaine to Hannibal and back, and that since they were going anyway, Emma and Spence could go too without charge.

"Mr. Barton and Cdr. Hoover and I also believe that your security protection for this trip should remain high," said Morelli. "Cdr. Hoover will provide you with medical assistance if needed, and she and Lieutenants Anderson and McGuffy also will be assigned security duties for the trip to Hannibal and back."

Elaine thanked Morelli, then she and McGuffy headed back to the hospital, accompanied by their two security guards.

"Well, Elaine, with your Mom and father-in-law in town tomorrow, I'll make myself scarce so you can have some private time with them," McGuffy told her. "You know you can reach me at work if you need me, but try my cell phone first. I'm not sure whether I'll be working in or outside the office."

"OK, Bob. It was so great being with you today, and great being able to get outside of this hospital," said Elaine. "I've been treated like royalty here, but I feel like I'm about to get cabin fever. Thanks for all you have done to help me get my life back."

Before McGuffy could say anything, Elaine reached up to him, put both arms around his neck and kissed him.

"I know you will have a lot of other things to do tomorrow, but while they're in town, at some point, I really would like for you to meet my Mom and my father-in-law," said Elaine.

"I'd like to meet your family, Elaine, at some appropriate point, but they will be trying to deal with grief as they make funeral plans tomorrow, and I'm not so sure my presence will make it any easier on them," said McGuffy.

"You know I will have security duties as well as my usual co-pilot duties on our trip to Hannibal and back; so perhaps they should meet all three of the Coast Guard officers who will accompany you to the funeral, or perhaps the entire team, rather than meeting just me. I'm just thinking it could get a little awkward if I'm too prominently present."

"You're probably right, Bob," said Elaine. "I wasn't thinking about how Papa Spence might feel, having to deal with someone else besides his son Tommy Joe keeping his daughter-in-law company so soon after his son's death.

"It might look a little out of place to him, and it may be a little out of place, actually. As far as I'm concerned, though, you are honoring Tommy Joe by helping to see that his killer is brought to justice.

"You're kind, Elaine, but let me pass on meeting your folks unless you want to bring them by Cdr. Hoover's and Chief Morelli's office toward the end of the day tomorrow and let them meet the whole team," said McGuffy.

"That's a good idea," said Elaine. "Tomorrow it is, then."

"Right. See you at Chief Morelli's office tomorrow afternoon," said McGuffy.

Elaine then boarded the elevator with her two security guards and pushed the button for the 11th floor.

She turned in early and was sleeping soundly when the phone rang. She fumbled around for it in the dim light of her hospital room, picked it up wondering at first who could be calling her at that hour, then she heard her mother's voice:

"Elaine, it's Mom. We're in town, safe and sound. See you at breakfast," came the voice on the phone.

"Hey, Mom. Don't be in such a rush. I'm awake now. Did you have a good flight?" asked Elaine.

"Yes, but I had to take off my shoes and socks so the security folks could see I wasn't hiding any plastic explosives," said Elaine's mother. "And I thought we were never going to get out of Atlanta. But we'll tell you all about it all in your room, say about 9 a.m."

"Well, if you want to wait that late for breakfast. I usually eat between 7:30 and 8," said Elaine.

"Well I do, too, and I'm sure Spence does, but we wanted to make it late enough so you'd be through with breakfast and we wouldn't disturb you," her mother said. "We'll probably eat at Hardee's around 7 if I know Spence."

"Well, look, why don't we compromise?" asked Elaine. "You're definitely *NOT* going to disturb me. For goodness sake, you're my mom and father-in-law. So why don't you all come to the hospital cafeteria on the first floor, just inside the security checkpoint, say around 7:30, and I'll meet you there and we'll have breakfast together?

"They'll make you jump through a few security hoops here, too, because the hospital's secure medical cells are full of injured pirates and drug traffickers and kidnappers and killers right now, and the place is probably swarming with their cohorts and family members who are still running free. But show your driver's license and another photo ID, such as your wholesale club card. I have told the federal investigators that you're coming in, and they're probably monitoring this call right now. So they're expecting you."

"So they're just letting you traipse all over the hospital by yourself now, are they?" asked Ms. Preston.

"No, there are two guards here on the eleventh floor suite with me, and they go with me wherever I go, like they did when I had lunch in the cafeteria today," said Elaine. "So you'll see them keeping a close watch on me and on whatever thug out there may be itching to harm me. Just treat them with respect and they'll be no trouble to you."

"Elaine, this is Spence," came Foster's voice on the phone. "Tell your mom to hang up so we can all get some sleep. I want to hear from you too, but I'm worn out from the trip and security folks putting me and my stuff through a ringer and everything. Right now, we just all need our sleep, don't you think? Oh, and did I hear you all discussing a change in plans for breakfast?"

"Yeah, Papa Spence, unless you want to sleep late and have breakfast at Hardee's or some place on your own schedule. I'm suggesting that you join me for breakfast here in the hospital cafeteria around 7:30 a.m. I'm sure they've got a big selection of breakfast items, and that way we could talk over breakfast."

"Yeah, that's fine. I usually get up with the chickens anyway, but if you want to eat at 7:30, that would suit me fine," said Spence. "OK, I'm going to give the phone back to your mother and you two hurry and hang up. I'll see you at breakfast."

"OK, Papa Spence. Mom, you heard that. We've got to hang up, and I'll have breakfast with you at 7:30 in the hospital cafeteria," said Elaine, who was now wide awake.

About the time she drifted off to sleep again, it was time to get up and the alarm sounded. She quickly showered and dressed in her white pants suit and got to the cafeteria just as her mother and Spence had arrived at the security checkpoint.

"Mom! Papa Spence!" Elaine shouted as she hurried to the check point to greet them, just as the security guards made them show their picture IDs and walk through a metal detector. Then they x-rayed her handbag.

"Hey, Elaine. We'll be with you soon I hope," said Ms. Preston.

"Yeah, Elaine, we got a powerful big supply of hugs we've been saving for you all the way from Hannibal, which I aim to deliver as soon as these security boys get done checking us out," said Spence. "But we appreciate you folks checking," Spence said, facing the guards. "Don't get us wrong. We're glad you're here and checking."

"OK, Ma'am, Sir, you may enter the first floor lobby and the cafeteria as you wish, but if you plan at any time to go to other floors in the hospital, you will need to come back to this checkpoint for special authorization," said the checkpoint security officer. "You will be required to carry a special security badge for the other floors. OK? So you folks have a good day."

"Thank you, officer, we will. You, too," said Spence. "Now come here, child, and give me a hug," he said as he gave Elaine a bear-hug, lifting her off the floor. Then he said to Elaine, "Oh, my, I forgot your injury. I didn't hurt you, did I?"

"No, Papa Spence," said Elaine. "You didn't do any damage. That was all in my head, you know, and I have been needing a hug like that since I got here."

"Well, save one for me," said Elaine's Mom, who gave her another big hug but without trying to lift her off the floor. And for a long while Ms. Preston and her daughter held each other and cried.

Finally, she asked Elaine, "Are you sure you're alright? I can see that big bandage under your hair, there. How long will you have to wear that?"

"Not much longer, I hope, Mom," said Elaine. "Now you all go through the serving line and get whatever you want, then you pay for it at the cashier over there. My breakfast is already on my plate in the warming closet, and already on my tab, I guess, so I get to skip the cashier."

"Then you must have some kind of clout around here," said Elaine's mom.

"No, just the opposite," said Elaine. "When you have nothing at all and you're a patient here, they take pity on you. Seriously, they have treated me really well here, Mom. Dr. Sutherland, my main doctor, has been fabulous, and he says I am making really good progress. He has said I may be here a month to six weeks, depending on my rate of healing. I'm coming up Monday on a full two weeks here and my progress is good, so I may be out of here in another two weeks or so."

Emma and Spence had little to say during breakfast, but each of them knew the unspoken subject of the day had to be planning Tommy Joe's funeral, and they postponed that as long as possible.

"Well, I may as well mention it. We need to plan the funeral," Spence said eventually, "but I'm not sure I can talk about that yet. I just can't believe my boy is dead. I mean, I can just blink my eyes and I can see him all the way from the time we brought him home from the hospital as an infant," Spence said, suddenly sobbing. "All the times we let him off at school or at the ball park or at the movies, and a good deal of the time, I think you know, Elaine, where we found Tommy Joe, we also found you. Ain't that right?"

"That's right, Papa Spence. All those days run continually through my mind, too, and until yesterday morning, I was only able to remember them in bits and pieces," said Elaine.

"But the doctor operated on me Monday morning and removed the splinter that had punctured the membrane around my brain, and within a few hours I was recalling great gobs of my past. I mean it was just flowing in like water over a waterfall."

"Well, what does the doctor say you need to do to get well," asked Emma.

"After Dr. Sutherland releases me from the hospital, whether it's two weeks from now or later, he wants me to enroll in some kind of community support residential facility such as the ones the medical schools run to train their interns to care for brain-injured people," said Elaine.

"He said they will help me get over the emotional trauma and will help me with practical things like transportation, getting my driver's license, finding a temporary job so I can make some money, and just generally put me with other TBI. That's what they call us, traumatic brain injury people, so we can share experiences and help each other recover."

"Well, that will be great," said Emma. "I mean, we'd love to have you back in Hannibal immediately and permanently, but we sure want those investigator folks to try and convict those pirates. So you may as well enroll in some programs here that will help you recover while you wait. Also, Spence and I may be able to stay here with you for a few days until you get settled."

``Well, Mom, I would really appreciate it, but I know it will be expensive for you all to stay down here that long," said Elaine. ``Also, Dr. Sutherland said these volunteer community programs have turned out really nice and helpful to recovering TBI folks. So I think I'll be able to make it alright for a few weeks."

``Well, where's that young Coast Guard sailor I heard on the phone at the hospital yesterday?" asked Ms. Preston. ``Won't he be able to help you with things until you get back on your feet so to speak?"

``Oh, you mean Lt. McGuffy. I'm sure he will help me, Mom," said Elaine. ``He seems to be real fond of me and all. Anyway, we'll meet him and the other members of the special investigating team, including Cdr. Hoover and Chief Morelli, who have been really great. Of course, they're mainly interested in seeing that Tommy Joe's killer and my attacker are brought to justice, either in prison or maybe the death chamber, whatever the judge and jury decide."

"I'd vote for the death chamber in a minute if I had a vote on that jury," said Spence.

"I don't care what they do with him, so long as he can't ever get out and knock somebody else's daughter in the head with a plank," said Ms. Preston.

"Yeah, you and me, too, Mom," said Elaine.

As Elaine and her mother and father-in-law finished their breakfast in the hospital cafeteria, a nurse's assistant approached their table.

"Excuse me, Elaine, and I believe this is your mother and father-in-law with you?" the assistant asked. "I'm sorry to interrupt you, but Dr. Sutherland said I'd probably find you here. He asked me to tell you that he would very much like to meet your family and discuss your progress and the outlook for further recovery if you have time sometime today."

"Sure. We'd love to meet Elaine's doctor," said Ms. Preston. "When does he want to see us?"

"He could see you all now if that would be all right with you," said the assistant.

"Well, I don't know why not, do you Elaine? What do you say, Spence?" asked Emma.

"Sure. It suits me," said Spence.

"Well, I know we've got other things to do today, but I can't think of a better way to start the day than to let you meet Dr. Sutherland and talk with him about how far I've come and what's ahead for me," said Elaine. "I'd kind of like to hear it all again myself. Tell him, we'll come up to his office right away."

"Well, if you come with me now, you will avoid some of the security red tape," said the assistant. "I have handed a note from Dr. Sutherland to the security checkpoint guard and he has a couple of badges you'll need to wear on the upper floors of the hospital."

"Here you are, Ma'am," the security guard said, handing Spence and Emma their badges. "You folks have a nice day."

"Thanks. We will," said Spence as they boarded the elevator with the two ever-present security guards. They all got off on the 11th floor and headed for Sutherland's office.

Sutherland introduced himself and invited them in, but the guards waited in a hallway outside his office.

"You folks have a seat," Sutherland said. He clicked on a large monitor showing a full-color image of a human skull and brain, with a straight-line mark through the lower right side. It was obviously a scanned image of Elaine's brain, showing the splinter that was removed during surgery on Monday.

"There are a lot of good things we can say about Elaine's recovery," said Sutherland, spinning his chair first toward Elaine and her family and then back so he faced the scanned image on the screen. "This mark here is a splinter that entered her brain at the point and time of injury. It penetrated the membrane surrounding her brain here, and then went nearly two inches inside it," Sutherland said, pointing out the splinter with an infra-red pointer as he talked.

"While it was intrusive and potentially a massive carrier of bacterial infection as well as a destroyer of memory and processing cells, the splinter may very well have saved her from further injury and possibly saved her life. You see, the splinter provided an exit point for blood and other fluid that accumulates inside the skull following a severe brain injury.

"With anti-inflammatory medication, we were able to hold the fluid buildup to a minimum, and the channel around the splinter allowed not only the fluid but the bacteria that entered through the puncture point to flow out and away as well. We administered massive doses of antibiotics, so that when we operated on Monday there was no sign of bacterial infection, and there has been no indication of any infection since then. So we dodged a very big bullet there.

"Finally, there was ample and complete drainage following the removal of the splinter, so that healing has occurred and continues to occur in the former pathway of the splinter. The main risk besides infection at this point is that the fluid will continue to build up after the exit channel heals shut, which it almost has done at this point.

"We're continuing to monitor for symptoms of a buildup of fluid and the resultant inappropriate pressure on the brain, and we are prepared to reopen the drainage point at the first sign of buildup. We will monitor her closely for at least another month, because in our experience, bleeding and swelling sometimes occur three weeks or longer following a severe injury. But if there is no buildup, Elaine will be essentially well physically in about a week except for the skull's knitting back together. Now are there any questions before I go into other aspects of her recovery?"

"No, Doctor, you've made it pretty clear," said Spence. "Even I could understand it, and it sounds like good news to me."

"Good. We think it is good news, Mr. Foster," said Sutherland.

"I've got a question, Doctor," said Ms. Preston. "You mentioned Elaine's skull. I understand that the plank that struck her head shattered the bone into tiny pieces. Will those pieces cause her any trouble, and will they eventually grow back together? And what should she do meanwhile?"

"An excellent question, Ms. Preston," said Sutherland.

"It sounded like several questions to me," said Spence.

"Well, they were all good questions, and the answers are kind of tied together," said Sutherland. "You are right, Ms. Preston, about the pieces. As severe as the fracture of Elaine's skull was, the pieces you mentioned stayed in the same plane and were not driven inward into the brain like projectiles, which would have severely impaired Elaine's mental and physical functioning, or possibly could even have caused her death.

"As it was, having the cranial cavity more or less flexible in the early hours after her injury helped to eliminate what pressure build-up there was, and it continues to provide something of a safety net against pressure build-up as her healing continues.

"Bottom line, by the time those fractures grow back together in a few weeks, which they should do without any help from us in the form of a cast or any other device, we expect the brain injury itself to be healed and Elaine will be physically well. She will need to prevent any bump or impact on that area meanwhile, of course, because the unprotected brain will be quite vulnerable. We will provide a special cushion for her to use during any aircraft flights, which I understand you expect to be taking in a few days."

"We are expecting to fly back to Hannibal for the funeral of her husband, but what you've said sounds like excellent news, Doctor," said Emma.

"It certainly is good news, I believe," said Sutherland. "In fact, I'm going to conditionally release Elaine from the hospital effective with her enrollment in the TBI rehab center a few blocks from here sponsored by the local university med school. I'm familiar with their program. It's excellent. Gives high quality care, although it's staffed entirely by med students and community volunteers.

"Just bring me a signed admittance slip from the rehab center and you will be processed out of the hospital," Sutherland told Elaine. "I'll still expect you to come in for checkups each Monday morning for the next three weeks. Then if you've not had any further adverse episodes, I'm going to dismiss you except for twice-annual checkups.

"But for the rest of our session this morning, I have asked Dr. Horton, our staff psychologist, to come in and make a few comments about the outlook for Elaine's emotional recovery. You can come on in, Doctor," said Sutherland as he saw Horton in his outer office. She came in, exchanged handshakes with them all, and then sat down in a chair facing them.

"I'm glad to meet with you today and to give you a good report on Elaine's emotional recovery up to now, and to give you the outlook we see for her continued recovery in the days ahead," said Horton.

"The first thing I'll mention is grief. As the famous cartoon character reminds us, not all grief is bad. In fact, a certain amount of grief is good and healthy even while it stems from emotional pain or distress, because it's a natural process of cleansing and restoration following an emotional trauma such as you have just experienced," said Horton.

"We can see the bandage on Elaine's head, although congratulations, Elaine, you've done a good job of hiding it so that we really have to look for it to see it," said Horton. "However, we cannot see or possibly even detect the marks of the psychological injury Elaine and you, her family, have suffered and to some degree will continue to suffer for some time, perhaps for an extended period.

"While you three will have a lot in common in that grief process, much of what you will experience is uniquely personal. Elaine will deal with it as the loss of her life's mate, which I understand was also her childhood sweetheart. You, Mrs. Preston, will share vicariously your daughter's pain. And you, Mr. Foster, will experience in your own personal way the loss of your beloved son.

"For you, Elaine, as you begin to build new relationships, you will find that the pain of losing Tommy Joe will be acute at times, and you may find yourself almost uncontrollably withdrawing suddenly from the new relationships you are developing.

"This will be very real to you and at the same time perhaps puzzling to you as well as to everyone around you. These episodes may come and go, without there seeming to be any connection between them nor any way to predict them nor control them.

"But slowly, if you understand these emotional episodes as part of the healing process, they should become less frequent and hopefully less severe. You will not, and you should not, ever completely escape the pain of your loss. That is the legacy you carry with you from a trauma like this.

"But you should and I believe you will, in time, be able to manage the pain so that it does not keep you from going ahead with your life. Now, let me ask you if what I have been saying makes any sense to you? Elaine? Anyone?"

"I know it will be very difficult for me as well as for Mom and Papa Spence to make arrangements for Tommy Joe's funeral, as we will have to do sometime today," said Elaine. "We know that we must go forward with that, no matter how unpleasant. But when the pain seems too intense at times to bear, what can we do to manage it then?"

"An excellent question, Elaine," said Horton. "You minimize the effects of those painful times, which inevitably will come, by maintaining good physical health and fitness and by good emotional preparation ahead of time. Now let me explain what I mean by that.

"We know we function better mentally and emotionally when we are physically healthy and fit. I don't need to say anything more about that. But we may feel, if we go into a grief episode unprepared, that we are stuck in the present, that life has stopped and left us nailed down to an unbearably painful present.

"We should tell ourselves ahead of time, and remind ourselves during those times, that the shortest distance out of pain is straight ahead. Am I being clear on that?"

"Is it like saying, no matter how bad it gets, that as the old saying goes, 'This too shall pass'?" asked Emma.

"Exactly," said Horton. "And we may feel during those times that we are being disloyal to our loved one if we do anything to move forward.

"Well, we should tell ourselves ahead of time that we have to move on. We cannot have a healthy life if we insist on living in the past. Our loved one wouldn't want us to do that. We are honoring, not diminishing, the memory of our loved one if we celebrate the good times of our past life and move forward out of the painful present, hopefully to a happy future.

"Now, I know this is all easier to say than to do. I remember thinking I would never be able to get over the loss of my father. That was many years ago, and it still hurts dreadfully when I think of the pain he went through.

"I know he wanted his daughter to live a happy life, and I knew I couldn't do that by staying stuck in the past. I have moved forward, carrying with me the vivid memories of a huge load of happy times we shared together in the past. Now, any more questions or comments?"

"I think we understand, Doctor. We need to take time to grieve, but then we need to move on and take the best of the past with us. Isn't that what you're saying?" asked Spence.

"Exactly, Mr. Foster," said Horton. "Now there's another topic I want to touch on, that of the need to avoid the emotional pitfall of finding an immediate and unhealthy substitute for a lost relationship rather than building over an extended time a truly new relationship with a new person.

"As we heal from an emotional trauma, our emotions seem to jump around almost at random, high and low and in between, like a roller coaster, without notice or warning, and essentially out of our control.

"We may break into uncontrollable crying, or to the opposite extreme, laughter that seems excessive and unseemly. Part of emotional healing is gaining or perhaps regaining control over your emotions, and you should call time out on them when they seem to be speeding along, going their own way.

"A final precaution is almost the exact opposite of the one I've just mentioned," said Horton. "While it would be unhealthy to fall immediately into a substitute relationship instead of building a new relationship over time, it would be unhealthy as well to withdraw from people out of a mistaken idea that you are thereby honoring the memory of your loved one.

"The catch here is that we may go, almost at random, back and forth between these two extremes, seemingly without our control. To a degree, both of these extremes are normal and part of the healing process, and we should not load ourselves up with guilt if we find ourselves in either one of these extremes.

"The key, as before, is awareness, advance preparation, and realizing that no matter where we are on a given day, we shouldn't stay fixed there. In other words, we should apply the principle of moving forward. Now that's all the advice I have. Are you ready to have a good and productive day today?"

"Yes, we are, Mary. I think of you as much my friend as my doctor, and I do think you have given me excellent advice," said Elaine.

"And what do you plan to do today," asked Horton.

"Of course our main task is to plan Tommy Joe's funeral, but I want us to save time to drive around Miami, and maybe Mom and I can go shopping for some clothes for me as well."

"Well, I'm here if and when you need me, Elaine," said Horton. "Ms. Preston, you have a wonderful daughter, whom we here at Miami General have come to care a great deal about. We're glad to have had a tiny part in seeing her move toward what we believe will be a virtually full recovery."

"Well, thank you, Dr. Horton," said Ms. Preston. "And you, too, Dr. Sutherland, certainly."

"Sure. You folks have a good day. Be sure you coordinate with security, and we'll see you back here tonight, Elaine," said Sutherland.

"OK, Doctor, thanks," said Elaine as she and her mother and Spence boarded the elevator with the two security guards and rode it down to the first floor.

Spencer Foster called a rental car place and had them bring a minivan to the main entrance of Miami General Hospital. Then he and Emma Preston and her daughter, Elaine, and two security guards climbed in for a leisurely drive around Miami. They drove close enough to see the ocean in places and stopped at shopping malls a few times, where Elaine and her mother bought several new outfits.

At the end of the day on Wednesday they stopped by the Special Tactical Law Enforcement Team's offices to meet Cdr. Jeanne Hoover, the team's commanding officer, and Chief Walter Morelli, its operations officer.

Elaine told Hoover and Morelli of their plans for Tommy Joe's funeral in Hannibal at 2 p.m. on Saturday and were prepared to leave Friday morning and return Sunday morning.

"That will be just fine," Morelli told them. "Of course we will fly Tommy Joe's body to Hannibal for burial. Ms. Preston and Mr. Foster, you are welcome to fly to Hannibal and back with Elaine and our team members if you wish. That's up to you."

"We appreciate your kindness, Chief," said Spence. "We would like to ride with you if that's all right."

Thursday went quickly with more shopping and sight-seeing and a visit to a local community-based TBI rehab center where Elaine obtained enrollment forms.

On Friday, the flight to Hannibal began as scheduled at 6 a.m. as Elaine, Spence and Emma gathered in Morelli's office before boarding the chopper with Anderson, McGuffy and Hoover.

On the way, Spence stopped at a coin-operated newsstand box on the sidewalk and bought a copy of *The Miami Herald*. He took a quick look at the front page before rolling the paper up and carrying it under his arm.

"Federal Grand Jury Indicts 18 on Piracy Charges," the banner headline screamed across the front page.

"I see you and your team made the front page, Chief," Spence said as he walked into Morelli's office with Elaine and her mother.

"Well, we certainly played a big role in it, that's for sure, although U.S. Attorney Barton and his top assistant, Milton Richards, deserve a huge amount of credit," said Morelli. "We gathered a ton of powerful evidence, but it was still the lawyer boys who had to get it into some kind of order and run it past the grand jury. Now that the grand jury has indicted them, we do it all over again at trial. Then the judge hopefully will send them away for good."

Before Anderson boarded, Morelli pulled him aside:

"You will report upon your arrival in Hannibal to Capt. Ed Mitchell of the Coast Guard Cutter *Ambassador*," said Morelli. "Mitchell said you guys will have the run of the ship, but primarily he's offering you and McGuffy a bunk for two nights.

"Cdr. Hoover will be pulling a security shift with Elaine and her mother, either at Elaine's house or her mother's, their choice; I'm trying to get Mitchell to swing for Saturday dinner for you guys and for Elaine and her family aboard the *Ambassador* after the funeral, but he's still swimming in red tape on that one.

"He says the town of Hannibal is going to do something for them, too, and he doesn't want to seem to be competing with them. If he can get it worked out, it will be a joint act of hospitality between the town and the Coast Guard, although it will be held at the captain's table aboard his ship.

"It should be simple enough to arrange, but you know what they say about us bureaucrats, that we can jam up a one-car funeral. Don't hold your breath on that one. He'll inform you if it's happening. Any questions?"

"No, sir, I believe we're ready. I think I hear McGuffy starting the engines, which means all are aboard but me. I'll see you when we get back Sunday night, Chief," said Anderson.

"Well, call ahead. I'll be here if it's not too late. Main thing is, remember we've got precious cargo, and I don't mean just the dead man's body," said Morelli.

"Right, Chief. See you Sunday night," said Anderson, who swapped a salute with Morelli and went out the back door of the office to the helipad.

Morelli listened as the engines revved and the sound of the whop-whop-whop of the rotor grew louder and faster and then dimmed as the chopper rose over the city and headed north.

"Let them get there and back safely, Lord," Morelli said as he poured himself a mug of coffee, sat in his swivel chair, put his feet on his desk and read his own copy of *The Miami Herald*. "Yessir, we've got to do this one right."

Hoover sat next to Elaine in the second row of seats behind Anderson and McGuffy. Elaine's father-in-law sat behind Hoover, and her mother sat behind Elaine.

"This may seem like an inconvenience to you Elaine, but I've got stern orders from Dr. Sutherland that I'm supposed to put this special pillow on the area of your skull fracture," said Hoover as the helicopter reached its top speed. "The pillow will protect you from injury if we were to hit turbulence in flight or if you were to fall on the way to the porta-potty or for any other reason were to bump your head.

"So if you'll lean your seat as far back as you can, I'll attach the pillow with these self-adhesive strips. It's really a self-inflating air pillow, as you can see, and it has been configured from the scans Dr. Sutherland ran to exactly fit your head and the location of your fractures."

"Sure, he mentioned it to me, I believe," said Elaine, leaning her seat back. "I think I'll feel more secure on this flight with the pillow in place, although I remember flying in this same helicopter without anything at all on my wound nearly two weeks ago when Lieutenants Anderson and McGuffy rescued me from that sandbar island in the Gulf. And that, of course, was before Dr. Sutherland had removed that two-inch splinter from my brain. So I trust these guys in the front seats up there to get us there safely."

"Thanks for that compliment, Elaine. Flattery will get you anything we've got on this ship," said Anderson.

"Yeah, even including peanut butter and cracker sandwiches," said McGuffy. "I'm sure Joe's got a supply of them in his shirt pocket."

"No, Bob. This time I loaded the chow lockers. There's a whole bag of those sandwiches, but they're back there in the locker with some more substantial food," said Anderson. "And in case you didn't hear Chief Morelli back at his office there a few minutes ago, we have two refrigerator lockers full of sandwiches, enough to feed us both lunch and dinner tonight, and we have everything you can easily imagine as far as variety, I think. Same's true of the soft drinks, although I know Elaine's favorite is Diet Dr. Pepper, so we've got several bottles of that."

"Thanks, Joe. You're right on that," said Elaine.

After Hoover attached the special pillow on Elaine's head, she returned her seat to the upright position but leaned her head back on the pillow.

"This is really, really comfortable," said Elaine. "Much better than the ride that morning from the sandbar island. And of course, a big difference is I don't have a splitting headache today."

Over the next several hours, Elaine gave the crew, particularly her mother and Spence, a full report on what she had been through since she and Tommy Joe left a festive celebration in Hannibal now nearly three weeks ago on the Fisher King yacht, *Nautilus*, bound for Cancun.

Elaine recounted their kidnapping and their eventual showdown with the pirates.

"When my husband realized that they planned to torture and kill us, he made an attempt to escape while the pirates were on board the Colombian ship, and only the captain, Joe Brannigan, and his second-in-command, Vince Perkins, remained on board the pirate ship, *The Silver Bullet*," said Elaine.

"Unfortunately, Tommy Joe only had two bullets, and both of them missed their mark. So he threw down his gun and raised his arms, yelling 'Don't shoot!' but Brannigan began to make him dance by firing and just narrowly missing his feet," said Elaine.

"Then he told Perkins, who also had run out of bullets and had a beam lifted above my head, to let Tommy Joe see what they were going to do to me before they shot and killed him. And that's all I remember until I regained consciousness on the beach of that island two weeks ago this coming Monday morning."

Team members who knew the story well nevertheless listened again with as much rapt attention as Spence and Elaine's mother, who hadn't heard it before.

When Elaine finished, she seemed tired and asked to be excused for a few moments. Then she unfastened her seat belt, walked to the back of the cargo section, and knelt down at the metal vault that held the frozen body of her deceased husband. She spread her arms over the vault and lay her head against it and wept for a long time.

Chapter Eighteen

From the comfort and safety of a high-rise hotel less than a block from Miami General Hospital, Mose and Marty Perkins continued their surveillance of Elaine Foster's whereabouts and her steady recovery from a near-fatal brain injury inflicted by the Perkins boys' brother, Vincent.

Vincent, or 'Vince' as they called him, remained hospitalized in a secure medical cell on the third floor of the hospital with severe gunshot wounds to his left hip and shoulder and right calf. He was shot when Coast Guard SAS teams took over the suspected pirate ship *The Silver Bullet* on which Vince was second in command.

Vince knew he had seen Brannigan shoot Tommy Joe in the back, and he was pretty sure Brannigan heard but didn't see him swing the beam that knocked Elaine overboard. Thus, as far as Vince knew, Elaine was the only living witness to what he had done to her, and he wanted her dead by any means possible so she couldn't possibly testify against him in court.

Vince didn't know and didn't suspect that Elaine's brain injury had wiped out her memory of Vince's hitting her on the head. So he had persuaded his brothers, Mose and Marty, to travel to Miami from their home in Brownsville, Texas, either to help him escape federal custody or to find and kill Elaine and thus prevent her testifying against him.

Mose persuaded Marty to delay any plans to try to help him escape as well as any plans to capture and kill Elaine, in view of beefed-up security at the hospital, until she had recovered enough to venture outside, where she would be relatively unprotected.

Through high-power binoculars from his 12th-floor hotel room, Mose watched Elaine and McGuffy Tuesday afternoon as they walked to and from a local bank and to and from Viscaya Museum and Gardens a block or so from the hospital. And he spotted the two security guards who ran ahead of them to sniff out any danger and then tagged along behind them keeping watch over them.

Mose watched as Elaine and her mother and father-in-law and two security guards left the hospital parking deck Thursday morning in a rented van and traveled across town to a residential community support facility for TBI or traumatic brain injury patients.

Mose and Marty followed the van at a discreet distance in their own rented vehicle, a black Mercedes sedan.

While they waited from a shaded parking space in the rear of the facility's parking lot, Marty used a laptop computer and a cell phone connection to do a Google search on the facility. Marty learned and passed on to Mose that the facility was sponsored by a university medical school and staffed entirely with volunteers from the surrounding communities and by medical school students doing training as interns.

While Elaine and her mother and father-in-law were in the facility, the two security guards separated, with one remaining at the van and doing an occasional visual survey of the parking lot while the other stood just outside the door of the facility. Mose told Marty that one of the guards apparently had seen them parked but hadn't made any attempt to come their way. Before Elaine and her mother and father-in-law left the building, however, Mose told Marty it was time to go on back to the hotel.

At the hotel, Mose called the facility on his cell-phone and said he was interested in volunteering to serve as a member of the support staff if they needed any help. He said he understood that a friend of his who had a brain injury was seriously considering enrolling at the school, and that he was seriously considering volunteering to be of any help he could be to her.

"What is your friend's name?" asked the woman who answered the phone at the facility.

"Why, it's Elaine Foster, but she has been considering other options and may have changed her mind," said Mose.

"And what is your name, Sir?" asked the woman.

"Clay Houston," Mose lied, using the name of the unlicensed doctor that had treated Brannigan for the wound near his heart. "I was a licensed physician at one time, but there were some questions about some of my work in medical school, and while they were considering that and its possible effect on my license, I agreed to surrender my license. I'm telling you that in the spirit of full disclosure, but I want to make it very clear that I am considering volunteering solely as a layman."

"Well, Mr. Houston, I see your name on-line here, and it does appear that you have been at one time assigned a medical license," said the woman. "But as you said, it is marked 'on temporary hold.' So, solely as a layman, we'd be happy to consider you. And as far as your friend, Elaine Foster, is concerned, I am not at liberty to confirm or deny anything at all.

"OK, Ma'am," said Mose. "I'll be by later today or tomorrow and fill out my application. Bye. Good talking to you."

"Bye, Mr. Houston."

On his cell phone, Mose Perkins called Clay Houston, who was free from federal custody on $100,000 bail on charges of aiding and abetting piracy and a battery of other charges.

"Houston," he answered.

"Doc, this is Mose Perkins," said Mose.

"Yeah, what do you want?" asked Houston, with a tone of anger in his voice.

"Oh, I think you know what I want," said Mose. "Just in case Uncle Sam is listening to this call, though, which I suspect he is, I just wanted to see whether you are having a pleasant day and are expecting to have any more pleasant days in the near future."

"It was pleasant until you called," said Houston. "Look, I'm a busy man. I have things I need to do. I don't have time to play games. I asked what do you want?"

"Well, Doctor, I doubt seriously that you are a busy man, since you currently don't have a license to ply your usual trade, which is medicine, I believe," said Mose. "In fact, I suspect that you have quite a lot of time on your hands, waiting for your trial on federal piracy charges, isn't that right?"

"I don't have time for this. If you've got anything to say to me, say it," said Houston.

"Well, let's just keep it friendly, Doctor," said Mose. "I was going to suggest that you might have time to enjoy a greyhound race with me today. So if you'll meet me at the front office of the greyhound park in Hialeah exactly one hour from now, maybe we can talk with a bit more privacy for the both of us. What do you say?"

"Well, I guess I can move some of my appointments around so I can accommodate you," said Houston. "An hour from now you say?"

"That's right, Doctor," said Mose. "That will make it just about noon. So why don't we get a brat and suds lunch at one of the stands there. I'll treat you, and we can sit in the bleachers, where there should be plenty of room and plenty of privacy. What do you say?"

"I reckon I can do that. I'll see you at the front gate," said Houston. "How will I recognize you?"

"I'll be wearing my Stetson hat, Doc. See you there," said Mose as he ended the call.

Mose was at the sandwich stand at the greyhound park early, and the woman behind the counter had their order almost ready when Houston walked up and spoke to Mose, the only man around wearing a Stetson hat.

"Mr. Perkins?" Houston asked.

"Doctor Houston! Glad you could make it!" said Mose with fake enthusiasm, handing him his sandwich and beer. Houston nodded in the affirmative but said nothing, then Mose led Houston to a spot in the virtual center of the almost empty bleachers, far out of earshot of anyone else.

"Now, Doctor, before we begin, I've got a little medical apparatus here which I'm sure will be for our good health," said Mose. "This little scanning device will tell me immediately if you're wired with a hidden mike and whether what we're saying is being recorded by the good old FBI in one of those apparently empty panel trucks over there in the parking lot. It won't hurt a bit."

Mose waved a tiny metal wand quickly around the doctor.

"There, you're clean. Didn't hurt much, did it?" Mose asked him.

"Look, you don't have to keep dragging this out. I'm not stupid enough to wear a wire, simply because I'd just as soon the government not know that I'm talking to you at all," said Houston. "Now if we can reach an arrangement that will be to the good of both of us as far as the feds are concerned, I'm willing within reason to see if I can work out something. Now if I remember our last conversation, you wanted me to say on the witness stand in court that your brother Vincent did everything Brannigan told him, and was completely acting under Brannigan's orders on everything he did, without bucking him or in any way leading a mutiny."

"That's right, Doctor. You have a good memory," said Mose. "What else do you remember?"

"I remember telling you that I would have no trouble testifying to that, because that is exactly the full truth as far as I know it," said Houston. "Now my question to you is, what will Vincent testify about me?"

"Ah, now that's where the whole testimony thing gets a bit cloudy and Vince's memory becomes a bit uncertain," said Mose. "If, under the pressure of the courtroom, Vince simply is unable to remember seeing you offering any medical treatment at all to him or to Captain Brannigan, that would be greatly to your benefit, I understand. But on the other hand, if Vince remembers seeing you giving him and Brannigan shots of antibiotics and morphine, checking their pulse and blood pressure and such things as that, then you are at risk of feeling a bit uncomfortable in the courtroom. Have I understood your situation, Doctor?"

"Yeah. Yeah. So what do you need me to do that would be ethical for me as a physician?" asked Houston.

"Tut-tut. That's a few rungs higher than the proper standard, Doctor Houston," said Mose. "I have been using the term 'doctor' as a courtesy title. We both know, don't we, Doctor, that your medical license is on hold, and of course if you were to get convicted of piracy, kidnapping, murder and such unethical things as that, then you would be unlikely from the confines of the federal death chamber to reclaim your physician's license, wouldn't you."

"So what do you want me to do?" Houston asked again.

"I was hoping you would ask that question in just that way, Doctor," said Mose. "Let me answer it this way: One of my brother's very favorite people in the whole world, a Ms. Elaine Foster, less than two hours ago visited a nearby residential rehabilitation facility operated by the local university medical school. She filled out an application to live there starting next week, possibly as early as Monday. That rehab facility is there for two very good reasons: one, it's the Miami-Dade community's way of reaching out to people who have suffered traumatic brain injury."

"TBI. I'm familiar with it," said Houston. "What about it?"

"Well, as I'm sure you know, Ms. Foster suffers from TBI, and another reason rehab facilities are there for people suffering from TBI is to train interns and students at the local med school on how to properly care for brain-injured or TBI people," said Mose. "As you might imagine, these interns and students are there for the experience, and are paid virtually nothing, just like the dozens of volunteers, some doctors, some nurses and some laymen, who volunteer their time there without pay."

"Yeah. I said I was familiar with it. What's your point?" asked Houston.

"Well, now that your medical license is on hold, and it wouldn't be exactly ethical, much less legal, for you to resume your rather profitable medical practice, Vince and I figured you'd have a little extra time on your hands, such that you could volunteer your services as a layman at the rehab center, where as I said, one of Vince's favorite people in all the world will be enrolling next week, perhaps as early as Monday," said Houston.

"You want me to volunteer as a non-medical volunteer at the rehab center and be there when Elaine Foster gets there next week?" asked Houston.

"Bingo!" said Mose. "By dogies, I think you've got it."

"Well, what do you expect me to do? Empty bedpans?" asked Houston.

"Now that might fit your training and experience perfectly, Doctor, but Vince and I expect you to be a bit more creative than that," said Houston. "We expect you to meet and introduce yourself to Ms. Foster and after a while to use your magnetic personality to win her confidence and trust. We would hope that you also would win the trust of the volunteers and medical staff and security officers as well, so that you would have free access to her room, day or night, without raising any suspicions."

"It sounds like you're trying to get me killed," said Houston.

"No, Doctor, we mean you no harm, and we will do everything we can to see that you come to no harm, because as we discussed earlier, my brother, Vince, needs your testimony in court," said Mose. "So we have a plan that will be of no real danger to you at all."

"What kind of plan?" asked Houston. "Don't you realize that if that girl moves to that rehab facility, the FBI and other federal agents will be swarming all over it, day and night, and I'm sure they'll check me out immediately and discover that I'm a physician without license, free on bond, pending trial on federal charges. You guys have got to be crazy to think a lame-brained scheme like that would work. As I said, it's a good way for me to get the death penalty on the spot, before I even get to trial."

"Not if you do what we tell you, Doctor," said Mose. "Now here's the plan, which will be timed to Ms. Foster's testimony in federal court. We may get very little advance notice as to the day and time she's going to testify.

"All you have to do is to use your knowledge and expertise, Doctor, to see that on the morning that she is scheduled to testify, she oversleeps a bit, say, three or four or five hours. In fact, I'm sure they will check and find that she was so distressed that she took an overdose of sleeping pills, which she won't remember taking. Poor memory is just one of the symptoms of her injury. Now, we don't even want you to try to pilfer those pills from their pharmacy stock, because I'm sure they monitor who gets what very carefully. But I'm sure you have drugs in your black bag or know a pharmacy where you can get them over the counter, that will make Ms. Foster want to stretch out her nap time by several hours."

"So you want me to add overt murder to all the other charges against me," said Houston. "I hope to practice medicine again someday, I'll have you know. I simply won't be dragged into another murder!"

"Oh, Doctor, you misunderstand. We're not asking you to murder anybody. Anybody else, I guess I should say. Now, to be sure, if you are careless enough to give our

Ms. Foster a lethal dose of sleeping pills, then she would be dead, tsk, tsk, and you would hardly qualify as an ethical future practicing physician it would seem," said Mose.

"But if you are as careful as the good doctor you claim you someday want to be, then you will select just the right sleeping compound and just the right degree of overdose, and just the right time to administer it, so that Ms. Foster will be very, very late for court. Then when and if she does finally get there, she will be too sleepy to testify.

"Then if the feds are persistent enough to re-schedule her testimony for another day and time, and if the judge permits it after her first performance, then we would expect you to administer a second dose, or rather overdose, in just the right degree so that Ms. Foster again is late at best and then again too sleepy to testify if and when she makes it to court. It wouldn't hurt if jurors thought she was either drunk or incoherent because of her terrible brain injury.

"Then after Ms. Foster is removed from the witness stand, without her testimony, she will be able to catch up on her sleep in the safety of her new rehab quarters and will be none the worse for wear and tear. Now, Doctor, don't you consider that a quite ethical alternative to sliding on a greased rail into the death chamber?"

"Don't toy with me, Perkins," said Houston. "If you push me too far, I may recall that I saw your brother leading a mutiny against Brannigan and in fact was the man who shot him and narrowly missed his heart. Do you hear me, Perkins? Think about it! I'm out of here!"

Houston left the park, threw the rest of his sandwich and bottle of beer in a trash can at the entrance, stormed angrily back to his car and sped away. Mose looked at his watch and quietly finished his meal and left the park as it began to fill with customers for the next dog race. Then he drove back to his hotel room and shared the rest of the morning's events with Marty.

"It seems you may have pushed the good doctor too far," said Marty. "I thought you were smarter than that, Big Brother."

"Don't get sassy with me, kid," said Mose. "I'll turn you over my knee and whip you with an electric cord if you smart off to me. Mom should have named you Smarty instead of Marty."

"Wo! I touched a nerve there, did I, Big Brother?" asked Marty. "Well, tell me this. What do you plan to do to get the good doctor back on track?"

"He's not off track," said Mose. "He's just smarting off like you were. He'll figure out which side his bread is buttered on when he cools down a bit. You wait and see. When he thinks it over a while, he'll realize my plan was doggone good for him as well as for Vince, and he'll call me back. I think he knows Vince would just as soon send his no-good hide to the death chamber as to look at him. Yeah. He'll call back. You wait and see."

At that moment, Mose's cell phone rang and he answered it, "Mose."

"Mr. Perkins, this is Clay Houston," came the voice on the phone. "I'm sorry I stormed away like that. I reacted in anger, and I apologize. I think your plan has merit, and I should be able to carry it out without a hitch."

"That's good, Doc. I was hoping you'd see it that way," said Mose. "Now I have taken the liberty of calling the rehab center, you might say on your behalf. In fact, I borrowed your name for just a few minutes, told the young lady on the phone that Ms. Foster was a friend of yours and that you were considering volunteer work at the rehab center so that you could spend more time with her.

"I also mentioned that you were applying as a layman, but in the spirit of full disclosure, mentioned that your medical license has a temporary hold on it because of some questions about some work you did in medical school. The young lady verified your license suspension on-line and said it shouldn't hinder you from volunteer work as a layman. Finally, I told her you'd probably be in to fill out the application as a lay volunteer."

"Mr. Perkins, your crass presumption that I'm going to do your bidding from now on has got to stop," Houston said. "How dare you 'borrow my name for a few minutes.' You are guilty of ID theft and outright fraud! If I didn't have these charges pending against me, so help me I'd prefer charges against you immediately, you can believe that. And it better not happen again, or I'm ready to go down with the ship and take Perkins and Brannigan with me. Do you hear me?"

"Loud and clear, Doctor," said Mose. "Just don't get bent out of shape. Now I would suggest you mosey on out to that rehab center and fill out all the paperwork and red tape to volunteer your services. You want to know the lay of the land quite well when Ms. Foster checks in on Monday. Is there anything else?"

"Yeah. Who's going to keep me posted on when I am to do this? You?"

"Yours truly, Doctor. I'll keep in touch," said Mose, ending the call. Then to Marty he asked, "Now is there anything you want to tell your big brother?"

"Yeah," said Marty. "You da Man, Mose! You da Man!"

"See that you don't forget it."

Chapter Nineteen

As the Coast Guard helicopter carrying Elaine and her mother and father-in-law and the body of her deceased husband made its way up the Mississippi River, Anderson, the pilot, called out the names of cities along the way like Memphis and St. Louis that were ablaze as virtual seas of bright lights.

But as they neared Hannibal, Anderson told Elaine she might want to look out her window to see below them the landing pad marked with a lighted "X" and in the riverside park, hundreds of lighted candles in small mounds of sand inside brown paper bags that spelled out the words, WELCOME HOME, ELAINE!

She was overcome with emotion and wept for several minutes as her mother and Hoover tried in vain to comfort her.

As the chopper landed, the *Ambassador*'s captain, Ed Mitchell, carrying a wreath of red roses, and Hannibal Mayor James Steadman, carrying a golden ribbon and a cardboard cutout of the key to the city, greeted Elaine and her family. Elaine dried her tears and met them with the biggest smile she could muster. A huge crowd cheered as Elaine and her mother and father-in-law stepped off the chopper.

"Elaine, we're happy to welcome you and your family back to your town and ours," said Steadman, handing her the key. "It's a time for celebration as well as sadness, as we all mourn the loss of our brother and your dear mate, Tommy Joe Foster. We honor you with this token of our esteem and expression of our sympathy, and may you be known from this point forward as `The Unsinkable Elaine Foster.'"

The crowd cheered again and Mitchell spoke.

"Elaine, we, the men and women of the United States Coast Guard, mourn your loss and that of your family and this community, and we take this opportunity to pledge to you all that we will not rest until the perpetrators of this violence against you and your husband are brought to justice," said Mitchell to another round of applause and cheers.

"We were advised that this day, as you left Miami, where you have found safe haven and healing, the good citizens of that city have returned a grand jury indictment requiring that these accused of piracy on the high seas must now stand trial in a court of law. May it hasten the day that all of them will have received just recompense for these crimes," said Mitchell, placing the wreath of roses on a stand as the crowd again cheered.

"Thank you all for coming out to welcome me home, and thank you, Mayor, and you, Captain Mitchell, for your kind expressions of sympathy," said Elaine. "It means a lot to me and my family. As you may know, we will have my beloved husband Tommy Joe's funeral at the First Presbyterian Church tomorrow at 2 p.m. We invite as many of you as can to join us as we bid him our last farewell in a memorial service at graveside. As you may not know, I will be returning on Sunday to Miami, where I expect to testify against our attackers in the days ahead in a federal court trial. I look forward to the day, however, when I shall return to Hannibal to renew old friendships and establish new ones. Now, if you'll excuse us, we have had a long and tiring journey and, we'll say goodnight until the funeral tomorrow. God bless you all and good night."

Hoover accepted Elaine's invitation to join her and her mother at Elaine's home for the night, while Anderson and McGuffy got Mitchell's permission to accept Spence's invitation for them to spend the night at his place. Members of Emma's, Elaine's and Spence's church groups promised to bring a full Saturday morning breakfast to Elaine's house.

After breakfast, as they waited for the funeral hour, Elaine, Emma and Spence took Anderson, McGuffy and Hoover on a quiet and peaceful walk through Hannibal's riverside park and some of the other nearby sights, including the Fisher King boat shop where the *Nautilus* was built. They also visited Mark Twain's birthplace and had lunch at Elaine's from food again brought in and left by neighbors. Tommy Joe's brother, J.T., and Elaine's sisters, Angela and Marcia, and their spouses and children joined them for lunch and conversation and visitation at the church before the funeral.

Jeffrey Sides, CEO of Fisher King, the boat manufacturing company where Tommy Joe had worked for years, expressed to Elaine his sorrow at Tommy Joe's death. He repeated his previous offer of a full-time job for Elaine if and when she moved back to Hannibal.

Helen Petree, friend, former classmate and loan officer at the Bank of Hannibal who helped her get money from her checking account wired to Miami on Tuesday afternoon, came by with her boss, Roger Hall, president of the bank. Elaine thanked them both for helping her out of a financial tight spot.

Hall repeated his suggestion on the phone Tuesday that Elaine should touch base with him when and if she decided to return to Hannibal and to help build another yacht to replace the *Nautilus*.

Elaine's biggest surprise, however, came from Teddy Johnson, the insurance agent who had sold Sides a $1.5 million policy on the *Nautilus* and had sold Elaine and her husband a $1 million life insurance policy on each other for their trip to Cancun. Johnson, a part owner of the insurance company, said he was prepared to present her with a life insurance claim check for $1 million plus a separate $150,000 check for her share of the claim for the loss of the *Nautilus*.

"I have the paperwork filled out, Elaine," said Johnson. "I have taken statements for my records from your Cdr. Hoover as to the results of her autopsy on Tommy Joe and the physical evidence of the destruction of the *Nautilus*. All you'll need to do is come by my office and sign the papers. I have the checks already cut with your name on them in my top desk drawer. I figured that might come in handy for you during your remaining days in Miami."

"Why, yes, I guess it will," said Elaine, who turned suddenly pale and seemed to have a momentary difficulty maintaining her balance. "Unfortunately, Teddy, we're headed back to Miami early Sunday morning, and I know that you're closed on Saturday afternoons, so I guess we'll just have to take care of that later."

"Oh, I will be open for a while this afternoon, if you think you could come by," said Johnson. "And I see Roger Hall is still here. I would just bet he would open his bank a few minutes on Saturday afternoon if he thought a good customer wanted to deposit more than $1 million in his bank. Would you like for me to ask him for you?"

"Uh, Teddy, I don't know. I've never done any of this before and I'm not sure just how to handle it, I'm afraid. What would you suggest?" asked Elaine.

"What I've just said is my suggestion. Come by my office, sign the papers, pick up the checks, and I'll go with you to the bank. Certainly you don't want to be carrying that kind of money around even in the form of a check," said Johnson. "And I'm not an investment counselor or anything, but that much money in a certificate of deposit would earn a tidy sum of daily interest."

"Well, OK. If you'll talk to Mr. Hall for me I'd appreciate it, and if you could go with me to the bank I'd appreciate that as well," said Elaine.

"Glad to. What I'm here for. Don't mention it," said Johnson, who seemed instantly gone and suddenly was some distance away talking to Hall, who was smiling broadly and shaking his head up and down in the affirmative.

"It's all worked out, Elaine," Johnson said moments later. "I'll be at my office after the funeral."

"Thanks, Teddy," said Elaine. "I'll see you then."

Elaine and her family took the funeral home's recommendation and didn't have an open casket ceremony. They did have a private viewing for family members at Elaine's request, but only she and Spence and J.T. viewed the body.

"I didn't recognize him when I buried him in the sand on the island the other morning, and I haven't seen him since I regained my memory, so I simply have to see his face one final time," she said.

"It's really you, my precious," she said softly as she stood alone by the open casket and let her tears flow. "I'll see you in heaven."

After the ceremony in the cemetery, Elaine and her family were invited to Capt. Mitchell's private suite on board the *Ambassador*, where they and Anderson, McGuffy and Hoover were to be served a complimentary early evening meal. Before the meal, however, Elaine asked for a brief time off for errands. She and Hoover went by Teddy Johnson's office. Elaine signed the insurance papers, then Johnson gave them both a ride to the Bank of Hannibal, where Roger Hall processed the deposit of her checks totaling $1.15 million and gave her $2,000 in cash from her account at her request for "spending money."

After the meal with Capt. Mitchell and a period of quiet reflection and conversation around his table, Elaine and family and the special team's members left the Coast Guard cutter and spent the night as they had done the night before, with Hoover, Emma and Elaine at Elaine's house, and Anderson, McGuffy and Spence at Spence's house.

They all met at a fast-food restaurant for breakfast at 6 a.m. Sunday before loading their sandwich lockers for the trip home, boarding the chopper and heading back to Miami. They arrived in Miami sometime after dark. Morelli was on hand to greet them.

"Welcome back, folks! Glad you made it back safely. That's an answered prayer. Thank you, Lord," said Morelli.

"Good to be back, Chief," said Anderson as he killed the chopper's engines and they all stepped out on the pad.

"They're having an arraignment before Judge Steele for Brannigan, Perkins and cohorts at 9 a.m. on Monday," Morelli told them. "Nothing says you have to be there for the arraignment, because it's a preliminary appearance, where they show up if they want to or send their lawyers if they don't and enter a formal plea to the government's charges, guilty or not or no contest. Do as you like. Judge Steele is likely to set the date for trial at that time, so that will let us know when the fireworks really begin. My recommendation, do as you like, but sleep late if you want to."

"Well, I thought we might help Elaine tomorrow with a few more of her chores, like getting her driver's license, getting her some kind of car, and maybe some more clothes," said Spence.

"Oh, yes. I wanted to help her buy some more clothes, and I wanted to go back out to the rehab center with her, see if they've processed her application and have agreed to accept her as a resident," said Emma. "Then if so, we'll help her get situated in her new apartment. Dr. Sutherland said he would at that point dismiss her as a patient at the hospital. Then I guess Spence and I can discuss how much longer we need to stay down here. I'd like to be here when the trial is going on, but that may take weeks, and I know we can never afford that. What do you think, Chief Morelli?"

"I think it could get expensive, yes Ma'am, but that's an excellent plan to get Elaine situated tomorrow, it seems to me," said Morelli. "I believe tomorrow morning while they're in court would be the perfect time to get Elaine out to the rehab facility and get her checked in without any of those thugs or their lawyers or the media seeing her.

"I've asked for two new security guards to stand watch with you on the 11th floor of the hospital tonight, Elaine, but I'm going to ask Lt. Hoover and Ensign McGuffy to work security with you tomorrow as you go out to the rehab center.

"And we'll work out security arrangements for Tuesday and beyond after that. So you folks have a pleasant evening, and I'd appreciate it if you will check back with me Monday afternoon around five. Is that alright?"

"That's great, Chief," said Spence. "We'll post you on what we were able to get done at that time."

"See you then," said Morelli as they bade him goodbye.

"I guess we'll meet you for breakfast in the hospital cafeteria again tomorrow morning before heading out to the rehab center, Elaine. Is that all right?" asked Ms. Preston.

"That's fine, Mom. I'll see you both then," she said, hugging her mom and father-in-law good night before they went their separate ways for the evening.

Elaine got a snack and took it to her room, while Spence and Emma went to the restaurant in their hotel for their evening meal before turning in for the night.

Mose and Marty Perkins were among several dozen people in U.S. District Judge Francis Steele's courtroom Monday at 9 a.m. for the arraignment of Joe Brannigan, Vince Perkins and others on piracy and other charges.

Brannigan and several other defendants had their own lawyers. Steele appointed lawyers for Perkins and others, whom he declared indigent and not able to hire an attorney based on their sworn affidavits.

Brownsville, Texas, lawyer Jeb Smoot, representing Brannigan, and just-appointed lawyers representing most of the other defendants, filed waivers and pleas of not guilty with the clerk of the federal court. A few defendants, including Clay Houston, the Miami physician whose license was temporarily suspended, stood as the judge's clerk called their names and told Steele, "Not guilty, Your Honor."

Assistant U.S. Attorney Milton Richards then stood and addressed the judge:

"Your Honor, the United States asks leave of the court to withdraw the indictment and its stated charges as to some defendants who will be identified following trial in exchange for their testimony against other defendants charged in this case," said Richards.

"As Your Honor knows, the federal Racketeering Influenced and Corrupt Organization or RICO statute authorizes the United States, in the interests of justice, to grant immunity from prosecution to one or more members of a corrupt organization in exchange for their testimony in the prosecutions of other members of the organization."

"Does the United States contend that the defendants in this case were engaged in a common enterprise of corruption, Mr. Richards?" asked Steele.

"We do, Your Honor," said Richards.

"What is the name and nature of the alleged enterprise, Mr. Richards?" asked Steele.

"The enterprise, Your Honor, was maritime piracy, as our indictment alleges, and it was being waged mercilessly and with shameless violence upon unsuspecting and defenseless travelers in the Gulf of Mexico by one Joe Brannigan of Brownsville, Texas, captain of the pirate ship *The Silver Bullet*, and his second-in-command, Vincent Perkins, and the crew, surviving members of whom comprise all the remaining defendants."

"Objection, Your Honor," said Smoot, attorney for Brannigan, who wore his trademark red shirt, brown jacket, black boots and a black felt hat which he placed on the counsel table in front of him.

"Identify yourself and your client for the record, Mr. Smoot," said Steele.

"Certainly, as Your Honor knows, I am Jeb Smoot, attorney for defendant Joseph Brannigan," said Smoot.

"State your objection, Mr. Smoot," said Steele.

"The indictment cited by Mr. Richards is defective, Your Honor, and should be quashed, voided and rendered of no effect, because it violates the constitutional rights of my client and all others named under it to due process of law, authority for which certainly no citation is necessary," said Smoot.

"In what way do you contend your client's rights are being violated, Mr. Smoot?" asked Steele.

"Your Honor, the charge of piracy, though admittedly mentioned in the language of the Constitution, is so vague as to its contents and components that it is impossible for my client, Mr. Brannigan, to know what the United States complains of and accuses him of having done against the peace and dignity of the people," said Smoot. ``To know with particularity what one is accused of is the bedrock, the essence, of due process of law, which certainly even Mr. Richards knows, yet which the indictment he has ventured to offer in this case runs over recklessly and roughshod. Thus, Your Honor, we renew our motion to throw it out."

"Mr. Richards. Your response," said Steele.

"Your Honor, I'm surprised that Mr. Smoot would cite the language of the Constitution itself in its reference to the crime of maritime piracy, since the drafters certainly intended for such crime to be prosecuted and left it up to Congress to fashion its content and boundaries," said Richards.

"Perhaps in perusing his copy of our nation's organic law, Mr. Smoot may have noted that the framers of our Constitution mentioned the crime of piracy as a crime against all mankind and civilization itself, and is punishable by civilized peoples everywhere by the sentence of death. The United States, incidentally Your Honor, intends to request the death penalty against his client, Mr. Brannigan, and his cohort in crime, Mr. Perkins, upon their convictions in this case."

"Your Honor, despite Mr. Richards' rhetoric, he has failed to give Your Honor and my client any definition of piracy which identifies it with the requisite specificity and circumscribes the offense which this wholly deficient indictment accuses my client, Mr. Brannigan, of having committed," said Smoot.

"Well let me advise you, Mr. Smoot, and you as well, Mr. Richards, that you both are to address your comments in this case to me and not to nor toward your fellow counsel. And I could use considerably less rhetoric from you both," said Steele. "And you, Mr. Richards, need to address the content of Mr. Smoot's objection to your indictment in your next turn at bat, or I'm going to declare you and your indictment out of this proceeding. Now let's go."

"Yes, Your Honor," said Richards. "I would state to Your Honor that Mr. Smoot's objection is meritless, since for nearly 200 years the U.S. Supreme Court has held that maritime piracy, quite simply and specifically, consists of robbery on the high seas. The United States intends to prove, Your Honor, that Mr. Brannigan and others named in this indictment also committed a battery of other crimes, including murder, kidnapping, destruction of private property and drug trafficking, which fit the pattern envisioned by Congress in its passage of the RICO statute."

"Thank you, Mr. Richards. What was the citation on that U.S. Supreme Court holding?"

"It was U.S. v. Smith, dated Feb. 25, 1820, Your Honor," said Richards, offering a copy of the ruling to Steele's clerk. She stamped it and passed it on to Steele, who then scanned it and handed it back to her.

"The court rules that the indictment meets the specificity requirement of due process of law. Mr. Smoot, your motion is denied," said Steele.

"Your Honor, I would like to request further argument and the citation of additional holdings in support of my motion," said Smoot.

"Denied," said Steele. "Now a word to counsel in this case. I have seen the catalog of the government's evidence, which appears to be both clear-cut and substantial, and I consider the maximum penalty upon conviction in these cases to be death. Now the government is prohibited from using the death penalty as leverage to obtain a guilty plea, but the government is authorized to use the offer of leniency to obtain testimony from defendants under the RICO statute. So I say to you whom I have appointed this day as counsel, that you should seriously consider negotiating with Mr. Richards as to a revised plea for your client or clients.

"Now a word to defense counsel about arguments as to the law. I consider the application of the RICO statute in cases such as these to be settled law, for which citations are legion. You may argue and cite authorities to the contrary, to which Mr. Richards will be given the opportunity to rebut. However, we won't take up courtroom time for that purpose. Offer your citations and arguments in a brief and file it with my clerk. I will scan it, and if you haven't received a positive ruling from me by the start of the trial in this case, consider your motion denied.

"Now, the key question. How much of the next two weeks will it take defense counsel to prepare for trial?" asked Steele. "I understand the government is ready now to proceed."

There were gasps and moans from the defense counsel, and Steele struck the gavel.

"I'll have order in the court," he said.

One lawyer who had been named moments earlier to represent one of the defendants stood and addressed Steele.

"Your Honor, as Your Honor knows, I was just named a few minutes ago to represent one of the defendants in this case, a member of the crew of *The Silver Bullet*," said the lawyer, Roberta Sparks. "I have conferences and court appearances scheduled virtually around the clock in other cases for the next two weeks. I won't have time even for an initial visit with my client in the next two weeks. It should be clear to the court that two weeks' preparation for a case of this magnitude is totally unrealistic and impractical."

"And how long do you think it would take a conscientious attorney to meet with and interview your client in this case and prepare for trial, Ms. Sparks?" asked Steele.

"Three to six months, Your Honor," said Sparks.

"Then it seems that you have made a very good case for what I suggested earlier," said Steele. "Unless there are activities of your client which the government has charged are separate and apart from those of the rest of the crew in this case, and which the government has said it intends to draw out and offer evidence against them separately, then I would suggest you should consider plea negotiations with Mr. Richards. Failing that, Ms. Sparks, I would suggest you might ask to resign your appointment as counsel for that particular client and I'll name a replacement."

"Your Honor," said another attorney, Mike Henson, standing up to address Steele. "I would agree with Ms. Sparks, Sir, that two weeks is not enough time for me to prepare for trial, but after having read the indictment just now, it seems like an extremely straightforward case about which there is likely to be virtually no dispute as to the facts, and in view of Your Honor's rulings today, no dispute as to the law as well. I will contact my client today as to a revised plea and will be prepared to make our decision known to the court by this time tomorrow."

"In view of the comments of Ms. Sparks and Mr. Henson, I'll delay my decision for 24 hours, and I'll see you gentlemen and ladies at 10 a.m. on Tuesday. Court is dismissed," said Steele as he gaveled the proceeding closed and walked out of the courtroom.

Before the defense lawyers in the piracy case left U.S. District Judge Francis Steele's courtroom after arraignment proceedings on Monday morning, Richards told them he would be available immediately in the courtroom and throughout the day in his office to discuss a recommendation of leniency for each defendant who would offer to testify for the government or to plead guilty.

"What exactly are you willing to do for my client, Mr. Richards?" attorney Roberta Sparks asked him.

"I don't know, Ms. Sparks. Who is your client?" asked Richards.

"I was named this morning to represent Vincent Perkins," said Sparks.

"Let me put it this way, Ms. Sparks," said Richards. "The clear and complete villains in this case in our view are Joe Brannigan and Vince Perkins. They organized and carried out their regime of piracy, kidnapping, drug trafficking, destruction of property and murder.

"But they also enlisted and directed the crew, who went along with their schemes instead of resisting them. Thus we'll ask the jury to return a guilty verdict against them all, kingpins and crew alike.

"And if they are so convicted, as we expect, the United States intends to ask Judge Steele to impose the death penalty on them all. And I think you know his past record in that regard.

"However, if the crew as a whole, who slaughtered the crew of the *San Pedro* and carted off its cargo of illegal drugs but didn't kidnap the man and his wife from Hannibal, Missouri, and didn't shoot him in the back and bludgeon her with a wooden beam in an effort to kill her, and didn't blow up their yacht, and didn't booby-trap *The Silver Bullet* to blow up and murder two Coast Guard sailors in cold blood, then I think justice would be served by offering rank and file crewmen an opportunity to plead guilty to a lesser charge of maritime piracy, for which we are prepared to recommend a more lenient sentence than death."

"Mr. Richards, it appears clear in summary that you expect the jury to convict Brannigan and Perkins and everyone else who refuses to plead guilty to piracy under the broad terms of the general indictment, and that you intend to ask Judge Steele to send them all to the death chamber," said Henson

"That's right, Mr. Henson," said Richards.

"On the other hand, you are prepared to recommend a lesser sentence for those who plead guilty to simple piracy, is that right?" asked Henson.

"Correct, Mr. Henson," said Richards.

"How much of a lesser sentence are you prepared to recommend if my client pleads guilty to the general piracy count only?" asked Henson.

"Well, that will depend to some extent on the evidence, Mr. Henson," said Richards. "The starting point for everyone other than Brannigan and Perkins will be a recommendation of thirty years in prison on a plea of guilty to general piracy. If the evidence, however, shows that a particular crew member obeyed orders from Brannigan or Perkins or both to booby-trap *The Silver Bullet* so that it would blow up and take the lives of two Coast Guard sailors, or to shoot the man from Hannibal in the back or bludgeon his wife in an attempt to kill her, or to blow up their yacht, then a guilty plea to piracy in those instances where murder was carried out or attempted would carry a recommendation of life in prison. In the case of destroying the yacht, we would recommend forty years in prison."

"Well, I'll have to consult with my client on this, but I may be in a position after I've reviewed the facts of his involvement or lack of involvement to discuss a revised plea, or perhaps immunity in exchange for his testimony, Mr. Richards," said Henson.

"I look forward to talking with you, Mr. Henson, and with any of the other counsel in this case," said Richards. "I'd recommend to defense counsel that you talk with your clients today, then let me know by 8 a.m. tomorrow if your clients intend to change their pleas. If I don't see or hear from you by then, I'll expect to lock in the plea filed today and proceed to trial."

"We'll let you know," said Henson.

"And I'll call you after I've talked with Mr. Perkins," said Sparks.

"Good enough. I'll see you tomorrow morning, then," said Richards, gathering up the papers on his desk as though preparing to leave the courtroom. Then when only he and Henson remained, Richards stopped and faced Henson.

"Oh, by the way, Mr. Henson. Who is your client?" Richards asked.

"Jim Cummings," said Henson. "I've never met him, and the court's appointment paper says he is being held in protective custody at his own request at an undisclosed location. Can you shed any light on his situation, where he is being held, and how I can talk with him?"

"Perhaps I can, Mr. Henson," said Richards, speaking in hushed tones.

"We interviewed Mr. Cummings at length while he was awaiting medical attention on the *San Pedro*. His account of the multiple crimes committed in this case clearly and completely implicate Brannigan and Perkins in the most serious of the crimes," said Richards. "We consider his testimony for the United States to be absolutely vital to the successful prosecution of Brannigan and Perkins, thus we are prepared to offer him absolute immunity from prosecution as to each and every charge in our indictment.

"He is being held in protective custody at his own request at an undisclosed location because he believes and we believe his life would be in danger if Brannigan and Perkins even knew he was alive, but particularly if they also knew his location," said Richards. "We are prepared, Mr. Henson, to make him available to you, with appropriate security force present, at whatever time and place you suggest."

"Well, can you bring him to my office downtown or would you prefer to take me to him?" asked Henson.

"Mr. Henson, you would have no way of knowing it, but Mr. Cummings was severely injured. He says that he took no part in the attack on the *San Pedro*, but his arm was practically shot off during the assault; so Brannigan, Perkins and crew left him to bleed to death or to go down with the ship, which later sank in the Gulf.

"Unknown to Brannigan, Perkins and crew, however, the Coast Guard rescued Cummings after the pirates left the area. We provided good and swift medical help for him and were able to save his arm. But he is still in serious condition. So it would be better if you could interview him in his hospital room, but there is a conference room nearby if you prefer that."

"What hospital are we talking about?" asked Henson.

"Miami General, which is practically next door," said Richards. "But the security measures are extensive, so we would have to issue special badges to you. So why don't you meet me at my office at 1 p.m. and I'll walk you over?" asked Richards.

"Fine. I'll see you then," said Henson, who walked out of the courthouse with Richards, but the two men then turned and walked in different directions.

Chapter Twenty

Elaine Foster met her mom and her father-in-law at the hospital cafeteria for breakfast early on the Monday morning after Tommy Joe's funeral on Saturday.

"It's been exactly two weeks today, Mom, since I washed ashore unconscious on that sandbar island," said Elaine as she pushed her tray through the serving line.

"It seems like an eternity ago, but so much has happened. I have come so far since then. That morning, alone on that beach with the worst headache of my life, and without food, water or medical care, I thought the rest of my life was about to pass by in the next few minutes. I really thought I was dying, and I believe I was near death."

"Well, what got you on such a morbid track this morning?" asked Elaine's Mom, Emma Preston.

"Oh, it's not morbid to me!" said Elaine. "I know we have all been through a heart-wrenching trauma in the loss of Tommy Joe, and I'm still sore and numb too from that, but I can't avoid feeling thankful that God has spared my life for his purpose, which only he understands. And as I search in the days ahead for his plan for my life, I'm going to do my best to be thankful for what he has given me instead of bitter about what and who I have lost.

"I'm overcome with gladness that God seemingly miraculously rescued me, from that deserted island and from death itself, and I just can't express how thankful I am for that."

"You seem to be doing a pretty good job of it," said her father-in-law, Spencer Foster. "But if you're that thankful, why don't you bless our bacon and eggs so we can eat them before they get cold?"

"I'd be glad to," said Elaine. "God, thank you for this day, for this family, and this food. Thank you for the miracle of healing and restoration you have given me over the past two weeks. Thank you for sending Mom and Papa Spence to be with me today, and while I haven't had an opportunity yet to share the news with them, I thank you also, Lord, for the tremendous financial bounty you caused to be poured out on me on Saturday as we prepared to leave Hannibal.

"And I'd like to thank my dear husband Tommy Joe, who's there with you now, for his part in providing the bounty that now has come my way, although I would trade it all for him back in a heartbeat. I know you know that, God, but I wanted to tell him. Now bless us we pray, this day, and thank you again for our food. Amen."

"What was that about?" Emma asked Elaine, staring her in the eye.

"That was a prayer of overflowing thanksgiving for the overflowing bounty God has poured out on me," said Elaine, taking her first bite of scrambled egg.

"Don't talk in riddles, Elaine," said her father-in-law. "What bounty are you talking about?"

"Well, it's a good thing you all are sitting down, because what I'm about to tell you would make you faint, I'm sure. In fact, it just about did make me faint when I first heard about it Saturday," said Elaine.

"Elaine, you're not making any sense at all. Are you losing your mind again?" asked her Mom.

"OK. I'll tell you. First, let me show you this stub," said Elaine. She opened her purse and pulled out two stubs that had been attached to two insurance checks: one for $1 million and the other for $150,000.

"I got the checks on both of these stubs Saturday from Teddy Johnson at his office, then he went with me to the bank to deposit them," said Elaine.

"Glory be!" said Emma. "I can't count all those zeroes, so I can't tell you how much it is, but I know I've never seen that much money in my life."

"Shhh. Hold it down some, Mom," said Elaine, as people at the next table turned around to look their way.

"Let me see that," Spence said then, reaching for the stub. "That's one-two-three-four-five-six zeroes and a one. Must be pretty close to a million dollars there, I'd say. How in the world did you get that?"

"Was there some mistake?" asked Emma. "Surely the insurance didn't pay no $1 million. You didn't have that much life insurance on Tommy Joe, did you?"

"Yes, it was Tommy Joe's idea," said Elaine. "That's what I meant in my prayer by thanking him for his part in my bounty. He said he knew it would be a dangerous trip and we needed a lot of insurance to cover our risks, but I think he was thinking more about the weather or engine trouble than pirates. We bought $1 million in term insurance on each other for the trip. We intended to cancel it when we got back from Cancun. And the $150,000 check was for our 10 percent ownership in the company yacht, the *Nautilus*, which Tommy Joe and I devoted many weeks to building without pay."

"Well, why don't we hurry and finish up with breakfast and see if we can get out of here and start spending some of it?" asked Emma.

"We may as well. I've done lost my appetite," said Spence. "You should have waited until after breakfast before springing news like that on us."

"Well, that's the reason I waited this long," said Elaine. "I kept looking for what I thought was the right time, and I couldn't decide, so I guess it just kind of slipped out when I started thanking God for all he has done for me. I just couldn't hold it in. Sorry."

"Oh, that's all right, but does that change our plans for today?" asked Emma.

"Well, I may pay a little less attention to the price tag on any new clothes I buy, and I may just rent Papa Spence that van for the rest of the week and your hotel rooms for as long as you want to stay down here," said Elaine. "But I still need to be enrolled in that rehab center, so I suggest we head out there first, get my official admission papers and then come back and get checked out of the hospital. Then, you all can help me get whatever housekeeping items I'll need in my new apartment and get me moved in."

Elaine and her mother looked up to see Hoover and McGuffy arriving at the hospital entrance security checkpoint and picking up their security badges. The two guards who had spent the night on the 11th floor and had followed Elaine to the cafeteria saluted Hoover and McGuffy for the official shift change.

"Well, everybody looks fit as a fiddle this morning," said McGuffy, smiling as he and Hoover greeted Elaine, Emma and Spence.

"So what do we have on the agenda today?" asked Hoover.

"That's what we were just talking about," said Elaine. "I think we're going to ride in Papa Spence's rented van out to the rehab center and get me officially signed in, then we want to come back to the hospital, say good-bye to the doctors and staff and get me checked out of the hospital. Mom and I want to go shopping for some clothes for me and for any items I'll need to set up housekeeping at the rehab center. Then I want to get officially moved in."

"Sounds like a full day, so we may as well get started," said McGuffy, offering to drive the rented van.

"Be my guest," said Spence, handing McGuffy the keys, and they soon were at the rehab center, signing Elaine in. She picked up her admission papers and got a list of items she would need in her apartment besides clothes.

Towels and toiletries were furnished, and there was a coffee-maker in the room but no coffee or creamer and no food. There was a desk and chair and a low sofa and a Gideons Bible in the desk drawer but no pens or paper, no dictionary or other books. There was a small refrigerator, but nothing in it but a small tray of ice. There was a small microwave oven but nothing to cook in it. There were sheets and pillows, one blanket and one spread.

"I think I can live here for a few days at least," said Elaine after giving the room the once-over. "I think getting to know the folks in the open common areas will be the most fun part of being here, though. I'm looking forward to sharing my experiences with others who have been going through much of what I've been going through. And maybe that will encourage us both."

At that point, they loaded back in the van and headed back to the hospital where Elaine made hurried stops at the offices of Drs. Sutherland and Horton, presented them with her enrollment papers from the rehab center and assured them both she would be only a short distance away and would contact them each Monday morning for a while as Sutherland suggested. Then Sutherland asked for her health insurance policy number which she didn't remember, but she told him the name of the company and its agent in Hannibal, Teddy Johnson, whose number she also didn't remember.

"That's OK, Elaine. We can take it from here. We'll get the number, call Mr. Johnson for your policy number, and submit the claim for reimbursement of our expenses," said Sutherland. "While we operate primarily from grant money and gifts from charities, we are required to seek reimbursement."

"I don't know how much of my bill will be covered by my insurance, but I would be happy to reimburse you for whatever the insurance doesn't cover," said Elaine.

"That shouldn't be necessary, Elaine," said Sutherland. "I am authorized to sign a waiver for expenses not covered by insurance where the patient has insurance. However, if you should ever wish to make a gift of any amount whatsoever to the Florida TBI Foundation, which helps us provide our services to the public, it would be accepted with gratitude. So, Elaine, take good care of yourself. Be especially careful with your fracture. Report any recurrence of symptoms, and we'll see you on Mondays for the next three weeks. OK?"

"OK, thanks for everything. You and your staff have given me my life back," said Elaine.

"No, God did that," said Sutherland. "But you did a major portion of the work yourself, Elaine. You are one tough lady."

"Thanks, Doctor. I'll see you on Monday," said Elaine as she turned and headed toward the elevator, where Horton and McGuffy stood waiting patiently. And for the first time since she regained consciousness on the beach of a deserted sandbar island two weeks ago, she felt really free.

The day went quickly as Elaine worked her to-do list, getting clothes and items for her room at the rehab center and checking in with Dorothy Goodson, the director, who shook hands with them and welcomed Elaine as a new member.

"We have a full schedule of activities, Elaine," said Goodson, handing her an information packet, which included a calendar of events that listed everything from games and fitness workouts and therapy sessions to hobbies, arts and crafts, TV and movies, music and sharing time.

"We encourage you to participate in at least one major activity each day, your choice," said Goodson. "We especially encourage you to relate as friends to as many of our members as you can, and remember that for those in the early stages of recovery, they are in some respects where you used to be, and with their hard work and your encouragement, they one day may be where you are. And as we learn and strive together, all of us reach heights that none of us would have achieved alone. That's what it's about here: friendship and encouragement produce healing and recovery."

"That's great, Ms. Goodson," said Elaine. "I'm looking forward to meeting and sharing experiences with the other members and the staff."

"Call me Dot," said Goodson. "We call each other by our first names only here, and nicknames are fine so long as the person you are referring to approves. We'll have our next get-acquainted session, where we make brownies and pop popcorn, after the evening meal tonight, so you'll want to participate in that. Now, are there any questions?"

"I have a few questions relating to security," said Hoover. "I'm Lt. Cdr. Jeanne Hoover and this is my associate, Lt. Robert McGuffy, of the United States Coast Guard. We're deputized you might say by the U.S. Marshals Service for today and perhaps to some extent in the future to ensure Elaine's security. We are here to help protect Elaine from any danger or threat of danger from those who attacked her in the Gulf of Mexico and inflicted her brain injury and who are soon to go on trial in federal court on criminal charges in connection with that attack."

"Oh, is that the case that's been on TV and in all the papers?" asked Goodson.

"Yes it is, Dot," said Hoover. "We not only want to protect Elaine for Elaine's sake. We also are charged with protecting her as a key witness in the federal court trial of the pirates. They kidnapped her and her husband, blew up their yacht, shot her husband in the back and killed him, and they bludgeoned Elaine with a wooden beam in an attempt to kill her. So we are dealing with the most vicious people I've ever had to deal with. They are desperate and apparently conscienceless, and I'm sure they would kill Elaine and those of us protecting her if they possibly could.

"Now, for that reason, two of our security officers must be on duty here at the center around the clock, seven days a week. We hope that after a while our presence here will hardly be noticed by your members, who are free to call us or any others assigned here by our first names.

"I'm Jeanne. This is Bob. We will be armed as covertly as possible and will wear casual clothes as we are wearing today. And it is imperative, if there are persons at any time who you don't know personally coming in the center here or are anywhere else on the campus, including the parking lot, you are to refer them to me or to one of the other security officers on duty.

"We do have what we call wands or portable magnetic detectors which we will use to scan those entering the building for the first time. They will not be allowed through our entrance checkpoint if they are not enrolled here or known to be family members or friends of those enrolled here. Now, I know that's sounds intrusive, Dot, and it is. But it's necessary for the protection of Elaine as well as everyone else at this center. Are we clear on that?"

"Yes you are. Jeanne, Bob, you will have our total cooperation," said Dot. "We understand the need for tight security for Elaine and the rest of us. I'm sure you will want to get to know our own security team, Art Snyder and Eva Brown, who are just coming in the door there now."

"Call us Art and Eva," said Snyder as they all shook hands.

"I'm Elaine's father-in-law and Emma here is her mother," said Spence as he and Emma also joined in the handshaking. "We're not members," Spence explained. "We're just with Elaine today to help her get moved in."

"Oh, I see," said Art. "Well, we have some security rules here in the center as well, which we won't take time to go over in their entirety.

"The main one we insist on is curfew. No resident is to be outside the center after 9 p.m. or before 6 a.m. unless they have obtained a signed security pass from one of us. That may prevent the necessity of your having your own security officers here through the evening hours, but that's your call. You're welcome to be here, make yourself at home in the staff lounge and help yourself to any goodies you find in it."

"I think we can work with you and may be able to clear you eventually as deputies," said Hoover. "That will ultimately be up to U.S. Attorney Joseph Barton, whose office is prosecuting the piracy case."

"Well, now that you're officially one of us, Elaine, make yourself at home," said Dot. "You may leave and return to the center at any time other than during curfew hours so long as you leave with an approved person who signs you out and signs you in when you return. The only other thing I've got to tell you is welcome."

"Thanks, Dot. I'm looking forward to spending time with you and the members here," said Elaine. "We're going to be gone most of the rest of the day, however, and I suppose you'll need one of these folks with me to sign me out."

"Either of the security officers will do, Elaine," said Dot, handing Hoover the logbook. "Your security folks are always approved, and we can approve up to five others at your request, with a reasonable advance notice, of course."

"I'll sign it for you this time, Elaine," said Hoover, signing the log book, then she and the others headed for the van in the parking lot.

After a long and tiring day of shopping, McGuffy drove the van to Morelli's office where he and Hoover gave him a report of their activities for the day. Then they went through a fast-food drive-through and picked up a sack of sandwiches and drinks and headed back to the rehab center. Hoover signed Elaine back in, and McGuffy helped her take several more sacks of clothes and other items into Elaine's apartment and hung them in the closet.

Spence and Emma said they'd be by around nine the next morning to see if they and Elaine could think of anything they'd like to do in Miami that day. Elaine thanked them and said good night, then two new security guards came in from the parking lot where they had been waiting and relieved Hoover and McGuffy on the security shift for the evening.

Then feeling a real pang of loneliness, Elaine watched them drive away into the night.

Chapter Twenty-One

U.S. District Judge Francis Steele gaveled his court into session at 10 a.m. Tuesday as Assistant U.S. Attorney Milton Richards, the federal prosecutor, and more than a dozen defense lawyers stood up.

"Court will come to order. Be seated please," said Steele as he sat down.

"Now I'll hear you, Mr. Richards, since you say you are ready for trial, on how you propose to proceed in these cases," said Steele. "Then I'll hear from defense counsel on any points of objection, on any revised pleas of your clients, and then your best judgment on how much of the next two weeks you will need to be prepared for trial. Mr. Richards."

"Your Honor, the United States plans to present eye-witness testimony on the major crimes at issue in this case," said Richards. "We have granted immunity from prosecution to certain defendants in exchange for their testimony. We expect them to tell how and by whom *The Silver Bullet* Piracy Conspiracy was created and carried out. We also would ask Your Honor, largely for security reasons, for leave not to announce prior to their testimony in this case which defendants have been granted immunity."

"Granted," said Steele. "Anything else?"

"We are prepared to show by abundant evidence that defendants Joe Brannigan and Vincent Perkins created and carried out this piracy conspiracy with the willful participation of some two dozen men they enlisted as members of *The Silver Bullet*'s crew," said Richards.

"We will seek the death penalty, Your Honor, on Brannigan, Perkins and any and all other defendants who insist on trial and are found guilty of the piracy and other crimes enumerated in this indictment. The United States is prepared to recommend life in prison for Brannigan or Perkins should either of them decide to plead guilty and thus spare the people and this court the time and expense of trying them, or, in the alternative, to present truthful testimony against the other.

"For those defendants, Your Honor, who plead guilty to general piracy on the high seas and if the evidence shows they also directly caused the deaths of the two Coast Guard sailors or the Hannibal, Missouri, resident, or who struck the Missouri resident's wife on the head with a wooden beam with the intent to kill her, we are prepared upon their guilty plea without trial to recommend a sentence of life in prison.

"We will recommend 40 years in prison on their guilty plea of directly causing the destruction of their yacht with an ammonium nitrate explosion.

"Finally, those defendants who plead guilty to the general charge of maritime piracy but did not directly kill or attempt to kill any of those victims enumerated in the indictment, the United States is prepared to recommend a sentence of thirty years in prison. As Your Honor knows and as we remind defense counsel, the sentences to be imposed in this case are totally without possibility of parole. With those parameters, Your Honor, the United States is ready to proceed to trial in this case," said Richards.

"Thank you Mr. Richards. What says defense counsel?" asked Steele.

"Your Honor, I am Roberta Sparks, counsel for Vincent Perkins, and I hereby repeat my previous statement in this court that I will need a minimum of three months to adequately prepare to defend Mr. Perkins on the charges in this indictment," said Sparks.

"I have considered Mr. Richards' generous offer to recommend life in prison for my client on his guilty plea, but I am firmly convinced, as a matter of ethics and professional responsibility, that justice demands that Mr. Perkins be given a full and fair trial on these charges," said Sparks. "Having said that, Your Honor, we are prepared to comply with Your Honor's order that we proceed to trial in two weeks."

"Your Honor, the United States would like to respond briefly to Ms. Sparks' comments, if I may, Sir," said Richards.

"The evidence against Mr. Perkins, Your Honor, is substantial that he was involved at the heart of this piracy conspiracy at every step of the way, in that he was second-in-command to Brannigan, and thus the enforcer of every murderous command Brannigan gave save one, Your Honor, and that was when Vincent Perkins took it totally upon himself, on his own motion, to summarily execute one Elaine Perkins, wife of the Missouri resident, by bludgeoning her on the head with a wooden beam."

"Objection, Your Honor," said Sparks. "Mr. Richards, totally out of order, is testifying against my client without having been sworn, for purposes of poisoning the jury pool with pretrial publicity, using inflammatory and sensational language to try him in the press and the electronic media."

"Sustained," said Steele. "Make your point, Mr. Richards, if you have one, and make it fast."

"Yes, Your Honor, I recited what the evidence will show is Mr. Perkins' extensive and overarching involvement with the separate crimes in this case not to prejudice his right to a fair trial but rather to support Ms. Sparks' contention that she may indeed need more time to prepare to defend Mr. Perkins. The United States would join in her request for more time for Ms. Sparks to prepare for her client's defense or possibly to enter a guilty plea, Your Honor, and we wouldn't object to two additional days beyond the two weeks mentioned by Your Honor before commencing trial."

"Thank you," said Sparks, who then sat down.

"Any other defense counsel want to be heard, or on behalf of their clients, want to amend their plea?" asked Steele.

"Your Honor, for the record, counsel for eight defendants filed guilty pleas on behalf of their clients as of the start of court at ten o'clock," said Jane Simmons, Steele's clerk. "Four others have since pled guilty, Your Honor, leaving only four defendants remaining: Joe Brannigan, Vincent Perkins, Clay Houston and Jim Cummings."

"Thank you, Ms. Simmons. Now to you counsel whose clients have now pled guilty, as you know, the court will have to examine each and every one of them in person. Have your clients here at 8 a.m. tomorrow. I will set the start of trial for the remaining defendants for two weeks and two days from today. That means jury selection will begin at 8 a.m. two weeks from this coming Thursday. Are there any other matters we need to take up today? Hearing none, court is dismissed," said Steele, striking his gavel.

Ralph Meese, attorney for Clay Houston, called Richards Tuesday afternoon and asked for an appointment for him and Houston to come by and talk over "some important pending matters," as Meese put it.

"Certainly, Mr. Meese. I'd be happy to talk with you and your client," said Richards. "May I assume that Mr. Houston is still interested in an agreement to testify for the United States?"

"That's what we want to talk about, Mr. Richards. So when could we talk?" asked Meese.

"How does two this afternoon sound? I've got some time then," said Richards.

"Two o'clock is fine," said Meese. "We'll see you then."

A few minutes before 2 p.m., Meese and Houston arrived in Richards' outer office and he invited them in.

"Sit down, Mr. Meese, Mr. Houston. Can I get some water or coffee or fruit juice for either or both of you?" asked Richards.

"No, thanks," they told him. "We just need to discuss some important pending matters with you, Mr. Richards," said Meese.

"Yeah, you said that on the phone. So what do you want to talk about, Mr. Meese? But before you answer that, I wonder if you'd like my secretary, who is a notary, to swear in your client, so that the substance of our conversation could be recorded, transcribed and filed as an affidavit with the court. I'm assuming you want to talk about the pending piracy case."

"That's right," said Meese. "Mr. Houston and I have no objection to your making a tape recording of our conversation, but we would ask for a copy of it, and if portions of it need to be put into writing in the form of a sworn affidavit and filed with the court, we have no objection to that, either."

Richards called his secretary, who set up the recorder and administered the oath to Houston.

"State your name for the record, please, Mr. Houston," said Richards' secretary, Myra Jones, flipping the recorder on.

"George Claybrook Houston," said Houston.

"Mr. Houston, do you solemnly swear or affirm that the statements you will make in this cause will be the truth, the whole truth, and nothing but the truth, so help you God?"

"I do," said Houston.

"You may proceed," said Jones.

"Mr. Richards, I'll let my client speak for himself, but he has shared with me two things which I want to mention and discuss with you, and the first of these is whether you are prepared to offer him a recommendation of leniency or perhaps total immunity from prosecution, in exchange for his testimony in the pending piracy case in federal court," said Meese.

"Yes, Mr. Meese," said Richards. "The United States is prepared to offer you, Mr. Houston, total immunity from prosecution on the charges enumerated in the indictment in this case in exchange for your truthful testimony. Are you willing to testify truthfully as to each and every question that will be put to you concerning your own actions and those you observed of any of the other defendants in this case?"

"I am," said Houston. "What do you want to know?"

"First, Mr. Houston, we will ask you whether you received a call from Joe Brannigan some two weeks ago requesting that you come alone by boat to his ship, *The Silver Bullet*, approximately five miles south of the port of Miami and to bring your doctor bag?" asked Richards.

"I did. And I asked him what for, and he said 'I've been shot real near the heart and I want you to operate and get the bullet out'," said Houston.

"What did you tell him?" asked Richards.

"I told him that was the quickest way to kill him, that it likely would cause septic shock, that there could be cardiac arrest or that he could bleed to death since I didn't have access to blood or plasma for a transfusion," said Houston.

"And what did he say to that?" asked Richards.

"He said, 'Well, I'm about to bleed to death as it is, and I can't take morphine, so bring me some good stuff for pain, and get here quick or I'll be gone'," said Houston.

"And what did you do?"

"I went out and examined him, checked his vital signs, cleaned his wound, put on the best bandage I could, gave him some antibiotics and something to slow down his blood loss and gave him a shot of oxycodone for pain and told him I'd be back the next day to repeat the process, but I strongly suggested that he arrange to get to the nearest hospital as soon as he could for more appropriate treatment than I could give him on his boat," said Houston.

"What did he say?" asked Richards.

"He said, 'Good. Come back tomorrow and we'll see how I'm doing then'," said Houston.

"And did you return the next day, which would have been Thursday, I believe?" asked Richards.

"Right. It was Thursday. I repeated the process exactly. Mr. Brannigan was in more pain, his fever was substantially higher, and the wound near his heart looked swollen and substantially discolored and inflamed," said Houston. "I told him he could be dead in 24 hours if he didn't get help."

"What did Brannigan say or do then?" asked Richards.

"He called Vincent Perkins and told him it was time to rig the wiring of the ship so that it would blow up if the Coast Guard was to take it over and try to start the engines.

Perkins said he had the diagram for doing that, which he took out of his billfold. It was folded up, but he waved it in front of Brannigan and said, 'I've got it all figured out right here, see, and I'll take care of it.' Perkins then left Brannigan's cabin and I never saw him again. Then I left and never saw Brannigan again. I was on my way back to my home in Key Biscayne when two men in a Coast Guard chopper landed on my lawn and took me into custody and threw me in jail, where I stayed several days without being allowed to see or call my lawyer."

"But eventually you got up with Mr. Meese, I see. Is there anything else you want to tell me, Mr. Houston?" asked Richards.

"Yes, there is something else, but before we leave the matter I just told you about, I would like to ask you if that information about what I did for Brannigan would have to be presented to the Medical Examiners Board," said Houston. "As you probably know, Mr. Richards, my license to practice medicine is suspended. And I am concerned that my license may be permanently revoked if anyone complained about what I did for Brannigan, and if the board were to consider that practicing medicine without a license."

"Well, I'm not intending this to sound flippant, Mr. Houston, but would you prefer to have your medical license revoked or to be found guilty of aiding and abetting piracy and the murder of two Coast Guard soldiers who died when that booby-trapped pirate boat blew up?" asked Richards.

"Mr. Richards, I consider that remark flippant at best and out of order," said Meese. "My client has been honest with you and is prepared to testify truthfully for the government as to those things he has just told you. It would appear that the federal government is not legally bound to disclose to the Medical Board the details he has just shared with you."

"Get serious, Mr. Meese. You both agreed to have his remarks recorded and filed in court, which as you very well know, is public record. We could, of course, ask Judge Steele to seal any documents not actually filed as evidence, but he may not approve our request. More importantly, however, we definitely intend to use Mr. Houston's comments here today as evidence in the case. I would say this, however, which is the best I could do for you, Mr. Houston, that once the information about Mr. Houston's medical practice is offered as evidence, the U.S. attorney's office would not be required to file any complaint with the Medical Board, and I could assure you that we would not do that. Would that be helpful?"

"Yessir, it would," said Meese. "Now as to the other matter I mentioned, you may prefer that Dr. Houston's remarks not be recorded."

"OK. Turn off the tape, Myra," Richards said to his secretary. "Now what did you want to tell me?"

"Mr. Richards, Dr. Houston felt, and I concurred, that he was under a legal duty to report a matter that perhaps falls under the category of a federal felony, namely the corrupt tampering with a witness in a federal court case," said Meese. "And if you'd like to hear about it, Dr. Houston as before will tell you in his own words."

"Of course, I want to hear it, but I think I do want this recorded. Do you object?" asked Richards.

"No, of course not," said Meese and Houston together.

"Flip the machine back on, then, Myra, and proceed, Mr. Houston."

"All right, well, a few days ago Vincent Perkins' brother, Mose I believe he called himself, called me, had got my number from a lawyer, not Mr. Meese, and said he wanted to discuss the piracy case with me privately. I told him OK, and after a discussion on the phone, we met at the dog track in Hialeah, and talked privately up in the bleachers there before the crowd for the next race started arriving. He scanned me to make sure I wasn't carrying a hidden microphone, then wanted to know what my testimony would be as to Vincent Perkins' role on board the pirate ship.

"I told him that Perkins seemed to be passing on and carrying out Brannigan's orders, and that's what he wanted me to say, so he could contend, I guess, that he was just following orders and wasn't himself guilty of stuff.

"But I asked him what Vincent Perkins would testify about me, and he said he might forget to mention that I was practicing medicine without a license, or on the other hand he might remember to mention it.

"I told him that I didn't have to prove I wasn't practicing medicine, but that the government would have to prove I was, and if Vincent were to say he didn't remember seeing me treating Brannigan's wound, it might help me with the Medical Board. He seemed to be saying Vincent would do that, but then Mose Perkins said as payment for helping me out, I would have to help him out."

"And how did he say he wanted you to help him out?" asked Richards.

"He came up with this elaborate scheme for me to sign up at a brain injury community program rehab center as a volunteer, because he had learned some way that Elaine Foster was about to be moving there for the rest of her recovery," said Houston.

"And what did he want you to do at the rehab center?" asked Richards.

"He wanted me to get real cozy with the staff and the security officers and the residents, particularly Ms. Foster, and then on the night before she might be scheduled to testify against Vincent in court, that I was supposed to administer an over-dose of sleeping pills to her," said Houston.

"So he wanted you to kill her, then?" asked Richards.

"No, that's what I thought at first. And maybe he did want me to kill her, but what he said was that he wanted her to be so out of it that she showed up late in court if at all and then would be so sleepy and incoherent she would be disqualified as a witness. I mean, he said Vincent Perkins, his brother, really, really didn't want her to testify."

"So did you agree to participate in his scheme?" asked Richards.

"Well, yes and no. It seems that he decided to force me to go along by calling the rehab center, using my name, and telling them I wanted to volunteer to help out. He even went to the length of telling them my medical license was on hold, and that I was disclosing that in the spirit of full disclosure, but that I was wanting to volunteer for menial things like janitorial work or something. So, bottom line, I was afraid he had already gone too far and that it was going to create a public flap about my license, so I told him I'd sign up."

"And did you sign up, Mr. Houston?" asked Richards.

"Yes, I did. And I understand that Ms. Foster has already signed in out there too. So Mose Perkins thinks I'm going to give her an overdose of sleeping pills more or less at his signal. That's the way I left it, but if there's any chance that I could cooperate with the government without letting him know, that's my preference," said Houston.

"Well, Mr. Houston, you've done the right thing. I will consult with my boss, the U.S. attorney, Joseph Barton, and we may be able to work something out that's mutually acceptable," said Richards. "I know he will have some concerns about your being in such close proximity to Ms. Foster, but if you are willing to help us bring Mose to justice, perhaps we can create a security net that protects Ms. Foster and nabs him at the same time. I would suggest that you go ahead and put in your scheduled time out there as a volunteer and not let Mose Perkins know you're cooperating with us. Can you do that at least for a few days until we can come up with a plan to nab him?"

"Sure, I can," said Houston. "I'll just go ahead and work as a volunteer and see if I can get to know the folks out there, including Ms. Foster. And I'll expect you, Mr. Richards, to let me in on your plan to nab Mose."

"That's exactly what we would expect you to do, Mr. Houston," said Richards.

"Now, Mr. Richards, my client would like to know what incentives you can offer him for the cooperation and testimony we have outlined," said Meese.

"Assuming we can work out some way to nab Mose Perkins, as I said, and particularly if Mr. Houston can testify that Vincent Perkins took personal charge of booby-trapping the pirate boat, the United States will offer him absolute immunity from prosecution in this case," said Richards. "I would state to you, Mr. Meese, on behalf of your client, and particularly to you, Mr. Houston, that if you veer in any way from the course of action you have outlined for me here today, you remain under indictment and would be prosecuted for aiding and abetting piracy. So you will remain a defendant in this case, Mr. Houston, until after you have testified. Then we would ask Judge Steele to let us withdraw the charges against you. Do you understand and accept those conditions, Mr. Houston?"

"Yes, I do," said Houston.

"We do, Mr. Richards," said Meese.

"Well, let's shake on it then," said Richards, as he shook hands with Houston and Meese and they left his office.

Marty Perkins took the elevator up to the 12th floor of the hotel near Miami General Hospital where he and his brother, Mose, were staying. Marty bounded off the elevator, ran down the hallway and knocked three times on the door.

"Who is it?" came the muffled voice of Mose from inside.

"It's me, Marty. Open up," said Marty, so excitedly that he was almost out of breath.

"Marty who? I don't know any Marty," said Mose, who after a few seconds' wait flung the door open with a hideous laugh. "Gotcha there for a minute, didn't I Marty? Thought you had the wrong door there for just a bit, didn't you? Come in. What's bugging you?"

"Have you been drinking? Mose, you've got to lay off the sauce," said Marty, still obviously trying to catch his breath. "And don't use the term 'bugging' around me. We probably are bugged."

"Why do you say that? And what has got you so riled?" asked Mose, who frowned and seemed suddenly concerned.

"You will not believe what I've just seen," said Marty. "I mean I don't think you'll believe it. I'll bet, in view of your little conversation with old Doc Houston last week, that you think you've got him all teamed up with us and that he's going to give that Foster girl an overdose of sleeping pills the night before she's supposed to testify in federal court, don't you?"

"Yes, I do have him teamed up, tighter than a jug, and I happen to know that he's already put in some time over there as a janitor or general helper or something," said Mose.

"Well, you're the one who's tighter than a jug," said Marty. "I just saw Houston and a lawyer-looking guy coming out of Milton Richards' office. They seemed awful glad about something, particularly for a guy who's got to stand trial on piracy charges."

"How do you know he's got to stand trial?" asked Mose. "I happen to have been in federal court this morning when Old Judge Steele's clerk read out the list of those who didn't plead guilty and are going to have to face trial. But I can tell you, Houston will have to stand trial. He's one of the last four defendants."

"That's just it, Mose," said Marty. "Sure Houston is still listed as a defendant, but that don't mean he's going to stand trial. If he cuts the right kind of deal with Richards, you can bet he won't stand trial. And I'll just bet Houston and his lawyer were trying to cut a deal, and from the smiles on their faces when they walked out of Richards' office, they have cut it."

"I'm telling you, Marty. I heard his clerk read out the list of defendants," said Mose.

"I was there. I know his name was read out. But the trial ain't over yet. A lot could happen between here and there," said Marty.

"Houston is one of four defendants left, the clerk said. Then she named Brannigan, Vince, Houston and a guy named Cummings, same name as that turncoat that drowned when the *San Pedro* sank," said Mose. "I say Houston's got to stand trial, and I'll bet his coming out of Richards' office just means they're over there whining, not that Richards has cut them loose."

"Bingo. You said it," said Marty. "They're whining. But if they're over there whining, that means they're trying to cut a deal, and if they're happy, it means they have agreed to hand over Vince's head on a silver tray, and that also means we can't rely on

Houston to overdose that Foster girl out at the rehab center on sleeping pills. And that means we've got to come up with another plan to take her out."

"Oh, you're just jittery, Marty," said Mose. "You always assume the worst. Remember what you said after I met with Houston at the dog track? You know what you said after old Houston called me and said the plan is on?"

"Yeah, I remember," said Marty.

"OK. Then tell me what you said. Go on. Tell me," said Mose.

"I said 'you da man, Mose. You da man'," said Marty.

"Well, am I da man, or not? Huh? Talk to me," said Mose.

"Let me put it to you this way, Mose. If you don't see the situation I'm trying to tell you about, then I say 'you da drunk man, Mose. You da drunk'."

"Now you're back to smarting off again," said Mose. "So let's do this. Why don't you and me go out to that rehab center, spy it out, and see if we see old Houston out there emptying any bedpans. Are you game for that?"

"Yeah, I'm game. But he can't be out there and in Richards' office at the same time," said Marty. "And I'm telling you, I know it was him coming out of Richards' office."

"Well, get in the car. We'll drive out there and see if he's there, and then we'll know, OK?' said Mose, heading out the door. "Bring your binoculars."

"OK," said Marty as he picked up the binoculars, and he and Mose rode the elevator down to the hotel lobby. "But you'd better let me drive," said Marty.

They got in their rented car, drove over to the rehab center, and parked on the curb at the back of the parking lot under the same shade tree they had parked under previously. They waited for a good thirty minutes without seeing Houston or anyone else, then a girl in hospital coveralls and a man in khakis wearing a white shirt with the sleeves turned up a couple of turns walked out and leaned against the building. The girl pulled out a pack of cigarettes and the man lit one for her but didn't light a cigarette for himself.

"See if you know who that man is, Marty," said Mose, handing Marty the binoculars.

"Well, I'll be a monkey's uncle if it ain't Houston," said Marty. "I may have been wrong about that being him coming out of Richards' office, really not that long ago."

"And you were wrong about me being drunk, too, little brother," said Mose. "Now I insist on an apology. I wasn't drunk, although I admit I had sampled the bottle a few swigs after breakfast, you know, just to wash the ham and eggs and biscuits down. But I wasn't drunk. OK?"

"OK, Mose. You may not have been over the legal limit, but you for sure were not feeling much pain. I think I may have scared you sober with what I said about Houston," said Marty.

"Yeah, but what have you got to say now? Huh? Go on. Say it," said Mose.

"OK, Mose. I'll say it. You still da man," said Marty.

Clay Houston and Elaine Foster were the two newest residents at the rehab center's get-acquainted meeting after the evening meal on Monday night. They all gathered in the large meeting room, while the smell of fresh-popped popcorn filled the place, and a couple of staff members in green coveralls took two big trays of brownies out of the oven.

Those who were able to get samples for themselves did so and then helped the others to get samples as well. Some of them sat still in wheelchairs. Others wheeled around the room with ease. Some walked smoothly and easily and some used a cane or a walker. When everybody was served and seated, Dot spoke to the group.

"We're glad to have two new people with us tonight," she said. "We have Elaine over there, who you may or may not recognize as the girl who has been in the news lately. She's a victim of a pirate's attack in the Gulf of Mexico but has made really great progress. Say hi to us, Elaine."

"Hi," she said and waved.

"I'm sure she'll have more to say as the evening goes on and as she meets and gets to know several of you," said Dot. "We also have a man who has practiced medicine for several years but is offering his time and energy to us totally as a volunteer helper and friend, and I'll let him introduce himself."

"Hi. My first name is George, which I've never really liked that much," said Houston. "But I really like what you all are doing here, and I'd kind of like to be known as George. I'll tell you why. You know you hear the saying sometimes, 'Let George do it.' Well, I hope you'll let me help you with anything at all. I'd like for everyone to think, if you need something done that you can't do for yourself, that you'll call George and let George do it. I really want to help."

"OK, George. Thank you for that. And we'll take you at your word," said Dot. "We need someone to make sure everyone has something to drink. If you didn't get a drink or if you need a refill, call George and let George do it. Thanks again, George."

As the evening wore on, Elaine took time to spend a few minutes with each of the more than two dozen residents and nearly a dozen staff members. Some of the residents had been unable to adapt well to life after their brain injury. Some had trouble talking or walking or coordinating eye and hand movements.

Others were confused about everything because they had lost much of their memory and couldn't read anymore, didn't know their family members, and seemed unable to control their emotions. Some sat and cried, others engaged in horseplay or robust laughter. Others sat at a table and practiced making their ABCs.

Elaine reminded each of these that she had similar symptoms just a few days ago, but as her wound healed she regained virtually all of her memory, in bits and pieces at first, and then much more. Those she talked to seemed to understand her and to be encouraged by her example and words.

Finally, Elaine spoke to George and shook hands with him. As they talked, he glanced at the two security guards seated just inside the room who were shaking their heads back and forth in the universal negative sign to him. Then one guard did the familiar "cut" signal, turning his hand on edge like a knife and symbolically slashing his throat. George took the cue.

"It was good to meet you, Elaine. I'll see you around," George said as he walked away and started a conversation with someone else. Elaine had not seen the guard's hand signal. Eventually, the activity session wound down and the residents turned in for the night.

Elaine woke up refreshed Tuesday morning after her first night in her apartment at the rehab center. She went in the kitchen where some of the residents were cooking oatmeal, and others were seated at tables having cereal or pancakes or scrambled eggs and bacon. She could smell fresh coffee brewing and poured a mug of it for herself.

As breakfast continued, a cheerful tone began as a small spark in one corner and then increased until the sounds of laughter could be heard across the dining room where at least two dozen residents had now gathered.

Elaine ate and chatted with a few new friends, read the paper briefly then went back to her apartment, showered and dressed for a day outside. Her Mom and Spence arrived as agreed about 9 a.m. and signed her out, promising to bring her back at the end of the day.

"You know, I really enjoyed getting to know so many people who were injured as I was, some of them more seriously and some less," Elaine told her mother. "I didn't realize so many people suffer from TBI each year, but I heard today that it's into the hundreds of thousands. Maybe more should be done to publicize the problem, so folks who are struggling to get their lives back can be helped and encouraged."

"I'm pleased that you're thinking of others, Elaine," said her mother. "That's a good sign. But what would you care to do today?"

"I know it's crazy, but I'd really like to go down to the pier and see the ships, particularly the yachts. I'm sure they've got a big and active yacht club here," said Elaine.

"But there I go, being selfish. I know that you and Papa Spence couldn't care less about yachts, could you?" asked Elaine.

"No, we really couldn't, Elaine. Which brings us to a point I'm reluctant to make," said Spence. "Your mother and I have talked about wanting to be here for you as long and in whatever way you need us. But our priorities are to be here during the trial, number one, which is a whopping sixteen days away. I know that sounds like almost no time to those lawyers, at least that's what they were quoted as saying in *The Miami Herald*, but sixteen days is a long time for me and your mother to be away from home."

"What are you saying, Papa Spence?" asked Elaine.

"Well, what I'm saying, and I think your Mom is with me on this, is why don't we fly on back to Hannibal for a while and then come back when the trial starts? We really, really want to be here when you're a witness. But now that you're in your new quarters, and you're making a lot of new friends, which you said your doctors told you you should do at this phase of your recovery, your Mom and I really feel like we're just taking you away from them and we're not doing you a bit of good. Selfishly, I think I'm on the edge of being bored silly," said Spence.

"Well, why don't you go ahead and get new tickets for 16 days from now, Papa Spence, for you and Mom, and I'll pay for them. Now, how's that? What's wrong with that plan?"

"Nothing's wrong with it as I see," said Spence. "I know it makes me and your mother feel a lot better."

"Well, consider it done then," said Elaine.

"Well, why don't we spend today looking at yachts with you, Elaine, then leave early tomorrow morning for Hannibal?" asked her Mom.

"Let's do it," said Elaine.

The day went quickly. Elaine beamed as she walked in the sunshine, admiring yachts and sailboats and cruisers and even Coast Guard cutters in the harbor as two new security guards she didn't know tagged along. At the end of the day, Elaine treated them all, including the guards, to steaks at a steak house, then Spence and her Mom went back to the hotel where they exchanged hugs and just a few sniffles and tears, and she sent them on their way. One of the guards drove her and the other guard out to the rehab center, where she checked in just moments before curfew.

And as she went to her room, she realized she needed time alone, just with herself and God. She pulled the Gideons Bible out and began to read her favorite scriptures, starting with *Psalm* 23. And then she read the words of Jesus from the *Gospel of John*, Chapter 15 and verse 15, where Jesus told his disciples as he was ready to leave them that he no longer called them servants ***"because a servant doesn't know his master's business. Instead, I have called you friends, for everything I learned from my Father, I have made known to you."***

"God, I don't know your business, and I don't know or understand your plan for my life, but I pray that you will make your plan known to me," Elaine prayed softly.

"I long to be your friend, and I want you to be my friend, which I trust you already are. Thank you for overflowing me with your blessings, even as I'm torn apart by my loss of Tommy Joe, the lifelong friend you sent to me but now for some reason you have called him home.

"I don't understand why, God. But I know that I will fear no evil, because you are with me, always with me, even when my world looks dark and dreadful, even when I walk through the valley of the shadow of death. I know you are there, protecting me from my enemies.

"Now I pray, God, that you will lead me to new friends, and that all of us truly can be your friends. And please protect Mom and Papa Spence as they fly back to Hannibal tomorrow. Amen."

Elaine didn't feel like going back to the great room to chat. She didn't understand the conflicting emotions she felt. But she reminded herself that she needed to learn how to be resilient and to bounce back as she learned to bring her emotions back under her control again.

She turned her light off then and slept soundly. And when she awoke, she vowed to meet at least three new friends this day. She told her security guards that she would be spending the entire day at the rehab center.

About noon, George called Mose. "We need to talk," he said.

"About what?" Mose asked.

"I've been thinking this thing over, Mose, and I'm not sure I can do it," George told him. "I guess you could say I'm getting cold feet."

"Well, I think Vince is going to be able to provide the only evidence the government will have that you were there providing medical care to Brannigan without a license. You can kiss the remainder of your medical career goodbye if you get cold feet now."

"Well, Mose, I've hit a snag on getting close to Elaine," said George. "Those two guards the feds have posted on her around the clock have so dampened what I'm able to do, that you may as well say I'm shut out. And they're on duty not 15 feet from her door at night, so I think it would be virtually impossible for me to get in there without their seeing me."

"Well, you'll just have to sneak the overdose of sleeping powders into something in the kitchen you know she's going to eat, like a hamburger or a pizza or something. She may notice that it's bitter or something, but if you use the right stuff you can hardly taste it, and a couple of good bites of it will do the trick," said Mose. "We've just got to keep that gal Elaine from getting on the witness stand, because Vincent thinks she may be the only one who saw him hit her over the head, and now that she's got her memory back, she probably remembers that too. But whether she does or not, we can't take that chance. Do you hear me, Houston? We can't take that chance."

At that point, Mose heard a click and the phone went dead, and simultaneously there was a knock at the door of his hotel room.

"Who's there?" Mose asked with a worried tone in his voice. When no one answered, he asked again, "Who's there?"

When there still was no answer, Mose ran angrily to the door, cursing.

"Marty, if that's you playing one of your smart-alec tricks on me, you're going to be sorry," he said, throwing the door open. He was greeted by two FBI agents in dark suits, carrying handcuffs.

"You will need to come with us, Mr. Perkins," one of them said, clamping the cuffs quickly on Mose's wrists as they led him from the room.

"And by the way, neither of us is named Marty," the agent said as the three of them boarded the elevator.

Morelli then called Houston.

"Mr. Houston, I've been authorized to tell you thanks for your cooperation. Thanks to you, we have foiled a plot by Mose Perkins to keep Elaine Foster from testifying in the upcoming piracy trial of his brother Vince and others," said Morelli.

"I've also been authorized to tell you, Mr. Houston, that you are no longer expected to remain at the rehab center. You're free to go on about your business, but just stay in the area. We'll be expecting you to be on hand to testify in a couple of weeks. And of course, we'll have to assign some security folks to stick with you pretty much 24-7 for a while."

"I'll be on hand, Chief Morelli, and I understand the need for the guards," said Houston. "But I must say that I've come to really enjoy my volunteer work at the center. I believe the residents here are being healed and restored, and that's something I may be able to participate in and help with. I know it's the most noble service I've ever done, although I'm sticking to emptying bedpans and taking out the garbage and helping the residents in the fitness room and playing games and stuff like that. I promise you, I'll not fudge on my medical practice until the Medical Board frees up my license."

"Well, I heard Mr. Barton say that he would be willing to write you a letter of recommendation to the Medical Board should it ever consider placing you in a program to rehabilitate your license, such as medical service in a federal prison, for instance," said Morelli.

"Thank you, for that, Chief, and I'll thank Mr. Barton when I see him," said Houston.

After her mother and father-in-law flew back to Hannibal on Wednesday morning, Elaine Foster resolved to spend that day and most of her time each day for the next two weeks at the rehab center where she was going through the final phases of her recovery from TBI. She made several new friends, male and female, ranging from children to older adults, all with the same thing in common: they had suffered a traumatic brain injury.

Their abilities and challenges were different, based on the severity and the location in the brain of their injuries. But she liked to believe that they all had the ability to improve, even though they might not be able to reach the same degree of recovery.

Elaine spent her most meaningful hours helping a girl who had been in the sixth grade at school who was having to learn how to read again.

And a woman old enough to be Elaine's grandmother was learning to walk again, and over the two weeks Elaine was there to help her, she heard her say, "Hey, Elaine! Look! I can do it with my cane, now! I don't need my walker!"

"That's great, Anna! Keep up the good work. But be careful, so we don't have to pick you up off the floor," Elaine told her.

Elaine made fast friends with a teen-age boy who had lost his sight in one eye, and was unable to talk clearly and walked with a limp.

"My picture was in the yearbook last year as the most popular guy on campus," said Rupert Landes. "I had more dates than I could afford or had time for. But I bet none of those girls would go out with me now. They just don't want to get close to a cripple."

"Oh, now you don't know that, Rupert," Elaine told him. "I'll bet you any girl worth having will be thoughtful and considerate of you. And you've already learned that you can re-learn any skill you lost if you put your mind to it and work hard and just refuse to give up. You remember when you could stand up but not walk? Now look at you! You can hardly tell you have a limp. And I'll bet that will go away as you continue working out."

"Yeah," said Rupert. "But I won't be able to talk to a girl with my speech problem and my bad eye looking so bad."

"Now Rupert, you know that isn't so. You're talking to me, aren't you? And you're improving your speech every day. And you know they promised to give you an artificial eye that you can turn just like your real eye. When that happens, you'll be the only one who can tell you have an eye problem, and I'll bet you can see a girl well enough to kiss her with that one good eye, don't you think? I mean, I'm sure it's happened before."

Rupert laughed.

"You're right, Elaine. I knew that. I just needed to hear you say it. And you think the really good girls will still like me?" asked Rupert.

"I know it," said Elaine. "Now do you see that little girl in the pink dress over there in the corner? Why don't you go over and talk to her. She's probably told herself no boy will speak to her now. Why don't you prove her wrong?"

"Hey, I think I will. Thanks, Elaine. You know, talking to you just makes everything better," said Rupert.

Elaine talked regularly to several women and several guys at the center who were close to her own age and degree of recovery, and over time she considered each of them her friend. She actually became good and close friends with George, the former doctor and fellow witness-to-be in the upcoming piracy trial in federal court.

But her most enjoyable days were those when McGuffy got the security detail assignment at the rehab center. She would sit in the parlor with him, and they would talk about their past lives and their future dreams.

After a few days of practice, Elaine got her driver's license back. After that, she seemed to check out of the center almost every day and drive with her two security guards to a shopping center or take in a matinee movie or visit a park, or her favorite stop, down at the pier where the yachts and other boats were docked.

When she was with McGuffy, the time seemed to rocket past, and she was with him frequently enough that almost before she realized it, jury selection had begun on the piracy trial.

Lawyers Jeb Smoot, for Brannigan, and Roberta Sparks for Vince Perkins, tried to convince Judge Francis Steele that pretrial publicity had prejudiced their clients' right to a fair trial. But Steele ruled that the trial would go on with such jurors as they could find, and at the end of the second day of selection on Friday, they had 12 jurors and two alternates who said they either hadn't heard or read about the facts of the piracy case or didn't have an opinion on whether the defendants were guilty. All said they could render a fair decision, so Steele ruled the panel acceptable and said the trial would begin at 7 a.m. on Monday.

Elaine called her mother to remind her that the trial was starting.

"I know it. Spence and I have been counting the days," her mother said. "We'll see you Sunday night."

"See you then," said Elaine.

Chapter Twenty-Two

Emma Preston and Spence Foster arrived in Miami from Hannibal on Sunday night and checked in with Elaine by phone. They decided they'd have an early evening meal with Elaine and turn in early. Their flight had been tiring, and they knew they would have to be up early the next morning. Elaine reminded them that she had to be back in the rehab center by the 9 p.m. curfew hour.

Hoover and McGuffy were assigned to the security detail for Elaine on Sunday. Elaine had learned to drive the rented van they had used for the past week to drive around Miami, so Hoover and McGuffy rode with her to Sunday morning worship services at McGuffy's church. They sat on either side of her during the services, then let her drive wherever she wanted to go around Miami most of Sunday afternoon.

When the evening meal was over, McGuffy suggested that he would drive Elaine back to the rehab center and would let Spence and Emma off at their hotel on the way. Then McGuffy said he and Hoover would bring the van back to the hotel parking deck and leave the keys with the desk clerk so Spence could pick them up the next morning.

McGuffy also suggested that Spence might want to leave the van in the hotel parking deck and get a ride to the courthouse in the government van that would be going out to the rehab center after Elaine. That way, McGuffy explained, Spence wouldn't have to bother with trying to find a parking space at the courthouse or with feeding the parking meters all day during the trial but the van would be available if they wanted it.

"I'll be happy to leave word at the security desk that whoever gets security duty for Elaine tomorrow can just swing by the hotel for you and Ms. Preston, if you like, on their way out to pick up Elaine," said McGuffy.

"That sounds like a good idea, Emma," said Spence. "I know we're going to want to be in the trial during the day anyway, so why don't we just catch a ride with the security folks to the courthouse as Mr. McGuffy suggests. Is that alright with you? We can walk anywhere we need to go during the day, you know."

"It's fine with me," said Emma. "It sounds like the simplest way to go."

"So, yeah, Mr. McGuffy. Just tell the security desk to have their guy stop by for us and we'll ride with him," said Spence, "And I'll pick up the keys to the van later."

"Got you covered, Mr. Foster," said McGuffy. "Now you and Ms. Preston remember to be at the hotel's front desk a few minutes before 6 a.m., because security will pick you all up first before heading over to the rehab center for Elaine."

"We'll be ready, Mr. McGuffy. Thanks," said Spence.

When the hotel desk clerk arrived at his post at 5:30 a.m. on Monday, he already had a customer.

"May I help you, Sir?" the clerk asked.

" I'm Spencer Foster in Room 916, and I understand you've got some keys for me," he said.

"Surely, Sir. They're right here on a peg on my bulletin board," said the clerk, who handed the man the keys and watched him drive away in a tan rental van.

A few blocks away at the rehab center, Elaine was up early, waiting at the front door for her guards to sign her out for federal court.

As she waited, she thought about this being finally the day that the piracy trial was to begin, and she thought of Vince Perkins and shuddered. She eventually reassured herself that this was to be the start of the trial that would bring him and the other pirates to justice. Then she saw the tan rental van she and Spence and Emma had been using for several days arriving with two new security guards she didn't know in it.

"I'm right here ready to go," Elaine told them as they walked in.

"Well, get in the van, then, and we'll get you to federal court," one of them said.

"Oh, you guys haven't had security duty for me before, have you?" asked Elaine. "You know you will have to sign me out like a library book and list the date and time and destination in the log book here before I can leave. Didn't they tell you this?" she asked. Then she handed the driver the log book, and when he had signed it, they all walked out to the van together.

"But I thought you guys were coming for me in the government van today," said Elaine as she climbed in.

"We had planned to take the government van, but we had trouble cranking it this morning," the guard said. "So we had to make a last-minute change of plans. Rather than fiddle with trying to start the government van, they told us to just get the van you've been using all week. So we picked it up over at the hotel where the other guards left it last night."

"Oh, I see," said Elaine. "And I notice Mom and Papa Spence aren't here, either. I guess they changed their minds about riding with me to court. They had said last night that going on the government van would keep them from having to find a parking space at the courthouse and having to feed parking meters all day."

"Yes, Ma'am, they changed their minds on that," said the driver.

As she leaned back in her seat on the front passenger side, the man who had ridden in that seat earlier helped her snap her seat belt, then he got in the seat behind her.

Moments later, the man in the back seat reached over Elaine's shoulders and with both hands put a flat vinyl strap over her head and neck and pulled it so tightly she couldn't yell or even breathe. She tried to grab the strap, scratching at it where it pressed upon her wind pipe just below her voice box, but to no avail.

"Go ahead and put the chloroform rag over her nose and loosen the strap before you kill her, Cyrus. You know good and well Marty told us to take her out of commission so she can't testify in court, but he was very insistent that we not kill her," the man driving the van said. "You know he said that now, don't you?"

"Yeah, I know what I'm doing, Jack. You drive. I've got the chloroform rag in this plastic bag, and I'll have it over her nose in a jiffy. There. That should about do it," he said, loosening the strap as Elaine gulped for air, flailing her arms wildly, but gulping a strong dose of chloroform instead. Then she passed out and slumped down in the seat.

Jack Bostwick drove the van back to the hotel parking lot and got out, leaving the keys in it. Then he and Cyrus Snead loaded Elaine into the back seat of a van in which they had come from Brownsville, Texas on Thursday, and they drove north on I-95 out of Miami.

At 6 a.m., two security guards driving a black van with a U.S. Government tag arrived at the front entrance to the hotel where Elaine's mother and father-in-law were staying. Spence and Emma had been waiting for a ride to the courthouse, so when the men in the black van arrived, they spoke, identified themselves and climbed in.

A few minutes later, they stopped at the rehab center for Elaine. But she wasn't there. Dot, the rehab center director, explained why:

"Elaine checked out a good thirty minutes ago, with two guys wearing security uniforms just like yours," Dot said.

"What kind of vehicle were they in? Did you see it?" asked the guard.

"Yes, of course I saw it. It was a tan rental van like the one Elaine has been driving around Miami all week," said Dot.

The guard ran out to his car and radioed the security desk at the courthouse.

"This is Code Red, Officer Reid Mazursky for Chief Morelli. Come in, Sir," the guard said over his police radio. "Chief Morelli, come in, please. This is Officer Mazursky, Unit 3 calling, Code Red."

"This is Morelli. Go ahead, Mazursky," Morelli virtually barked over the radio.

"Sir, someone has kidnapped Elaine Foster, Sir. We're at the rehab center now to pick her up for the start of the trial, and the center director told us two men dressed in security uniforms signed her out and left with her about thirty minutes ago. We're awaiting your further orders, Sir," said Mazursky.

"Where are Elaine's Mom and father-in-law?" asked Morelli. "You were supposed to pick them up at their hotel before picking up Elaine. Did you do that?"

"Roger, Chief. They're right here with us," said Mazursky. "We're awaiting your further orders, Sir."

"Stand by at the rehab center, Mazursky. I've got your report. We're going to be busy at the office here for a while, but we'll be back to you. Stand by. Morelli out."

"Yes, Sir. Mazursky out," he said and went back inside to talk again to Dot.

From a cell phone somewhere in Miami, a call came in to U.S. Attorney Joseph Barton's office. It was before his office normally opened, but he was there early this morning, making last minute preparations for the piracy trial set to begin before U.S. District Judge Francis Steele at 7 a.m.

"There are several canisters of ammonium nitrate and diesel fuel at key places in the federal courthouse," came the man's voice on the phone. "Two of them are set to go off at 8 a.m. Two more will be remotely detonated at 10 a.m. unless the scheduled trial in Judge Steele's courtroom is indefinitely postponed. A final canister is in a vehicle of undisclosed make and model located somewhere in Florida. It will be detonated if the vehicle is located and any attempt is made to remove one of its passengers, a woman by the name of Elaine Foster. You have been warned. Good-bye," and the call ended.

Barton immediately dialed Judge Steele's chambers, identified himself, and told the judge he had something he needed to hear.

"What is it?" asked Steele.

"It's a bomb threat, Your Honor, and they've kidnapped Elaine Foster," said Barton, suddenly gasping for breath. "I suggest you and your staff leave the courtroom and the building as soon as possible, Your Honor. Our FBI bomb squad will do an immediate search and try to disarm it if it's not a hoax. I have the caller's words on my office voice mail and I'll play it for you if you want to stay and listen to it, but I'm telling you, Sir, that I'm not going to wait for it to play. Do you want to hear it?"

"Well, sure I'd like to hear it if we've got time," said Steele. "When is the bomb supposed to go off?"

"The caller says the first is set to go off at 8 a.m. It's not yet 7, so that's more than an hour away, but we may not have that long, Your Honor," said Barton.

"Play the tape," said Steele.

Barton pushed the play button on his office recorder as sirens began to go off. He then called Morelli and his Special Tactical Law Enforcement Team and the FBI's Miami chief and key deputies into his office shortly after 6:30 a.m.

"We have major problems, folks, to put it mildly," Barton told those he had alerted as they filed into his office, except for Steele, who still hadn't left his courtroom. Then lastly Steele filed in, after Barton had begun to talk.

"Come in, Your Honor," Barton told Steele. "I had just said what we all already know, judge: We have major problems here this morning. Elaine Foster has been kidnapped, we're pretty sure we know by whom, and we also have an active bomb threat in the courthouse.

"Thanks for coming to my office so quickly in response to my alert. But our first order of business is to leave here as quickly and in as orderly and safe a fashion as possible for the Dade County Courthouse a block from here.

"I understand there is a vacant courtroom in the county courthouse which we can use for the piracy trial, whenever Judge Steele and my office can determine that it's safe and advisable for us to commence it.

"For our security work, several county deputies based on the first floor of the courthouse have agreed to vacate their offices for the duration of this emergency and let us use their space as a temporary command center. We will assemble there immediately. This meeting is adjourned."

Security personnel on the federal courthouse grounds quickly put up a yellow police ribbon and forbade anyone else, including several judges and their staffs, from entering the building. Other security personnel and Miami police blocked both lanes of traffic on all four sides of the courthouse.

Moments later, from their temporary command center, Barton laid out the challenge:

"I will excuse the FBI folks at this point and let you guys complete your search of the federal building to determine whether this explosion threat is real or is a hoax. The rest of us will remain here until we hear from you," said Barton.

"Next, I would like to hear from Chief Morelli about what we need to do and how we need to proceed to rescue Elaine Foster at the earliest moment and with the least risk possible to her," said Barton. "Chief Morelli. Any ideas?"

"Thank you, Mr. Barton," said Morelli. "From what we know at this point, the guys who kidnapped Elaine were wearing uniforms similar or identical to those worn by our regular security guards, thus their arrival at the rehab center raised no suspicions or concerns, not even to Elaine apparently until at least she was inside the van and it had left the premises.

"They were traveling in a tan rental van which Elaine has been using regularly over the past couple of weeks, accompanied at all times by two security officers. We believe the kidnappers left the rehab center in the van by my watch exactly 34 minutes ago. We believe, therefore, that it and they are either still in Miami proper or are within a 30-mile radius of the city, most likely, we believe, on Interstate 95, because we think they would try to take Elaine as far away from Miami as possible.

"We believe the kidnappers are friends, family members or cohorts of defendant Vincent Perkins, who as you know is being held without bond and is one of the defendants set to go on trial in Judge Steele's court today.

"We foiled an earlier plot by Vincent's brother Mose to keep Elaine from testifying. We took Mose into custody two weeks ago and he is being held without bond on federal charges of tampering with a federal witness.

"We know there is a younger Perkins brother, Marty, still in the area, and we suspect he's behind this kidnapping, with possible help from a couple of other guys from Brownsville, Texas, who came to see Vincent right after he was hospitalized in Miami General Hospital with severe gunshot wounds. But they haven't been seen in the area to our knowledge since then.

"Now what I will say next doesn't need to leave this room," said Morelli.

"We are using some security tracking devices that we do not discuss publicly, but in anticipation of just such a situation as we face now, we installed a signaling device in the rental van when Elaine began to use it regularly some two weeks ago.

"This device, in tandem with our global positioning system, should permit us to track Elaine and her captors covertly, so that we can know exactly where they are without them knowing where we are until the moment when we believe we can take her away from them with the lowest risk of injury to her. We are preparing to take the initial readings from this device momentarily.

"Finally, and this also should be considered departmentally classified as not for public discussion, Elaine has at least three other devices with her that should prove invaluable to us," said Morelli.

"The first device is a homing signal, just like the one we installed in the van, which is sewn into the lining of her purse, in case the other device stops working or if they change vehicles.

"She also has a miniature cell phone sewn into a strategically located item of underclothing which can be activated and used without removing it. As you might guess, it gently vibrates instead of playing a tone if we were to call her on it.

"And finally, we call this the Maxwell Smart option, the heel of one of her shoes also contains a miniature cell phone which can be activated by stomping her foot on a sidewalk or other hard surface and which will pick up and transmit voices clearly from several feet away. My team and I will do our best to locate Elaine and pass word of her location on to you folks in a timely fashion.

"Lt. Anderson and Lt. McGuffy are standing by for helicopter duty if it turns out we need airborne tracking at any point, but my hope is that we'll be able to spot the van on the interstate with the signaling devices, then have have four unmarked patrol cars manned by plain-clothed deputies from law enforcement agencies upstate from us, waiting on the on-ramps ahead of them to pull onto the interstate on our signal.

"These cars will ease quickly and as unexpectedly as possible into positions on either side and in front of the kidnappers as well as behind them, at which point we can simply muscle them off the highway onto the shoulder and use such force as is necessary to neutralize them and rescue Elaine.

"With that, Mr. Barton, we'd like to clear out of here and rescue Elaine."

"Thanks for that report, Chief. Go get 'em," said Barton. "Now, Your Honor, those of us who are left will be glad to hear your plans as to postponing or commencing with the trial."

"Thank you, Mr. Barton. My first choice would be that the bomb threat turns out to be a hoax and that we can return to the courthouse and commence the trial as scheduled," said Steele. "Before I give you my second choice, I'd like to ask you what the chances are that the bomb squad could make a definite determination in the next 10 or 15 minutes."

"Well, they have several floors to check, but those bomb-sniffing dogs are really good and really quick. I've seen them do a practice run in 15 minutes or less, but depending on what they find, it may take them longer," said Barton. "Now what was your second choice?"

"My second choice also is that the bomb threat turns out to be a hoax, but we would postpone the start of trial for one hour, which should give the bomb squad ample time to check out the courthouse, and it should give us time as well to move back into the courtroom in an orderly fashion. As you can tell, Mr. Barton, neither of those options involves scrapping the trial or delaying it more than the minimum necessary."

"I understand your position, Your Honor, and I can assure you the United States is eager for the trial to commence as soon as you give the word to do so," said Barton. "Chief Morelli assured me a few minutes ago that his team has all the scientific evidence locked in steel and reinforced concrete vaults in the Coast Guard forensics lab, so presumably it would be safe even if the worst comes and a bomb goes off in the federal building."

"That's good to know, Mr. Barton," said Steele. "Now if you'll excuse me, I brought some briefs in my satchel that I need to find a reasonably quiet place to read. Keep me posted on what the bomb squad finds."

"I certainly will, Your Honor. Hopefully it will be good news and it will be quick."

Chief Walter Morelli's Special Tactical Law Enforcement Team quickly transformed one corner of a former deputy sheriff's office into a command center and monitoring station. Morelli hooked up his laptop computer to a projector, which cast maps of Miami area streets and the state of Florida on the wall.

Morelli flipped images back and forth on the two screens, and somewhat to his surprise, he was getting two sets of glowing dots, which he interpreted as signals from two separate locations on his maps.

The city map showed a blinking red dot staying in a fixed location just a few blocks from the county courthouse. The Florida state map showed a different blinking light, this one bright yellow, heading north on I-95 about forty miles from downtown.

"Why and how could we be getting two separate signals?" asked McGuffy, staring over Morelli's shoulder at the projections.

"The rented van is the one shown at a fixed location on the city map, and I have no idea what the one north of the city is," said Petty Officer Sam Mendez, the team's law enforcement specialist.

"What we know is that the rented van is about six blocks from here, probably in the parking deck of the hotel where Spence and Emma have been staying. My first thought is that the kidnappers have changed vehicles and have left the rented van at the hotel to try to throw us off. If they've got another vehicle headed north, naturally they'd like for us to be looking for the wrong vehicle.

"Fortunately for us, however, the signal in Elaine's purse is sending out the blinking yellow light, so we know that's where she is. I should say there is a chance that Elaine is in neither vehicle and that they are carrying her purse in the vehicle headed north to further throw us off course. But I don't think the Perkins boys and their buddies are that smart. I hope they don't prove me wrong.

"I'd suggest we signal the four unmarked cars to come onto I-95 ahead of the vehicle we think is carrying Elaine and let them slow down in a random pattern until the kidnappers are surrounded on all sides. Then we can eyeball the inside of the vehicle to see if we can see Elaine and tell what kind of restraints they are using on her, what condition she's in, and whether there are any weapons."

"That sounds good to me, Mendez," said Morelli, who approved the plan and ordered it carried out. He reached those outside the command post by radio.

"All units, this is Morelli. Our global positioning system indicates that an unknown vehicle carrying the signaling device Elaine has in her purse is traveling north on I-95 at 70 mph, apparently taking no risk that they will be stopped for speeding.

"They appear to be nearing the sixty-mile marker now, so the four unmarked units should enter I-95 at this point traveling about 60 mph so our kidnappers can catch up to them. We think our signaling system is accurate enough to pick the exact vehicle you want to surround, so we don't get egg on our faces and make somebody really, really mad at us. Before you do the surround move, give us their tag number so we can determine if they're driving their own vehicle or have stolen it. Morelli out."

The four unmarked cars driven by plainclothes deputies moved out on Morelli's signal, creating four separate blinking blue lights on Morelli's screen. At this point, Morelli's phone rang. It was a TV news reporter.

"This is Brad Patch of Channel 40 News, Chief. Our news helicopter is in the air over the four deputies who have just pulled onto I-95 at the 60-mile marker. Can you tell us if the deputies are in any way involved in the effort to rescue Elaine Foster, the alleged piracy victim and likely witness in the piracy trial set for today which we've just learned has been delayed by a bomb threat on Miami Federal Court?"

Morelli motioned for Barton, now seated at a desk adjacent to Morelli, to pick up on the line, and he did so.

"Mr. Patch. I have U.S. Attorney Joseph Barton on the line with me, and he can correct me if I'm wrong, but I think he will tell you that if you screw up our rescue of Ms. Elaine Foster, a victim of piracy and a witness in the pending federal piracy case, then you should expect to be charged with obstruction of justice and prosecuted to the full extent of the law. Now get away from those deputies before we send some armed fighter planes your way to help you find someplace else to be. Do you get my drift, Mr. Patch?"

"I stand by every word he just told you, Mr. Patch," said Barton. "You are dangerously close to screwing up a major law enforcement effort, and I can assure you, you and your organization will feel the consequences if you do."

"Guys, guys, come on now. Surely you've heard of a little thing called the First Amendment," said Patch. "However, it was never our intent to obstruct justice or to hinder your operation in any way. We simply didn't know. Sorry."

"Now you know. And when our mission is accomplished, we'll be happy to talk about it. Good day, Mr. Patch," said Barton, hanging up the phone.

"Tell us what you see, guys," Morelli told the plainclothes deputies who now were only a few car lengths ahead of where the signal producing the yellow blinking light on Morelli's map appeared to be located.

"Traffic's pretty steady and mixed here, Sir, between cars, trucks, pickups and vans," said one of the deputies. "There's a navy blue van pretty close to my tail light and a silver minivan in the lane to my right."

"Well, my signal is showing the van immediately behind you is the one to watch," said Morelli. "Can you see anything inside?"

"Well, yes, there appears to be a man with a scruffy beard driving the van and a woman kind of slumped down in the front passenger seat, looks like maybe she's asleep, and then there's another guy in the seat right behind her. I can't get a good look at him, though," the deputy said. "Wait a minute. He's pulling around me in the lane on my right. I guess I should be able to see his tag in a minute. Yep, it's a Texas tag and an emblem on the back door that says Tony's Used Cars, Brownsville.

"Sounds like our man," said Morelli. "Now you say there's a woman apparently asleep in the front passenger seat. Describe her for me."

"Well, she's got brownish blonde hair and is wearing some kind of bandage on the lower right side of her head, said the deputy.

"That has to be her," said Morelli. "Now you guys get in position without making any abrupt or surprise moves. Stay with the flow of traffic as much as you can and just observe for a while. Keep us posted on what you see, particularly if you see any guns or weapons of any kind."

"It looks clean as to weapons, and it looks like the guy in the back seat is reaching between the driver and the woman, and he's fiddling with something on the dash, like maybe a radio or CD player or something. And she still seems to be totally out of it," said the deputy. "Wait, she's stirring a bit, and the guy in the back seat is putting a cloth over her nose. OK, now she's slumped back down again. That must have been chloroform or some kind of knockout stuff."

"Exactly," said Morelli. "That means we won't be able to coordinate what we do with Elaine. If we could talk to her, we could suggest she go to the restroom or something, anything to get her away from them so we could take them out without hurting her. But we don't have that luxury. So what we do, we're going to have to do soon. Are you guys ready?"

"Ready, Sir," the deputies in all four unmarked cars said.

"Well, I want you to hug them close and just move them off the highway to the shoulder, strong-arm style. But before we do that, I want to remind you what we're dealing with here.

"As you know, the bomb threat caller said the van was booby-trapped with an ammonium nitrate explosive charge, which would be exploded if any effort were made to remove Elaine from the van. We have just got word from the FBI bomb squad that the courthouse is clean, and at least their threat to explode a bomb at the courthouse on a timer at 8 a.m. appears to be a hoax.

"We know those pirates really did booby-trap their own ship to blow up in Miami harbor, which it did, killing two Coast Guard sailors. So I want to remind you that their threat as to the van may be real, and that you are risking your life when we move against these guys in a few minutes.

"I will tell you that Mr. Barton and my entire team and I are agreed that we must move on them and take our chances. Are any of you guys getting cold feet?"

"No, Sir, we're game, Sir. We risk our lives every day, Sir. That's our job," said one deputy. "That's right, Sir," said the others.

"Well, it's time. Squeeze them dry," said Morelli as the four unmarked cars moved against the van at the same instant. The driver of the car directly in front of the van slammed on his brakes, causing the van to rear-end the deputy's car and triggering the van's front seat air bags. The other three cars then muscled the van off the highway and to a complete stop on the shoulder in a matter of seconds.

The deputies then rushed the van, opening the driver's door and the middle passenger door. They grabbed the driver and the male passenger by their arms and yanked them out onto the ground, pulling their shoulders out of socket and thereby temporarily incapacitating them in one swift yank. Then two other deputies unfastened the woman's seat belt and moved her to the back seat of one of the deputies' cars.

"It appears to be Elaine, Sir, and I believe she's not injured, just out on some kind of anesthetic substance. There's a plastic zipper bag on the floorboard with a rag in it which smells like chloroform to me, Sir," the deputy said.

"That's really good work, and tell the other guys I said so," Morelli told him.

"Glad we could help, Sir," he said.

At that moment, a Coast Guard chopper manned by Anderson and McGuffy landed on a grassy area farther down the shoulder from where the deputies had forced the van off the highway.

"We'll be able to take your passenger on back to Miami for you, Sir," McGuffy told one of the deputies he had seen placing her in the back seat of his car. "And I want you to know that that was one fantastic piece of rescue work, and I say that as one who makes his living rescuing folks."

"It really was some top-notch work, guys. I'm glad we could be here to see it," said Anderson. He and McGuffy once again lifted Elaine into their chopper and headed toward Miami.

A crowd had gathered outside the Miami federal building when the helicopter bringing Elaine Foster back from her kidnapping ordeal landed across the street on the rooftop helipad of Miami General Hospital.

Elaine was whisked quickly to the examination room of Dr. Jonas Sutherland, her surgeon, who ordered several scans to determine if she had received any additional injuries when she pitched forward against the airbag.

"Young lady, you must have some powerful folks looking out for you," Sutherland said after reviewing the scans of Elaine's brain.

"Why do you say that, Doctor?" Elaine asked him.

"Well, you sustained enough of an impact to have caused considerable damage if it had been in a slightly different location," said Sutherland.

"I'm guessing that you were protected from injury by the fact that you were unconscious from breathing chloroform, and you were thus relaxed to a far greater degree than you would have been if you had been riding alert in that seat.

"Also, because you were sprawled forward in a sidewise position, the brunt of the impact appears to have been more toward your shoulder than toward your head. The bandage on your original injury shows no sign of additional drainage, which basically means, taken all together, that you appear to be no worse for the wear. You're OK to testify in court, in my professional opinion.

"Now you may experience a headache slightly more severe than usual, but this would be more from stress after the fact than from any new injury. In short, you should get any relief you need from a couple of acetaminophen tablets, which you should take with water before going to the courtroom. You're free to go, but I still want to see you on Monday morning for your usual checkup."

"Thank you, Doctor," said Elaine. "Now I think a whole bunch of people over at the federal court house are looking for me. So I'd better get over there. Thanks for all you continue to do for me."

"I wish all my patients responded as well and as quickly as you, Elaine. As I've told you before, you're one tough lady," said Sutherland.

"Thanks, and I'll see you Monday," Elaine said as she and Anderson and McGuffy climbed back into the helicopter. Anderson started the engines and lifted off the pad, only to land again across the street on the Coast Guard's own pad outside the forensics lab.

The crowd, which had continued to stand by to get the word on whether Elaine was injured during the kidnapping, cheered and applauded when she and Anderson and McGuffy stepped down from the chopper. She smiled and they smiled and waved before entering the lab through a back door.

The crowd of law enforcement personnel who had gathered in the lab to welcome her and her rescuers back also broke into applause and cheers.

Barton said several TV and newspaper reporters were outside wanting to interview him and everyone else involved in the rescue. But at Judge Steele's request, Barton told them he would release a brief factual statement and all other details of the rescue would be released at the conclusion of the piracy trial, which was expected to last the rest of the week.

Steele told Barton and defense counsel in the case that he would begin the trial promptly at 1:00 PM, and that all motions to delay the start of trial for any reason would be denied.

Chapter Twenty-Three

When the courthouse clock struck one, Steele and his clerk walked into the court-room from his private office suite.

"All rise!" the clerk shouted, and everyone in the audience and at the counsel tables stood. "The U.S. District Court for the Miami District is now in session. God save these United States and this honorable court. Be seated please," she shouted, and every-one sat down.

At the defense table sat Jeb Smoot, attorney for defendant Joe Brannigan, and Roberta Sparks, attorney for defendant Vincent Perkins. They sat next to their clients, who wore business suits through which could be seen prominent bandages.

Smoot wore his traditional brown coat, red shirt and black boots and a black string tie, and he placed his black western-style hat on the back side of the counsel table behind a stack of papers. Sparks wore a black pants suit with a white blouse. Barton and Richards, the U.S. attorney and his top assistant, sat at a separate table, both wear-ing standard dark business suits.

"Are the lawyers ready?" Steele asked, and Sparks and Smoot stood and said in unison, "We are, Your Honor."

"The United States is ready, Your Honor," said Barton, also standing.

"I will allow opening statements, 20 minutes per side, and then Mr. Barton, we'll hear your first witness," said Steele. "Bring in the jury and alternates."

Moments later, jurors were seated, and Barton approached the lectern.

"Your Honor, ladies and gentlemen of the jury, my name is Joseph Barton, the United States attorney for the Miami District. My job is to enforce federal laws in this district by prosecuting those who violate those laws against the peace and dignity of the citizens of this district," said Barton. "With me at the counsel table is my top deputy, Assistant U.S. Attorney Milton Richards, who has done much of the work in prepara-tion for this case and may assist me from time to time during the trial.

"There are two defendants on trial here today. They are seated here at the table with their lawyers. Certain others may be identified later," said Barton.

"This is defendant Joe Brannigan, who we believe the evidence will show was the organizer and the active force behind the piracy conspiracy we allege in this case," Bar-ton said, standing near the table where Brannigan was seated.

"And this is Mr. Brannigan's attorney, Mr. Jeb Smoot, who will be representing Mr. Brannigan in this trial." Brannigan and Smoot nodded to the jury when their names were called.

"And over here is defendant Vincent Perkins, whom we believe the evidence will show was the second-in-command to Mr. Brannigan. We believe the evidence will show that Mr. Perkins was Mr. Brannigan's enforcer, who carried out his orders on board their ship, which they named *The Silver Bullet*.

"We allege that their vessel was a pirate ship engaged in missions of kidnapping, murder, destruction of private property, transport of illegal drugs, and, in short, maritime piracy, an activity so offensive to governments and private citizens alike, to human civilization and to mankind itself, that it has been punished for centuries with the sentence of death. The United States will seek the death penalty in this case should you ladies and gentlemen of the jury find these defendants guilty as charged."

"Objection, Your Honor," said Smoot, jumping to his feet. "Mr. Barton has invaded the role and function of this court by attempting to set the penalty for alleged crimes that absolutely no evidence has been offered to support."

"Well, of course no evidence has been offered, Mr. Smoot. That's what we're holding this trial for," said Steele. "Ladies and gentlemen, I will inform you that Mr. Barton has absolutely no authority to set the penalties in this or in any other case, nor do you. The Congress has set penalty limits in the law which the court may impose, including death or prison time, should the evidence and your findings support it. Go ahead, Mr. Barton."

"Thank you, Your Honor. Now I was about to point out to you, ladies and gentlemen of the jury, that Mr. Perkins also is represented by counsel, Ms. Roberta Sparks here," said Barton, as Perkins and Sparks nodded to the jury.

"Now it's my job and the job of my assistant in this case to present in an orderly fashion the facts or evidence which we believe will support the charges in the indictment," said Barton. "Remember that what I say, or what Mr. Richards or Mr. Smoot or Ms. Sparks will say is not evidence. Neither is the indictment, which enumerates the government's charges against the defendants in this case.

"The indictment is just the mechanism for getting this case to court. The indictment is the grand jury's way of saying the evidence in this case should be reviewed by you jurors to determine if the defendant or defendants are guilty as charged or not.

"The evidence in this case is what you will hear coming from the witnesses on the witness stand, who will be sworn to tell the truth, the whole truth, and nothing but the truth. It is Judge Steele's job to preside over the orderly presentation of the evidence and the arguments of the attorneys and to tell you what the law is."

"Your time is about up, Mr. Barton," the judge said after Barton's comments went on and on.

"Thank you, Your Honor. I will conclude my remarks by saying that if you find that the evidence you will hear in this case is sufficient to convince you beyond a reasonable doubt that the alleged crimes have been committed by either or both of these defendants, then your duty will be to return a verdict of guilty as charged.

"I'm sure you've all heard public officials from time to time say they will send a message to lawbreakers that crime won't be tolerated in our communities nor in the waters off our shores. Well, it is you ladies and gentlemen of the jury who will send the real message to criminals by your verdict. Because if you return a verdict of guilty against these defendants, you will have told them and all would-be pirates like them, that maritime piracy won't be tolerated by the people of South Florida.

"I urge you to give them the equivalent of what our ancestors have told pirates for centuries, `You aren't welcome here. We hang pirates!'"

"That will be about enough, Mr. Barton," said Steele. "Now we'll hear from Mr. Smoot and Ms. Sparks, who have 10 minutes each. Ms. Sparks, I'll hear you first."

"Thank you, Your Honor," said Sparks, standing.

"I won't repeat what you have heard already about your role and that of us lawyers, ladies and gentlemen," said Sparks.

"Just remember that the defendants, Mr. Perkins and Mr. Brannigan, have no duty or responsibility to prove they are innocent," said Sparks. "Under the Constitution and laws of the United States, every person accused of a crime comes to court presumed to be innocent, and that presumption of innocence goes with them throughout the presentation of all the evidence, through all the arguments you will hear from us lawyers, and through all of Judge Steele's instructions on the law.

"The presumption of innocence will stay with these defendants unless and until you ladies and gentlemen find that beyond a reasonable doubt they are guilty of the offenses charged in this indictment.

"And I will remind you, ladies and gentlemen, that it is as much your duty to prevent an innocent person from going to jail as it is to send a guilty person to prison. Remember that, and my client, Mr. Perkins, and I, thank you."

"Thank you, Ms. Sparks. Now we'll hear from Mr. Smoot," said Steele.

"Thank you, Your Honor," said Smoot. "I too will seek to avoid telling you what you've heard already, ladies and gentlemen. But using what Ms. Sparks said as a starting point, I'll mention that Mr. Barton and Mr. Richards will try to pin on my client, Mr. Brannigan, what some two dozen other folks did. Now they both like to use the term `pirates,' trying to conjure up in your minds the grisly images of the evil robber barons of the high seas over hundreds of years, and which by right have been and by rights should have been made to walk the plank or hung from the yardarm, or dispatched to Davy Jones' locker, I could go on…"

"See that you don't, Mr. Smoot," said Steele.

"Yes, Your Honor," said Smoot. "Mr. Barton and Mr. Richards will tell you about death and destruction, robbery and intrigue, but I will assure you, ladies and gentlemen, that they won't show you one shred of evidence that any of those bad things were done by my client, Mr. Joseph Brannigan.

"In each case, the things they allege as maritime piracy against my client, if seen in their true light, will be acts committed by others, pirates if you will, who have rebelled against the honest and true leadership of Mr. Brannigan. Now, we don't contest the government's evidence that Mr. Brannigan was the captain of *The Silver Bullet*. He was its captain until the crew mutinied and took the command away from him.

"Regrettably, those who would have been able to attest to the mutiny have all been killed by the Search and Seizure teams of the U.S. Coast Guard. And I think you will find, ladies and gentlemen, that they will attempt to show by what they will contend is circumstantial evidence that my client, Mr. Brannigan, acted alone when he allegedly shot a man in the back.

"They will call it circumstantial, ladies and gentlemen, because they don't have any real evidence. They will be unable to present any witness who can truthfully testify that Mr. Brannigan shot anyone. On the contrary, however, even the government's witnesses will confirm that the man from Hannibal, Missouri, shot my client just inches from his heart in a failed attempt to kill him. Because Mr. Brannigan is innocent of each and every crime of which the government has accused him, I ask you to return a verdict of not guilty."

"Thank you, Mr. Smoot," said Steele. "And Mr. Barton, let's hear your first witness."

"Your Honor, the United States would like to call Jim Cummings," said Barton as Cummings, wearing an arm swing on his left arm, was escorted into the courtroom from a hallway on the judge's left and took his seat on the witness stand.

"Stand and face the jury and raise your right hand, Mr. Cummings. And please state your full name," said Steele's clerk.

"I'm James Earl Cummings," he said.

"Do you swear or affirm that the testimony you will give in this cause will be the truth, the whole truth and nothing but the truth, so help you God?" asked the clerk.

"I do," said Cummings as the clerk said, "Be seated please."

"Mr. Cummings, do you know the defendants, Joe Brannigan and Vince Perkins?" asked Barton.

"Yeah, that's them sittin' over there," said Cummings.

"Let the record show that Mr. Cummings has identified the defendants," said Barton.

"Tell the ladies and gentlemen of the jury how long you have known the defendants and where you first met them."

"Well, I guess I've been knowing them both nigh unto 20 years. A long time. I met them in Brownsville, Texas," said Cummings.

"And tell us when and where you most recently saw them," said Barton.

"Well, I most recently saw them on board Brannigan's ship, which he named *The Silver Bullet*," said Cummings.

"And how did you come to be on board their ship, Mr. Cummings," asked Barton.

"Well, I signed up as a member of the crew," said Cummings.

"And what did they tell you was the mission and business of *The Silver Bullet?*" asked Barton.

"They said they were going to have some fun with some drug runners, like steal their cargo and dump it in the gulf, and try to make them sorry they had been in the drug business. I got the idea, they might rough them up a little and maybe mess up their boats, but I didn't know they was going into kidnapping and torture and total destruction of private boats," said Cummings.

In careful and deliberate steps, Cummings over the next hour recounted how Brannigan and Perkins ordered the kidnapping of a man and his wife from Hannibal, Missouri, Tommy Joe and Elaine Foster; the capture of their yacht and the destruction of it by blowing it up with ammonium nitrate and diesel fuel at the same time that they used the explosion to cripple a Colombian freighter, the *San Pedro*.

Cummings said he also heard Brannigan and Perkins order the slaughter of the captain and crew of the *San Pedro*.

Cummings testified that he was made to load the ammonium nitrate aboard the Missouri couple's yacht, the *Nautilus*, after he had told Brannigan and Perkins that he didn't want to participate in any killings or kidnappings or torturing of the man and his wife or even hauling drugs.

Smoot and Sparks asked Cummings repeated questions about whether he led a mutiny, but Cummings just as repeatedly insisted that he wasn't attempting to lead a mutiny and never led one.

"Call your next witness, Mr. Barton," Steele said as the direct testimony and cross-examination of Cummings concluded and he stepped down from the witness stand.

"The United States calls Elaine Foster, Your Honor," said Barton as Smoot stood and objected.

"What's the basis of your objection, Mr. Smoot?" asked Steele.

"On the basis of her likely mental defect, Your Honor," said Smoot. "As Your Honor will take judicial notice I'm sure, Ms. Foster unfortunately sustained a severe blow to her head and lost most if not all of her memory, and thus isn't competent to testify in this or any other court of law. And as of this morning, Your Honor, she has sustained additional mental shock perhaps additional physical injury from the collision of the vehicle in which she was riding, which triggered the discharge of a front seat air bag."

"What says the United States? Do you have evidence that would qualify your witness, Elaine Foster, as a witness in this case, Mr. Barton?" asked Steele.

"We do, Your Honor. We have Dr. Jonas Sutherland, whose office is nearby, who not only was Elaine's surgeon following her injury but has been constantly monitoring it for most of the past month. He also has examined her this morning after she came into contact with the airbag."

"OK, ladies and gentlemen, I will ask the marshal to escort you back to the jury room. We'll take a 10-minute break while the government brings in its witness. You are welcome to get something to drink or go to the restroom, but be ready to come back to the courtroom in 10 minutes. Marshal, escort them out. Court is in recess for 10 minutes," Steele declared, striking his gavel.

When the recess ended, jurors were ushered back in. Sutherland took the witness stand and was identified and sworn. He testified as to his academic degrees and experience in the area of TBI, and Barton offered him without objection as an expert witness.

"Dr. Sutherland, are you familiar with the injury of Elaine Foster, and could you tell this court and jurors whether or not she is sufficiently recovered from her injuries as to be a reliable witness in this case?" Barton asked.

"I am familiar with Elaine's injury. She has been under my direct care for about a month now, and I find that she has made a remarkably complete and full recovery from TBI," said Sutherland. "I consider her totally competent to testify based on any measure of her mental ability and memory."

"Did you also have an opportunity, doctor, to examine Ms. Foster following her contact with an airbag that discharged in front of her in a vehicle in which she was riding this morning?" asked Barton.

"Yes, I examined her this morning after she came into contact with the airbag, and I found no evidence of further injury and no aggravation of her existing injury," said Sutherland.

"OK, Doctor, if you'll answer questions from the defense lawyers or the judge," said Barton.

"Doctor, I'm Jeb Smoot, attorney for Joe Brannigan in this case, and I'd like to ask you, Sir, if persons who receive traumatic brain injury, or TBI as you called it, virtually 100 percent of the time, suffer some memory loss that they never recover. Isn't that right, Doctor?"

"That is correct," said Sutherland.

"And you're not telling this court and these jurors, are you Doctor, that Ms. Foster, unlike virtually all other TBI people, has suffered absolutely no memory loss?" asked Smoot.

"I am not," said Sutherland.

"Isn't it a fact, Doctor, that Elaine Foster is virtually certain to have suffered some permanent memory loss and thus couldn't remember, much less reliably testify, that she saw my client, Mr. Brannigan, shoot her husband Tommy Joe Foster in the back as alleged in this indictment, or that she saw the other defendant, Mr. Perkins, strike her on the head with a wooden beam, as also alleged in this indictment?" asked Smoot.

"My professional opinion, as the surgeon who operated on her a few weeks ago and who has intensely monitored her recovery since then, is that she is totally capable of giving reliable testimony on events she and her husband experienced while on your client's ship except for events occurring within a span of a few minutes before or after her injury," said Sutherland.

"Thank you, that's all the questions I have, Your Honor," said Smoot.

"Ms. Sparks?" asked Steele.

"Thank you, Your Honor. Dr. Sutherland, if Ms. Foster were on the witness stand and Mr. Barton were to ask her whether she could remember my client's striking her on the head with a wooden beam, and she were to testify that she could remember it, would you be inclined to disregard that testimony as unreliable?" asked Sparks.

"Objection, Your Honor. It calls for speculation on the part of the witness," said Barton.

"Overruled," said Steele. "You offered Dr. Sutherland as an expert and the defense didn't object. He's entitled to give his opinion if he has one. Do you have an opinion on the matter you were asked about, Doctor?"

"I do, Your Honor," said Sutherland.

"And what is that opinion, Doctor?" asked Sparks.

"I would tend to disregard as unreliable any testimony about events within a few minutes before and a few minutes after a TBI that has caused temporary loss of other memories," said Sutherland.

"I have no more questions, your honor," said Sparks.

"No more questions, Your Honor," said both Smoot and Barton.

"Dr. Sutherland, you're excused, Sir. Thanks for being with us today," said Steele.

"Hope I was of some help," said Sutherland as he left the courtroom.

Elaine Foster was sworn in and took the stand as the government's next witness while her mother, Emma Preston, and her father-in-law, Spencer Foster, watched from the audience. They were seated next to each other, and Elaine smiled at them.

"Elaine, defense attorneys in this case, before you took the stand, questioned whether your TBI erased your memory of key events in this case. From your first-hand knowledge and observation, tell the jurors what you can remember and what if anything you can't remember about the incidents described in the indictment," said Barton.

"Well, sir, I cannot remember anything immediately before or immediately after my injury, but I have regained all of my other memories from the time I regained consciousness on a sandbar island several weeks ago to right now, and backward from a few minutes before my injury all the way back to my childhood," said Elaine.

"Can you tell the judge and jury whether you remember seeing your husband, Tommy Joe Foster, shot in the back and killed?" asked Barton.

"No, I cannot remember that. But I do remember seeing him shot at by Mr. Brannigan several times," said Elaine. "Brannigan fired several shots into the deck really close to Tommy Joe's feet and told him he wanted to see him dance. And then he told Perkins, who was holding a beam above my head, that he wanted Tommy Joe to see what they were going to do to me before they killed him."

"Now, Elaine, tell the judge and the ladies and gentlemen of the jury if you can remember anything else that you saw Brannigan and Perkins do before the time you say Perkins was holding a beam over your head and Brannigan was shooting at Tommy Joe's feet and making him dance," said Barton.

"Well, my husband and I were on our yacht. We had come through stormy weather, and immediately we saw Brannigan's ship, *The Silver Bullet*, as though it had been waiting for us to come through the storm. Perkins called out to us from the top deck.

"Perkins said Brannigan, the captain of *The Silver Bullet*, would like to help us with repairs to our yacht and wanted to invite us to come aboard for a party. We went aboard as invited, then Brannigan ordered his crew to make Tommy Joe drink more and more liquor until he was drunk, and then they started saying crude things to and about me and threw me down on the deck and started to abuse me.

"Brannigan, Perkins and several members of the crew had guns of various types, and Tommy Joe grabbed a small caliber pistol and started firing it. One shot hit Brannigan near the heart. He ordered us locked up in their brig, and then one of their crewmen, Mr. Jim Cummings, came to our defense and tried to talk them into putting him and my husband and me back on our yacht and letting us go our own way.

"Brannigan and Perkins wouldn't agree to it and they threw Mr. Cummings in the brig with us. Mr. Cummings had a gun which we later used to try to escape, but they ordered Mr. Cummings to load our yacht with ammonium nitrate, which they later detonated near a Colombian freighter, the *San Pedro*."

"Then what happened, Elaine?" asked Barton.

"When the freighter had moved in real close between *The Silver Bullet* and our yacht, the explosives were detonated. The explosion obliterated our yacht and blew a big hole in the freighter. Then after a couple of hours, Brannigan gave the orders to invade the freighter and kill all the crew and then to load on board *The Silver Bullet* what they suspected was the Colombian ship's cargo of cocaine, marijuana and other contraband and a little bit of coffee. Tommy Joe and I broke out of the brig while they were all on board the *San Pedro* except for Brannigan and Perkins and one young man they left guarding the brig," said Elaine.

"Tommy Joe tried to use the two bullets he had left in the pistol Mr. Cummings had left us to kill Brannigan and Perkins, but he missed and threw the empty gun down. And as I've told you, that's all I remember before I regained consciousness on a sandbar island five or six hours or so later."

"That's all the questions I have, Your Honor. Thanks, Elaine. Now the defense may have some questions," said Barton.

"We do, Your Honor," said Sparks. "Ms. Foster, may I call you Elaine?"

"Sure. That's my name," said Elaine.

"But isn't it true that for a long time after you regained consciousness after you received your TBI, you didn't know that Elaine was your name?" asked Sparks.

"That's right. It was several days before I knew for sure. And I didn't recognize Tommy Joe as my husband at first, either. But he had a homemade tattoo on his arm that he put on there when he was a kid. We were childhood sweethearts, and he put my name ELAINE on his arm with a ballpoint pen."

"Well, tell us, Elaine, if you remember, how you happened to remember Tommy Joe and that your last name was Foster, the same as his," said Sparks.

"Well, it was after my surgery to remove from my brain one of the splinters that our forensic scientists determined through DNA and tissue examination had come from the beam that was used to hit me on the head. Lt. McGuffy, one of the two Coast Guard sailors who rescued me from the sandbar island, showed me some pictures and wanted to know if I knew who they were. I said I did," said Elaine.

"And had Lt. McGuffy or anyone else at that point told you who was depicted on the photos?" asked Sparks.

"No, not at all," said Elaine.

"That's all the questions I have, Your Honor," said Sparks.

"I have one question, Your Honor, and I don't intend any redirect," said Barton.

"Go ahead," said Steele.

"Elaine, tell the court and the jury who you saw depicted on those photographs that caused you to remember your husband's name if you will."

"Certainly. The photos were of Joe Brannigan and Vince Perkins. Those two guys sitting right over there," said Elaine. "I knew immediately that they were the two guys that had tormented and tortured my husband and me. And then I instantly remembered Tommy Joe and that his last name was Foster."

"Anything else of this witness?" asked Steele. "If not, call your next witness, Mr. Barton."

"Your Honor, I'd like to call Mr. Clay Houston," said Barton. Houston was sworn in and took the stand.

"Mr. Houston, there has been testimony in this case that the ship the United States contends is a pirate ship, *The Silver Bullet*, was booby-trapped to blow up if anyone tried to restart the engines after it had been taken over by the Coast Guard. Do you know anything about that?" asked Barton.

"Yes, I had been invited by Mr. Brannigan to come on board *The Silver Bullet* to give him medical treatment for a gunshot wound near his heart. I overheard a conversation between Brannigan and Vince Perkins in which Brannigan told Perkins it was, his words, `time to set the trap.' At that time, Perkins pulled out a piece of paper from his billfold which had what looked like some kind of wiring diagram on it, and he said he would `take care of it,'" said Houston.

"Your witness, Ms. Sparks, Mr. Smoot," said Barton.

Sparks stood up.

"Mr. Houston, you said you heard Mr. Brannigan give the order to booby-trap *The Silver Bullet*, is that right?" asked Sparks.

"That's right, but I also said I heard Mr. Perkins tell Brannigan he would take care of it," said Houston.

"And Mr. Houston, you used to practice medicine in the state of Florida, is that right?" asked Sparks.

"Yes, I did," said Houston.

"And you practiced medicine on Mr. Brannigan at his request aboard *The Silver Bullet*, is that right?" asked Sparks.

"That's right," said Houston.

"And can you tell the ladies and gentlemen of the jury whether you were practicing medicine on Mr. Brannigan without a valid license," said Sparks.

"Yes, my license has been suspended," said Houston.

"As part of a settlement in a drug trafficking case, is that right?" asked Sparks.

"Yes, that's right," said Houston.

"No further questions, Your Honor," said Sparks.

"Call your next witness, Mr. Barton," said Steele.

"The United States calls Dr. Jeanne Hoover," said Barton. Hoover was sworn in and took the stand.

"Dr. Hoover, can you give us another title by which you are also known?" asked Barton.

"I am a forensic medical specialist with the United States Coast Guard," said Hoover. "I have the rank of lieutenant commander, and I am the commanding officer of a Special Tactical Law Enforcement Team which investigated this case and gathered evidence in support of the prosecution of the defendants in this case by the United States."

"Now tell us generally, Dr. Hoover, what you expect the scientific evidence you have gathered in this case to show," said Barton.

"I believe the evidence will show that Vincent Perkins swung the wooden beam that struck Elaine Foster on the head, depositing a splinter that pierced the membranes surrounding her brain," said Hoover. "I believe the evidence also will show that the beam and Elaine together went overboard into the ocean and that both floated ashore on a sandbar island.

"Our DNA tests have shown that the tissue on splinters which I removed from the hands of Vincent Perkins is the same as the tissue on the wooden beam which we recovered from the ocean. The tests also showed that other tissue on that beam is the same as the tissue on the splinter that was surgically removed from Elaine's brain."

"I see you have a stack of documents there. Can you identify what those documents are?" asked Barton.

"Yes, these are written reports on each of the DNA tests we performed to establish that Vincent Perkins swung the beam that struck Elaine Foster on the head and injured her brain, and we believe that shows his intent to kill her," said Hoover.

"We have in this bag the wooden splinter that was removed by Dr. Jonas Sutherland from Elaine's brain."

Hoover held up the bag containing the splinter.

"I was present when this splinter was removed, and I placed it in this plastic bag, and it has been locked in the vault of the FBI's Miami branch forensics lab until just before this trial commenced this afternoon," said Hoover.

"And I see you have a rather large beam there. What is that, Dr. Hoover?" asked Barton.

"That's the beam which we recovered from the ocean, which contains DNA of both Ms. Foster and Mr. Perkins," said Hoover.

"And based on your knowledge as a physician and as a scientist, Dr. Hoover, what would you say are the chances that Vince Perkins used this beam here to bludgeon Elaine Foster upside her head?"

"I would say the chances that Vince Perkins used this beam to bludgeon Elaine Foster are trillions and trillions to one, or a virtual certainty approaching the same degree of certainty as that the sunrise will be in the east tomorrow morning," said Hoover.

"Thank you, doctor. You may answer the defense's questions," said Barton.

"No questions, Your Honor," said Sparks and Smoot.

Barton continued to call witnesses as to various elements of the maritime piracy and related crimes enumerated in the indictment, and shortly before noon on Friday, after almost four full days of testimony, Barton rested the government's case except for a final surprise witness he said he wanted to put on the stand after the break for lunch.

Smoot hit the ceiling.

"Objection!" he shouted, jumping to his feet. "This is just one more blatant attempt by the government, Your Honor, to prejudice and if at all possible, by hook or crook, to deny my client's right to a fair trial. The defense moves for a mistrial!"

"Mr. Barton, have you furnished the required JENKS material on this witness to Mr. Smoot and his client?" Steele asked.

"No, Your Honor. We only moments ago knew for certain that our witness would testify," said Barton.

"Well, as you very well know, Mr. Barton, if your proposed witness has made any prior statements at all related to this case, Mr. Smoot and his client are entitled to them. They must be furnished a copy before the witness testifies," said Steele.

"The scant prior statements of our proposed witness have been reduced to writing, Your Honor, which we're happy to furnish at this time to Mr. Smoot and his client," said Barton, handing copies of a typed statement to both Smoot and Sparks.

"We renew our motion for a mistrial, Your Honor. The lunch hour is insufficient time for the defense to prepare for Mr. Barton's 11th-hour witness," said Smoot.

"Denied," said Steele. "Court is adjourned until 1 p.m."

Promptly at 1 p.m., Steele strode back to the bench and sat down.

"We will hear your final witness, Mr. Barton. Proceed," said Steele.

"Your Honor, the United States would like to call as our final witness, defendant Vincent Perkins, for the very limited purpose of testifying about a matter mentioned in the government's complaint but which otherwise may lack specific supporting evidence," said Barton.

"What says the defense, that is, counsel for Mr. Perkins?" asked Steele. "I've already heard from you, Mr. Smoot, and your objection is overruled."

"Within the parameters outlined by Mr. Barton, Your Honor, Mr. Perkins has no objection to taking the witness stand," said Sparks.

"OK, Mr. Perkins, take the stand, please, and raise your hand to be sworn," said Steele.

"Do you swear that the testimony that you shall give in this cause will be the truth, the whole truth, and nothing but the truth, so help you God?" asked the clerk.

"I do," said Perkins.

"Be seated, Mr. Perkins," said Steele.

"Mr. Perkins, you have a right under our Constitution, as I'm sure counsel Ms. Sparks has reminded you, that you are free to refuse to answer any question concerning the allegations enumerated in the indictment in this case on grounds that your answer might tend to incriminate you, as prohibited by the Fifth Amendment," said Barton. "Are you aware of that?"

"I am," said Perkins. "However, I have discussed this with my attorney and on my own motion, I wish to testify as to a crime I saw committed in my presence which I had absolutely nothing to do with."

"And what was that crime, Mr. Perkins?" asked Barton.

"I saw the fatal gunshot in the back that killed Tommy Joe Foster," said Perkins. "It looked like cold-blooded murder to me, because the man had his hands up, begging not to be shot. When Foster saw his wife knocked into the sea with a blow to the head with a wooden beam, he jumped overboard as well and was shot in the back as he jumped.

"Did you know the person who shot Tommy Joe Foster, and could you identify that person if you were to see that person again, Mr. Perkins?" asked Barton.

"I knew him. I can identify him, and I will identify him. He's sitting right there by Mr. Smoot. His name is Joe Brannigan," said Perkins.

As Perkins spoke, Brannigan slammed his fist on the counsel table, shattering a pane of heavy glass that sat on top of it, and he cursed Perkins with a stream of loud profanity.

"Get that man out of my courtroom and don't bring him back in here," Steele said angrily from the bench as the marshals escorted Brannigan out to a holding cell down the hall. When Smoot got up and started to leave, too, Steele shouted: "Mr. Smoot, sit down! I didn't give you permission to leave my court."

Smoot sat down quickly and Barton spoke again.

"That was our final witness, Your Honor. The United States rests," said Barton.

"Thank you, Mr. Barton. Now I will ask you, Ms. Sparks, and you, Mr. Smoot, if you have agreed on your witnesses and the order of their testimony to be presented?" asked Steele.

"Your Honor, defendant Vincent Perkins rests. He will present no further testimony or evidence of any kind," said Sparks.

"Defendant Joe Brannigan also rests, Your Honor," said Smoot. "We will offer no testimony but contend as we have from the outset that the government has failed to present credible evidence to rebut the presumption of innocence that travels with my client through this trial. We renew our request that the indictment be voided."

"Denied," said Steele. "Now if counsel for the United States and counsel for the defendants wish to present closing arguments, I'll hear you one hour from now. Then I will instruct jurors as to the law, and deliberations will begin. Is there any other matter we should take up before we recess?"

"I have one matter, Your Honor," said Barton.

"Let's hear it," said Steele.

"The United States asks leave of the court, Your Honor, to withdraw the indictment in this case from the other two defendants not previously identified, that is Jim Cummings and Clay Houston," said Barton.

"Granted and they are dismissed as defendants," said Steele. Then striking his gavel, Steele said, ``Court will be in recess for one hour."

When the trial resumed after the break, Barton and the defense lawyers made closing arguments which sounded very much like their statements at the beginning of the trial. Barton however said the government had proved its case and said the defendants should be found guilty as charged. Defense lawyers said the U.S. had failed to make its case and that the defendants should be found not guilty.

Steele explained the law to jurors, particularly on maritime piracy and the RICO statute and a few other legal matters, and the case then went to the jury. At five minutes to five, on Friday, the jury signaled it was ready to report.

"We, the jury, find the defendants guilty as charged and urge the death penalty for them both, Your Honor," said Tom Hawkins, the jury foreman.

Cheers went up in the courtroom, among the loudest from Spence and Emma, before Steele gaveled the audience to silence and then adjourned the trial.

"The defendants are turned over to the custody of the attorney general pending sentencing, which will be considered in this court exactly three weeks from now. Bail will remain as previously set," said Steele, who then got up and left the courtroom.

"Well, Elaine, this calls for some celebration, don't you think?" asked Spence, who had come to the counsel table to thank Barton and congratulate him on a powerful case well presented. Emma thanked him too and hugged Elaine.

"We want a turn," said Chief Morelli and the other team members, who gathered around and hugged Elaine, including last of all McGuffy, who hugged her almost twice as long as everyone else.

"Thank you all so much, Chief, Cdr. Hoover, Ensign Hess, Petty Officers Meacham and Mendez and Lts. Anderson and McGuffy, whom I've gotten in the habit of calling Bob, for some reason," said Elaine. "No matter where I go from here or what I do, I will never be able to thank you wonderful people enough. I like to say, and I really mean it, you, and my doctors of course, have truly given me my life back."

"I know it sounds trite, Elaine," said Morelli. "But that's what we're here for. We won't forget you, either, young lady."

"Well, I see the TV cameras outside and Mr. Barton is already in front of them," said Elaine. "I suggest we go out and face them for a few minutes, and then get on with the rest of our lives." And they left the courtroom.

Chapter Twenty-Four

On the Friday night after Brannigan and Perkins were convicted, Elaine and her mother, Emma Preston, and her father-in-law, Spencer Foster, sponsored a steak dinner in the ballroom of the hotel in which Emma and Spence were staying.

Elaine invited Barton and Richards, Hoover, Morelli and other team members; Doctors Jonas Sutherland and Mary Horton; Jim Cummings and Clay Houston; Pastor David Hanson of the Davie Independent Baptist Church, and Dot Goodson, director of the Miami TBI rehab center.

At Elaine's request, Hanson asked God to bless the food and fellowship. Hanson also thanked God for rescuing and protecting Elaine through many harrowing trials and for restoring her memory of past events in her life. Hanson also asked God's blessing on Barton, Hoover, Morelli and the team for devoting their lives to public service in general and law enforcement and rescue in particular.

"Finally, God, thanks for answered prayers, particularly our prayers for Elaine, that she will discover your plan for the rest of her life and live it out. In your name, Jesus, we pray, Amen."

The steaks were served and enjoyed, and one by one the guests bade Elaine good night and good luck, and finally Emma and Spence said good night, too, and left the ballroom where only Elaine and McGuffy and a piano player remained.

"Where do we go from here, Elaine?" McGuffy asked as the pianist played, *It Had To Be You.*

"I don't know, Bob. This night is so wonderful, I wish it could last forever," said Elaine.

"Maybe it can," said McGuffy, getting up and inviting Elaine to a slow and intimate dance beneath the majestic chandeliers of the ballroom.

"What do you mean?" asked Elaine.

"I mean we have choices, and the choices we make will fill all our tomorrows, and I don't see why all our tomorrows can't be filled with the most wonderful thing about this day," said McGuffy.

"And what is that?" asked Elaine.

"Being with you, wonderful you," said McGuffy, as the pianist continued to play.

"Bob, you're so sweet and romantic," said Elaine, placing her head softly on McGuffy's shoulder as they continued to dance. "What do you think I should do about going back to Hannibal, where all of my family lives — my Mom and father-in-law, and of course Tommy Joe's brother, J.T., and my sisters and their husbands and all my nieces and nephews. One can't just go away on a yacht trip that goes way south, literally, and never come back, can one?"

"I think you should follow your heart, Elaine," said McGuffy. "For Tony Bennett, it was San Francisco. I think you have to decide where it is with you."

"Hmm. I think you're right, Bob. It's just that I don't know if I really know my heart. My heart was ripped out of me when Brannigan shot my precious husband, Tommy Joe.

"My heart has a hole as big as the *Nautilus* in it, and I fear that it's a hole nothing will ever be able to fill. And you have to know, Bob, that I care deeply for you. But I'm not sure it would be fair to you, doomed to spend your tomorrows with someone who's forever pining away for her childhood sweetheart she'll never see again and a lost dream of a ship named *Nautilus*, adrift on a smooth and silent sea.

"It's like I'm forever doomed to sit in front of a lifeless statue of Tommy Joe, complete with the bullet hole that gouged through him, and on his head sits a dreadful, horrid black bird, squawking, repeating, the word **NEVERMORE** forever."

"Elaine, you have a right and an uncompromising need to grieve for your lost husband, your lost ship, your lost dreams, your lost life," said McGuffy. "And I know that the grief process lasts a long time, at least a year, I've heard, and for some, much longer than that, and for a few it seems to be permanent, where happy days never return.

"That's why you need to determine the depth and length of your grief. Neither I nor anyone else can do that for you, but we can be waiting in the wings, supporting you with our prayers, checking softly from time to time to hear the glorious chimes that say you're ready to move forward into the rest of your life.

"I'm willing to be that friend to you, Elaine, for as long as it takes, because for me, I know where my heart is and where it will be. Whether you stay in Miami or go back to Hannibal, or set up shop in some new place, a compromise location, like the Big Easy, the new post-Katrina New Orleans, my heart will forever be where you are.

"But I'm old enough and hopefully mature enough to know, that's my problem, not yours. I'm just telling you, Elaine, that I have a permanent case of you, and you are the only doctor I know who can cure it."

"Awww, Bob. Tell me you can wait until my heart is healed and I am able to move on with my life, because I'm just not there yet, Bob," said Elaine.

"I can wait, because I have to wait," said McGuffy. "For me, the choice is easy. There is no choice but you."

"Play it again," McGuffy told the pianist, who had stopped playing and was quietly watching him and Elaine.

For a few more moments, neither Elaine nor McGuffy said anything, and then Elaine broke the silence:

"I don't know why it took me this long to find it, but I know what we should do," said Elaine.

"What?" asked McGuffy.

"Will you join me in a prayer that God will show us HIS will? After all, as the Bible says, we are not our own. We are bought with a price, and we belong to the One who paid the price. We both know Jesus paid the price with his life, and we have accepted his sacrifice on our behalf. We have given our hearts to Him, and now we belong to Him. And all our tomorrows belong to Him. So, Bob, let's stop trying to decide what WE want and ask him to show us what HE wants. Can we do that right now?" Elaine asked.

"Sure, we can," said McGuffy, who bowed his head with Elaine, and they both prayed, promising to live out God's plan for their lives as he showed it to them.

"So let's just spend this weekend listening to whatever word the Lord gives us," said Elaine.

"Good. And why don't we spend tomorrow down on the beach and then go to my church on Sunday and ask Pastor Hanson and his congregation to pray with us and for us?" asked McGuffy. He gave the pianist a $20 bill and told him he could go home now if he wanted to.

"Good idea, Bob," said Elaine, who then looked at her watch and exclaimed, "Oh, look at the time. I've missed curfew!" It was a minute to midnight.

"I'll call Dot at the center and tell her I'm spending the night with Mom in her room here in the hotel, and that I'll be in tomorrow to check out," said Elaine. "Then I'd better call Mom and ask her if it's alright that I stay with her. I'll bet she was asleep two hours ago."

"Good night, Elaine. I'll be by for you tomorrow for that day on the beach. Is 9 a.m. alright?" asked McGuffy.

"That's fine, Bob, Good night," Elaine said and they kissed a long passionate kiss good night.

On Saturday, Elaine got checked out of the rehab center, and Dr. Sutherland agreed to let her skip her scheduled checkup on Monday but said he'd like to see her again in six months. On Sunday, she and McGuffy and Emma and Spence went to worship services at Pastor Hanson's church. Hanson and the congregation promised to continue to pray for Bob and Elaine that God would show them his will for their lives.

Then on Monday morning, bright and early, Bob helped Elaine and Emma and Spence load their bags in the rented van and drove them to the airport. Outside the security checkpoint, Elaine gave Bob another long passionate kiss before she and her mother and father-in-law walked through the curtains of a metal detector and disappeared into the airport.

"I'll send you an e-mail every day," Bob shouted after them.

"I'll call you on my cell-phone when I get home," Elaine shouted back, then they both yelled a final "Bye!"

Back in Hannibal, Elaine told Jeffrey Sides that she would take him up on that offer for her to work in his boat factory if he would agree to build another yacht like the *Nautilus*.

And Roger Hall, president of the bank of Hannibal, told her he'd like her help to convince Sides that he should add a new section to his factory that would build only yachts. Sides eventually said he'd create a yacht section if Hall would provide the financing and if Elaine would head up that section and run it. She agreed, and a new yacht identical to the *Nautilus* began to take shape.

McGuffy was able to finagle assignments to Coast Guard stations in the Chicago-Great Lakes area as well as in Alaska and even New Orleans and Mobile. And while on these missions, he often was able to stretch out time and distance to take in a stop in Hannibal to see how work on the yacht was progressing and how Elaine was doing, although definitely not in that order.

A year passed quickly, and the yacht was done. This time, however, Elaine bought all the outstanding shares, including those retained by Sides. So the new yacht was exclusively hers and she invited McGuffy to fly his chopper up to Hannibal and help her christen it.

McGuffy was on hand for the ceremony, along with the mayor and Sides and Hall and a good portion of the townspeople.

Elaine and McGuffy held a bottle of champagne together and broke it on the hull, and the crowd cheered. Then Elaine removed a golden silk banner from the front of the yacht to reveal the name in gold on black borders: *Friendship*. Again the crowd cheered, and McGuffy held up both hands to ask for silence.

"I am glad to be invited and able to be here today and to help christen Elaine's new yacht," said McGuffy. "And after seeing the name, which she kept secret from me as well as from all of you, I guess, I just have one important question I'd like to ask, right here in front of you and God and everybody: **ELAINE, WILL YOU MARRY ME?**"

"**YES!**" she yelled close enough to an open mike that they knew her answer throughout the city and some said at least 10 miles north and south, east and west of Hannibal.

The fruit trees had flowered and the trees had put on fresh new green leaves when McGuffy's proposal and Elaine's answer came in mid-April, but Elaine proposed that the wedding itself be held in June. After some grumbling from McGuffy that June was way too long to wait, he agreed and the invitations were sent.

Elaine insisted that an old-fashioned paddle wheel boat from New Orleans would come up river to Hannibal for the wedding, then it would turn around and steam back to New Orleans and back for the reception and all-night on-board party.

When the time came, Pastor David Hanson was flown up from Davie, Florida, to conduct the ceremony. Music for the wedding came from a New Orleans jazz band, who played such favorites as *When the Saints Go Marching In, Put Your Hand in the Hand of the Man from Galilee,* and of course, the most amazing rendition of *Amazing Grace* that anyone at the wedding other than the band had ever heard.

After Bob and Elaine had said their "I do's," Elaine said she wanted to read one verse from the Bible, which she said she wanted to dedicate "to my wonderful friend and husband, Bob McGuffy, who taught me the true meaning of friendship."

"I will read from *The Gospel of John,* Chapter 15, verse 13: *Greater love has no one than this, that he lay down his life for his friends.* May God bless you all."

The crowd cheered and applauded again, and the jazz band again broke into *When the Saints Go Marching In.*

At this point, out on the top deck of the paddle wheel riverboat, a tall, lanky, white-haired man with a white mustache and wearing a white hat, suit and shoes, came to the edge of the deck, put one foot up on the lower bar of the banister and raised his hands. A hush fell over the crowd and the band softened and went silent.

"I'd also like to add my blessing to these children," said the man, opening a large, black, leather-bound book. "And to do that, I'd like to read a passage of Holy Scripture, too, from the *King James Authorized Version, The Gospel of Matthew*, Chapter 19, verses 4 through 6.

"Now these are the words of Jesus, Our Blessed Lord, and lest some of you out there who know me better than others point out indelicately that I didn't always believe in Him, I will state that I've had some time since I rode the Mississippi into eternity, to reconsider the alternative, and thus I'm quite proud to be here today," and then he read from the book:

"And Jesus answered and said unto them, Have ye not read, that he which made them at the beginning made them male and female, and said, For this cause shall a man leave father and mother and shall cleave to his wife: and they TWAIN shall be one flesh? Wherefore they are no more TWAIN, but one flesh. What therefore God hath joined together, let not man put asunder."

The crowd remained silent, and slowly and softly the band began again to play *Amazing Grace* as the old man walked back toward the captain's cabin. And when he could no longer be seen, the crowd broke into applause and cheers again.

"That was a great stroke you added there, Elaine," said the mayor, referring to the man in the white suit. "That guy was really good. Where'd you find him?"

"Oh, I didn't do that. I assumed you or the Chamber of Commerce did that," Elaine said.

"We didn't do it," said a Chamber official.

"Maybe the riverboat management added him extra at their own expense. I know I didn't hire him," said Elaine.

"We didn't do it either, Ma'am," said the riverboat management official, sipping on champagne. "I don't know where he came from." And nobody in the wedding party or the town of Hannibal ever found out, either.

THE END

About the Author

STAN BAILEY has four decades of experience writing and reporting for daily newspapers in six states, covering law enforcement, victims' rights, state and federal trial and appeals courts, prisons, state government and politics for 32 years ending August 2005 for *The Birmingham News*, Alabama's largest daily newspaper.

He also did general assignment reporting for newspapers in Hollywood, Florida; Harrisburg, Pennsylvania, and Montgomery, Alabama; interned at newspapers in Jackson, Mississippi, and Memphis, Tennessee, and was editorial page editor and editorial writer for *The Savannah Morning News* in Savannah, Georgia.

He is a graduate of Mississippi State University, B.A. degree in English; was features editor of MSU student newspaper, *The Reflector*, and editor, student literary magazine, *Inscriptus*. He was valedictorian, Class of 1960, at Vardaman High School, Vardaman, Mississippi, sweet potato capital of the world. Grandpa to Britton, Rivers, Breanna, and John Benton. Dad to Stephen and Cheryl; true love/husband to Bobbie since 1970.

Printed in the United States
204283BV00002B/229-330/P